CHAMPION

JAKE BRANNIGAN

aethonbooks.com

CHAMPION
©2024 JAKE BRANNIGAN

ALSO IN THE SERIES

ACT I: A TORTUROUS CLIMB

ONE
A CAPTAIN'S REPORT
BECKA

"So that's everything we've learned," Glenn concluded as Becka stood silently at his side. "Leo was last seen leaving the chapel this very morning. He met Sara on the docks, and they had lunch there after Sara secured a boat to take us to Caelfall. They then both traveled to the Old Fishing District, where the Town Guard on duty confirmed they entered alongside Ripper. After that, they vanished."

Following Glenn's lead, she and Glenn had spent most of last night verifying the facts Glenn had just laid out for Captain Marion Hawkshadow. The aging Blazer watched them impassively from the seat behind her scroll-covered desk in her office in the Lakebrooke Blazers Guild. Leo and Sara were missing. There was no question they were missing. So the only question was what to do next.

Once Glenn finished relaying his tale, Marion turned her gaze on Becka and practically burned her with a scowl. "So if I understand what you're saying, what you're telling me is that your so-called urgent mission to compete in the <Sandsea Cup> was not urgent at all. Which means you, Coldbreaker, spent all afternoon yesterday spinning me up and wasting my time."

"That's not it at all," Becka said soothingly. "It's still vital Glenn compete in the cup and scan the clergy gathered there. We won't have another chance to find this many secret Deathcasters. We simply can't complete the journey to Caelfall without Sara and Leo. Without Sara's ship and Leo's—"

"Aiden can easily get you on a ship," Marion interrupted. "After I approved your Quest, all you had to do was ask. We can also have someone else track down the location of the Shrine of Ralun and send it through phantom correspondence once you arrive. But if you're going to reach port and make the trek to the **<Sandsea Cup>** in time to put yourself on the roster, you need to leave Lakebrooke tomorrow on a boat. Which means none of what you've told me is your problem."

"We can't leave Lakebrooke until we know Sara and Leo aren't in trouble," Glenn said patiently. "They're our party members, and our friends besides. They—"

"Are Blazers perfectly capable of taking care of themselves, likely even more than you two," Marion again interrupted. "Despite how special you may think the Gods have made you, Graybreaker, saving the entirety of Luxtera does not rest upon your shoulders."

Glenn frowned. His hurt expression suggested he didn't think of himself as special but couldn't immediately come up with a way to insist he wasn't. Becka would have leapt to his defense had she not been convinced it would only irritate Marion more. They had to handle this delicately.

"We don't need you to verify Leo and Sara were taken by someone, if they were taken at all," Marion continued firmly. "We don't need you to rescue them. We can do that. In case you forgot who we are, we're the largest, most powerful guild in Luxtera. Nobody abducts our people or gives us trouble... or if they do, they only give us trouble *once*."

The Shadowers Guild would argue differently, but Becka didn't bring that up.

Marion's scowl remained hard as she stared Glenn down with determination that made even Becka uncomfortable. "If Leo and Sara have gotten into trouble, we'll find them. If they need help, we'll rescue them. We don't need you to do that. In fact, you won't be doing that at all."

Becka hid her grimace as she struggled for a way to salvage this rapidly deteriorating situation. Glenn should never have pushed Marion this hard.

"Captain—" Glenn started.

"You're officially done looking into Leo and Sara's so-called disappearance," Marion said. "That's an order from your superior officer in the Blazers... that's still me, by the way... and one you'd be a fool to ignore."

"But what if—"

"Even if someone did snatch those two up, we can't have you and your bleeding heart mucking up the search because you're worried about your friends. You focus on packing for your trip to Caelfall and making sure you're ready to scan every member of every branch of the church who shows up to cast [-Resurrect-] on the contestants. Others with higher levels and better focus will look into this."

Glenn had looked like he was going to continue arguing until Marion said those words. "Are you going to send Brennon after them?"

Becka had no doubt Brennon Shadesinger could find two missing Junior Blazers. She doubted there was much Glenn's mentor, one of the most celebrated Truth Seekers in all of Luxtera, could not accomplish. But she also knew one unfortunate and discouraging fact.

Marion Hawkshadow wouldn't assign Brennon Shadesinger to a task this... small.

Marion confirmed Becka's unspoken thought. "Shadesinger's busy. But I give you my word, Glenn. If Leo and Sara are missing, we'll bring them home. Blazers don't abandon their own."

Glenn's grimace had returned. Since he looked like he might argue again, Becka grabbed his hand and gripped it tight. When he glanced at her, she incrementally shook her head. *Not here.*

Marion continued as if she hadn't noticed anything. "Now, I need you to find the captain Sara convinced to ship you to Caelfall and confirm you're still on board. Can I trust you to handle that monumental task yourself, or do I need to send someone with you?"

Becka squeezed Glenn's hand as hard as she could manage. She prayed she could convince him to stop digging before he ruined any chance of them getting back into Marion Hawkshadow's good graces.

Glenn's incremental nod was a huge relief. Even so, he couldn't lie to Marion. He couldn't lie to anyone, at least not well. That was her job.

Becka turned to face Marion. "We'll be on that boat. You don't need to worry about us."

"Good," Marion said curtly. "I appreciate the head's up regarding

Leo and Sara's absence. I'll get someone looking into it today. Now, you're both dismissed."

Glenn still looked like he might be about to say something else, or launch another doomed plea to be put back on the quest to find Leo and Sara. Before he could do that, Becka turned and dragged him off... or tried. It was like trying to yank a full-grown tree right out of the ground. When Glenn glanced at her in protest, she offered the most pitiable look she could muster.

That convinced him. He never could resist her pitiable gaze. Once he agreed to move, she added a knowing wink that immediately perked him up. He'd gotten the message, finally.

We're not giving up, Becka assured him silently. *But we're not getting anywhere in here.*

With the last of his attempts to sway the unswayable Captain Hawkshadow from her chosen course concluded, Becka led Glenn out of Marion's office by the hand and into the hallway on the second floor of the Blazers Guild. The inside of the guild was not a good place to plan their next move—too many eyes and ears—so Becka dropped Glenn's hand and led him down the stairs.

Aiden Goodfellow sat at a round table nearby speaking with two Blazers. Becka immediately recognized them as Jackson Marshcutter—a muscular, brown-haired 24-year-old Shadower—and Jessica Rainfall, a comely, dark-haired 22-year-old Guilecaster. She quietly catalogued this new information away with the reams of other facts she carefully organized inside her head. Blazers constantly came and went from the guild and zone, and it was always good to know who was around.

After all, the only reason she'd been able to convince Marion to assign Glenn a Quest to go to Caelfall, enter the <Sandsea Cup>, and use [-Soul Scan-] on every last high level Spiritualist and Shamanist there was because she had known Marion was in town for the week. Becka kept tabs on the comings and goings of Blazers almost as well as Aiden Goodfellow, the guildmaster.

Jackson and Jessica weren't supposed to be here, or at least there had been no plans for them to be here. Both had been reassigned to the Blazers Guild in Cullfield last year after officially leveling out of Evolan. Some unexpected matter must have brought them back to Evolan recently.

As Jessica glanced up and in her direction, Becka smiled warmly. The other woman smiled back. She elbowed Jackson, who took one look at Becka and Glenn, then looked back to Aiden.

Becka had taken a liking to Jessica the moment they first met. They were both Guilecasters and both blessed with strong, loyal men who were sometimes too thick about matters for their own good. Jessica was simply a few years further along in her journey, and Becka was grateful for any advice the older woman offered.

Becka didn't know Jackson nearly as well. Unlike Glenn, Jackson tended to keep to himself unless Jessica forced him to be sociable. Still, he seemed like a good sort. She also knew from Sara that Jackson had retrieved her namesake mace—Becka—from the Redwood home the day after Glenn "died," and that Jackson and Sara (then Svara) had trained together and been friends.

Their presence here could be useful if she needed to call in a favor to help Glenn find Leo and Sara. Their presence here could be useful for other matters as well. Even so, Becka had no immediate need to enlist either of them in her latest scheme. She turned her eyes to the door and led Glenn out.

The moment they emerged, she turned to Glenn in full sight of the windows on the second floor of the Blazers Guild. Windows she suspected Captain Hawkshadow was looking out of right now. Marion, unfortunately, knew just how clever Becka could be. She had to make this look good.

Right now, Marion was wondering if Glenn was *really* going to follow her orders or go do something else. Something rash. Before Glenn could say anything, Becka wrapped her hands around the back of his head and pulled him down for a kiss in full view of the second floor of the guild.

He resisted her, but likely only out of surprise. "Hold on. Is this really—"

"Kiss me like you mean it," she whispered. "They need to think we're heading off to bone."

"Oh." Glenn blinked. "Well, I guess if—"

Becka ended the last of his resistance by hopping up on her tiptoes and planting a kiss on his waiting lips. He had no problem slipping into his role after that, and Becka didn't really have to act in this regard. She loved teasing Glenn. She only wished they truly had time to get serious.

Once she was certain anyone watching them from the windows of the guild would have a *very* clear idea where they were going next, Becka once again took Glenn's hand and led him off in the direction of the Iron Scabbard. They would speak in Glenn's room. [+**Shadow Sense**+]—her Blessing that allowed her to detect hidden mortals and Demons—would alert her if anyone followed to spy on them.

The trek to the Scabbard ended without issue, and Becka made sure to kiss Glenn a lot more once they arrived outside, just to make sure no one saw through their clever ruse. Finally, they headed upstairs, and it was only once they were alone inside and the door was closed that she let herself incrementally relax. Glenn now watched her with hopeful eyes.

"We're not giving up on them," he said quietly. "Right?"

Becka offered the most offended gaze she could muster. "What do you think?"

He grinned with visible relief. "So, what's your plan?"

"I thought I made my plan for you clear outside."

He rolled his eyes at her. "Other than that."

"You understand what you were doing wrong back there in the guild, don't you? With Marion?"

"I... suppose."

"So what were you doing wrong?"

"I imagine I was trying to break through a brick wall with my head."

Becka nodded in approval. "You can't simply badger a woman like Marion into agreeing with you. Pressing her to change her mind when she's already made it up simply causes her to dig in deeper. You know that. That means she might actually be right about some of what she said."

Glenn frowned. "What do you mean by that?"

"You're very close to Sara and Leo. Are you absolutely certain your worries for them as friends aren't going to interfere with your ability to complete this investigation as a Truth Seeker? Impartially? Because if it is—"

"I won't let my feelings for them interfere with my investigation. I can separate my worries for them from my work. Marion might not believe that, but you do, right?"

"If you help me." She waited. "So help me believe you, Glenn."

His features calmed. She watched the man she loved as he mentally moved away from her, from this, from the world, and then returned re-centered and refocused. "I can do this."

"Good." She absolutely believed him. "So, let's start by summarizing where we are now. Marion expects us to be on a ship to Caelfall by midday tomorrow. That gives us the rest of the day and perhaps tonight to find something that will change her mind about sending us away."

Glenn's brow furrowed. "But you just suggested I couldn't change her mind."

"I suggested *you* couldn't change her mind by arguing with her about the limited evidence we've already gathered, which she's already absorbed and dismissed. So we simply need to gather new evidence before our new deadline. Something to make her look at the facts with fresh eyes."

Glenn's eyes widened as he caught on, which amused and relieved her. He was a talented and capable warrior, a veritable savant in regards to solving the obscure and odd cases Brennon had slowly been assigning him as part of his training, and an absolutely phenomenal lover. But while he could often read people like a book, he still had little idea how to *manipulate* them.

Glenn's open nature could get even the most untrusting people to trust him, but he couldn't trick them into doing what he wanted. He could offer an impassioned plea that would melt the hearts of even the most stoic curmudgeon, but he couldn't convince them that helping him was in their own best interest. Becka didn't enjoy manipulating other people into helping her get her way, but she *was* good at it... so she should simply continue to aid Glenn where he was weak.

Just as he aided her in the same way each and every day.

Glenn visibly considered their options. "So we can't convince Marion to let us keep searching for Sara and Leo with nothing but the word of a Town Guard that they were last seen in the Old Fishing District. But if we gather hard evidence that they've actually been abducted—"

"And where we might start looking for them," Becka added.

"—she might have to reconsider her orders," Glenn agreed with visible relief. "And as you said, she's not wrong about all of it. The evidence we have now is rather flimsy, and I am close to both people involved. I need to give Marion real evidence and prove I'm up to the task of finding them."

Becka smiled warmly. "Now you're talking like the Glenn Graybreaker who saved the Marshvale Fishing Company from financial ruin. So. We have one more afternoon, evening, and night to gather evidence about Leo and Sara's disappearance that changes Marion's mind."

"Right. Though... we've already been to the docks and the church, and we've all but walked the length of the Old Fishing District. We need to figure out where to go next."

"May I offer a suggestion?"

"Please do. You're amazing at all this. I'd be lost without you."

From anyone else Becka would have assumed they were buttering her up, but from Glenn, the words came straight from his heart. He might be a bit thick-headed sometimes, but his genuine devotion to her and to helping others more than made up for that. No one could be good at everything.

"Brennon's unavailable, and we can't go to Marion until we know more," Becka said. "But there's one other person in town who I think might help us. In fact, I can almost guarantee she will."

"Who?" Glenn asked hopefully.

Becka pictured the kind face of her first and most formidable mentor in the Blazers. "Jenny Ambersun."

Glenn stared at her in surprise and, she noted, with a visible hint of worry.

"She returned from her latest recruiting trip just two days ago. She'll be here in Lakebrooke for another three days before she heads out on the next one. She also knows both Sara and Leo personally."

Glenn's brow furrowed. "But Jenny knows who I am, doesn't she?"

"She knows Glenn Redwood. She never got to meet Glenn Graybreaker. Unless you're worried that Guilecaster charm around your neck has somehow broken in the past three months, I think it's past time I introduced the two of you."

"Right," Glenn agreed... hesitantly. "But can we really risk her realizing who I am?"

"We might as well. She knows I have a man now, and she has asked about you. If I keep finding excuses to keep her from meeting the man I'm spending my nights with, she might begin to wonder if I'm ashamed of you... or if I really am secretly boning the same Glenn she knew."

"And she would want to help us. She did train Leo, after all."

"And Sara. And me. In fact, I like to think we've grown quite close since she took me under her wing two years ago. Finally, Jenny and Marion don't really get along."

Glenn's brow furrowed. "And that's... good somehow?"

Becka patiently reminded herself that one of the reasons she loved Glenn so much was because of how he could never, ever manipulate people into doing something against their best interest.

"It means Jenny's unlikely to casually mention to Marion that we've come to her about this matter. Which makes it likely Marion won't hear about us not quite following her orders until when we have some evidence that proves we had good reason to do so."

Again, Glenn nodded. She could see his keen mind absorbing these new facts. "Then I think you're right. If we tell Jenny Leo and Sara are missing, she may be able to offer some ideas about where they might have gone or what might have happened to them. So, where do we find her?"

"This time of night, after being gone for three weeks on a recruiting mission, I believe she would be on her way to enjoy a delicious supper at the Golden Minnow. She might be content to eat trail food while on the field, but the woman loves her crab legs."

His expression grew more interested. "So... noble clothes for supper, then?"

She batted her eyes at him. "You can't tell me you aren't already looking forward to seeing me in another **[Noblewoman's Dress]**. Perhaps the frilly blue one you bought me last week?"

Glenn's grin widened. "That would work."

She offered a mock frown. "Just don't get distracted. We're going to supper on a quest, not so you can spend the night ogling me in my lovely, frilly, low-cut dress."

"Sure," he agreed. "We certainly wouldn't want me doing that."

TWO
A CAVERNOUS ARENA
LEO

The six captives Teacher and his Desouled had gathered around the tables in one corner of the large cavern had finished eating their soup and bread long ago, and Sara had been gone longer than Leo was comfortable with. He glanced at the six people he needed to rescue once more. It was going to be a real chore to get them all out of here alive, but that didn't mean he wasn't going to try his best.

Erick (a level 14 Shadower) now sat by himself on the corner of a bench, facing away from the others. He had his arms crossed like he was sulking. That was odd, since no one had said anything since the group at the table had finished introducing themselves. Perhaps, as a Shadower, Erick simply carried an instinctive distrust of Blazers.

Evie, the red-haired level 13 Guilecaster who hadn't said a word since she introduced herself and her class, stared at the table and nothing else. Meanwhile, Maria, the level 19 Harmcaster who had yelled at Evie when she gave her name and class, continued staring down the tunnel into which Sara had disappeared with Teacher. Maria looked even more cross now than she had earlier.

Meanwhile, Kenneth (the level 15 Brutalist) and Cyrus (the level 13 Anchorite) talked in tones too low for Leo to make anything out. Had Leo not known how low their levels were, their ages would have assured him they had already each chosen an Evolved Class. Yet the whole reason these people were here (in Teacher's eyes) was because they had abandoned Luxtera's Climb.

Just like Tom Brightbow, a level 10 Auracaster. Leo's best friend. His big brother, and the man he'd initially come here to save. And right then Tom walked around a table, climbed up on a bench, and thumped down on top of the table beside Leo.

Tom smiled. "Looks like you get to bail me out once again."

"This one isn't your fault." Leo kept his eyes fixed on the tunnel down which Sara, Ripper, and Teacher had disappeared, willing them to emerge. "No one plans to be abducted by a crazy person."

"I don't know. Sometimes I wonder if he's so crazy."

Leo offered him a sharp glance. "What do you mean by that?"

"He showed us the scripture. All of us have read it. Kind of makes you think."

"What scripture?"

"The Scripture of Ralun. It... well, it says things. Like why we should level, and what's going to happen to us if we don't."

Leo scoffed. "You can't possibly believe that. Scriptures of Ralun don't exist."

Tom offered a surprisingly lucid gaze. "Did the church tell you that?"

Leo hesitated only a moment before firming his scowl. "The church isn't perfect. I'd be the first to admit that. But if there actually were Scriptures of Ralun out there, they would have spoken to us about them. Even the church wouldn't dare hide the word of the Gods from the faithful of Luxtera."

"There's a lot about the church we don't know. Anyway, I can't say I'm fully convinced. The words of the scripture leave a lot to interpretation. The one thing I do know is that I don't want to get my head ripped off by an Antlion, so until I know for sure that I'm going to wander in the dark forever if I don't get back on the ladder, I'm not going to risk my life leveling."

"But we have to start climbing the ladder again," Evie said quietly from the other side of the table. "If we don't... there's no afterlife waiting for us. Not a good one."

"There's no warm afterlife waiting for us no matter what we do," Maria said darkly. "The Gods are spoiled children tossing around their playthings. You think they care about their toys after we break? They'll toss us on the rubbish pile and move onto whoever entertains them next."

Kenneth frowned at her. "You shouldn't talk about the Gods that way."

"Why? If They were going to smite me, They'd have done so by now."

"I don't know if They plan to reward us in the afterlife or not," Kenneth said angrily. "But I do know I wouldn't want to make Them angry before I die."

"But that's what you're already doing every day, if you believe Teacher. When was the last time you leveled anything other than your drinking tolerance?"

Kenneth glared. "It's tough to level solo in Evolan. I'll get back to it. I will! I just need some more training and I'll be ready to go out and level again."

"I just hate that they make us fight and kill," Cyrus said sullenly. "We shouldn't have to kill Monsters to stay in Their good graces. Isn't the fact that we worship Them enough?"

Kenneth chuckled and shoved him in the arm. "You're not mad about having to do more than worship. You're just afraid to take a punch."

"So why aren't you? I never wanted to be an Adventurer. I would have been perfectly happy raising crops outside town!" Cyrus shook his head. "I hate fighting."

Tom sighed. "You and me both. I always wanted to be a Merchant instead."

Maria scoffed. "If you'd chosen that Class, you'd be even poorer than you are already."

Tom scowled at her. "What do you know anyway? All you do is complain!"

"And all you do is daydream. It doesn't matter how many of Teacher's games we play or how many of his hurdles we clear. He's never letting us leave this cave. And even if we did escape, we'd just die in some empty field when a Monster or Demon manages a lucky strike." Maria looked up. "Damn the Gods and Their decrees. I'm done playing Their games."

Despite his desire to be patient with these people, Leo was getting rather tired of their defeatist attitudes. No one would ever claim fighting Monsters and leveling was easy or safe, but with a good party and good sense one could still make progress. As much as he didn't want to agree with Teacher about anything, the man was right that these people had absolutely given up on leveling.

Even so, abducting them and *forcing* them to fight Monsters wasn't the answer. There had to be a better way to motivate them to start climbing the ladder again. Though... if he'd been unable to convince Tom Brightbow, a man who was as close to him as a brother, to do that...

The toll of a single bell echoed through the cavern. Everyone stiffened, including Leo. He didn't know what that bell meant, but the others obviously did. He glanced at Tom. "What's that mean?"

"Time to earn our supper." Tom looked at the table. "Tomorrow's supper."

"How?"

"By fighting Monsters."

Cyrus set his jaw. "I don't want to fight today. I'm *not* going to fight today. If he sees I'm not willing to fight today, he'll have to let me out of the arena. I don't care if I don't eat."

"And what if he doesn't let you out?" Kenneth asked angrily. "You plan to just let some Goblin stab you in the gut?"

To Leo, this was sounding worse and worse. "Teacher forces you to fight Goblins down here?"

"Among other Monsters," Evie said timidly. "Each of us has to kill at least one Monster a day or we don't eat. Goblins are the worst though. They just... they enjoy hurting people."

Leo had only fought Goblins a few times with a full party of Blazers. Second to Demons, they were one of his least favorite Monsters to fight. It wasn't just the fact that they were humanoid, which felt disturbingly like killing other Adventurers. It was the feral way their eyes lit up when they spotted human prey and what they often did with the corpses of those they defeated... which was eat them.

Normal Goblins were only level 10-12, but they were fierce fighters. Goblin Archers were usually lower level, 9-10, but they were frustratingly good at shooting poisoned rancid arrows or blow darts and fleeing before they could be struck down. And Goblin Champions could easily be level 14 or higher. Those Monsters carried shields, primitive armor, and **[Bone Axe]**s that could crush bone and tear flesh.

Anyone who died in a fight with a Goblin pack and whose body wasn't retrieved by their party was almost certain to meet the Forever Death, because Goblins, like Minotaurs, enjoyed nothing more than the taste of a dead Adventurer. Even worse, unlike Minotaurs... Goblins didn't bother to cook the body first. No Spiritualist could [-Resurrect-] an Adventurer whose body was devoured by Goblins.

Worse, Goblins rarely fought alone except for their scouts, and they generally clustered in underground caves where only a full party of experienced Adventurers dared venture. They were rabid, smelly, disgusting creatures that always targeted the weakest members of a party, always fled from superior numbers, and always set ambushes in their underground caverns.

Still, fighting one Goblin wouldn't be so bad. The ravenous little Monsters were a terror in a pack, but each individual Goblin was relatively weak and easy to kill... though the way they sometimes fought, with no regard for their own well-being, almost ensured anyone without adequate armor would be bitten or scratched. Goblin saliva was mildly venomous, as was the poison they put on their claws.

Leo already knew Teacher was an Evolved Deathcaster, though he might be dual classing. What would he do if one of his captives got scraped or bitten by a Goblin during their daily battles? Leo had seen firsthand how goblin bites and scratches swelled and quickly became infected.

When Leo had fought Goblins with the Blazers, they always had an experienced Lifecaster in the party to use [-Cleanse Body-] and [-Flash Heal-] on any wounds before they could fester. So did Teacher have a Lifecaster working for him as well? He had mentioned human disciples as well as Desouled.

Leo was finding it difficult to concentrate on anything while his partner remained missing. Where was Sara? He struggled to remind himself that she was just as capable of taking care of herself as he was, but... they were the captives of a high-level Deathcaster. The man could easily murder either of them, regardless of how strong or brave or clever they were. The level difference alone assured that.

Maria sighed and rose. "Guess we'd best get on with it then." She walked toward the tunnel guarded by the Silver Colossus. "Unless you want to get carried into the arena again."

Leo watched them file off and then glanced at the desouled corpse of a Silver Colossus, a towering six-armed humanoid with gleaming silver skin that could completely shrug off any spell one cast at it. "Carried?"

As he fell into step behind the line, Tom glanced back at him. "If we refuse to go to the arena, Teacher just sends one of his Desouled to carry us there. We don't like been carried about like a sack of potatoes, so we go."

"And where *are* we going now?" Leo once again resisted the urge to draw his [Steel Spear] and take his chances with one of the high-leveled Desouled in the cavern. Where was Sara?

"Just keep walking," Tom said. "It's easier to see it than describe it."

Leo glanced at the tunnel down which Sara had disappeared several times as they approached the tunnel guarded by the towering desouled corpse of the Silver Colossus. What little he recalled of how Deathcasters manipulated their puppeted corpses told him a Deathcaster had to be within sight of the corpse to actually make it do things. Otherwise, it simply stood dumbly in one place.

As they approached the tunnel, the Silver Colossus shuffled aside. Yet Leo didn't see any sign of Teacher or Sara, so was it possible there was more than one Deathcaster down here? As a form wearing a long set of dark robes and a dark-colored mask similar to Teacher's stepped from the tunnel, Leo realized he'd guessed correctly. This must be one of Teacher's "disciples"... assuming they were alive.

As he peered closely, he was fairly certain he could pick out the subtle rise and fall of the slim figure's chest. Their dark, thick robes made it impossible to ascertain anything else, including sex. He hoped the person would speak, allowing Leo at least one fact to archive in regards to their identity.

Instead, the figure simply stood aside and motioned with one hand as the procession filed through. Maria led with her eyes stubbornly fixed forward, followed by Kenneth, Evie, Cyrus, Erick, and lastly, Tom. Leo followed at the rear and paused at the tunnel entry. He stared the figure down.

"You have to know this is wrong," he said firmly. "You can't *force* people to fight Monsters."

The disciple in the robes and mask remained silent.

"Is he forcing you to help him? Are you under duress? Why are you doing this?"

Once again, the figure simply motioned with one hand. As they did so, the Silver Colossus flexed all six of its arms and took one step forward, a thunderous single pace. The meaning was obvious. Continue up the tunnel after the others... or be carried there in the arms of the Silver Colossus.

Teacher's disciple obviously had no intention of offering anything other than gestures. Leo abandoned his efforts to coax words out of them and followed the others up the tunnel. His worry for Sara remained, but he couldn't help her if he got grabbed by a level 30 Desouled.

The journey continued for what Leo estimated was five or so minutes, though he couldn't be certain. In addition to gradually sloping up and down, the tunnel wound back and forth enough that Leo would easily have gotten lost if there were any offshoots. Yet the tunnel went only one direction.

The floor, walls, and ceiling of the tunnel were also unusually smooth and round. It was either the work of a Builder or some sort of Monster that could burrow in the earth. Perhaps a Rock Spider? Leo doubted the rock-eating Monsters would build these tunnels on their own, but Teacher could easily kill some and enslave their corpses. A desouled Rock Spider could tunnel as easily as a live one.

Finally, they emerged into another cavern that, while smaller than the one they'd just left, was obviously built for a single purpose. The center of the cavern contained a large bowl with high stone walls all around it, with another tiered ring around that. Even had Tom not mentioned this was an arena, the design would have made that obvious. It was also already occupied.

Teacher stood on a raised overlook above the second ring, and Leo was greatly relieved to see Sara standing beside him with Ripper close at her side. He saw her visibly nod when he exited the tunnel, and he didn't miss the way she subtly relaxed as she saw that he, too, was still alive. Still, the cast of her features assured him she was troubled. Her worries didn't appear to be an act.

Leo would compare notes with her later. For now, with assurance she was still safe, Leo took in the rest of Teacher's "arena." The bowl wasn't empty. At least six metal cages stood around the edges, four of which were occupied. Leo spotted three different Goblins, one locked in each cage, and what was obviously a very agitated Antlion in the fourth cage. The last two cages were empty.

There were also six small wooden boxes in the arena, gathered around the edges. All were closed. What was in those boxes? Potions? Weapons? Teacher couldn't expect his captives to fight Monsters bare-handed. Even if Cyrus could manage that, as an Anchorite, the rest certainly couldn't.

Also, did Teacher's disciples go out and capture these Monsters themselves? They didn't appear to be Desouled, so Leo wasn't sure how they could capture them... unless Teacher had his Silver Colossus grab them and carry them bodily back to this cave. Leo supposed that would work well enough.

Perhaps one of Teacher's disciples was a Guilecaster or Mindbender? They could easily **[-Charm-]** a Monster of equal or lesser level and bring it back for capture. Leo knew that was how events like the <Sandsea Cup> acquired the Monsters they had Adventurers fight in its contests of strength, guile, and will. Guilecasters and Mindbenders spent months collecting Monsters to sell to the cup.

Two more robed figures waited in the arena below as well, each dressed similar to the one Leo had seen at the entry to this tunnel. So Teacher had at least three disciples working with him. That was discouraging. It was bad enough that this man believed his wild tale about the Gods punishing those who refused to level in the afterlife. Apparently, he'd convinced a number of followers as well.

Even Teacher's current captives seemed to be close to accepting the man's wild claims about those who refused to undertake Luxtera's Climb. Tom had always been one of the most skeptical people Leo knew, and yet he was already half-worried Teacher might be correct about divine punishment. Even Maria, callous as she acted, seemed to believed Teacher. She simply didn't care.

The others, from what Leo had overheard, all believed Teacher's words in one way or another, but they had reacted differently. No one seemed to have flat out told Teacher he was wrong. Their captor was charismatic and persuasive, but Leo reminded himself he didn't need to convince Teacher he was wrong or even convince these captives. He just had to get them out of here.

As they entered the cavern, the two robed disciples on the middle ring lifted the end of a wooden ramp cobbled together from planks and long poles. They slammed the end down on the highest level of the ring, the level onto which Teacher's captives (and Leo) had arrived. So that was how they allowed transit between rings. Leo spotted a similar ramp leading down into the lowest ring, or arena.

From the platform above the highest ring, Teacher called out. "Cyrus! Evie! Form your party and step into the arena! Protect your adventuring partner and honor the Gods!"

Cyrus paused at the edge of the ramp leading down to the second ring and angrily shook his head. "I won't do it. He can't make me fight anything today."

Evie clutched his hand, only to have him angrily rip it away. "Please, Cyrus. I can't fight them alone. They're *Goblins*. I don't want to get bit, and I can't hold off a Goblin on my own."

"Then take Kenneth with you," Cyrus said irritably. "He's killed plenty of Goblins."

Kenneth glared at him. "She can't take me with her, you oaf. You heard Teacher. You're first into the arena today. You know what happens if we refuse to fight."

"Cyrus! Evie!" Teacher's voice grew stern. "Step into the arena! I will not ask again!"

Maria turned on Cyrus in exasperation. "He's just going to have some corpses toss you in there if you don't go willingly. You'll fight better without a twisted knee or broken foot. So go!"

Cyrus stepped back and crossed his arms. "I refuse."

"Please!" Evie asked desperately.

Leo had heard enough. "I'll go with her."

All of their eyes snapped to meet his.

"You can't," Kenneth said.

"He won't let you," Erick said crossly. "It's Teacher's rules or nothing. That's how this works."

"Cyrus is refusing to enter the arena!" Leo called up to the platform. "I volunteer to fight alongside Evie Greenfeather instead!"

"That is not your place," Teacher responded ominously. His voice echoed unnaturally through the cavern. "It is also not your climb. Cyrus, Evie. Enter the arena or we will throw you into it."

That seemed to be the last warning Evie would tolerate. She hurried down the ramp without a look back. Just what would happen if she refused?

From behind them, something chittered. And as Leo looked up in horror, a desouled Rock Spider burrowed directly out of the earth. When Cyrus saw it, he shrieked.

The moment he attempted to run, a second desouled Rock Spider burrowed up from the ground on his other side. Despite moving slightly slower than a running human, Cyrus seemed too petrified to move. Both spiders closed on him from either side. Leo drew his [Steel Spear] and stepped forward.

"Do not interfere, Leo!" Teacher called from above. "My spiders will not harm him! I swear to you by Celes! Stand down and allow me to teach them how to survive!"

Leo mentally debated until Sara called out from above as well.

"Listen to him, Leo!" Sara yelled down. "For now, you need to let them fight!"

Leo stared up at Sara in shock. What game was she playing at? Why would she willingly allow this man to place these Adventurers in danger?

Yet as he stared up at his partner, the firm cast of her features told him this was no act. She really did want him to let this man toss Cyrus into the arena alongside Evie. Sara wouldn't do that if she didn't have a good reason. He didn't trust Teacher, but he trusted Sara.

Sara must know something he didn't, something she had learned from her interrogation of Teacher after they left together. As much as every instinct in his body urged him to attack the desouled Rock Spiders and stab them until they turned to dust, he sheathed his spear and stepped back.

Cyrus finally made a run for it, but far too late. A desouled Rock Spider leapt and pinned him. He shrieked as the other skittered over, palps pulsing. Between the two of them, the Rock Spiders picked up a thrashing Cyrus and scurried down the ramp to the second level.

The disciples down there had already lowered the last ramp. Evie hurried down the ramp, evidently in no mood to be carried into the arena by Rock Spiders. Once she was on the ground floor, the two disciples pulled up the ramp. That was about the time the spiders and Cyrus arrived.

"Don't!" Cyrus screamed. "I don't want to... agh!"

The spiders simply tossed Cyrus into the arena. Leo winced as he heard something visibly snap once Cyrus landed on the rocky ground. His howl of pain made Leo physically uncomfortable, but he was an Anchorite, wasn't he? A fall like that should only make him stronger, and he could simply use [-Aura Mend-] to heal whatever injury he'd just suffered. Couldn't he?

Evie hurried over and attempted to help Cyrus to his feet. Instead, the man visibly pushed her away. He rolled onto his rear, drawing his knees up to his chest. He wrapped his arms around his knees and sat stubbornly, like a child angry about being punished for defying his parents.

"Gather your weapons!" Teacher called from above. "The cage will open in thirty seconds!"

Evie gasped and hurried to one of the crates. She pulled the lid off, which at least assured Leo it wasn't locked. She pulled out what looked to be [Ring-Mail Armor], armor suitable for both low-level casters and melee classes, and also, thanks to its cloth-like nature, a piece of armor she could easily slip over her own head. That would offer some protection for her chest and waist, but her legs and arms remained bare. Even caster robes, which covered the full body, didn't protect those.

Evie rummaged desperately through the crate and picked up what Leo immediately recognized as a plain but well-maintained [Steel Dagger]. He hoped she at least knew [-Shadow Blast-]. If she got one or two of those off before the Monster closed in on her, she could blind it and then stab it to death.

If she didn't, she could get bitten or scratched very quickly. This "arena" was scarcely bigger than the common room of a small tavern. There wasn't much room to run from a fight and no tables to use as cover, so without a melee class to hold the Goblins at bay, she would be overrun quickly.

Cyrus remained sitting on the floor, clad only in his commoner's clothing. Was he seriously going to let himself get murdered by a Monster today? No... he likely planned to let Evie do his fighting for him. What kind of an Adventurer would let his friend and party member fight a Monster alone?

One of the cages snapped open.

Leo stepped forward and once more gripped his spear as a slavering Goblin stumbled out of the cage. Its beady red gaze immediately alighted upon Cyrus and then away, as the Monster... which had an almost humanoid intelligence... decided he was no threat. Evie, on the other hand...

The Goblin charged her with a blabbering snarl. Its only weapon was a rusty-looking [Commoner's Dagger] and it wore no armor save for a filthy loincloth, but its poisoned claws and drool-stained teeth were far more deadly than any common blade. Two level 13 Adventurers should be able to easily dispatch a lone Goblin, but Cyrus was obviously in no mood to fight.

Evie raised one hand as black and purple energy swirled in her palm. She unleased what Leo recognized as [-Shadow Blast-], but the Goblin was fast enough that she looked terrified. Arm trembling, her blast went wide. The Goblin then leapt for her, screeching in triumph.

"Dive!" Leo shouted.

His shout reached her at the last moment. Evie dived sideways as the Goblin came for her, and the frenzied Monster missed taking her down by a hair. It slammed into the rock behind her as Evie stumbled back, but it was back on its feet in another moment... just in time to take a [-Shadow Blast-] to the face. The Monster shrieked and stumbled backward. Blinded, it batted at its shadow-cloaked eyes.

Its red Health Bar appeared for the first time in the fight, assuring everyone who now watched that the blast had struck home. Better yet, Evie's [-Shadow Blast-] had ashed what looked to be a tenth of its bar. That suggested this Goblin was level 10 at best, three levels below her. Any lower than that and killing the Monster wouldn't even yield experience.

While [-Shadow Blast-] didn't blind a Monster every time it hit, especially if that Monster was high level, there was always a chance. Evie had three levels on this Goblin. Yet as the Monster snarled and stumbled about, stabbing blindly with its dagger, Evie backed away. Unless she pressed the attack, the Goblin would soon regain its sight, and she might not get so lucky again.

"Attack it now, while it's blinded!" Leo shouted. "Go for its legs!"

Evie glanced up at him with visible worry.

"Stab it in the legs!" Leo shouted. "You have to slow it down before your blind wears off!"

Desperation or resignation took Evie as she went back on the offensive. Leo's heart leapt into his throat as the Goblin stabbed at her blindly, but she somehow slipped past the blow. Her **[Steel Dagger]** plunged into the Goblin's side, then its thigh. The beast shrieked and slashed blindly as its Health Bar ashed further, though not by much. Evie's Strength must be rather low.

Evie shrieked as well as the rusty blade sliced a deep and bloody line into her upper arm, but the blade glanced off her **[Ring-Mail Armor]** instead of striking an organ. She stabbed again and again, and both strikes plunged deep into the Goblin's flesh. It stumbled and fell to one knee as it slashed at her again, but again the blow glanced off her armor instead of cutting flesh.

Evie's Health Bar had appeared once the Goblin struck her, revealing over a fourth of it had ashed from just that single glancing strike. Her Vitality must be as low as her Strength. Not good. Still, more of the Goblin's red Health Bar had ashed with Evie's strikes. It was obviously in worse shape.

The Goblin was down to less than fifty percent Health now, and its tortured wheezing and snarls assured Leo it was hurting. His experience with fighting Goblins with the Blazers continued to come in handy. They remained relatively weak Monsters one-on-one.

"Run to the other side!" Leo shouted from above. "Hit it with more spells!"

Evie finally seemed to be listening. She ran to the other edge of the arena, then turned when she reached it to put her back against the wall. The Goblin angrily shook its head and stumbled forward as the shadow cloaking its eyes melted away. Its red eyes fixed on Evie as it stumbled after her.

Yet she already had another **[-Shadow Blast-]** forming in her palm. This time, as it became obvious to everyone that the Goblin could, at best, manage a lumbering jog, her aim was true. Her next **[-Shadow Blast-]** slammed into the Goblin and seared its flesh. That ashed its Health Bar to under a third. It shrieked and waved its dagger madly, but Evie's earlier strikes had hobbled it.

Evie unleashed another **[-Shadow Blast-]**. It slammed into the Goblin and knocked it onto its back, leaving but a sliver of Health Bar. Yet Evie also dropped to her knees. The fact that her skin was now disturbingly pale told Leo she had, perhaps, spent the last of her Blood using her Skill.

Becka could easily toss eight **[-Shadow Blasts-]** without pausing to quaff a Blood Potion, and she was only level 12. Evie must not have as much Wisdom as Becka if she could only manage four **[-Shadow Blast-]**s before she collapsed. Still, the Goblin was barely a threat any longer.

"Finish it with your knife!" Leo called. "You have to finish it now!"

Grimacing, Evie stumbled to her feet. She walked, shakily, toward where the barely conscious Goblin lay on its back with a sliver of red Health Bar remaining. As she approached, Leo saw the Goblin's blackened fingers tighten around the hilt of its rusty **[Commoner's Dagger]**. That was the only warning Leo had that it was conscious... and he was glad he had been paying close attention.

"Stop there!" Leo shouted. "It's playing dead!"

Incensed by Leo's words, the Goblin lumbered to its feet... but its many wounds and the impact of so many **[-Shadow Blast-]**s left it clumsy and slow. Evie had no trouble stepping back to avoid its attacks. It slashed at her, once, twice, thrice, before collapsing onto its face in exhaustion.

"Now!" Leo shouted. "Take it down!"

With a little snarl, Evie jumped on the back of the Goblin and plunged her dagger into its back. She howled with respectable fury as she stabbed again and again, and again. Leo wanted to cheer as the Goblin burst to ash below her, but he didn't want Teacher to think he was enjoying watching... this.

Panting and pale, Evie tumbled to the rocky ground on a rapidly dissipating pile of ash. A purple, glowing life crystal the size of a grapefruit appeared where the Goblin had fallen. Evie had won!

As she grabbed her arm and winced, however, it was obvious from the small icon on her Health Bar and the way it ashed incrementally every few seconds that she was bleeding. Leo looked around and then stared down at the disciples. "What are you waiting for? She won the fight. Heal her!"

Teacher's voice filled the cavern. "Evie Greenfeather, today you have honored the Gods. Rejoice in your accomplishment. The life crystal is yours. Take it with my blessing."

Evie scooped up the life crystal as best she could. She still looked pale and weak.

"Cyrus Hillmane!" Teacher called. "Once again, you have failed to do as the Gods demand! You also allowed your adventuring partner to fight a Goblin alone and made no move to help her!"

Cyrus said nothing. He still didn't move.

"For refusing to resume Luxtera's Climb and for allowing your partner to face danger without you, you will spend a day in the hole."

Now, at last, Cyrus reacted. He jumped up and stared wide-eyed. "No, you can't!"

Maria chuckled darkly at Leo's side. "Bloody fool. Maybe this will get him off his arse."

"Don't do that!" Cyrus shouted madly. "I'll fight! Send out another Goblin!" Yet even as he spoke, the same desouled Rock Spiders from earlier burrowed up from the floor of the arena.

Before Leo could do more than draw his spear and step forward, the spiders below spit bursts of sticky rock at Cyrus. They bound his feet and legs together. He toppled and then struggled to escape the spiders, moving like an inchworm while he screamed. As the spiders closed on him, Leo glanced up desperately at the platform. Sara watched him from above.

Again, she shook her head. She didn't want him to intervene. How could he not intervene?

From below, Cyrus's cries ceased. Leo looked down again to find that the Rock Spiders had bound him up in rock like a cocoon, leaving only his nose and terrified eyes visible. One spider spun and visibly opened a hole into the earth, then skittered through it. As it did so, a strand of rocky web dragged Cyrus, feet first, after it. He disappeared into the hole, followed by the other spider.

"They won't kill him," Maria said from Leo's side. "But he'll have a rough night stuck in a hole, alone, with only the dark for company."

Leo glared at her. "Don't you care about any of these people?"

Maria glared back in response. "It's because I *care* about them that I don't need you doing anything stupid, Blazer. You may think this is barbaric, but Teacher will do far worse to us if you attack him. I don't need you getting us thrown in the hole because you decided to be a hero and failed, again."

The hole in the floor of the arena vanished. There was no more sign of Cyrus Hillmane, but the disciples had not lowered the ramp that connected the floor and second ring. Were they going to make Evie fight another Goblin? What were they waiting on?

Evie answered Leo's silent question a moment later. She rose, stumbled to the crate she'd opened, and tossed in the **[Steel Dagger]** she'd used to fight the Goblin. Then she pulled the **[Ring-Mail Armor]** off over her head and tossed that in as well. Finally, she replaced the lid on the crate.

Only then did the disciples lower the ramp from the second floor to the lower floor into place. A pale-faced Evie stumbled up it, clutching her bleeding arm. As she did so, golden energy washed across her body. Leo was relieved to see one of the disciples had just cast **[-Flash Heal-]**.

So one was a Lifecaster! A Lifecaster working for a madman. Did they also believe in this "Scripture of Ralun" Tom claimed Teacher possessed?

Evie's ashed Health Bar healed to full before vanishing. The fact that a single **[-Flash Heal-]** had topped her off was more evidence of her low Vitality. Perhaps this was why she was afraid to fight Monsters on her own. An Antlion or Minotaur could likely kill her with one or two lucky strikes.

Teacher's voice boomed once more from the platform. "Kenneth Tallwood! Tom Brightbow! You are next into the arena! Protect your adventuring partner and honor the Gods!"

Kenneth crackled his knuckles and then rolled his head around on his shoulders. "Time to earn our supper, Brightbow. I just hope we don't get the Antlion."

Tom stepped to Kenneth's side. "**[-Marching Rose-]** or **[-Morning Dew-]**?"

Leo knew those Auracaster Skills. The former raised the Strength of all members in a party, while the latter passively healed 5 Health Points every 10 seconds. At least Tom had spent enough time leveling to gain two of an Auracaster's most popular Skills. He just didn't like using them.

"Let's go with Rose today," Kenneth said. "I want to get this over with quickly, so I'll just beat the Monster into submission. Just don't let it hit you."

Tom smiled cheerily as they proceeded down the platform together. "Of course not." He glanced back at Leo as he reached the second ring. "Any tips for this one, little brother?"

Leo watched him with more worry than he expected. "Stay behind

Kenneth. Don't be afraid to stop playing if the Monster runs at you. Only play if you're sure its attention is already on your partner."

Evie returned to the party as Kenneth and Tom walked down. She glanced at him as she arrived, her lips pressed together. Was that gratitude he saw on her features?

"Thank you," Evie said. "Cyrus was just... I'm glad you were here."

Leo nodded. "You fought well down there. You need to work on holding your arm steady when a Monster is coming at you, but you did well to avoid the Goblin's blade. Overall, I was impressed."

Evie's eyes widened as he spoke, but he didn't miss the way her shoulders squared up and her stance firmed as she absorbed his words. Leo knew enough from working with younger Blazers that a little encouragement could go a long way. Evie would remember his words... and hopefully, gain the confidence she needed to help her in the future.

She didn't say anything else. But as she joined everyone else in watching the next fight in the arena, she looked far more interested than she had been. She would be paying close attention.

Below, Kenneth and Tom entered the lowest level of the arena. Both headed to different crates, and both pulled out what he expected. Kenneth pulled out another set of [Ring-Mail Armor]... perhaps that was all they had available... and a gleaming [Steel Greatsword].

So he was already fighting like a Cleaver despite having not Evolved his Class. It was just as Leo had suspected. Kenneth had stopped leveling since Demons would ruin him, and because few parties would take a Brutalist who didn't know [-Taunt-] or use [-Mighty Smash-].

Tom produced what looked to be a serviceable [Minstrel's Lute] from another crate and strummed it experimentally. "Hold a moment," he said. "Need to tune this before we start."

"No time," Kenneth said. "Just try not to be entirely off key."

From ahead, a cage clicked open. It was the cage containing the Antlion. As Kenneth and Tom both realized this, their curses came in unison. With a roar, the Antlion clambered out.

Yet Leo couldn't help but be a bit proud of how they both immediately leapt to the attack.

THREE
A MENTOR'S REINTRODUCTION
GLENN

When they reached the gate to the fine dining district where Glenn had met Brennon Shadesinger for lunch more than two levels ago, the same Town Guard who'd been there that day was once again on duty: Trevor Mosscloud. Glenn now used **[-Soul Scan-]** instinctively on all those whose identity he couldn't verify by visual inspection, even though he felt guilty about it afterward.

Yet it would be irresponsible to run into a problem at this juncture simply because his inconvenient moral scruples got in the way. Sara and Leo were missing, and Jenny Ambersun might be the only Blazer ranked high enough to change Marion's mind about who would go and rescue them. She was also the only Blazer whose rank was high enough to actually challenge Marion.

As Becka had said, Jenny and Marion were rivals... to an extent. Glenn hated the idea of taking advantage of discord between two Blazers he respected, but Becka wasn't wrong about their ability to do so. She'd never been wrong about the complexities of interpersonal relationships before, so Glenn had no reason to doubt her this time. He was so grateful for her counsel.

The trip through the gate was painless—Glenn and Becka both showed their Status Sheets to Trevor, who nodded and waved them through—and then they were once again on the lovely and well-maintained boardwalk that ran along the river leading to the bay. The smells from the expensive restaurants clustered along this walk were delightful, and Becka looked *fantastic* in her blue **[Noblewoman's Dress]**. Then again, she looked fantastic in everything.

If only this could simply be another night out on the town. Another date. Yet Glenn could never relax and enjoy himself, even when he had such a beautiful and intelligent woman on his arm, while his friends languished in an unknown prison somewhere. He had to find and rescue them.

While Becka visibly clung to his arm as they walked, he subtly let her take the lead. She knew better than he where to find Jenny this time of night. They walked the full length of the dock as Becka subtly scanned the restaurants, but didn't stop. They were halfway back, and Glenn was starting to worry when Becka's subtle pull on his bicep suggested they change course. Glenn let her lead him.

They walked to the entry to a restaurant at the same moment a tall blonde woman dressed in a white-and-yellow **[Noblewoman's Dress]** almost as low-cut as Becka's strode off of a restaurant the sign identified as the Flying Fish. Her blonde hair rested atop her head in an elaborate series of braided curls, and narrow silver pins held it in place. What might be real emeralds dangled from her earlobes.

Glenn blinked in surprise. He recognized the same brave Blazer recruiter he'd met for the first time over two years ago on the Dewdrop Hills outside Grassea... but only barely. Dressed up for a night on the town, Jenny Ambersun rivaled the richest nobles he'd seen in Lakebrooke. He suspected she would blend into any high society party in the city, even one thrown by the Marshvales.

Jenny smoothly slowed and smiled as she spotted Becka's approach. She motioned incrementally with her head for Becka to meet her out of the way of others who might be exiting or entering the restaurant. Becka released Glenn's arm and took the lead as she did so.

Glenn followed reluctantly, praying the effect of his Guilecaster charm would hold strong. Jenny should see the man she remembered... but not remember him as that man. Time to find out if this Guilecaster charm was worth whatever Aiden Goodfellow had paid for it.

Once they were standing in the shadow of the Flying Fish and far enough from the tables they wouldn't be overheard, Jenny spoke. "This is not a chance meeting, is it? You came looking for me."

"I did," Becka said. "I'm sorry to bother you on your night off. I know you have so few of them, but you were the only person we could turn to regarding an urgent problem."

"Well, I can't say that doesn't sound interesting. How can I help you tonight?"

Jenny sounded just as confident and friendly as Glenn remembered from over two years ago. And while she had offered him a curious once-over as he approached, he'd seen nothing in her features that implied she recognized him. So his charm was working... or she was a talented actress.

Becka smiled wide. "Before we talk about that, I want to introduce you to my partner. This is Glenn Graybreaker." She paused. "And by partner, I mean we're dating. To be absolutely clear."

Jenny offered Glenn a casual nod. "A pleasure, Glenn. I'm Jenny Ambersun, level 23 Spiritualist."

So Jenny had gained three levels in Spiritualist in the past two years despite continuing with her recruiting duties across Luxtera. She truly was something special.

He answered her polite greeting with his own. "Glenn Graybreaker, level 14 Brutalist. And it's a pleasure to meet you finally, Miss Ambersun. Becka told me she's really enjoyed training with you."

"It is a coincidence, though," Jenny said. "That she would be dating another Glenn."

Glenn blinked. "I'm sorry?"

Becka touched Jenny's arm. "Before we get to the problem I mentioned, I genuinely do want to know how you've been. How was the trip out to Aquarine?"

Thank the Gods. Becka was redirecting the conversation.

Jenny sighed and brushed back her blonde hair. "Not as productive as I'd hoped. The candidate showed promise, but it also became clear as the interview continued that she simply wasn't ready to step away. Others in Bredon confirmed my suspicions, though not intentionally. She was too attached to her parents and Lindow Village to leave it all behind. It would become a problem."

Lindow Village, Glenn remembered, was the starter town in Aquarine's starter zone of Bredon. Anna Bronzelight, the only other Soulseer in Luxtera, had leveled there for a time before she fled to Wolfpine and encountered Glenn and Zack, though Anna actually hailed from Frostford, Aquarine's equivalent to Lakebrooke. Jenny really did travel the world in her quest to recruit new Blazers.

"I'm sorry to hear that," Becka said sympathetically. "But I suppose it would have been unwise to recruit someone who would eventually grow desperately homesick."

"It certainly would be. So how are you doing, Becka? Since Wolfpine?"

Gods! Jenny was talking about the incident where her childhood love, Glenn Redwood, had died... or so Jenny must believe. She spoke of it so casually he wondered if she was talking about something else.

"I'm doing well enough," Becka agreed cautiously.

"I'm glad to hear that. I know the news from home was difficult to process. I want to state again that if you ever want to talk to someone about it, I'm here."

Jenny meant the news regarding the deaths of Glenn Redwood and Zack Silverstone, Becka's childhood friends. Was Jenny implying she knew at least some of those deaths were faked?

"I appreciate your offer," Becka said. "But I assure you, I'm coping. As we discussed that day you first recruited me, we can only move forward, not back. I need to move forward."

"A good plan," Jenny agreed calmly. Once more, her gaze fell upon Glenn.

He couldn't swallow. He smiled instead. He tried to look as natural as he could.

"So, Glenn," Jenny asked. "How did you and Becka meet?"

Glenn's mind stuttered as her seemingly innocent question threw him for a loop. How had he met Becka? What was the story they'd settled on when Ashley Bloodbraid asked the same question?

Becka offered a rueful sigh. "It's a fun story, but it will have to wait for another night. Leo and Sara are missing, and I was hoping you could help us look into the matter."

Jenny's playful expression hardened as she visibly set aside any attempt to tease the story of how Becka had met the *second* Glenn she had ever dated. "Tell me everything you know."

Becka summarized the results of their investigation with a precision Glenn could only marvel at. When she finished, Jenny nodded and once more brushed her bangs back from her face. "Leo would never fall out of contact like this, nor would Sara. And Marion truly wishes you to let this go?"

"She gave explicit orders that Glenn and I are not to look for them. She also promised she would have someone look into it, but you know how many issues she handles on a daily basis. Issues that spawn the zones and may seem more pressing. You can see why we aren't exactly eager to jump on a boat tomorrow and leave our good friends to their fate."

"Yet perhaps you should," Jenny said calmly.

Before Becka could say anything, Glenn stepped forward. "Not you too!"

Jenny glanced at him and offered what looked to be a sympathetic smile. "Tell me, Glenn Graybreaker. Do you believe you deserve to be a Truth Seeker?"

"Of course I do." Yet something in her tone gave him pause.

"And as a Truth Seeker, a Blazer who focuses on facts and evidence above all else, do you truly believe that the best person to search for Leo and Sara would be a party member who cares dearly for them and would do anything to keep them safe? Someone who lacks objectivity?"

"I can remain objective."

"The way you reacted when I suggested you should both keep your appointment with the boat suggests differently," Jenny said... though not unkindly. "So I will ask you the question you should be asking yourself. Are you the best choice to search for your missing friends? Think before you answer."

Glenn almost answered her before he caught himself. Of course there were better options to find Sara and Leo. He'd said as much to Marion when she refused to let him handle the search himself.

Brennon had far more experience with finding missing people and also had connections across the city Glenn which lacked. Jenny also seemed well-connected and well-respected throughout the city, especially by the Blazers she'd trained or worked with. Either would be a better choice to look for Leo and Sara than him, especially since his feelings about them might color his perceptions.

"I'm the best option of those available," Glenn answered calmly.

Jenny nodded. "That's a fair answer. Still, nothing you've told me makes me confident I can convince Captain Hawkshadow to change her mind. While we don't agree on all aspects of training our new recruits or how we deploy them, in this case, I feel her concerns are warranted."

Becka grimaced. "Then you won't speak to her?"

Jenny turned back to Becka and gripped her hands. "I wish I could, if only because of how much I truly care for you. But I also don't like it when you lie to me."

Becka's features went calm. "How have I lied?"

"You're not convinced Glenn is the best option to find Sara and Leo either."

Glenn gasped as Becka's unflappable, confident mask fell for just long enough to assure him what Jenny said was true. He wanted to yell at them both, to insist they were wrong and hadn't considered all the facts, but he couldn't deny the facts any longer. Truth Seekers didn't do that.

"Gods," Glenn said. "You're right. I really am too close to this to be objective about it. If I let myself get distracted or overcome with emotion, I could miss something. I could fail my friends."

Becka looked absolutely crestfallen as she stared at him. "Glenn, I'm—"

"—too close to *me* to be objective. You didn't want to tell me this because you care about me too much."

Becka said nothing. She merely wrung her hands. They both knew he was right.

Jenny walked over and placed one warm hand on his shoulder. "The fact that you're willing to consider this speaks to how much you care about them. It's no weakness to recognize there are people out there who may be better qualified to solve a problem that drops into your lap. It's a sign of a rational mind that puts the well-being of others above concessions to their own ego."

Glenn sighed. "But even knowing this, I can't step away. I may not be the best choice to find them, but no one else is stepping up to take my place. Unless you know someone better?"

Jenny smiled at him. "I'd be willing to look into it."

Glenn stared at her in relief. "You would be?"

"Of course. Like you, I care deeply for Leo and Sara, but unlike you, I've also had a bit more... experience... in separating my feelings about those I care about from my responsibilities to keep them safe.

This isn't a matter I'd be comfortable handling on my own, but I know people I trust to help me. People who have excellent tracking skills. Together, we can find them."

Glenn smiled wide. "That would be wonderful."

"But we need more than you have to begin. What you've given us isn't enough to start searching for them, so until it's time to hop on that boat, I see no reason why you shouldn't continue to investigate this matter on your own. Just be ready to hand it off to us when you know more."

"But Captain Hawkshadow ordered us not to investigate this matter further," Becka said. "If she finds out we're still looking into it, that could cause a problem."

Jenny glanced at her. "What were her exact words?"

"She ordered us to focus on packing for our trip to Caelfall and preparing Glenn for the **<Sandsea Cup>**. Our boat leaves tomorrow afternoon."

"Then you should focus on preparing Glenn to compete in the **<Sandsea Cup>**. A good first step might be ensuring he believes the search for his friends is in good hands before he leaves. Otherwise, he'll be constantly distracted in Caelfall and could be injured in a tourney match."

A faint smile crossed Becka's face. "Preparing Glenn for travel *is* what Marion asked us to do."

"I will admit I'm surprised she agreed to let you step away from training to attend the cup."

"As are we. But she is right about something else. If we don't hop on that boat tomorrow, we'll arrive too late to join the rolls of Adventurers participating in the **<Sandsea Cup>**. They don't take latecomers." She looked to Glenn. "And unless we enter it and win, we may not level as fast as we hope to level."

In other words, he might not reach level 15 in time to complete his Quest to resurrect Zack. Before now, choosing between Zack's life and his worry over Sara and Leo's disappearance had seemed like an impossible choice. But with Jenny to look into it...

Glenn looked back at Jenny. "Thank you for offering to do this."

"I can't do it yet. I mean what I said. I need more than you have gathered so far before I can justify devoting more resources to finding our missing Blazers. Right now, they've simply stepped away from their training. We have no proof they've been abducted."

"Other than that they'd never step away from the Blazers."

"A fact you, Becka, and I accept. Our personal impressions and opinions of two Junior Blazers are not what gets us the Blazer resources we need. We need evidence."

"I'll find more evidence," Glenn said. "And I'll find it before tomorrow afternoon."

"I believe you. But since you've come all this way, could I offer a suggestion?"

Glenn smiled gratefully. "Please."

"You should offer a Quest in the Old Fishing District for information on Leo, Sara, and Ripper from anyone who might have seen them or saw where they went."

Glenn gasped. Hadn't Leo done the same back in Wolfpine when he needed to track down Anna and Alan in a town full of people desperate for experience and coin? Those had been healthy Adventurers. The people in the Old Fishing District would be even more desperate.

"That's a lot of coin," Becka said cautiously.

Glenn smiled happily. "But I can afford it, thanks to that huge stipend I got from the Marshvales for saving their business." He looked at Jenny again. "It's a good idea. Thank you."

Jenny smiled back. "I simply hope my suggestion bears fruit. Now, as much as I might enjoy catching up with Becka or getting to know you better, Glenn, I do have other plans tonight. I've kept them waiting longer than I feel comfortable with. So if there's nothing else..."

Glenn stepped aside. "Of course. How do we get in touch with you once we know more?"

"Becka can leave a letter with the details at the usual place. I'll check tomorrow after lunch, and if you've given me what I need, I'll get the search party organized."

"Thank you," Becka said. "And... I hope you and your plans have a good time."

Jenny smiled fondly. "We always do. Good night, you two."

She turned and strode down the docks toward the exit still

guarded by Trever Mosscloud. Glenn glanced at Becka. "Is it safe to leave a message about this with Aiden? He might tell Marion."

Becka eyed him in amusement. "He would tell Marion. Which is why we aren't leaving the message with him, or leaving anything at the Blazers Guild."

"Oh," Glenn said... reluctantly. "So you and Jenny have another way to communicate outside of the official Blazer channels?" That almost sounded illegal.

"I didn't say outside. I just said different. But we'll have plenty of time for me to explain all that while we walk. If we're going to commission a Quest tonight, we need to do it quickly."

"Right! I'm glad we spoke to her. I just wish she was less... well, insightful."

"You and me both. I knew we couldn't fool her."

Glenn glanced at Becka in alarm. "Fool her about what?"

Becka calmly stared into his eyes. Without words, he knew. Jenny knew too. Jenny Ambersun knew the true fate of Glenn Redwood. She'd likely known the truth for some time.

Glenn rubbed the back of his head. "Am I really that bad of an actor?"

"This one's on me. Jenny knows how much I loved Glenn Redwood because she was the first Blazer to meet and recruit us both. She saw me pine for you during training, when we were both convinced we might never see each other for twenty years. When you died..."

He gripped her hands.

"When I thought you died," Becka continued softly, "it left me rather out of sorts."

"I'm so sorry I made you feel that way." As he remembered the extra week he'd spent in the Deepscorn Woods leveling Ripper, he remembered that he'd also let Becka think he was dead for at least that long. He'd only learned later that no one had told her until she returned from Aquarine.

"Once I learned the truth, I did all I could to appear as if I grieved, but Jenny knew me too well to believe it. I think she suspected the moment I learned the truth and my attitude changed."

"When you learned I wasn't dead."

"Yes. And the moment she saw the way we looked at each other, I knew I couldn't keep it from her even if I wished to do so. I trust her to keep this matter to herself, and I obviously love you far too much for us to have only met a few months ago. So... that's my weakness."

Glenn pulled her close and kissed her. She responded eagerly, and Glenn only remembered they were still in public when a patron at one of the tables in the nearby restaurant *loudly* cleared their throat. Blushing and overcome with emotion, Glenn glanced in their direction, offered a nod of apology, and headed off to find a Merchant with Becka clinging to his arm.

"So you're certain she won't tell anyone?" Glenn asked.

"She won't. She'll also do everything in her power to track down Sara and Leo. We just need to make sure we set her on the path before we leave."

"That we can do. At the moment, I'm just frustrated I didn't think of her idea myself."

"Learn and improve, love. Now, do you already have a Merchant in mind?"

"I do, and I think he'll be eager to help us and get his cut."

FOUR
AN EXPENSIVE QUEST

It was now less than an hour from dawn on the day he was supposed to hop on a boat to Caelfall and sail away from Lakebrooke, and Glenn could barely keep his eyes open. It didn't help that he was stuck sitting in a small shack near the gate of the Old Fishing District, or that he'd spent the entire night following its many denizens around the district chasing down one bad lead after another on his missing friends. He'd never give up on either Leo or Sara, but he would need to sleep soon.

Jenny's plan to find them had seemed so brilliant when she first brought it up. Glenn still had a large reserve of moons from the reward Lord and Lady Marshvale had given him for saving their fishing business. A little over two-thirds of his remaining coin would be enough to create an official Quest to bring him verified information regarding the whereabouts of Sara Cinderflare and Leopold Argentshade... and their looming Arctic Wolf. It was difficult to miss Ripper.

People in the Old Fishing District talked, and someone had to have seen *something*. The people who lived here wouldn't talk to a Blazer under normal circumstances, not for free, but this was an actual Quest that provided both coin *and* experience. Glenn had known even the most jaded resident of the district would eagerly jump at the chance to make some easy experience and coin.

Of course, Glenn couldn't create an official Quest on his own. He wasn't Townsfolk. He did, however, know a local Merchant who had agreed to create the Quest on his behalf.

Glenn had given the Merchant the coin to pay the Quest submission fee to the city and also provided the Quest reward. Paying for both (and paying the Merchant's ten-percent commission on top of all that) had savaged his once impressive savings, but he still had a reasonable nest egg. Just not enough to buy Becka any more dresses or enjoy another meal of fine crab legs.

Still, he was now completely out of debt, and he could always kill more Monsters, sell more life crystals, and earn more moons once he concluded his journey to the <Sandsea Cup>. No amount of money was worth more than the lives of his friends. Glenn's Quest had inspired dozens of tips from the locals living in the Old Fishing District... though so far, none had proven useful.

After a whole night of listening to, following around, and investigating tips from the locals that had offered no real new information, the disappearance of Sara Cinderflare and Leopold Argentshade remained unsolved. They had entered this district... that was certain... but the unsolved mystery of how they'd vanished *vexed* him. They hadn't left through the gate, there was no way to leave this district otherwise, and they certainly hadn't left Lakebrooke. He'd asked at all the gates.

If Sara and Leo were tied up or otherwise imprisoned in some dilapidated building in the Old Fishing District, someone would have found them by now. The residents were certainly motivated to complete his Quest, and they knew every nook and cranny of this section of Lakebrooke far better than he did. Since no one had claimed his Quest reward, they truly hadn't found his friends.

Even encountering a Voidstrider like Arthur Everglow wouldn't explain how Leo and Sara had exited the district. They could have used a Voidstrider's teleport abilities to slip out of the district itself and enter the city, but even a Voidstrider's teleports couldn't take them through town walls. Just like Monsters, Demons, and others, the Gods forbid Adventurers from bypassing the walls of a city through teleportation magic. Otherwise, it would be trivial for ne'er-do-wells to avoid Town Guards.

The other possibility... and it was a terrifying possibility... was that Leo and Sara were dead. If a Deathcaster had killed them, he could have placed their bodies in an [Unfilled Bag] and smuggled them out with no one the wiser. Even so, Glenn couldn't believe that. Some event had befallen the two of them, something that prevented them from making contact, but they had to be alive.

Believing anything else would depress him too much to continue looking.

Another knock on the door jolted him from his disappointed musing, but he immediately recognized it. That was Becka's knock. He didn't bother getting up from his chair since he needed to save energy. There had been many knocks in late afternoon and after night fell, but visitors had fallen off rapidly as Glenn spoke to each of them. None had offered the information to complete his Quest.

Becka entered without being prompted, smiled as she spotted him sitting in his chair, and walked around to the back of it. She wrapped her warm arms around his chest from behind. She kissed his shoulder and sighed. "Still no luck?"

Glenn shook his head.

"You really do need sleep," Becka said. "I got in at least four hours. I'm good for the day, and we agreed we'd sleep in shifts as we waited for people to turn in tips. It's your turn to sleep."

Glenn sighed heavily. "I know. I did promise." He reached up to wrap a big hand around one of her forearms. "I just hate leaving a task unfinished. I really thought this Quest would unearth something more than the fact that people saw them walking through the district. We already knew that."

"At least you can get your coin back," Becka said soothingly. "Or some of it. Right? You can refund some of the cost of commissioning a Quest if no one manages to complete it in a week."

"I won't even be here to do that. We'll be on a boat to Caelfall."

"Then simply have your Merchant friend handle the refund. He's the one who officially filed the Quest anyway. But if you can, try to bargain them down from ten percent."

Glenn glanced back at her. "I honestly don't know what I'd do without you."

Becka kissed his ear. "You'd certainly be having a lot less sex."

He couldn't help but chuckle at her constant teasing. She never stopped trying to cheer him up. She always did all she could to take his mind off his troubles, and it was working... sort of.

"Now, to bed with you," Becka ordered. "If any resident of this lovely district brings me information that explains where Leo and Sara wandered off to, I will rouse you immediately. But you will be useless to everyone if you're stumbling around like a Desouled."

"I think I might just sleep right here. In the corner. With a blanket."

"Only if you *promise* to sleep. No faking with your eyes closed."

Glenn rose from the chair as Becka gamely hung on with her arms wrapped around her chest, and she huffed playfully as her feet dangled off the ground. He turned... slowly, so as not to dislodge Becka... and walked to one corner of the room. She finally dropped off him.

Glenn yawned. "I don't think I could fake anything now. I'm *really* tired."

"Then sleep well, love. I'll handle any tips that come in for the next few hours."

There wasn't really anywhere comfortable to sleep in the old dilapidated shack he'd paid a local a full moon to "rent" for the day, but there was a pile of hay in the corner. Glenn had slept on worse. He settled down and had just gotten comfortable when a quiet knock sounded.

"I'll get it," Becka said before he could say anything. "Don't you dare move."

Glenn let his eyes close as the creaking of steps on wood announced Becka walking to the door. Still, he couldn't fall asleep. Not until he knew who this was and why they had come to see him. He heard Becka open the door and then a man's whisper. He couldn't make out the words.

The door closed once more. More whispering continued. Glenn couldn't hear what their visitor was saying, so he opened his eyes and sat up.

Becka grimaced as she stepped back and a thin, older man stepped inside. He had weathered skin and gray hair, and while it could be rough living, Glenn had the impression he was at least fifty. Why was he whispering?

The old man's eyes widened as he spotted Glenn in the corner. "You! You're Graybreaker?"

"I am." Even as Becka frowned his way to discourage him, he rose to his full height. "And it's awful late, Mister... what do I call you?"

"Everett Commoncloud," the old man said stiffly and proudly. "Level 16 Merchant."

So this man was Townsfolk. Interesting. Most of the people who'd approached him tonight had been down-on-their-luck Adventurers, so at least having a Merchant approach him was novel. The problem was, Glenn was rather low on coin at the moment. He didn't have the capital to make a deal.

Still, this man obviously had something on his mind. Glenn was desperate enough he wouldn't turn down any opportunities right now. Becka spoke before he could.

"What can we do for you this morning, Mister Commoncloud?"

Glenn had almost forgotten it was morning. Gods. The sun would be up in an hour or so, and he hadn't slept for almost forty hours.

If only [-Guardian's Heal-] also regenerated his energy! Even [+Regrowth+], which could keep him going for a long time when fighting constantly, was obviously reaching its limit. His rare Town Guard Blessing couldn't let him stay awake forever.

Everett cleared his throat. "First, I need your word that you will not speak of the information I offer to anyone who lives here. I want to complete the Quest anonymously. I need your guarantee that no one will know I completed it. Not the Blazers, not the Town Guard, not even the city."

Glenn perked up despite his exhaustion. No one who had contacted them previously had said anything about wanting to complete his Quest anonymously. That suggested that Everett, at least, believed he had something more than "I saw them over here!" or "They passed this way."

"That won't be easy, Mister Commoncloud," Becka said diplomatically. "It will also cost more to add anonymity to the Quest, and obviously, Mayor Earthwhite will have to meet you in person. You know no Quest can be certified as complete without the blessing of the mayor."

"That's fine. The mayor's not who I'm worried about. It's all the people who live here with me. If they find out I've spoken to you, I'll never make another deal again."

"Spoken to us about what?" Glenn asked.

Everett stared at him. "I know how the people you're looking for got out of the city."

Glenn felt a rush of triumph and tempered it with all the disappointment he'd suffered tonight. Could this be it, finally? Could the answer be within reach? Everett certainly *looked* confident.

"How?" he asked.

Everett's features hardened. "Your word, Graybreaker. Swear to me you'll make the Quest anonymous and that you have the coin to do so. Swear that you'll not share my identity with the Town Guards or the Blazers. Swear to it by Celes."

Becka glanced at him, face pensive. This was a big request. Glenn held her eyes a moment before making his decision. It was going to cost him another chunk of savings to alter the Quest in this way—anonymity regarding Quest completions was *expensive*—but he wouldn't have to pay if the man didn't have good information. He would phrase his oath carefully.

"Very well, Mister Commoncloud. I swear by Celes that if the information you offer does lead me to learn how Sara Cinderflare and Leopold Argentshade left this district, I will change the Quest to anonymous and keep your name from everyone, including my fellow Blazers."

Everett nodded, satisfied. "Fine. Good. So..." He took a deep breath. "Here's your answer. Your friends most likely left through a narrow alley that leads to the east wall of Lakebrooke. I can't take you there... someone will see me... but I'll draw you a map."

"How did they leave the district? Is there a tunnel leading to another district?"

Glenn's research on the area had told him the ground beneath this district was too soggy to dig any sort of real tunnel, but perhaps that research had been wrong. He should have consulted more sources, but he'd been in a rush. Did this mean the Builder census he'd read was incorrect?

"It's no tunnel, Graybreaker. There's a hole in the town wall."

Becka gasped. Glenn stared. He was absolutely certain he had misheard the man, likely because he'd been up for forty hours without sleep. Had he fallen asleep without realizing it?

"A hole—" Becka started.

"—in the wall," Everett repeated. "Locals have been using it for months to slip in and out of the city and pass contraband to the Shadowers Guild and others. They've made enough moons doing that to make your head spin, and they pay the locals who do know about it enough to ensure they'd never talk." Everett shuddered. "Not to mention what would happen to them if they did talk."

"That's impossible," Glenn said, even though those were the two words Brennon had once warned him a Truth Seeker should never utter. "The Gods won't allow the walls of a city to fall."

"I didn't say it *fell*. I said there's a hole in it, one hidden by trash in the alley. It's big enough for a person to squeeze through, and maybe just big enough for that big white wolf who was with the blond Blazer you described. They could all easily get out of the city through the hole."

"Did you see this happen?"

Everett glared at him. "No, of course I didn't *see* it happen. I don't go over there. I only know about the hole because I've been buying and selling in this district for over a decade now."

"And? What proof do you have?"

"A few months ago, several of my competitors got unreasonably flush with coin, and locals who couldn't get a moon together suddenly started hitting the booze and eating real meat. There was way too much coin flowing through the district, and I needed to know why. I got it out of a friend when I got him really drunk."

Glenn could almost believe this man's wild story. The sudden abundance of coin in this poor portion of Lakebrooke was certainly hard to explain. "And you think there's been so much coin floating around the district in the past few months because the guild and others have been using this... hole... to sneak illicit goods into and out of the city?"

"Which is exactly why I need that Quest to be anonymous. I had to wait outside this shack half a night to be sure no one would see me sneaking in here to talk to you. I knew no one else in this district would be willing to risk the wrath of the Shadowers Guild."

Gods, what if this was true? A hole in the walls of Lakebrooke would be absolutely priceless to a group like the Shadowers Guild. Even high level Voidstriders and Timestriders couldn't easily sneak in or out of the gates of Lakebrooke, and Town Guards could search those entering the city at any time.

But a hole in the wall... a hole would allow the guild to bring in or ship out practically any illegal substance they could acquire in the city or abroad. They could meet a ship at a covert meeting away from the official docks to acquire any illicit substance they wished.

Worse, once their contraband was inside the city's walls, they had more than enough resources to smuggle it around so long as they used unassuming couriers. Town Guards rarely searched people moving between gates *inside* the city. There was no reason to do so, since the gate guards supposedly handled all that.

"Gods, Glenn," Becka said. "If he's right..."

"The Shadowers Guild will never forgive anyone who gives up a secret this valuable," Glenn agreed grimly. He also knew, from his investigation for Lady Viktoria Marshvale, that the guild was willing to murder if the price was high enough. "So why would you risk telling us this?"

"I want out," Everett said grimly. "I've done my time on the climb, forty-eight years of it, and I'm ready to step off the ladder. I've been building a nest egg over the past decade, and the reward from your Quest will give me enough to leave here for good." His expression went distant. "I'm going to retire to a nice place in the center of the city. Small house, but it's real cozy. I don't want visitors."

Everett focused on Glenn. "And I'm not just talking Shadowers. I'm talking Blazers too. If Mayor Earthwhite wants to give me some sort of medal or recognition for exposing this hole in Lakebrooke's defenses, I'll politely ask her to keep her mouth shut. I don't need any recognition, just the gold."

"And you can't show us this hole yourself, can you. Because you'd be spotted."

Everett nodded. "Which is why I'll draw you a map. A real good map. But first, I need to hear you say it. I've told you what I know. Does this information complete your Quest?"

Glenn grimaced. "I'll have to verify your claims. But if you're right about this—"

"I'm right! Just follow my map."

"Then... yes. Having explored all other alternatives, I don't know of any other way my friends could have left this district other than using the hole you describe. If it exists. And if it exists..." He sighed.

"Then there's a whole lot more going on here than just the disappearance of two Junior Blazers."

"Good." Everett grinned with satisfaction. "Now, I'm going to leave before someone else happens by. I'll expect you to verify my information tonight. Two days from now, I'll make a trip into the city to complete the Quest... *anonymously*. I'm not coming back here again."

"We'll have the Quest updated and ready for you. Again, assuming I can verify everything you've told me."

Everett crossed his arms. "Then you'd best get walking. For what it's worth, I hope you find your friends."

Once Everett had left them alone again, Glenn glanced at Becka. "Think this'll be enough for Jenny to get the Blazer resources she needs to find them?"

Becka ruefully shook her head. "If there really is a hole in the wall, it won't just get Jenny the people she needs to look for Leo and Sara. It's going to put the whole guild in an uproar."

"Just so long as someone focuses attention where it needs to be."

"That's why we have Jenny. Now, let's go find this hole."

"Not without backup," Glenn said.

Becka winced. "You're right. Leo and Sara may have discovered this hole just as we did, and the fact that they didn't return suggests someone is watching it closely. We won't save anyone if we get abducted before we can share what we've learned with others."

"Chancing upon this hole could even be the reason they were abducted," Glenn agreed darkly. "The Shadowers Guild could have imprisoned them to ensure word wouldn't get out. Even now, they could have them both sitting in a cell with a poisoned chalice."

Becka clenched one fist. "I pray they wouldn't go that far."

The Law of Consent forbid even members of the Shadowers Guild from harming others without their consent. But someone who was locked in a cell and denied food and water for long enough might grow desperate or feverish enough to accept the cup of cool, clean water sitting in their cell. Poison.

"So, who can we ask to help us?" Glenn asked. "Marion?"

"She's out of the city again," Becka said. "She's also a few levels higher than you are now, so I don't know that she'd make that much of a difference in a fight."

Glenn winced. Marion was so intimidating in person he'd forgotten that the Devourer in the Temple of Balance had reduced her from a truly powerful high level Blockader to a simple Brutalist who was only a few levels ahead of him... without the powerful Blessings of a Town Guard.

"But I do know two high level Adventurers who could back us up. Jessica Rainfall and Jackson Marshcutter. They're not Evolved, but they're a whole lot closer than we are, and Jessica likes me. I think they'd jump at the chance to tackle a problem this big."

Glenn smiled. "Then let's go find them. Also, what about Ashley?"

"If we can rouse her out of her cups. Maybe the others as well. There's no guarantee Owen will be in fighting shape this early, but Kate and Brian would give us almost a full raid. I don't think anyone the Shadowers Guild left guarding that hole would be ready for all of us."

"Then that's our plan! You go find Jessica and Jackson. I'll go find Ashley and whoever's not too drunk to join us. Then, we meet back here and leave to verify Everett's story."

"It's *a* plan. It's even a good one. But are you going to be able to stay awake?"

Glenn ran his hands through his short brown hair and then rubbed his eyes. "At this point? Not even one of Preceptor Fallowpeak's **[Sleep Potion]**s could keep me down."

FIVE
A FIGHT IN THE TOWN
LEO

Watching the people Teacher had abducted fight in his makeshift arena had taught Leo some very important things about their captor. First, despite his misguided intentions and criminal actions, Teacher did seem to genuinely wish to teach his captives to resume Luxtera's Climb. Every fight in his makeshift arena pitted two captives against one Monster of equal or lesser level, a challenge that would be reasonable for any Adventurers of the level of these captives.

Also, after the fight concluded, the anonymous Lifecaster working with Teacher healed anyone who was injured. And though it didn't happen during the three fights he observed, he suspected the second anonymous acolyte standing over the arena on the next ring up was there to kill any Monsters who got too close to killing those "training" in the arena. Watching out for them.

If Leo was being honest with himself, the challenges Teacher set for his captives weren't that different from how the Blazers trained new recruits. The biggest difference was that senior Blazers would escort Junior Blazers into the field the same way he and Sara had been escorting Glenn and Becka as Glenn leveled Soulseer. They didn't force them to fight caged Monsters in underground arenas.

Still, it was a relief to know that Teacher seemed to be telling the truth about his intentions with capturing these people. It still didn't make it right for him to abduct them, and it didn't change Leo's plans to free them. But it did assure him Teacher had no plans to kill or harm anyone by pitting them against Monsters they couldn't defeat.

That was one less worry for Leo to consider as he planned their escape.

Once everyone had killed their Monster for the day, all the captives save for Cyrus walked back to the central cavern using the same tunnel they had traveled down to get here. Leo made several attempts to learn more about where the Rock Spiders that had abducted Cyrus had placed him... a separate holding area apparently known as "the hole." No one would tell him anything, and he suspected the fact that an acolyte walked behind them in hearing distance was why.

Once they were back in the main chamber, Sara was waiting with Ripper. Leo heaved a sigh of relief at seeing her safe and unharmed. He also needed to speak to her about her actions during the arena battles today. Was she really in favor of letting Teacher force these people to fight?

As the remaining captives wandered off to the tables or the sleeping tents, Leo decided to leave them to their own devices for a time. He needed to speak with Sara. He needed to know what she and Teacher had talked about and fill her in on the levels and capabilities of the people they'd come to rescue. Perhaps she could come up with a strategy that would allow them all to escape.

Sara made a motion with her head that suggested he follow. Together, they walked to a distant corner of the cavern, one far from the tunnels guarded by Teacher's Desouled and the sleeping and eating areas occupied by the other captives. The only figures close enough to hear them speak in quiet tones were the beaten-up training dummies on posts nearby, and they didn't talk.

Once they stopped, Ripper flopped down on the cool earth with his paws forward and his tongue hanging out. He remained alert as his eyes scanned the cavern for threats, and Leo found himself glad for the backup. He didn't pet Ripper, though. Only Glenn and Sara could do that.

"What was that about today?" Leo asked quietly. "Why did you let those spiders abduct Cyrus?"

Sara merely fixed him with a level gaze. "Do you think we could have stopped them? Without endangering the other captives or angering Teacher?"

"I suppose not. Still, what if one of them gets injured? Or dies?"

"Teacher does not plan to kill anyone. He truly wishes to help these people."

Leo narrowed his eyes at her. "No one's listening now. You don't need to pretend."

"I'm not pretending." She took a breath. "I believe him."

Leo processed her shocking words and searched her features for any trace that she was only pretending because she knew something he didn't. Yet knowing her as well as he did, all he could conclude was that she was telling the absolute truth. Had a Mindbender gotten to her?

"Don't look at me like that," Sara said irritably. "I'm not saying that his choice to abduct people from their homes and imprison them down here was the best way to go about convincing them to resume Luxtera's Climb. But I do believe, now, that someone needs to do that."

Leo fixed his jaw in place before he spoke again. "He's a madman, Sara. The Gods don't punish those who refuse to level."

"Yes, they do."

Again, Leo was struck dumb by the certainty in her voice. Her words. She believed this. Gods, what had Teacher done to her?

"I saw the scripture. I read its words myself, and I... heard them. In my head."

Leo snorted derisively. "You actually saw a Scripture of Ralun?"

"The very same. I don't know why the church has hidden those scriptures from us for all these decades. Perhaps there's something in the scripture that argues against the outlawing of Deathcasters. It would be difficult for them to cite some parts of scripture and suppress others that opposed their laws, but if they simply suppressed the existence of the scripture in its entirety..."

For the first time, the certainty in Sara's words chilled Leo more than he expected. He fought off that chill. How could he believe this?

"Sara, you realize what you're saying, don't you?"

"What am I saying, Leo?"

"If what you say is true, the church has spent the last few decades dooming people who chose not to level to an afterlife equivalent to the Six Hells. Is that what you now believe?"

"I don't know if it's equivalent to the Six Hells. But otherwise, yes. That is exactly what the church has been doing."

Leo swallowed. It was so tempting to dismiss her as mad, but Sara wasn't mad. She was one of the most insightful, cautious, and experienced people he knew. So if she believed this...

Leo shook his head. "If Scriptures of Ralun were really out there, and they really said things like this, someone would know. Someone would reveal the truth."

"It's been over forty years since the church outlawed Deathcasters. Teacher said they suppressed the scriptures even earlier than that. Anyone out there who knows the truth and is still walking around free likely isn't foolish enough to spread it."

"We can't believe anything Teacher says."

"Yet I do. The leaders of the church have had forty years to arrest and imprison anyone who spoke out against them. Four decades to stamp out the truth. Even if some in the church still know, they've all agreed to keep it secret to honor their faith. No one dares violate their oath to Celes."

Sara sounded so certain that Leo was starting to believe as well, and her theory, while terrifying, was just plausible enough that he couldn't dismiss it out of hand. It also made him angry. He knew it was unreasonable to be angry about something that might be true, but he was anyway.

"So does that mean you're going to help him? Join his acolytes? Keep these people imprisoned down here and force them to fight Goblins and Antlions in a rocky arena or starve if they refuse?"

Sara's firm determination faltered. "You really think so little of me?"

Leo grimaced. "I..." He breathed deep. "I don't want to think that of you, no."

"Then remember who I am and how I think. We do need to free these people. That hasn't changed. But afterward, we need to let the Blazers and everyone else know the truth about what happens if you abandon Luxtera's Climb. We need to make sure everyone knows about this."

Finally, Leo saw how her perspective had changed, and he felt guilty for ever doubting her. Of *course* Sara still believed they should help these people. All that had changed was now she believed they needed to help more than the people in this cave. They had to help everyone in Luxtera.

And if what she said *was* true, even offering a whisper of this news would likely cause members of the Church of Celes to come after them with as much fervor as they had gone after Zack Silverstone and Glenn Redwood, Town Guard. The church could hire Shadowers Guild assassins to silence them.

Even so, even with that danger hanging over him, Leo had to consider Sara's reasoning and how they could spread this news... if they chose to do so. Because if it was true, he could no more keep silent than Sara could. Not now that he knew people's immortal souls were in danger.

Leo breathed deep and decided to mentally reason through their problems. "If the church is actively suppressing the Scriptures of Ralun, I doubt revealing that would go well for us. Even the Blazers may have trouble protecting us if we start openly spreading heresy."

Sara frowned. "Would it be better to abandon those who abandon the climb to a hell of their own making? If we keep this to ourselves, we're worse than Teacher. We'd know the truth about what happens if someone refuses to level and not even raise a finger to save them."

Leo forced a smile. "You really think so little of me?"

She watched him for a long moment. Then, she smiled back... though it was just as forced as his was. Even so, the sentiment behind her smile was real.

"So," Sara said. "How would we do it?"

Leo considered carefully. "Let's take this one step at a time. Before we can think about spreading this... new theory... we need to get these people to safety. That has to come before anything else. So, do you have any ideas in that regard?"

Sara nodded as she refocused. They were once more in agreement, and once more a powerful team. "You've spoken to them, haven't you? You know their levels and classes?"

"I do."

"Tell me."

When Leo finished, Sara frowned. She looked less sure of herself than she had a few moments ago. "They really have been neglecting their duty to level."

"Which is certainly the reason Teacher abducted them. Still, we have what we have, and we've both trained plenty of newer Blazers who don't even have the levels this group has. There has to be some way we can get past those Desouled and escape."

"I'm not sure that's our only problem. Even if we somehow got into those tunnels and past the Desouled, Teacher could simply have his desouled Rock Spiders close the path ahead and block us. Also, we don't even know if these tunnels lead to the surface. We know at least one tunnel *did* lead up there... the one we came down... but Rock Spiders could have already sealed it up by now."

"Plus we don't have whatever item he used to open that secret passage in the rocks up in the Bone Cage. So... we'll have to find a way to capture Teacher and steal his item."

Sara eyed him. "And how did our attempt to capture him go last time?"

"Last time, he had a hostage."

"And now he has six. So how would you suggest we 'capture' him?"

"If we can just get some cuffs on him, we should be able to handle his acolytes. I watched the arena battles closely today. The Lifecaster used [-Flash Heal-] and [-Cleanse Body-] once, but nothing more powerful. I don't think they're Evolved or as powerful as Teacher."

"Yet he still has three of them. There may be more elsewhere in this cavern."

"Which is why it may be up to you to cuff him and get whatever item he used to open the secret passage. You said you believe him, don't you? You actually believe he's right about what happens if you abandon the climb? And that he has a genuine Scripture of Ralun in his possession?"

"I know he does."

"So if you believe him... he must be starting to trust you. Right?"

Sara's lips pressed together. "He doesn't trust me enough to let me get my cuffs on him."

"Not yet. But for better or worse, the two of you seem to be on good terms. So if we have no other way, you should express interest in becoming one of his acolytes. Offer to aid him in this unpleasant business in other ways. And once he lets his guard down—"

"I betray his trust?" Sara interrupted softly.

Leo suppressed another surge of worry. Did Sara already genuinely empathize with Teacher now? This is what their instructors, and in particular Jenny Ambersun, had warned them about when they studied methods for gaining the trust of captives and eliciting critical information.

The goal of an interrogation was to make a captive sympathize with you by empathizing when them... but never to the point where you began to justify their crimes to yourself. Once you began to sympathize with the person you were trying to bring to justice, your judgment was clouded.

"I don't see any other way to free these people," Leo said. "Unless you have a better idea, or you're comfortable spending the rest of our lives living in a cavern watching arena fights."

Sara considered in silence for a moment. "What is clear is we need more information. That's how Jenny taught us to deal with situations like this. If you encounter a situation you can't solve, and you aren't in immediate danger—"

"—don't act until you have a solution," Leo finished for her. "And keep your eyes open. The solution may present itself even after you expect it to not."

Sara's faint smile returned. "For now, we'll trust Jenny."

"And Glenn."

Sara glanced at the people sitting at the tables across the cavern, quietly speaking with each other. "I don't know that Glenn will be able to help us this time."

"He's been solving mysteries for months now. If he can't solve the mystery of where the two of us vanished off too, then he really does need to step up his game as a Truth Seeker."

"It's a possibility," Sara agreed. "But we can't depend on Glenn or even the Blazers to help us this time. Getting these people out of this place safely will fall on us."

"And what about Teacher? If he opposes us, can you fight him?"

Sara's expression firmed. "I'll do what I must to protect you and our charges. I said I believed Teacher. I didn't say I thought everything he was doing was right."

Beside her, Ripper growled a deep assent.

――――

GLENN

"Gods." Glenn stared at the open space in the middle of the town wall that he had unearthed after moving a pile of trash. "That is an enormous hole." He could even see the greenery of Evolan on the other side of it. A straight path through to the zone.

Ashley Bloodbraid elbowed him in the ribs. "That's what he said."

"Hey!" Owen said loudly from behind her. "Don't go telling Glenn all my secrets!"

An exasperated sigh from Jackson Marshcutter reminded Glenn that pairing two veteran Blazers with Ashley and her band of bawdy drunken Adventurers hadn't been the best idea he'd had this week. Still, no one had tried to abduct them... yet. They'd have a hard time with it.

Becka was level 12 and he was level 14, but the rest of their investigation party? They had a level 17 Anchorite (Ashley), a level 19 Brutalist (Owen), a level 16 Harmcaster (Kate), and a level 16 Lifecaster (Brian). Once one added Jessica (a level 18 Guilecaster) and Jackson (a level 18 Shadower), they had a full raid that could tear apart even the Minotaur camp out at the Twin Sisters.

Glenn glanced back at the two experienced Blazers in the party. "Jessica? Would [-Detect Magic-] be of any use here?" If someone had used illusion magic to hide this hole, they might be able to get an impression of their echo... or some clue as to who had used it most recently.

"I don't sense anything," Becka said softly from his other side.

"She's right," Jessica agreed. She had to work hard to squeeze past Jackson in the narrow alley, and then again to squeeze past Owen, who occupied almost the whole thing. "But I can try."

Once she was standing almost on top of Ashley, Glenn, and Becka, Jessica raised her hands and closed her eyes. A moment later, she opened them. "Nothing. The only thing hiding that hole was those mundane piles of trash, but magic might have drawn attention. These Shadowers were clever."

"Not clever enough." Glenn pointed at the hole. "This has to be how whoever took Leo and Sara got them out of the district without being seen by others. *This* is how they were abducted."

This hole was all the evidence he needed to convince Captain Hawkshadow that she needed to mobilize the resources necessary to search for Leo and Sara. Jenny Ambersun, he knew, would do just that. He might not be able to find them himself, but he'd led the Blazers to the proper path.

"What? No!" Kate shouted from the back of the alley. "You can't do that! Stop that!"

Glenn turned around and almost sent Becka stumbling in the narrow alley. He winced an apology and squeezed past Jessica with Ashley right on his heels. Past Jackson, Owen, and Brian, he saw Kate staring down a large and menacing figure in well-used **[Steel Armor]**. He stood in the alley with his shield raised, and it was a massive shield: a **[Magesteel Pavise]**.

Glenn had always dreamed about owning a shield that large. Magesteel was inherently magic-resistant, so if one could afford an enchantment on top of the exorbitant cost of the shield itself, one could become almost immune to the bane of a heavily armored, slow-moving Adventurer... Monsters who could cast magic. This shield's glow suggested it was enchanted.

In this narrow alley, even Kate's slim frame couldn't squeeze past the shield. Not without getting pinned against a wall. The armored figure with the shield wasn't attempting to push her back, since he couldn't push her back without violating the Law of Consent, but he didn't need to. They were trapped.

Glenn looked up just as multiple additional figures appeared atop the pair of two-story buildings whose walls made up this alley. He counted six of them, and he actually recognized three of them: Zara Barrelblade, Tim Tallstrider, and Soren Shadecutter. He should have expected he'd see those three again. They'd been released after three months in prison on good behavior.

He used **[-Soul Scan-]** on the two of them to verify their identities and then used **[-Soul Scan-]** to size up the rest. He was pleased to find they actually had the Shadowers Guild outnumbered and outleveled. There were only seven of them, while he had eight, and the highest of them was level 17.

"Glad we brought backup," Glenn said.

"So am I," Ashley added hungrily. "Call for the arrest. I'm gonna break shield guy in half."

"Let's try and negotiate with them first. They might have been able to get away with spiriting away two Junior Blazers, but if four of us disappear, it'll draw citywide attention."

"And us vanishing won't?" Ashley challenged.

Glenn glanced at her and winced. "You said not to lie to you."

She laughed and thumped his arm. "At least you remembered that."

As Kate retreated into the alley, the shield bearer advanced relentlessly. Fortunately, Brian had the presence of mind to interpose himself between the shield bearer and the rest of them before he could gain too much ground. The man stopped and clanged his mace against his shield. Brian just smiled.

"That's a lovely tone. I didn't take you for an Auracaster."

The shield bearer growled. "Back up."

"No, I don't think I will."

Glenn's [-Soul Scan-] told him that this man, despite his impressive armor and equipment, was only a level 14 Brutalist. The Shadowers Guild could obviously afford to purchase the very best gear, just like the Blazers, but this man's gear felt excessive. Still, intimidation was a weapon like any other.

He, Ashley, and Owen all reached the front of the narrow line before the Brutalist could menace Brian into retreating. Only then did Brian squeeze past Glenn and saunter away. Glenn pulled his own shield off his back. He formed a wall that even this confident Shadower looked hesitant to challenge.

Glenn stared at the helmeted man with every ounce of confidence and menace he'd developed as a Town Guard. "You know I'm a Blazer, right? We all are."

"Doesn't matter who you are. You're not leaving this alley."

Glenn smiled. "Have you ever been arrested before?"

The man didn't answer, so Glenn looked up at those gathered on the buildings above. "Show of hands! How many of you have been arrested by the Blazers?"

For a moment, none of them reacted. Then one—Tim—actually started to raise his hand before Zara angrily elbowed him in the side.

Glenn considered their low mix of levels and the way they'd approached and immediately realized what was happening here.

This group wasn't here to capture them. They were here to stall them until high level members of the Shadowers Guild could arrive to deal with them. Those people wouldn't be dawdling in Lakebrooke, but they would be on their way. The Shadowers Guild had called for reinforcements.

He looked back at Owen and Ashley. "We're going to push through them and on out."

Ashley slammed her fists together. "Gods yes!"

"But don't kill anyone. This brawl falls under Blazer jurisdiction. If anyone dies while we're attempting an arrest, they get priority over all of you. Even us."

The man with the shield huffed. "You can't arrest us! We haven't done anything wrong!"

Glenn glanced at him as he raised his fist and made the motion they'd already agreed upon to ready his people for a fight. He didn't see it, but he suspected Jackson Marshcutter had just vanished into [-Shadow Walk-]. His people had been prepared for this. Waiting benefited no one.

Glenn made his voice boom even without the benefit of [-Public Address-]. "As a Blazer invested with the authority of Mayor Earthwhite, I order you to leave this alley and step aside. You are interfering in a Blazer investigation. If you refuse to step aside and do not allow us to leave peacefully, I will place you under arrest."

As he spoke, he activated [-Soul Scan-] again. This Brutalist might be level 14—the same level Glenn was—but his Strength was only a paltry 24. Glenn's, with his shield, was 35. His Soulseer Skill would allow him to see any Skill this man used the moment he tried to use it.

Had the Brutalist truly parsed the way Glenn had worded his ultimatum, he would have realized that the battle was already on. The Law of Consent had been suspended the moment he refused to step aside. Instead, the Brutalist made the mistake of glancing up at the people on the rooftops for orders.

Glenn slammed his shield into the man's pavise with all the force he could muster. Glenn hit him hard enough to literally knock him onto his back like a flipped turtle. His big shield clattered to the ground, and the fact that this man couldn't hold onto his shield when knocked on his back immediately made Glenn lose a great deal of respect for him. Still, he couldn't complain.

He leapt over the downed Brutalist. "Go!"

Shouts and war cries sounded behind him as Glenn charged out of the alley. A loud clang followed by a pained cry told him either Owen or Ashley had struck the downed Brutalist hard enough to drop him out of the fight. They had three and five levels on him, respectively, which was harsh.

Now Glenn had to get out of the alley before anyone managed to block it again. The sound of tumbling rocks warned him of the danger. He halted and set his feet as Ashley slammed into him from behind, nearly bowling him over. Owen slammed into her, at which point all three of them almost went down. Glenn grunted and grabbed exposed bricks on each side of the alley, holding strong.

Rock after huge rock smashed into the ground just ahead of him at the exit to the alley. That created a large obstacle and, had he not stopped, would have pummeled him repeatedly with large stones. Dropping a boulder at the edge of the alley was clever. It wouldn't violate the Law of Consent so long as the Shadowers pushed it over the edge *before* anyone was below to be struck by it.

If Glenn had kept running, he'd now be buried in a pile of heavy rocks and likely badly wounded as a result. It would be his fault for failing to look up. Another reminder never to underestimate the Shadowers Guild. Fortunately, even this makeshift earthen barricade wouldn't hold them for long.

Glenn flattened himself against the alley wall. "Ash! Punch the wall!"

Ashley dashed forward and pulled back her fist. A white glow manifested around it, as did small bits of swirling rock. From above, people shouted in audible desperation.

"She's an Anchorite! Stop her!"

"How? You just said she's an Anchorite!"

Ashley roared as she unleashed **[-Stone Punch-]** on the huge pile of fallen rocks. The rock in the center and the one beside it were all but disintegrated when her punch landed. The rest tumbled toward the exit of the alley or slammed into the walls.

Ashley's heavy blow left enough daylight in the middle of the pile for Glenn to shove his way into it. His shield, Strength, and targeted heaves pulled the blockade apart, and then he stumbled into the street. Ashley and Owen followed, kicking, punching, and slamming rocks with their shields and great Strength. Together, the three of them cleared a wide path for the others.

Six dark-cloaked figures ringed them in the narrow street beyond the alley, the same crew that had been up on the roof. Glenn was glad there were no Rangers among them. His armor and Owen's made them immune to arrows, but Becka, Kate, Jessica, and Brian's armor was too thin to protect them entirely. As for Ashley, a successful arrow strike would just feed her Strength and make her stronger.

And Jackson? He still didn't see Jackson. Yet he knew the man was ready to pounce.

"Anyone want to back off?" Glenn called to the surrounding Shadowers. "Last chance to run."

None of them answered him.

"Then you're all under arrest," Glenn told the six gathered around the alley.

And so the second fight began.

Attempting to arrest only one of these criminals at a time would allow the others to leap in and attack the person attempting the arrest with impunity, getting a free strike before they, too, committed a crime. So in this case, Glenn calling an arrest on all six of them under Blazer authority was the best way to handle the problem. That way, his group could bring their superior numbers to bear immediately.

The brawl in the street was short and brutal, but went about as Glenn would expect given the level difference. An overconfident Harmcaster hit Glenn's armor with a single blast of [-Burn-] before he went flying as he encountered a wide swing from Glenn's shield. Bone cracked audibly. It was still a kinder fate than what would have happened if Glenn had brained him with Becka, his heavy mace.

The rest of the group arrayed to stall them fell in short order. Tim Tallstrider cried out and dropped to his knees, screaming his lungs out as some mental Skill Jessica used terrified him beyond the ability for rational thought. One swing of Owen's mace dropped Tim flat and shut him up.

Zara, with the inky blackness of Becka's [-Shadow Blast-] clinging to her eyes, stabbed blindly at Kate, but the experienced Harmcaster easily danced away. Before Kate could toss a [-Burn-] at her, Zara got trampled by Owen. She wasn't getting up after that, and Glenn was freshly impressed by Owen's attention to his party. This was one Brutalist who never let his party members go unprotected.

As for Ashley Bloodbraid, the first punch she threw sent blood, teeth, and phlegm flying. The Skirmisher who'd foolishly stabbed her with his [Iron Spear] flopped backward and bounced like a child's doll. She'd broken his jaw. She wrenched his spear out of her side, tossed it away like a light stick, and roared in triumph. She was probably even stronger now.

From behind her, Brian sighed a put-upon sigh and raised one glowing hand. He tossed a [-Flash Heal-] on Ashley to seal her wound. No one else in the party had been injured in the melee, so Glenn's [-Guardian Heal-] wasn't needed.

Seeing how obviously outmatched he was, the last of the Shadowers... Soren Shadecutter... vanished in a puff of smoke. [-Shadow Walk-]. Yet the wet footfalls splashing in the muddy alley made it all too obvious the path he was running... away... and then he appeared again with a loud huff.

He slammed into a wall so hard he bounced off it and hit the ground. As he groaned and rolled onto his back, Jackson Marshcutter stepped from the air beside him. Jackson glanced their way.

"We only have four cuffs," Jackson reminded Glenn. "Who's going to jail?"

Glenn marched forward. "None of them. There's more on the way, higher level Shadowers who might actually be able to give us a good fight. We need to get to the Town Guard at the gate before they get here. We'll worry about arresting people after the guard is informed."

"You're the boss," Jackson said evenly.

Glenn was surprised to hear that, given Jackson had several years of experience and four levels on him. Still, the older Blazer's trust cheered him immensely. He didn't feel great about the mess they'd left in their wake—some of these people might suffer permanent injuries if they weren't treated by a Lifecaster—but at least they hadn't killed anyone.

Everyone who'd fallen had active Health Bars, though the Skirmisher Ashley had punched was charred down to a third. Glenn considered asking Brian to toss a [-Flash Heal-] on the wounded man before they left, but they needed to save Brian's Blood for if they encountered real trouble.

"Double time!" Glenn shouted as he moved into a jog. "Ashley! With me! Owen, Jackson, rear guard! Everyone else, stay between us and keep a sharp eye out!"

Glenn led, and his party followed, as they jogged through the narrow streets of the Old Fishing District. The place was a maze for the uninitiated, but he'd spent the last few days getting to know it well enough that he had no trouble leading his party by the most efficient route. The only question now was if they'd get to the gate in time... and what would happen if they didn't.

They soon encountered obstacles, seemingly at random. A large cart that had broken a wheel and blocked their path. A large crowd thick enough that they couldn't easily pass through it. Every time they encountered an obstacle, Glenn mentally visualized the streets of the Old Fishing District and led his party around and away. He'd always had a good memory for directions.

Glenn kept expecting high level Voidstriders or Timestriders or even a Shadowers Guild Deathcaster to step from the alley at any moment and bar their path. Yet other than a few more engineered obstacles abandoned by those who'd placed them, no one interfered. It seemed the Pantheon was with them... this time. When they finally sighted the gate, Glenn huffed in relief.

"Don't slow down! We're almost out!"

Town Guard Mosscloud turned to watch a party of eight out-of-breath Adventurers arrive one by one at his gate, some barely winded and others struggling for breath. Kate and Brian looked the most winded, with Brian clutching his knees and Kate wheezing heavily. As for Becka, she was breathing hard but still looked ready to run. Glenn grinned at her in relief. She might get a point of Stamina after this.

"Is there a problem, citizen?" Trevor asked calmly.

Glenn had no idea what the man must have thought when he witnessed eight high level Adventurers (at least by Lakebrooke's standards) fleeing toward his gate like they had a horde of Minotaurs chasing them. He wasn't going to keep the man in suspense any longer than necessary.

"We found a hole in the wall."

Only the years Glenn had spent wearing **[God Armor]** and watching his fellow Town Guards wear the same revealed that Trevor had just stiffened at his words. Glenn would have as well. The walls of the settlements of Luxtera did not have *holes*. They were Builder-made and God-blessed.

"A hole, citizen?" Trevor didn't sound like he believed it.

"There's also a large group of Shadowers Guild members back by the alley that leads to the hole. Some are injured. I don't expect any of them will stick around, but if anyone comes limping up to the gate who's been in a fight, you might consider arresting them."

"I see," Trevor said calmly. "Can I help you with anything else?"

Trevor knew who Glenn was, but he didn't know what he wanted. He remained bound by Kya's decrees to only ask formal questions when on duty. Glenn knew what to do next. He focused on the Town Guard and made his voice as confident as Brennon had taught him.

"My name is Truth Seeker Glenn Graybreaker, Blazer Rank 8. On my authority, I ask that you halt all traffic through this gate until my superiors can arrive and secure the district. To verify my request, you can contact Truth Seeker Brennon Shadesinger, Jenny Ambersun, or Captain Marion Hawkshadow."

Trevor nodded. "Understood, citizen. No one will enter or leave this gate until the Blazers arrive or I hear differently from my captain." He stepped aside. "I assume you'll want to leave first."

Glenn nodded gratefully and motioned his people through. "Everyone, outside, now."

As the brave people who'd come to protect him filed through the gate one by one, Ashley grinned and punched his arm hard enough he nearly lost his balance. Becka stopped when she arrived, and when their eyes met, she ran to him. He instinctively hugged her as he kept his eyes on the streets behind them.

"Are you hurt?"

"No. But I was rather scared for a moment."

Owen tossed Glenn a wry grin as he walked by. "Didn't think I'd get to bust any heads today. Thanks for the invite, Graybreaker."

Glenn shook his head ruefully. "Don't mention it."

He held Becka in his arms as the rest of his people filed through the gate. He kept his eyes on the street they had used to flee the district, still convinced a Desouled would come charging out of the district to attack them. And a form *did* flicker in the corner of the alley, causing him to gasp.

Becka broke from his embrace and spun about, raising a hand to call a **[-Shadow Bolt-]** if necessary. Yet whoever Glenn had seen, they vanished before he could use **[-Soul Scan-]** on them. Even though he couldn't see how was out there, he could *feel* them.

A chill washed over him as some malevolent presence watched him from the shadows in the Old Fishing District... and he was very glad he had a high level Town Guard standing at his back. He suspected Trevor Mosscloud's presence was the only reason whoever was out there hadn't done more than flicker. Even a high level Void-strider couldn't defeat a high level Town Guard in a fight.

Glenn was glad he'd realized what the Shadowers Guild group at the hole was up to. He was *very* glad he'd ordered his people to run instead of allowing that group to delay them until the real danger showed up. He didn't know how the guild could have made eight people, including four Blazers, simply disappear from Lakebrooke... but he suspected they'd done that with Sara and Leo.

But more than anything, Glenn was glad he had so many wonderful friends.

SIX
A GOBLIN HORDE
LEO

Until he spent the night there, Leo had never realized just how disorienting it was to live and sleep underground. There was no sunrise or sunset, no day or night, just the flickering light of torches that looked the same when he opened his eyes as when he closed them. It had been difficult to accept the idea of sleeping while captive in Teacher's cavernous underground lair, but Sara was confident Teacher had no plans to harm them (yet), and Leo continued to trust her judgment.

Desouled Rock Spiders had arrived in the night, returning a sullen and silent Cyrus to the group of tents. He'd finished his time in the hole... whatever that was. Leo considered trying to comfort him and gave up the moment Cyrus glared at him. The man obviously just wanted to be left alone.

Leo would very much like to see the Scripture of Ralun for himself, but after witnessing how Teacher's captives had to fight Monsters to earn their supper, he hadn't had another opportunity to speak to the man. One of Teacher's robed and anonymous disciples had delivered a meal of meat, bread, and mead (Leo, it seemed, did *not* have to fight to earn his supper) which he still hoped was *not* poisoned.

The reason he had eaten the meal was because Teacher had no need to resort to poisoned food. If Teacher wanted them dead, his desouled Silver Colossus could smash them easily, as could either of the big desouled Cave Trolls guarding the other exits from the cave. So in the end, Leo had eaten to keep his strength up and slept to avoid fatigue. And Sara, he saw immediately, was already up.

She sat on the second of two cots with Teacher's disciples. Ripper curled up contentedly at her feet. Even as she idly stroked the big white wolf's head, Leo could tell her mind was elsewhere. As her eyes rose to meet his, he could tell she was mentally grappling with something important.

"Do you want to talk?" he asked calmly.

A brief smile warmed her features. "I don't think talking will help."

"It might. Tell me what you're thinking about and I'll tell you what I think about that."

Sara scratched around one of Ripper's big ears, which the wolf's quiet growl assured them both he quite enjoyed. "I'm just thinking about all the others."

"Others?"

"Others across Luxtera who have abandoned the climb. None of them know that by doing so, they may be dooming themselves to an afterlife unlike the one they expect. After they die, they may end up wandering in the shadows beyond this world forever, blinded by the light."

"I thought you didn't believe in an afterlife."

He and Sara had discussed theology many times before, of course. Leo personally believed that Adventurers rejoined the Gods after death and could even return in a new body if they chose, taking another run at Luxtera's Climb and the world in general. But no one knew for certain.

"I didn't," Sara agreed. "I wish that was still the case. Oblivion would be more pleasant than what the scripture suggests awaits those who refuse to tackle Luxtera's Climb."

Leo worked to keep his features neutral. "I don't doubt you read what you read, but there's still the possibility we aren't interpreting it correctly. Even Preceptor Spiritualists often debate the meaning of the passions. Ralun's scriptures sound even more vague than those of Celes."

"I wish I could believe I was misinterpreting it. But when you hear the words of a God in your head, it's far more impactful than reading them on a page."

"So you still believe the voice you heard was Ralun?"

"I heard a voice unlike any I'd ever heard speaking in my head, yes. Whether it was Ralun Himself or some lesser deity devoted to Him, I can't say. But I can no longer doubt what it meant."

Leo considered before he spoke again. "Then we'll tell them."

"What do you mean?"

"I mean just what I said. I trust your judgment. You've never been one to hide from inconvenient truths or jump to conclusions without sufficient evidence. If you believe what you read in that scripture is the literal truth, then we will spread the news ourselves and warn everyone. Even if the church tries to suppress the idea or brands us as heretics, we'll save whoever we can. Except unlike Teacher, we'll do it by educating them rather than imprisoning them in a cave."

Sara gripped his hand. "Thank you."

"For what?"

"For not arguing with me, and reminding me we aren't helpless in this endeavor."

"I'm your partner." Leo smiled. "I'll always have your back."

Sara nodded and released his hand. The tents gathered across the cave remained closed with those inside... the Adventurers they had come here to rescue... still fast asleep. Teacher's disciples had given them a pair of tents away from the others. Leo was glad that gave him and Sara the privacy to plan their next move, but regretted that their special treatment marked them as aligned with Teacher.

He needed to gain the trust of the Adventurers Teacher had captured down here—Erick, Evie, Kenneth, Cyrus, and even Maria—if he wanted them to follow him in whatever escape attempt he eventually devised. Tom would follow him, of course, but he was no longer here simply to rescue Tom. After seeing what these people endured every day, Leo refused to leave them to their fate.

Ripper, who had until this point been contentedly relaxing at Sara's feet and enjoying having his ears stroked, abruptly growled deep in his throat. His head popped up as his narrowed eyes and keen nose fixed, with grim determination, on the back portion of the main cave.

Sara, who could sense his moods like her own by this point,

immediately looked in the same direction. She reflexively reached back to draw an arrow from a quiver she wasn't wearing. Neither of them was wearing armor, since sleeping in it was rarely comfortable. Now, Leo wished they had both been a bit more cautious before bedding down for the night.

Leo stood and reached into his **[Unfilled Bag]** for the **[Steel Armor]** he'd stashed there last night before he rolled into the cot, but hesitated to draw it out. "What is it?"

Sara reached into her **[Unfilled Bag]** and pulled out her bow, then quiver, equipping both with the practiced ease of the Sharpshooter she'd been before a Devourer from the Six Hells stole her levels. She scanned the gloom. Ripper rose to his full height, which now had his back up to the middle of Sarah's chest, and went scarily silent as his lips peeled back to reveal sharp teeth.

"Monsters are coming," Sara said grimly. "A whole lot of Monsters." She looked to Leo. "Rouse the others. We need to evacuate this cave."

Leo had no time to don his armor. Instead, he pulled his enchanted **[Steel Spear]** out of his **[Unfilled Bag]** and sprinted toward the large group of tents where the captive Adventurers slept.

As he crossed the dusky cave, he risked a glance in the direction Ripper had growled and found nothing to alarm him. The desouled Silver Colossus he'd seen earlier stood at an exit from the big cave as if nothing was amiss. Wouldn't it have reacted if something was wrong?

Ripper wouldn't react like this if something wasn't wrong, and Sara certainly wouldn't. "Get up!" Leo shouted at the tents. "All of you, up, now! Gather your things!"

A tent flap moved, and then Maria, blinking irritably, stepped out into the cavern wearing thick sleep robes. "What are you babbling about, Argentshade? It's the middle of the night."

"It might be later than you think." Leo reached the cluster of tents. "All of you, up now! Erick! Evie! Kenneth! Cyrus! Tom!" He knew shouting each of their names would rouse them in a way that a generic warning would not. "Out of your tents! Right now! There's Monsters coming!"

The people he'd called out soon stumbled out of their tents, half-dressed and bleary eyed. None wore any sort of armor, and none carried any weapons. Leo belatedly remembered that they had neither. Teacher only allowed them to don armor and pick up weapons when they fought in his makeshift arena, which would leave them defenseless against... whatever Ripper smelled.

A distant rumbling became audible from the tunnel toward which Ripper had growled. The Silver Colossus tasked to guard it broke from its statue-like stupor and stomped as it turned to face the tunnel. The rumbling continued to grow as Leo reflexively settled into a ready stance and pointed his **[Steel Spear]** at the back of the cave. Was this another of Teacher's tests? A drill? A trick?

Sara rushed toward them in nothing but her nightclothes with her bow held close and her quiver bouncing on her back. "Leo, we need to move! It's Goblins!"

He glanced her way as she and Ripper joined them. "How do you know that?"

"Ripper smells them. He smells a lot, far too many for us to defeat alone."

"But how could Goblins..." Leo realized it didn't matter. "Everyone, get ready to move out! We have to get somewhere defensible before we get mobbed."

"How could Goblins get into these caverns?" Maria demanded angrily. "What are you playing at, Cinderflare? Are you working with Teacher now? I'm not in the mood for games."

The rumbling grew louder, along with the sound of guttural shouting. It was definitely coming from the single tunnel leading deeper into the cavernous complex, and it was absolutely not human. It was the sound of growling, and howling, and screeching... the sound of inhuman things.

Wood creaked as none other than Tom Brightbow stepped up onto the wooden table on which he and the other captives took their meals. "Listen up! Leo and Sara are Blazers with years of experience fighting Monsters, and both have more combat experience than you can imagine! If they say there's Goblins coming, there's Goblins coming. Now move, move, move! Right now."

"I'm ready!" Evie said worriedly. "Just tell us where to go."

Leo took one quick look around at those gathered. While Maria still scowled, she looked more uncertain of herself the louder the disturbing noise in the distant tunnel grew. Evie and the others were all looking to him for leadership now, and he recognized their willingness to follow him from all the years he'd spent leading Junior Blazers around Evolan.

Sara was looking to him as well. Not because she couldn't lead these people out of the cavern, but because she *wanted* him to act as leader. She'd often assured him he was a natural leader, and as difficult as that was for him to believe, no one else was going to step up. If they did, everyone would just get confused if both of them started shouting orders. So it was time for him to lead.

Leo pointed at the tunnel exit directly opposite the one from which the ominous noise rumbled. "Everyone, grab only what you can't live without and head for that tunnel exit!" A desouled Cave Troll even now stood guard, but Leo could spear it in the leg and distract it temporarily if he had to do so. "Sara, Ripper, and I will cover your retreat. Now go!"

Tom leapt off the wooden table and took off in the direction Leo had pointed. "This way, folks! You heard the Blazer! Don't dawdle, or you'll get left behind!"

A pained roar echoed from the tunnel, concealing a danger Leo could only imagine, and then the desouled Silver Colossus moved again. It stomped to stand directly before the tunnel exit, lowered its weight, and spread its many arms as if readying itself to stop an avalanche. Was all that noise really being made by Goblins? Just how many of them were in that tunnel?

Leo's question was answered when the first of the green-skinned mob boiled out of the hole in a chorus of drool, spittle, and shrieks. Their wiry little bodies washed over the Stone Colossus like ants around a recently dropped chunk of meat. They stabbed uselessly at the Desouled's thick hide as it stumbled backward with the weight of them. Soon it went down beneath them, buried by the tide.

Leo's body grew cold as he observed how many Monsters were now flooding this cavern. There were hundreds of Goblins, far more than even a full raid of high-level Blazers could fight. If these Goblins reached the Adventurers he was charged to protect, they would kill them, eat them, and ensure everyone who was *not* a Goblin in this cavern met the Forever Death.

This sight, at least, was enough to send Maria scrambling after the others. As Leo glanced behind him, he was relieved to find that

Teacher's captives had gathered at the front exit from the cavern. The desouled Cave Troll still blocked their exit, but Leo could handle that. He exchanged one last glance with Sara before the two of them darted after Maria with Ripper snarling and dogging their heels.

They reached the Cave Troll to find it still barring the way. Leo pointed his spear at it and bared his teeth. "Out of the way! Can't you see what's coming? Go and defend your cavern!"

He was shocked when the Cave Troll, rather than continuing to bar their passage, did just that. The massive Desouled smashed its fists together, leaned forward, and thundered around the Adventurers huddled by the exit as it charged toward the Goblin horde. The first few screeched triumphantly as they spotted the people huddled at the end of the cave.

To Goblins, Adventurers were prey. To Goblins, Adventurers were meat. All the more reason to get into this tunnel where he could fight them a few at a time rather than being pummeled by a wave of slimy green flesh. "Sara! Take point with Ripper! Everyone else, follow Sara! I'll play rear guard!"

"Follow me, everyone!" Sara called warmly. "Single file and into the tunnel! Go now!" She snatched one of the [Smokeless Torch]s from its brazier and jogged into the tunnel with Ripper close on her heels. The big Arctic Wolf looked even more massive in the confines of the tunnel.

Erick was the first to dart after her, followed by Evie, Kenneth, and Cyrus. Maria stood impatiently at the tunnel exit beside Tom. Leo backed up and motioned angrily. "Go, now!"

"We're not letting you fight those Goblins alone," Tom said. He grabbed the torch from the other side of the tunnel. "Start a party. We'll help you hold back the tide until we're safe."

An Auracaster's buffs, even those of a lower level Auracaster like Tom, would be a welcome boon. Leo grimaced and nodded. "Tom Brightbow, join my party?"

A moment later, he felt a tug as Tom joined him.

"Me as well," Maria said. "Maria Rainfeather."

Leo didn't hesitate. "Maria Rainfeather, join my party?"

Another tug announced their trio was formed, and then Tom hurried into the tunnel followed by Maria. Across the cavern, the desouled Cave Troll waded into the spreading Goblin horde. It stomped some of the beady-eyed Monsters flat and kicked aside others. Even so, there had to be hundreds of them. As Leo retreated into the now open tunnel, the last to go, Tom spoke from behind him.

"[-Marching Rose-] or [-Morning Dew-]?"

Even without a lute, an Auracaster with a talented enough set of pipes could still use Auracaster buffs simply by singing a tune without musical accompaniment. Tom, for all his faults, had a lovely singing voice. When he wasn't deep in his cups, he could carry a perfect tune.

Leo turned and motioned for both of them to follow the others. "Sing Rose if we get in a fight. Switch to Dew if we take injuries. Now move. We won't turn to fight until we have no other choice."

Tom took off after the rest, sending light flickering through the tunnel with each step. Maria followed close after him, followed by Leo. As they scurried away from the tunnel entrance, the shrieks of the Goblin horde beyond grew more urgent and crazed.

The Goblins could now see their meal escaping, and the idea of losing *food* would make them all the more ravenous. Leo's only comfort was that the Goblins would be fighting in perhaps the worst situation possible for them: forced to move single file toward a Skirmisher whose spear could all but kill them in a single strike. He'd fought Goblins in close quarters before, so he knew he could easily slaughter the front ranks that came after them.

What he couldn't do was hold off the entire horde if they came at him all at once. Momentum alone would drive the Goblins in the back over the Goblins dying in the front, and eventually they would wash over him as they had washed over that desouled Silver Colossus and the desouled Cave Troll.

No one spoke as they all rushed, single file, through a smooth rocky tunnel that wound upward and around. The light of Sara's torch was barely visible from wherever she was, far ahead, and Leo was glad Tom had thought to snatch a torch as well. He wouldn't need his hands to fight.

The only sounds echoing through the tunnel were the shuffling of feet on rock and the heavy breathing of worried people. Beyond the tunnel, Goblins howled. Leo had no idea where they were going and didn't care so long as they continued to move away from the Goblins.

How had this happened? Where had this horde come from? He'd

seen no sign of Teacher or his disciples, but the Desouled in the cavern had reacted to the attack. Had Teacher left them orders to attack Monsters that entered the cave?

The sound of scrambling feet in the distance told him the first of the Goblin horde had entered the tunnel. There was no benefit to silence any longer. There was only one path through this tunnel, and they had found no forks. Barreling straight ahead, the Goblins would be upon them soon.

"Sara, anywhere to hide?" Leo shouted down the tunnel.

"Just a straight path so far!" Sara shouted back. "Ripper doesn't smell any threats ahead!"

"So at least we won't get pincered," Maria said grimly. "At least not all at once."

They continued retreating steadily. The sound of the scrambling in the tunnel grew louder and more ominous. How was Leo going to hold off an entire horde on his own?

"There's a sharp turn ahead!" Sara called. "It would make a good choke point!"

"Then that's where we'll make our stand!" Leo shouted back. "Everyone, keep moving! Through the choke point! We can't outrun these Goblins, so we'll find a way to push them back!"

He hurried after Maria, Tom, and the others as they continued to ascend. Sara was right. As he spotted the sharp turn Sara had recommended, he approved of her choice. The Goblins coming after them would have to run uphill in this tunnel, slowing their charge, and also squeeze around a tight right-angle turn. The turn would blunt their momentum and force them to move single file.

With Tom's [-Marching Rose-] to bolster Leo's Strength and [-Morning Dew-] to bolster his endurance, Leo could likely hold the Goblins on his own... but not forever. No Blazer could hold back a horde of Goblins forever. But if he could hold them off long enough to buy the others time to find a fork in the tunnel or somewhere to hide, they could evade the horde.

After that, Leo would simply have to hope he could escape without being overrun himself.

He reached the chokepoint Sara had called out and was pleased when he had to slip sideways to squeeze through it. It really was narrow, and the Goblins would have trouble coming through more than one or two abreast. He spun to face the rising tunnel as the terrifying clamor beyond grew and grew.

"Sara, find us a way out!" Leo shouted. "I'll hold them off as long as I can!"

Maria stepped up to his side in the narrow tunnel. "We'll hold them together."

Leo glanced at her. "I thought you were done playing the Gods' games?"

"The Gods can sit on a stick! I'm doing this so people won't die."

Leo faced the narrow corner and took a ready stance with his **[Steel Spear]** ready to thrust. "Seems we might be more alike than you thought."

Maria huffed. "Here's the plan, Argentshade. You and I will hold off the Goblins as long as we can. If it looks like we're going to get overrun, pull back so I can cast **[-Freezing Cube-]** on a Goblin as it tries to squeeze through that narrow stretch around the curve."

She was a more experienced Harmcaster than he'd thought. "You'll freeze the Goblin in the crack, forming a barricade the others can't break." Leo nodded in approval. "That's a good trick. **[-Freezing Cube-]** lasts a minute?"

"Yes, but it has a three-minute cooldown."

"So once you freeze the Goblin, we fall back as far as we can and take a new chokepoint. We'll keep it up until we find somewhere better to make our stand."

It was growing increasingly hard to hear anything. The Goblin horde was screeching and clamoring so loudly that the noise in the tunnels was deafening. They had to shout to hear each other.

"Just keep in mind I can only cast **[-Freezing Cube-]** three, maybe four times!" Maria shouted. "The spell isn't meant to be used often. It takes a good amount of Blood!"

"I think I can help there!" Tom shouted from behind him. "As we retreat, I'll switch to singing **[-Morning Dew-]** and help you regenerate your Blood! It's the least I can do!"

"It is that!" Maria agreed.

"All right!" Leo faced the tunnel as their desperate, dangerous plan came into focus in his mind. "Hold the line until Sara finds us a way out! Tom, don't you dare drop that torch!"

Moments later, the first of the Goblins stumbled around the curve in the tunnel, followed by two more. As Tom launched into a rousing a acapella performance of **[-Marching Rose-]**, Leo stepped forward with catlike grace and drove his **[Steel Spear]** directly through the foremost Goblin's chest. He could feel the difference Tom's song made. An extra five points of Strength was welcome.

His expert stab drove the Goblin back into its fellows as its Health Bar appeared and charred all the way black. Leo hadn't expected to hit it that hard. Its beady eyes went wide before it burst into purple ash, but the two behind it rushed forward before its life crystal even hit the ground.

Their blind hunger was their mistake. Their urgency meant they got stuck in the narrow tunnel as they fought to run through at the same time, at which point Maria stepped forward and motioned grandly with both hands before unleashing a burst of flame Leo recognized as **[-Burn-]**. It blasted one Goblin and charred its Health Bar down by over half, but Maria didn't finish it.

Leo saw his mistake at once. "Tom! Stop singing! We need to injure them, not kill them!"

Killing the Goblins wouldn't help them hold back the tide. Any Goblin he finished off burst into purple ash. He needed living but injured Goblins to become obstacles that slowed the rest of the horde. As the badly burned Goblin thrashed and batted at its fellow, Leo stabbed the other Goblin instead... but in the leg. Its Health Bar appeared and ashed by a third as it tumbled forward, but it didn't die.

Tom stopped singing.

Another Goblin wriggled into the gap, mindlessly clawing at its injured brethren. Leo thrust his spear directly into the face of that Goblin, driving it back. As the burned one cleared the tunnel, Maria cast **[-Burn-]** again. While that finished it off, it had been too close to getting past the chokepoint. They would have to choose who they hurt and who they killed.

More Goblins rounded the corner and wriggled, drooling and screeching, as Leo stabbed at kneecaps, shoulders, and bellies. Anything to hurt and slow the Goblins without finishing them off. Their tactics were delaying the horde, but it was obvious they couldn't keep this up forever. There were just too many Goblins, and they had seemingly abandoned all thoughts of self-preservation.

He and Maria were forced to take several steps back, then several more, with writhing, screeching Goblin bodies carpeting the tunnel as they retreated. More Goblins stomped over their fellows, some going down in a pile of arms and legs but others advancing and ignoring the blasts of flame or stabs from Leo's spear. They were insane!

Leo had hoped to buy more time in their first engagement, but it was clear to him now that the Goblins would break through any moment. They would have another chance. "Maria, use [-Freezing Cube-]!"

She stepped forward and expertly moved her palms and arms. A glimmer of blue light shot from her hands and impacted a Goblin that was almost out of the narrow chokepoint. Its eyes widened a moment before [-Freezing Cube-] hit it and instantly encased it in a heavy block of ice. While her Skill hadn't hurt the Goblin, she had turned it into a living barricade.

The Goblins behind the frozen one screeched and clawed at the barricade, but [-Freezing Cube-] was a skill bestowed by the Gods, backed by Their divine power. That block of ice wouldn't move for one full minute, and it completely filled the narrow tunnel. No Goblin could squeeze past it.

Leo spun about gestured with his spear. "Go! Tom, Maria, go! After Sara!"

The three of them darted down the tunnel and, not long after, caught up with the back of the procession hurrying through the tunnel as Goblins continued to screech behind them. All the while Tom continued to sing [-Morning Dew-] while on the run without an instrument, which impressed Leo all the more. Tom was a more talented musician than he'd known... when he wanted to be.

Cyrus, who had been relegated to the back of the line of escaping Adventurers, looked back with wide eyes. "Did you stop them? Are they dead now?"

"Still coming. Sara! Find us another chokepoint!"

"On it! Ripper smells greenery ahead as well! It might be a way out!"

Leo was exceptionally grateful to have Ripper's keen nose on their side. He also suspected it was taking all of Sara's bond with the big Arctic Wolf to stop him from rushing back down this tunnel and tearing into those Goblins. With his impressive Strength, he could rip them limb from limb... at least until their numbers overpowered him and they tore him apart with their claws and teeth.

Not long after, the thunder of feet announced that **[-Freezing Cube-]** had worn off. The horde was after them again, and they would need to hold the horde off for at least two minutes before Maria could cast **[-Freezing Cube-]** again and buy them more time.

Ahead, Sara called out. "New chokepoint! Everyone, through!"

The tunnel was now so narrow that Leo couldn't see past Tom's wide shoulders, and Maria was now ahead of Tom. The only light came from Tom's torch, and when he reached the chokepoint, he saw that it was even more narrow than the first one. It looked like the Rock Spiders that had dug out this tunnel (he could not see how anything else could do it) had joined two tunnels here. Leo had to scramble through.

Once he was on the far side of the chokepoint, he turned just in time to see the Goblin horde boil around a curve in the tunnel. He could barely see them in the flickering light, but their beady yellow eyes all glowed. They screeched, pushed, and slammed into each other as they raced each other to the hole... and supper.

Maria readied herself. "Buy me a minute and a half

Leo adjusted his stance and readied his spear. "I can buy you more than that."

The Goblin horde smashed into the hole and did their best to scramble through. Leo expertly stabbed arms, hands, and shoulders, slowing and injuring Goblins so they collapsed and blocked the hole. The horde behind pushed the injured Goblins forward, and as they did, Leo expertly finished each of them off with additional strikes. He was tiring quickly, but he couldn't slow. If he slowed, people died.

Just when he was certain he was going to collapse, Cyrus appeared at his side. "Step back! Let me stun one!"

Leo gratefully stepped back as Cyrus stepped forward, throwing a flurry of punches. One smashed into a Goblin's skull and locked it in place. An Anchorite stun of some sort! Leo wasn't familiar with that Skill... perhaps he could ask Ashley Bloodbraid about it the next time he saw her... but the stunned Goblin made a wonderful temporary barricade.

Then Kenneth arrived at Leo's other side wielding what looked to be a... kayak? Gods! That was Sara's kayak! The kayak she kept in her

[**Unfilled Bag**] in case the great storms that roamed Evolan flooded the rivers so much she could use it to get around.

"Clear a path!" Kenneth yelled.

Maria launched several [**-Burn-**]s that ignited the remaining Goblins, and then Leo stabbed viciously again and again. Goblin after injured Goblin burst to ash as life crystals poured out of the opening, and Kenneth launched Sara's kayak into the opening like a giant spear. It smashed into the opening and got stuck halfway in, which was exactly what they needed.

Leo dropped his spear in easy reach and joined Kenneth and Cyrus as they shoved the kayak further into the breech. The sound of wood being smashed and savaged sounded from the other side of the hole, but it was a thick kayak. It was also Sara's favorite kayak. He appreciated her quick thinking and sacrifice.

The doomed vessel shook and vibrated as the Goblin horde beyond continued to savage it, but it was almost as difficult as cutting through a tree from the top down. Leo and the others couldn't retreat, but the Goblins couldn't get through the opening. Finally, Maria shouted triumphantly.

"Ready!" she told everyone.

[**-Freezing Cube-**] was off cooldown. Had it been only a minute? It seemed like so much longer.

"Everyone, back!" Leo shouted. "Give her space!" He picked up his [**Steel Spear**] and danced back to lead by example.

Cyrus and Kenneth both dashed clear, and as they did so, the remains of Sara's kayak shook and then shattered. The first Goblin through the opening got a face full of [**-Freezing Cube-**], and then the hole was plugged up with an immovable block of unbreakable ice... for one minute. The furious shrieking of the Goblin horde behind the hole assured Leo they understood that.

He felt half dead on his feet, but then Tom launched into the next verse of [**-Morning Dew-**]. His gallant singing voice was audible even over the Goblin racket, and Leo felt strength flooding back into his limbs as Tom's singing restored both his Blood and Vitality. It was a good song.

"Keep moving!" Leo shouted.

The others were already on the way, and he caught a glimpse of Sara's brilliant blonde hair before she moved around another corner with Ripper hot on her heels. As he stumbled after the others, he glanced back at the frozen Goblin staring balefully at him from the hole. They had less than a minute to find a new chokepoint, and then they had to hold it for another two.

They could do it. They had to do it. Still... it would be nice if Sara had another kayak.

They ran. The huffing of eight people sounded impossibly loud in the narrow, torch-lit, Rock Spider-dug tunnel somewhere beneath the ground of Evolan. A loud crack announced Maria's block of ice shattering, freeing the Goblin it had imprisoned and the hundreds behind it. The horde would be after them again, and the tunnel was widening. Not narrowing.

"Move!" Leo shouted. "We have to outrun them!"

As the tunnel widened even more, it was soon as tall and wide as a hallway in the chapel of Celes back in Lakebrooke. There was no way he could hold back the horde on ground this open. The Goblins would run past him on either side and savage the others until they'd completely surrounded him, at which point everyone would die and become Goblin snacks.

This wasn't how Leo had wanted to die. He hated the idea that others would die because he had no way to stop it, especially Sara. But he'd always known dying like this was a possibility, and for that reason, he would fight until he fell. He would kill Goblins until he could kill no more, and then... would he enter a grand afterlife filled with mead and fellow Adventurers?

He supposed there was only one way to find out.

"There!" Sara called hopefully from ahead. "I hear water! Ripper smells it! It's an underground cavern of some sort!"

The party increased their pace as the clamor of furious Goblins grew louder. A wide round exit from the tunnel appeared, and while Leo couldn't see perfectly from his position at the back of the pack, it looked to open into an underground chamber that was far more massive than the one in which he and the other captives had slept before the Goblins arrived. What was out there?

A tall shadow in robes stepped into view at the tunnel exit, and Leo's heart sank. Another enemy? A threat that would smash them between itself and the Goblin horde? As the shadow raised its cowl, Leo spotted the alabaster mask with the red stripe down its center.

Teacher! Teacher was waiting in that large cavern outside of the tunnel to... what? Was Maria right? Had this all been a test?

Unleashing a horde of Goblins seemed like an unreasonable test. How was Teacher going to stop all of them? Even a Preceptor Death-caster could be overwhelmed by a horde of Monsters this large, and it would be impossible for Teacher to protect everyone else without more Desouled guardians.

"Hurry!" Teacher bellowed. "The Vaulted Gardens is just beyond! Get out of the tunnel!"

That name, plus Leo's brief look at the huge cavern beyond the tunnel, finally snapped together in Leo's memories. The Vaulted Gardens was Evolan's zone dungeon, an area reserved for elite Adventurers that was filled with powerful Monsters and dangerous traps. Worse yet, each zone dungeon contained a powerful dungeon boss who could easily trample an inexperienced party.

Zone dungeons only existed in zones higher than level 8, and Adventurers could only enter one once a week. A portal deep in the wilds of Evolan would allow a party entry to the dungeon, but that portal was controlled by the Gods. Finally, a zone dungeon existed in many states at once, and each four-person party that entered one experienced its own version of that dungeon. Thus, a party could not call for help from others after they entered it.

While a single successful trip through a zone dungeon could wield an impressive amount of experience, life crystals, and rare loot, a party could not leave the zone dungeon once they entered until they defeated the dungeon boss. That meant if the dungeon boss or the Monsters inside "wiped" the party—killing everyone—all four of them would meet the Forever Death. Once a party entered a zone dungeon, no one could follow them. Not even a level-capped Adventurer.

It was impossible for anyone outside the unique copy of the zone dungeon to retrieve the ensouled bodies of those who died there, which was why even Adventurers who could enter it often chose to stick to the wilds instead. Many brave parties of Adventurers had entered a zone dungeon hoping to emerge victorious, only to never be seen again. Only the bravest dared risk it... and now, he and the other seven people with him were on the verge of entering one.

"The portal is beyond the exit from this tunnel!" Teacher shouted.

"You will not enter the zone dungeon until you are ready. Now move! I've already called my spiders!"

Sara and Ripper reached the tunnel exit first and dashed out into the much larger cavern beyond. As the others stumbled out after her, Leo glanced over his shoulder without slowing his pace. As a Skirmisher, his Prowess assured he would not trip and fall on his face.

The Goblin horde was after them, but a whole line of desouled Rock Spiders emerged from the rock between them and the horde. Their palps spun as they spit chunks of sticky rock that rapidly formed a barricade between the horde and those running from it. Leo looked ahead just in time to dart around Teacher. The man marched past him, hands raised and covered in inky black.

Teacher tossed Leo a brown pack that he caught reflexively. As he clutched it, he realized it was an **[Unfilled Bag]**. Why was Teacher tossing him an **[Unfilled Bag]**?

"Keep moving!" Teacher yelled as he marched toward the horde. "I'll hold them back!"

The Goblin horde was too fast for the spiders to fully contain them. Even as the desouled Rock Spiders spun a new wall of rock, eager Goblins leapt, clambered, or tumbled over it. Some attempted to stab the desouled Rock Spiders and then screeched as they literally melted before Leo's eyes.

When Leo glanced at Teacher, he found tendrils of inky energy zipping off his hands and slamming into Goblin targets. Each Goblin afflicted in such a way melted into a noxious pile of goo. Teacher must be using a powerful Deathcaster Skill, and it was not one Leo would wish to encounter in battle. He suspected one strike from that Skill would melt him into goo as well.

He reached the cavern exit and turned to find Teacher and his quartet of Rock Spiders still struggling to close the tunnel behind them. There were simply too many Goblins! The nasty little Monsters stabbed at Rock Spider after Rock Spider, and several burst into ash. As the horde continued to advance, Teacher turned to face Leo and raised both arms.

"Get these people to the surface!" Teacher bellowed. "Saving them falls to you now!"

Leo stared in alarm. "How? We can't go through the Vaulted Gardens!"

Just above Leo and inside the tunnel, the rocky ceiling began to melt like the Goblins struck by Teacher's inky black Skill. Strong hands grabbed Leo and pulled him out of the entry as the whole tunnel trembled. Teacher was going to bring it down on top of himself!

"You must lead them to save them!" Teacher yelled. "Honor the Gods! All of you!"

The tunnel collapsed in a deafening rumble. Leo tumbled backward as chips of rock bounced his way like Rock Spider spit. When he rose again, he stared in disbelief at a pile of huge rocks and dirt that completely blocked the exit from the tunnel and, likely, had filled the space beyond. The Goblins, the desouled Rock Spiders, and Teacher were all beyond that barrier. Possibly, they were all buried alive.

Maria huffed. "That mad bastard. Why would he do that? That idiot!"

"He gave his life for us," Cyrus said mournfully. "Why would he do that? He was our captor!"

"All he wanted was for us to level," Kenneth said grimly. "Why did we stop? Why didn't we believe him?" He clenched his fists. "I don't care if I can't face Demons. I'm done hiding. I'm going to... I'm going to live and level. I don't want to wander in the darkness after I'm dead."

"So how do we get to the surface?" Evie asked plaintively. "How can we escape?"

As Leo wrenched his eyes from the sacrifice Teacher had just made to keep them all safe, he saw the way out at the same time as Sara. There was only one way forward and through this cavern, and it was a huge glowing portal the size of the Blazers Guild in Lakebrooke. There was no way to go around the portal and no way to go back through the tunnel. He glanced at the [Unfilled Bag] he still clutched, the one Teacher had tossed to him before he perished.

Even without opening it, he suspected he knew what this bag held. Equipment. Enough equipment to equip everyone who was now trapped down here, to give them a fighting chance to defeat the Monsters and Demons between them and the surface. Even in death, Teacher continued to challenge them. Except this time, refusing Teacher's challenge meant they'd meet the Forever Death.

That portal led to the Vaulted Gardens. The dangerous, trap-filled,

Monster-filled four-person zone dungeon which he and three others would need to complete in order to escape this place. They would need to make their way through the entire dungeon and defeat the powerful zone boss before they could return to the surface of Evolan, and that seemed impossible with this meager party.

But Leo was evidently going to have to figure out a way to do it *twice*.

SEVEN
A PLAN FOR SURVIVAL

S ara's warm hand rested on his arm. "We're safe for now. We should get you armored up. The journey through the gardens isn't going to be an easy one."

They would need to get through the Vaulted Gardens to escape. It was tempting to argue with Sara, but what would be the point? He knew she was right. This was the only choice they had if they wanted to get the people Teacher had abducted... and then given his life to save... back to Lakebrooke.

Leo set down the **[Unfilled Bag]** Teacher had given him and turned to take in the worried, harried, scared people who surrounded him. People depending on him to lead them to safety. Even Maria was watching him in a way that gave him the impression that she was willing to listen to him, even if she wouldn't follow his every order. So what now?

Counting him and Sara, they had eight people to save. The Vaulted Gardens only allowed a party of four to enter. That meant they would have to form two groups. Two groups of Adventurers who were both under-leveled and inexperienced for a challenge like the Vaulted Gardens. Worse, if the whole party fell in the isolated space beyond that portal, they would almost certainly meet the Forever Death.

Yet, if they stayed in this narrow alcove they would die from dehydration long before they starved to death, and it was doubtful anyone would find their bodies here either. That assumed that the Goblins didn't dig their way out of that rubble or more Rock Spiders didn't show up. Leo knelt and opened the [Unfilled Bag] Teacher had tossed him and slipped a hand inside.

The large 40-slot cabinet he was well familiar with stretched out horizontally ahead, and Leo verified that almost every slot within the bag was occupied. Teacher had likely stuffed every last piece of equipment he kept in his "fighting pit" into this bag before coming to save them from the Goblin horde. That meant, at least, that the Adventurers now in his charge wouldn't be fighting naked.

There were potions. Not many, but he counted ten [Healing Potions] and four [Blood Potions] in the bag, which was a massive boon when they didn't have any dedicated healing... other than Tom. He would decide how to parcel out the potions once he decided who would be in the two parties tackling the Vaulted Gardens. For now, it was simply comforting to have some.

As Leo pulled basic weapons and armor from the bag and arranged them neatly on the ground, he acknowledged the gear in this bag was far from ideal. Most Adventurers wouldn't dare challenge a zone dungeon like the Vaulted Gardens without the best enchanted gear they could purchase, and this... wasn't that. Leo completed a cursory examination of what was available, then set aside the bag and gazed at those gathered around him, looking to him for leadership.

"Has anyone here ever entered the Vaulted Gardens before?"

Everyone but Maria shook their heads. Leo focused on her. "You've tackled it before?"

"Once." She crossed her arms. "It was years ago."

"What level were you at the time?"

"Fourteen."

And she was level 19 now, which put her three levels ahead of the highest level Monster or Demon in the zone dungeon. That and her powerful Harmcaster Skills would give her party an advantage in the zone dungeon, though not as much as she would give them in the wilds of Evolan. Monsters and Demons in zone dungeons were tougher than those found in the wilds, and they also came in bigger groups. Still... a level 19 Harmcaster could almost solo the dungeon boss.

It was the others who would be in the most jeopardy during their escape. Evie was level 13, which was a respectable level for a Guile-caster with good equipment, decent Vitality, and a balanced group of slotted Skills. Evie had none of those advantages, and her low Vitality meant that a few false moves inside the Vaulted Gardens could quickly lead to her demise. She would need to be protected.

And what of Cyrus, the cowardly level 13 Anchorite who was terrified of being struck in combat? He would be dead weight unless he found the courage to use his Skills, and even then, his inexperience could easily lead to a party wipe. Kenneth, the Brutalist who lacked the ability to [-Taunt-] and preferred two-handed weapons over a mace and shield, seemed eager enough to fight, but he would have difficulty keeping his party safe. His slotted Skills were focused on offense, not defense.

Still, while the limitations of those three would cause problems, Leo could work with the rest. Erick, the level 14 Shadower, gave off the impression he knew how to fight. He could scout ahead for his party and cripple at least one Monster or Demon in every group. Finally, despite only being level 10, Tom had proven he could carry a tune even while fleeing a horde of Goblins. His buffs would be helpful in the Vaulted Gardens, and he could even heal them... slowly... with [-Morning Dew-].

Lastly, Leo had Sara... and Ripper. Ripper was a powerful Arctic Wolf with the ability to both pin enemies and tear them limb from limb. While Sara might only be level 14 at the moment, she had the experience of a level 23 Sharpshooter and some of the best gear available to someone of her level. And while Leo was not one to boast, he knew his own skills were sufficient to tackle the gardens.

So Sara would lead one party into the gardens, and he would lead the other. The people they'd come here to rescue (with the possible exception of Maria) lacked the knowledge and experience to tackle a challenge like this on their own. Moreover, allowing inexperienced Adventurers to enter a zone dungeon alone was like signing their death warrants. He took a breath and made his case.

"If we attempt to escape through the Vaulted Gardens, we will face a challenge unlike any most of you have ever encountered... a zone dungeon is nothing like the combat you may have faced in Evolan or the zones before it. The Monsters and Demons there cluster in packs, each individual is more powerful than an equivalent individual you'd find above, and the gardens are also a maze filled with traps and dead ends that can lead an inexperienced party to its doom."

"So we can't risk it," Cyrus said. "We should stay and wait for a rescue."

Leo frowned. "There's no rescue coming. No one knows we're here. Not the Blazers, and certainly not other Adventurers. Whether by design or by accident, we have only two choices before us. Tackle the Vaulted Gardens and escape, or stay here and die from dehydration."

"We could find an underground stream!" Cyrus protested.

"And what would we eat?" Kenneth demanded. "He's right, Cy. There's no way out of this cave except through the gardens. Stop being a coward for once in your life and help us."

Leo raised a hand to recapture their attention. "Being afraid of Monsters, and afraid of dying in combat, is normal. While the Gods charged us to level and grow stronger, being frightened of combat is something all of us have faced at some point. I have more experience than any of you, save Maria, and I'm still often frightened before I tackle a group of Monsters."

"But you're a Blazer!" Evie protested. "You can kill anything!"

While Leo appreciated her vote of confidence, he knew that presenting himself as unafraid and invincible wouldn't help the others. "Before a battle, I'm as afraid as the rest of you. I'd be mad not to be. Any battle could be my last, but sometimes battles are unavoidable."

Cyrus frowned and Maria narrowed her eyes at that, and Evie looked even more confused. Before any of them could get too discouraged, Leo continued. This was where he could either gain their confidence or lose it forever.

"The only difference between us is that I've had the best training you can get from the Blazers, and I'm wearing some of the best equipment you can acquire. Same with Sara. That doesn't make me less frightened of battle, but it does give me the confidence I need to survive. I've done it before. I can do it again. And if you follow Sara and me, you're going to survive and escape as well."

"So you've tackled the Vaulted Gardens before," Maria stated calmly.

"I have," Leo lied. "I can lead one party through it. Sara will do the same with another."

He knew Sara had tackled the Vaulted Gardens before, and also that she couldn't lead both parties. Admitting that he'd never entered his zone dungeon (or, for that matter, any zone dungeon) would only discourage the others. He trusted Sara to tell him everything he needed to complete this challenge before they entered it in two parties.

He swept his eyes across those gathered once more. "Now, you know what will happen if we stay here. You know what you have to do if you want to live and escape. It's up to each of you to decide whether you want to stay here, starve, and meet the Forever Death, or follow us into the Vaulted Gardens and accept a challenge from the Gods that will allow you to live." He pointed at the equipment scattered across the cave floor. "While you think about what you want to do, all of you can gear up. I need to talk with my partner so we can figure out the best party arrangement to get us both home."

He glanced at Sara, who smiled warmly at him before looking again to the others.

"Leo can do this," Sara said confidently. "All of us can do this. We're Blazers. We've trained to tackle this sort of challenge for almost as long as we've been adventuring. We are going to get every last one of you out of this dungeon and to safety. You have my word."

Maria was the first to step forward. As she knelt and inspected the gear Leo had tossed out of Teacher's **[Unfilled Bag]**, Leo strode as far from the others as he could in the confines of the cavern and was unsurprised when Sara followed closely. Ripper remained where he was, sniffing for threats with his ears up and his eyes alert. Today, the huge Arctic Wolf was a comforting sight. Once he and Sara were far enough away from the others, they could speak in privacy.

"I didn't know you'd tackled the gardens," Sara said. "I thought you avoided zone dungeons?"

"I lied," Leo admitted quietly. "But I know you have experience with this one."

"I see." Sara took a deep breath. "It's not going to be an easy trek, but the good news is that we don't have to make any detours. The gardens have multiple wings that offer all sorts of opportunities to gain experience and find rare treasure, but every one of those is filled with dangerous Monsters and Demons, and traps as well. Our best bet is to avoid all that."

"I'd hoped we'd have that option. So what's the most direct route to the zone boss?"

Sara reached into her **[Unfilled Bag]** and pulled out a rolled-up piece of parchment, then unrolled it on the ground and knelt beside it. Next, she pulled out a piece of charcoal and began drawing wide lines. Soon she had created a series of lines that weren't simple, but didn't look nearly as complex as Leo had feared. Large circles waited off the main lines.

She tapped her finger on the "southern" tip of one line. "This is the overlook where you'll arrive after you step through the portal. It's not the highest point in the gardens, but it's high enough you can see each of the four wings." She tapped the eastern circle. "This area is the Cursed Steppes. There's a large Demon population scattered throughout this part, though they're not much more dangerous individually than those you'd find in the Cloudy Divide. The difference is their numbers. There's also roaming Rock Trolls on the paths. Those can be challenging, even for a full party of level 16s."

"But we don't have to enter the Cursed Steppes?"

"Correct." Sara smiled tolerantly. "May I finish before you ask any more questions?"

Leo winced. "Of course. Sorry."

She tapped the western circle. "This area is known colloquially as 'the ruins.' If it has an official name, I've never heard it. It's mostly Goblins down there, but they roam in packs of three to five. Some even have pet Dire Wolves that could give Ripper a challenge."

Leo nodded to ensure he understood.

Sara tapped a circle to the northwest. "This is the Wicked Climb. It's a series of successive rising ledges built on the side of a cliff. It's less heavily populated with Monsters than the other wings, but the cliffs are slippery and the ledges narrow. It's not unheard of for an Adventurer to fall off as they attempt to ascend this, and a fall from that height will kill you far more quickly than a Rock Troll."

Leo nodded again.

Sara tapped the last and smallest circle to the northeast. "This is the Forsaken Crypt. It's the smallest of the four wings, but unfortunately it's unavoidable. The crypt has Fetid Skeletons in both Warrior and Archer variants, which range from level 12 to 14, as well as Rock Spider Matrons. These are larger Rock Spiders that attack solo but can surprise anyone who stumbles over one of their detection webs. Those are strung like tripwires throughout the space."

Leo desperately wanted to ask a question now but refrained. Sara smiled as if she'd noticed that. She tapped the edge of the circle on the northeast tip.

"This is the final room of the zone dungeon, the Forsaken Vault. You'll need to clear out all the skeletons in the Crypt before you pull the levers to open the vault. Pulling the levers before you clear the skeletons will cause all those skeletons you haven't cleared to come rushing up to defend it. The mob can easily overwhelm a party of inexperienced Adventurers."

Leo swallowed at the thought and nodded again.

"As boss Monsters go, the Skeleton Barbarian is a straightforward fight. It doesn't have any ranged Skills, but that doesn't mean it's just a brute. It has a piercing scream which can deafen party members, making it hard to shout orders once battle is engaged. It can also summon Skeleton Minions from the bones on the ground that will target your weaker party members. But so long as you are aware of and ready to counter those threats, it's a typical taunt-and-smash encounter."

In other words, one member of the party needed to generate enough Anger on the Skeleton Barbarian to keep it focused on them while the others pelted it with damage from behind or afar until it succumbed to its wounds. The only complication was the piercing scream, which meant Leo would be unable to change his strategy after the engagement. If it summoned minions, that could also prove challenging. He wasn't sure he could defend his whole party while occupying the boss.

Sara smiled. "You can ask questions now. Thank you for waiting."

Leo nodded. "What weapons does the Skeleton Barbarian have?"

"A big two-handed blade. It has a slowing enchantment, but that's only a problem if it manages to strike your weaker party members. Whoever's acting as the party's Shield will be up close and personal with it for the duration of the fight, so the slow means you can't easily retreat."

"And the Skeleton Minions? Is it possible to stop it from summoning those?"

"If you know the cue. The minion-summoning Skill only requires two seconds to activate, but the signal is obvious. The barbarian will step back and raise one hand, at which point purple energy will gather around its fist. If you can stagger or stun it before the Skill completes, you can stop it from summoning the minions and buy two minutes before it can try again."

Leo nodded thoughtfully. While he didn't have any stuns currently slotted, Erick (the Shadower) might have one. Kenneth would have one as well with [-Staggering Blow-]. The difficulty would be ensuring either of them knew when to use the Skill, since all of them would likely be deafened by the Skeleton Barbarian's piercing scream after the fight began.

"Let's step back to the Crypt itself," Leo said. "You said the Rock Spider Matrons spread tripwire webs throughout, but they won't attack you unless you touch the wires. You also said skeletons roam the area. So will the spiders attack the skeletons if the skeletons trip the web wires?"

Sara nodded approvingly. "That's one of the common strategies parties use to make the Crypt easier to traverse. It takes longer, and you have to deal with the Rock Spider Matron after it finishes with whatever skeleton or skeletons tripped the web, but the spiders always win and usually take some damage in the process. Of course, you can also avoid the tripwire webs entirely and focus on only taking out the skeletons. The Rock Spider Matrons won't attack unless you touch their tripwires."

"But if someone stumbles into one during a fight, you could end up pincered between whatever skeletons you're fighting and any angry Rock Spider Matron going for whoever touched the web."

"Yes. It's a danger no matter what path you choose. Still, if you think your party can handle the matrons, I recommend luring the skeletons into them and then finishing off the Rock Spider Matron after it deals with the skeletons. While a single matron is tougher than individual skeletons, it's just one Monster, which means your whole party can focus on it at once."

"That makes sense to me," Leo said. "What other threats do we face on the way to the Forsaken Crypt? If we stick to the main path and avoid the other wings?"

"So long as you stick to the main road, which does a bit of winding and has several forks I've marked on the parchment, you'll only encounter Monsters such as Goblin Warriors and Archers and Skeletons of the same type. There's a low chance that a patrolling Demon called the Vomitous Horror will spawn on the main path, but it's a rare spawn."

Leo grimaced. "We should be prepared to defeat it anyway. What can you tell me about it?"

"The horror is a level 16 and an elder Monster, so it's rather tough. It looks a bit like a rotund human with gray skin, though it's twice as tall as the average person. It has a big mouth, but no eyes or nose. It can spit black acidic vomit that can actually destroy weaker armor entirely, even Uncommon armor, which is why most people prefer not to fight it if they can avoid it."

Leo shuddered at the thought. "Getting your gear melted could make it impossible to escape the Vaulted Gardens, couldn't it?"

Sara nodded grimly. "Like all demons, the Vomitous Horror also moves into shimmer when threatened. Fortunately, it's slow, so anyone with a ranged Skill can stay out of vomit range, and any weapon with a Demonslaying enchantment can also hurt it rather badly. Still, I wouldn't recommend fighting it up close."

"We may not have a choice. Any suggestions for doing that?"

"Just be ready to run. It'll wretch several times before it vomits acid, so if you hear it belching and see its belly shaking, run away as fast as you can. And don't step in any puddles afterward."

Leo found himself increasingly impressed with Sara's depth of knowledge. "You seem to know this zone dungeon quite well. How many times have you completed it?"

"Many times. It was part of how I reached Sharpshooter ahead of most. I linked up with a party of all Rangers who had powerful pets, and we'd tackle the gardens once a week and clear as much as we could. With the four of us providing ranged damage and our pets stunning or Angering anything that tried to reach us, it was safe... relatively... so long as we paid attention."

"Smart. And it's lucky for us you know the gardens so well."

Sara sighed. "I often think we were simply lucky. There was another party similar to ours that tried the same thing. I didn't know them all that well, but we often had drinks after our runs. We would usually hit the gardens on the same day each week. Then, one week, we came out and they didn't."

Leo knew what that meant. The other party had fallen inside the zone dungeon, wiped out to the last. Because the zone dungeon was a pocket of reality that included them and only them, it had been impossible for anyone to look for or rescue them... so all had met the Forever Death.

"That's not going to happen to us," Leo said as confidently as he could.

Sara smiled. "Given how talented we are, why would it?"

"So you're fine leading one party while I lead the other?"

"I can't imagine doing it any other way."

"Good. Based on our party composition, I have a recommendation for how we split everyone up. Obviously, if you have concerns, we can discuss it."

"I'm listening."

"Since you have Ripper, I think he should serve as your party's Shield. While it seems like the only healer we have is Tom, using [-Morning Dew-], that's not entirely true in Ripper's case. You can heal him with your Ranger Skills after each fight."

"I can. That was going to be my suggestion as well."

"So for your party, I'd suggest taking Maria, Evie, and Cyrus."

Sara tilted her head as she considered him. "Maria can probably solo most of what's in there, and she's also a talented ranged attacker. Won't you need a ranged Adventurer as well?"

"Not the way I'm thinking we'll handle the gardens. Evie and Cyrus are also our..." He paused before saying "weakest," because that wasn't entirely fair. "Our most fragile members. I'm not excited about sending two fragile members with you, but I think your talent and experience, Ripper's Strength and Vitality, and Maria's high level will allow you to carry both of them if needed."

Sara nodded. "It'll also be simpler to coordinate. Since it seems like Cyrus is reluctant to engage Monsters anyway, I can hold him back to intercept anything that gets past Ripper while Maria, Evie, and myself attack whatever Ripper has engaged at range. That'll also work for the zone dungeon boss."

"We're thinking along the same lines."

"So that means you'll be taking Erick, Kenneth, and Tom. How do you see that working?"

"Kenneth has the Vitality to be a party Shield but lacks the Skills and temperament, so I'll be taking that role for myself."

"You're going to act as a paper Shield?"

Leo nodded. A paper Shield, unlike a traditional Shield, used their superior mobility to avoid most of the attacks of Monsters they Angered. While a traditional Shield would block and absorb attacks, a paper Shield simply avoided them while dancing around the battle-field and tormenting Monsters from just outside of their range. It was very easy for an inexperienced mobile Shield to blunder into other Monsters or trip, which is why it wasn't common.

"You can do it," Sara said confidently. "So how do you plan to use the rest?"

"Erick will scout for us and quickly take down targets I've Angered or weaker enemies when he pops out of [-Shadow Walk-]. Kenneth seems eager to just run up and hit things, so he'll serve as our party's second Knife. I think that's a role he might actually enjoy."

"I agree," Sara said.

"As for Tom, he's not a fighter, so he'll simply stand back out of the fray and play [-Marching Rose-] during battle, and then [-Morning Dew-] after battle to heal any wounds. We'll take it slow, engage one group at a time, and work our way steadily to the vault. I like the strategy of luring the skeletons into the tripwires, and between myself, Kenneth, and Erick, we should be able to wipe out a single Monster afterward. Tom will heal us up if we get banged up during each encounter."

Sara nodded. "All of that makes sense to me. You know, you might have a talent for leadership and strategy. Have you considered leading a party of your own?"

Leo rolled his eyes. "Anyone could come up with this."

"Not anyone." Sara patted his arm. "Me, of course, but not anyone else."

Leo chuckled. He was starting to feel like getting everyone safely through the Vaulted Gardens was possible, though it would still be exceedingly dangerous. Yet, he had a plan. Sara thought it was a decent plan. Her vote of confidence and the information she'd provided about the Vaulted Gardens meant he was far better prepared for this than he would be otherwise.

"I'm happy with what we discussed," Leo said. "Are you?"

"I am."

"Then let's go tell the others."

As they walked back to the rest of their party, Leo mentally parceled out the potions available to him. He would split the [Healing Potion]s five and five, but give all four [Blood Potion]s to Sara's party. No one in his party would be using Skills that consumed Blood, and Maria, Evie, and even Sara (who would be using Skills to heal Ripper) would be using quite a bit of Blood.

Leo looked at the ragtag group of various leveled Adventurers watching them anxiously. Everyone now wore armor and carried weapons based on their preferences, and Tom even had a real lute. While the strategies his group and Sara's would use to traverse the Vaulted Gardens and reach the zone dungeon boss were different, both were relatively simple and should be possible to execute even for inexperienced Adventurers like these.

They had a chance to survive. Often, a chance was all the Gods offered. As much as Leo still disagreed with Teacher's decisions and motivations for trapping all these people underground, he could, at least, respect the man's decision to give his life to give them that chance. Leo wouldn't waste it.

And if everyone survived, maybe these people would finally tackle the climb once more.

EIGHT
A DUNGEON DIVE

As Leo stepped to the edge of the irregular stone platform looking over the Vaulted Gardens for the first time, his heart pounded. Ahead waited an expanse of cliffs, ancient ruins, and over-grown architecture that looked to be the size of Lakebrooke. The underground cavern in which the gardens rested seemed too large to be real, and Leo didn't know how it could fit beneath the Bone Vault above.

Zone dungeons existed outside of Luxtera... some said they existed outside of reality... and until they defeated this dungeon's boss and escaped, he and his party were the only four mortals in the world. Seeing the Vaulted Gardens laid out below was like looking down at a massive stone labyrinth. The ruined and overgrown build-ings, many formed of stone and little more than pillars and rotting wood, formed a green-and-gray blanket of irregular alleys, cul-de-sacs, and dead ends.

In the distance, the tiered levels of the Wicked Climb stretched toward the cavern ceiling, all but obscured by a light fog. Finally, the abandoned stone buildings of the Cursed Steppes were lost in a thick purple mist that somehow *oozed* evil. Leo could almost feel the Demons lurking there, waiting for anyone foolish enough to wander into their domain.

He glanced back at those he'd promised to deliver from death. Tom, clad in a light **[Ring-Mail Shirt]** and clutching a weathered

[Minstrel's Lute], smiled encouragingly. Kenneth wore a battered set of [Iron Armor] and an open-faced [Iron Helmet] that had obviously seen plenty of combat, but both looked sturdy enough to weather a few more battles. He also easily carried a two-handed [Troll's Cleaver] that looked far too large for any normal man to wield successfully.

Finally, Erick wore a set of [Leather Armor] more appropriate for a Shadower half his level and carried two unenchanted [Iron Dagger]s. None of them were geared up to the point where they should be tackling the Vaulted Gardens today, and their party makeup was far from ideal. Still, despite his worry for how he could get them out of here, Leo found one small, cold comfort.

If he failed to get the three of them to safety, he wouldn't be alive to live with the guilt.

"Huddle up," Leo ordered. "We should be safe until we leave this platform, so it's time to walk you through our plan for escape."

He knelt and pulled out Sara's simple map as the others gathered around. He calmly repeated everything Sara had told him as if he'd always known it himself, including the fact that they planned to avoid all the dangerous wings and head straight for the exit. Once he explained his plan to lure the skeletons into the tripwire webs, Kenneth tentatively raised his hand.

Leo couldn't help but be a little amused at the situation. He was no instructor. Still, the others were now treating him like one. He nodded as he hoped an instructor might. "Yes, Kenneth?"

"Are you sure you don't want me to act as the party's Shield? I don't mind taking a few blows, and most everything I've ever Angered is happy to go after me after I chop its ally in half."

"We don't have the healing to support that." Leo offered Tom an apologetic glance. "[-Morning Dew-] can slowly heal small injuries over time, but we can't risk you taking larger wounds in battle."

"You'll get no argument from me! If you get your arm lopped off in combat, Ken, even the best rendition of [-Morning Dew-] I can offer might as well be your dirge."

Leo looked to Kenneth again. "We do have five [Healing Potions], but I want to save those for emergencies or grievous wounds. It's my hope we'll be able to avoid using those potions entirely, but without a

Lifecaster, I think having me act as a paper Shield is the best approach."

"Even in that heavy **[Steel Armor]**?" Kenneth asked doubtfully.

"He can do it," Tom said confidently. "You should see this man dance!"

Leo frowned at Tom. "I don't dance."

Tom wiggled his eyebrows annoyingly. "You don't dance with *girls*. But from what I've seen of you in battle, you dance with Monsters just fine."

Leo focused on Erick next. "Are you comfortable scouting ahead?"

Erick nodded. "Sure."

"No risks. Ideally we won't get any adds as we engage the packs along the main path, but there's always a chance. If you see something, whistle loudly. And once we engage the pack, pick off the weakest targets you can find. Don't be afraid to lead them to me if you're in over your head."

Erick scowled at him. "Why are you doing this? You don't know us. You don't owe us anything."

Tom jumped in before Leo could decide how to answer that. "He's a Blazer! Helping people they know nothing about is what they do. It's a compulsion for them."

Kenneth clapped Leo on the shoulder. "That's right. The Blazers are heroes, Shadower, like the legends of old. There's more to life than cutting purses and running away."

Erick turned his scowl on Kenneth. "You don't know anything about me, old man."

Leo raised one hand. "Peace. Save the fight for the enemy."

Kenneth thumped his fists together. "Then let's get onto the enemy, shall we? It's been too long since I've seen a Monster bleed."

Erick scoffed. "Don't act like you're eager to fight. You left the climb just like the rest of us."

"I stopped climbing because there were too many Demons out there and too many idiots who decided a Brutalist was only good for absorbing hits. Today, I'll show you different. Brutalists can be just as dangerous as any other Knife in a fight."

Leo couldn't help but disagree. Once a Brutalist reached twenty and took the Evolved Class of Cleaver, they could certainly serve as an armored Knife, but until that point they were far better as Shields.

Still, who was he to tell Kenneth how to complete Luxtera's Climb? At least Kenneth was eager.

"Let's move," Leo said. "Stay close until we spot our first Monster pack, at which point we'll adjust. Erick, save your **[-Shadow Walk-]** until I give you the order to scout ahead."

Leo half expected an argument from the Shadower, but Erick simply fell into step on one side of him with Kenneth on the other and Tom bringing up the rear. It still felt strange to him that people would actually listen to his orders. It might always feel strange... but he was even more determined, now, to ensure the orders he gave got them home.

Walking in a close diamond formation that was almost respectable, Leo led his ragtag party down repeated tiers of ancient stone steps. It took over five minutes to descend to the level of the large main road that meandered through the center of the Vaulted Gardens, a road that looked like it had once been fine cobblestone but which was now ruined and overgrown.

As Leo cautiously led his party forward, he wondered what had gone into the building of this place. Had the Gods built a pristine city that existed for hundreds of years and was eventually abandoned? Had They turned it into a zone dungeon afterward? Or had They built the Vaulted Gardens just like this... ruined and destroyed... from the moment They called them into existence?

He didn't have long to ruminate on the matter. After walking quietly through a narrow S-curve, Leo raised a fist and pumped it down. He and everyone close by dropped as one to kneel on the road. Around the corner and about fifty paces ahead, four bleached-white skeletons stood like statues as they watched the cobblestone road.

While they all wore a few pieces of armor—a battered helmet here, a worn pauldron there, even some rusted **[Iron Boots]**—none wore armor that would stop a good blow. Odder yet, only two of the skeletons carried weapons, rusting jagged blades that looked like they were as likely to give a target metal poisoning as anything else. The other two skeletons were unarmed.

If only Leo had Glenn's unique Skills! He could use that identification Skill Glenn favored and immediately know what level each of these four skeletons was, as well as what types of Skills it had and even how it might attack. A Soulseer, Leo decided, would be more than welcome in a zone dungeon.

But he didn't have one, so he was going to have to do this the old-fashioned way.

He turned back to his party and kept his voice low. "Erick, pop into **[-Shadow Walk-]** and sneak past that group. I want to make sure four animated skeletons is all we'll need to deal with for our first pull. When you've verified there's nothing beyond, give a whistle and wait for an opening. I'll draw their attention, and then you can attack anything that looks weak from behind with your best Skill."

"**[-Shadow Stab-]**," Erick said eagerly. "Even with this junk knife, I don't think it'll survive."

Leo nodded to show confidence in his scout. "Tom, as soon as I walk forward and gain their attention, I want you to launch into **[-Marching Rose-]**. I don't know what type of skeletons these are, but they look fragile. With luck, Kenneth can cut through them with a few good swipes."

"Just one," Kenneth said. "I can easily cut through weak Monsters."

"Save **[-Mighty Slash-]** for a bigger threat. I know it's tempting to disintegrate one of these Monsters in a single blow, but there's always a bigger one around the bend. I don't want your best Skill on cooldown if something truly dangerous shows up."

"You're the boss," Kenneth said cheerily. At least he sounded like he meant it.

Leo surveyed his party. "Everyone understand their roles?"

One by one, his party members nodded. Erick looked calm as ever, but Tom was smiling as if he was enjoying this. Kenneth was all but chomping at the bit to get started. They were as ready as they could be. Time to face Luxtera's Climb as a team.

"Go," Leo told Erick.

With a puff of smoke, Erick vanished into **[-Shadow Walk-]**. Leo motioned Kenneth and Tom a few more steps forward and waited patiently. A minute later a soft whistle, like a bird call, echoed down the street from behind the four skeletons. One pivoted almost curiously at the sound.

Leo rose to his full height and marched forward. "Tom, sing us a song. Kenneth? At my side. Don't attack anything until I've angered them first."

As Tom strummed a few notes on his [Minstrel's Lute] and then launched into a rousing refrain of [-Marching Rose-], Leo felt the extra five points of Strength provided by Tom's Auracaster Skill strengthening his muscles. All four skeletons pivoted on the two of them, and while the forward two raised their jagged one-handed blades and advanced, the other two reached skyward instead.

With a crackle of dark energy, spectral bows appeared in the hands of the back two Skeletons. Leo grimaced as he realized both skeletons were archers. Normal Monsters carried their equipment on their bodies in plain sight for Adventurers to see, but zone dungeon Monsters were trickier.

He didn't know how accurate these Monsters were at range and didn't want to find out. His [Steel Armor] would protect him, but Tom would be a sitting duck. Leo broke into a run.

"Erick! Hit the archer on the left and then distract the right!"

With Kenneth pounding the cobblestone at his side and the two blade-wielding skeletons rushing toward them, the back two skeletons simultaneously reached to smoky quivers that had appeared across their backs. As they both drew inky arrows that were halfway transparent, one archer unleashed a chittering cry. It dropped to its knees.

At the same moment, Erick appeared behind it with one [Iron Dagger] buried directly in its spine. The Skeleton Archer burst into ash and dropped a glowing purple life crystal the size of an apple on the cobblestones. A small rush of ecstasy rushed through Leo as the experience shared.

Leo noted that Erick's [-Shadow Stab-] had finished the skeleton in one blow. As he rushed toward the two melee skeletons, he lacked the ability to do the math to multiply the damage of Erick's [Iron Dagger] by six. Yet he knew, now, that these skeletons had less Health than whatever that value was. That would be useful information for later.

As Erick pivoted to attack the second Skeleton Archer, the Monster did its best to block his strikes with its bow. Yet it looked entirely unprepared to face a melee opponent, and Leo could see now that Erick knew how to use his daggers. It was time for a change of strategy.

"Kenneth! The left skeleton is all yours!"

Kenneth roared eagerly. With one Skeleton Archer already ashed and Erick occupying the other, there was no need for Leo to act as a paper Shield. It would be more efficient for him and Kenneth to simply engage one Skeleton apiece and strike it down as quickly as possible.

Leo ashed his skeleton with a few stabs of his enchanted [Steel Spear], easily staying out of the reach of its one-handed blade, but Kenneth was far more reckless. He drove straight in on his enemy and swung his giant [Troll's Cleaver] with all his might. The skeleton struck back.

Kenneth got lucky. The skeleton's strike glanced off his [Iron Armor] instead of penetrating, and then, as Kenneth had promised, his [Troll's Cleaver] cut through the skeleton's fragile spine and cut the Monster in half. It ashed at about the same time as Erick finished off the second archer.

Leo hid his grimace. Kenneth was too reckless. He was going to get injured sooner or later, so he would have to be careful to manage the man's bloodlust.

Yet the street was empty, and now everyone in Leo's party had just gained 8-10 experience. The first group of skeletons was ash. "Anyone injured?" Leo called.

Tom played one last jaunty chord with his lute and ceased his song. "I'm fine back here!" he called up merrily. "You all made that look easy!"

Kenneth grinned and pumped his fist. "And the Strength you gave us is why we cut them apart!" He chuckled merrily as he picked up one of the fallen life crystals and held up to admire it. "We're all doing our part, lad. This is easier than I remember!"

Erick crouched and gathered up the two life crystals left by the Skeleton Archers he'd killed. "Those Monsters were chumps. Don't expect them all to drop that easy. There's worse in this garden."

Kenneth scowled his way. "You really do take the fun out of things."

"And you don't seem to be taking this seriously," Erick groused.

"If you're going to serve as your party's Knife, your goal is to *not* get hit."

"Everyone did their part," Leo interrupted before Kenneth and Erick could get into another argument. "That was a textbook take-down of an enemy group. Erick's right that they won't all be that easy, but Kenneth's also right that we handled that well. Let's keep this streak going."

"That's the little brother I know!" Tom called happily. "Endlessly upbeat and cheerful."

As Kenneth sheathed his giant cleaver across his back, he looked down at his big hands and flexed his fingers. "I've forgotten how good it feels. Crushing Monsters. I'd almost given up on ever experiencing this sort of high again." He tossed the life crystal once and caught it. "And look? This'll buy me supper. I should have come out to these gardens years ago."

As Tom hurried up to join their party, Erick tossed a crystal toward Tom. "Head's up."

Though Tom almost fumbled the crystal, Erick's throw was expert. Tom caught it and frowned. "I didn't kill a skeleton."

Erick shrugged. "You supported us. In all the parties I've been in, we split crystals equally."

Leo nodded in approval. He was increasingly certain he'd misjudged Erick. He might be a Shadower, but he seemed to have as much honor and care for his party members as anyone else.

"Form up," he said calmly. "Same formation as before. Let's keep moving."

They moved along the road and almost immediately came up on another group of skeletons. Now, Leo could judge how many archers were in the pack by counting how many skeletons lacked a visible weapon. This group had two archers and three melee fighters, which was too many to engage in a frontal assault. He raised his fist, called his party close, and spoke quietly.

"Cooldown on **[-Shadow Walk-]**?" he asked Erick.

Erick grimaced. "Just under two minutes."

"Then we'll wait. We're not competing against an hourglass here. Slow and steady."

They waited. Kenneth fidgeted and looked to Leo hopefully from time to time, but he didn't break ranks. Erick waited silently, and Tom did as well. Finally, Erick looked back.

"[-Shadow Walk-] is off cooldown."

"Same drill as before," Leo said. "Erick, we'll trust you to handle the Skeleton Archers. This time, I'll draw the Anger of all three melee skeletons. Kenneth, once they're chasing me, run them down and kill them from the back."

His party all nodded their assent, and then Erick vanished. A little over a minute later, all five skeletons were ash and they had five more life crystals to add to their tally. Leo doubted the crawl would continue to be this easy, but then again, most parties only used this road to reach the entry to whatever wing of the gardens they wanted to explore. The road itself was trivial.

They would find no rare treasures along this road. Since a party could only enter a zone dungeon once a week, simply killing the skeletons along the road would net a fraction of the experience they could otherwise gather. In any other case, simply sticking to the central road would be a waste, but their goal today was not to maximize their experience. Their goal was to survive and escape.

So far, Leo supposed, they weren't doing half bad at that.

They continued up the road as before, waiting as necessary to refresh Erick's [-Shadow Walk-]. They used their first [Healing Potion] to fix Kenneth's broken arm after they were ambushed by a Rock Troll while fighting skeletons. In that case, Leo couldn't fault Kenneth for placing himself in harm's way.

Kenneth intercepted the troll before it could gore Tom, and there had been no way to stop it but to take a few blows. Leo finished the troll off and then offered the [Healing Potion] as thanks. Kenneth might not wield a mace and shield, but he remained focused on protecting his weaker party members.

The trek down the main road of the Vaulted Gardens continued at a glacial pace, but they took no further injuries. Leo felt like they'd been creeping along the road engaging in intermittent fights for hours, but it was impossible to tell. There was no sun in this giant cavern. Time seemed to stand still.

Still, he had balanced his party well. None of their abilities consumed Blood, and the only Skills they needed could be used repeatedly with only a wait for the cooldown to expire. Tom's frequent shifts to **[-Morning Dew-]** kept them healthy and free of fatigue long past when other Adventurers would have needed to rest and recover. When it came to steadily fighting Monsters in a situation where you could choose when to engage, Auracasters were consistently underrated.

Leo kept expecting someone to defy his orders and get injured, or for them to unexpectedly encounter the Vomitous Horror, but their luck held. They reached the entry to the Forsaken Crypt with three **[Healing Potions]** left. Leo had to consume one himself after taking a battering from a pair of Rock Trolls who ambushed them from the alleys while they were fighting the second-to-last group.

As Leo led his party forward, he recognized worn headstones in the grass along the path leading to the sealed door of the Forsaken Crypt. Who would be buried here? The Gods must simply have created these headstones as They created everything else. Their ways would always be strange to him.

Leo paused his party outside the closed door. He saw a large, obvious switch built into the wall beside it. Opening the door, it seemed, would be easy... but the inside would challenge them.

He turned back to his party. "First, all of you have done a fantastic job so far. Everyone followed orders, worked together, and kept their heads. All of you should be proud."

Kenneth thumped his fists together and grinned, and even Erick managed a small smile. It was the solemn expression on Tom's face that surprised him. He'd been expecting a joke.

Tom walked forward and placed a hand on Leo's shoulder. "We wouldn't be here without you."

"I'm going to get you out of here," Leo promised. "Only one area to go."

"That's not what I mean," Tom said. "I mean we wouldn't be alive without you. If you hadn't shown up to try and rescue us, we'd never have gotten out of our tents in time to stay ahead of that Goblin horde. And if you hadn't led us while we fled, we'd have fallen in those tunnels."

Leo frowned. "You'd still have fallen if Teacher hadn't shown up."

"But he put us down here, little brother." Tom's solemn expression didn't fade. "You got us out, and your leadership is why we were able to fight this far through a zone dungeon without getting our heads torn off. We're alive because of you. So... I just want to say thank you."

"The lad's right," Kenneth said. "You're a good sort, Blazer. I'd follow you into battle any day."

Leo had always been uncomfortable with compliments. Still, they were looking to him for leadership, so he did his best to nod stoically and acknowledged Tom's statement. "Let's keep it up. This crypt will be more challenging than what we've faced before."

He paused a moment as he remembered Glenn's worst fear. "Just to check, is anyone here arachnophobic?" The sight of a giant spider could paralyze even an experienced Adventurer if they were phobic or not expecting it to attack.

His party looked around at themselves, then shrugged.

"Nope."

"No."

"I think they're neat!" Tom added slyly.

Leo nodded in approval. "Good. Inside, I want every last one of you to stay behind me. Don't walk ahead. I'll spot the trip wires and trip them as needed."

Kenneth saluted, Erick nodded, and Tom grinned. They believed in him. They trusted him. Leo refused to let them down. He pulled the lever.

The Forsaken Crypt yawned as the door leading into its depths rumbled open.

NINE

A SPIDER'S MAZE

The interior of the Forsaken Crypt was gloomy and musty. Motes of dust floated freely and were visible in the beams of gray light that cut through the space from the occasional high window, but the space remained gloomy enough Leo wished they'd brought a [Smokeless Torch]. He motioned the others into a diamond formation behind him and advanced slowly into the crypt.

Towering square columns filled the space at regular intervals, carved with reliefs of what looked to be armored Adventurers. Large stone coffins were arranged in neat lines along the sides of the large and open room, though many of the lids were off-kilter, missing, or broken. Leo supposed that might be where all the skeletons had come from.

He spotted the first patrol of skeletons immediately ahead, and at the same time, the skeletons spotted him. It was four of them, three melee and one archer, but as Erick moved forward to attack the archer, Leo raised a hand. "Wait. I don't see trip wire webbing. We have to find that first."

As the Skeleton Archer pulled a smoky arrow from its smoky quiver and nocked it to its spectral bow, Kenneth growled low. "He's going to feather us!"

"Kneel down!" Leo ordered. "Tom, Erick, get behind us!"

The others, fortunately, obeyed. While Leo and Kenneth made themselves smaller targets and formed a barrier of steel and iron armor, Erick and Kenneth crouched down behind them. Tom launched into **[-Morning Dew-]** without being asked, which would likely heal any minor injuries they suffered if one of the Skeleton Archer's arrows managed to pierce their armor. Then, they waited.

The Skeleton Archer loosed an arrow. It flew over their heads. Meanwhile, the three other skeletons, armed with one-handed blades, marched forward with a loud chittering sound. The next arrow from the archer slammed into Leo's chestplate and bounced off. No damage.

The leading skeleton was only fifteen or so paces away when it tripped and stumbled. Its ankle was caught on something! Leo's eyes widened inside his **[Steel Helmet]** as a near-invisible strand of thick webbing around the same diameter as a good-sized rope glistened in the gloom.

Before the skeleton could free itself, a gray spider the size of Ripper dropped from the ceiling. It landed on the skeleton with a triumphant screech. The hapless Monster flailed away with its blade as the spider tore it apart, and then the other two skeletons joined the fray as well.

Their blades sliced off a single leg and cut deep into the spider before it finished both skeletons off, and then the spider rushed the single Skeleton Archer. It stupidly fired one more arrow, not retreating, before the spider took it down. It tore the archer's head off and then spun about, bleeding and seven-legged, to focus its eight eyes on the Adventurers huddled close by.

"Let it come," Leo said grimly.

The spider charged them, but with an off-balance gait that showed it was already wounded. The places where the skeleton blades had carved it open oozed, and its Health Bar, which floated above it as it approached, was well below half. The skeletons had done their damage.

When it was only ten paces away, Leo rose and rushed forward. He shoved his **[Steel Spear]** directly into the space below its eight eyes. His weapon pierced its skin and impaled it, causing it to screech in fury. It flailed with its forward legs but couldn't reach him.

Tom switched into **[-Marching Rose-]** as Kenneth and Erick rushed the spider from each side. The Monster seemed too stupid to back off after being impaled, and it stubbornly struggled forward as it forced Leo's spear deeper into its own chest. Only the extra Strength provided by Tom's [-Marching Rose-] allowed him to hold it at bay. Kenneth and Erick sliced its sides repeatedly until it ashed.

A life crystal the size of a pomegranate clattered to the crypt floor. Leo, breathing hard, glanced at his party and nodded. Normal parties would not use this strategy because it would allow that spider to steal 40 experience from the four skeletons it had torn apart in their place. But again, his party was focused on escape, not efficiency.

They could do this. They could reach the zone dungeon boss. For the first time, Leo allowed himself to internally believe escape was possible. Thanks to Sara, he knew how to get them out of here the safest way possible. Now he just had to execute.

They proceeded slowly through the large crypt as they had on the main road. They encountered four more groups of skeletons and dispatched one on their own, but the other three all stumbled across all-but-invisible spiderweb tripwires. This not only cleared the way for Leo's party to proceed but ensured they were never ambushed while in the middle of the fight.

Not long after, they sighted a closed set of stone doors in the center of the crypt. There was a lever beside those doors that would lead them down to the boss chamber; however, Leo remembered Sara's warning. Pulling that lever would summon every skeleton still active in the crypt, and those skeletons would trip over more webs and summon spiders as well. A recipe for a party wipe.

"There's the door!" Kenneth said excitedly. "We're almost out!"

"Not yet," Leo reminded them. "We need to clear all the skeletons first."

Working cautiously, they crept through the rest of the crypt and dispatched four more groups of skeletons. Only once they'd made another full circuit, careful to only travel along paths where the skeletons had already broken the spiderweb trip wires, was Leo satisfied. It was possible they had missed a group of skeletons somewhere... but nowhere he could see.

Once they returned to the set of stone doors, he looked to Tom. "Pull the lever and be ready to sing. The rest of you? Prepare yourselves. If we do get attackers, retreat into the hall beyond these doors and let Kenneth and I hold the line. We should be able to fight off even superior numbers if we use the hallway beyond these doors as a chokepoint."

"You're good at this," Tom said ruefully. "I always knew, I mean... I thought I knew. But I hadn't *seen* it before. My brother, the grand Adventurer."

Leo simply grunted in response.

"I'm pulling the lever," Tom warned. "Here goes everything."

A small metallic crunch followed by a loud, mechanical screech sounded from behind Leo. Stone rumbled against stone as the doors to the inner crypt slowly opened with enough noise to wake the dead... quite literally. Leo waited for more skeletons to attack and prepared himself for battle.

None came. They'd cleared the crypt in advance. He silently thanked Sara for her information.

Once Leo was certain nothing would harass them, he led the way through the stone doors. They almost immediately encountered a spiral staircase, but it led up, not down. Leo glanced at his party. "Erick, behind me, Tom, follow him. Kenneth, rear guard."

By necessity, they proceeded up the staircase single file. It seemed to wind endlessly, and Leo was surprised to find torches burning in the walls that lit the path. Who had placed those torches? Who had lit them? Who replaced them? More questions, he supposed, for the Gods.

Finally, after they had climbed what felt like at least twenty stories, they reached a level hallway. At the end of that hallway were two more big doors, though these were formed of oak and metal instead of stone. Leo led his party slowly down the hall, wary of traps or hidden Monsters. They were almost to the doors when both creaked open of their own accord.

Leo raised a fist to halt his party. Meanwhile, the doors swung open to reveal a sandy expanse of flat ground surrounded by a tall stone wall that had to be at least three stories high. As Leo's eyes swept past that wall to the tiers of empty stone benches ascending around them in rings, he realized what he was seeing. A colosseum. There was a colosseum deep beneath the earth.

Outside, he knew, the Skeleton Barbarian waited to challenge them.

"The zone boss is outside," Leo said calmly. "This is how we get out. This is the end of the zone dungeon. If we beat this boss, we'll be able to leave out of the same exit all Adventurers take at the edge of the Bone Cage." He turned to Kenneth and pulled out two [**Healing Potion**]s. "Take these."

Kenneth eyed him doubtfully. "Should you keep those? What if you get hit?"

Leo offered a rare smile. "I feel like you'll need them more."

Kenneth watched him a moment, then chuckled. "Too right."

Leo handed the last two [**Healing Potion**]s to Tom and Erick, respectively. "Save it for an emergency, but don't be afraid to use it. When the barbarian appears, let me anger it. Once we're certain it's focused on me, launch into [-**Marching Rose-**] while Kenneth and Erick attack."

"What about if it tries to call in its minions?" Tom asked.

So Tom had been paying attention during Leo's briefing. That was refreshing.

"I'm the party's Shield," Leo said. "I'll stop it from doing that."

Kenneth clapped him on the shoulder. "I'm ready, boss. Let's do this!"

Leo looked around. "Are the rest of you ready?"

Erick cracked his knuckles. "[-**Shadow Walk-**] is off cooldown. I'll make myself scarce when the battle starts and try to land a [-**Shadow Stab-**] once the barbarian is busy with you."

"Give me a bit to soften it up before you do that much damage," Leo cautioned. "You don't want to draw its Anger."

"I won't."

"Then I think we're ready."

"Wait!" Tom said in alarm. "You don't have a [**Healing Potion**]!"

"I don't need one."

"Balderdash." Tom held out his potion. "Take mine."

"I have armor. You don't."

"And you'll be going toe to toe with a Skeleton Barbarian zone dungeon boss! I'm quick on my feet. I won't get anywhere close to it. But if it injures you badly enough you can't escape, I'll run up to you to try to give you this potion, and then we'll both get killed. That'll be your fault."

"He's right, lad," Kenneth said. "You should take the last potion."

"I agree," Erick said. "You're quick, true enough, but the moment that Skeleton Barbarian hits you with its cursed blade, you'll be slowed down. You could still get hit."

Leo mentally debated. He knew he could refuse if he truly wanted to. He was this party's leader. Even so... perhaps Tom was right. Perhaps they were all right. Reluctantly, he took the last **[Healing Potion]** and hitched it to his belt. He wouldn't want to fumble inside his **[Unfilled Bag]** for it if he was engaged in close combat with a Skeleton Barbarian.

"Thanks." Leo stared at Tom. "Now you have no excuse to get anywhere near that boss."

"Oh, I won't. Now let's kill this trumped-up skeleton and go home!"

Leo took one deep, calming breath. He turned to face the sandy arena. He suspected that the Skeleton Barbarian would not present itself until they walked out into the colosseum. They could take as much time as they needed to get ready, but they were ready.

He exited the hall and walked out onto the sandy soil with his party behind him.

The moment all four of them had entered the colosseum, the big oak and metal doors behind them slammed closed. Leo suspected not even a Harmcaster's **[-Inferno-]** Skill could open them. There would be no retreat back into the crypt if the zone dungeon boss overwhelmed them. The only way was forward. As he stood with his party, ghostly chanting rose from the empty stands.

Spectral figures appeared in the stands, hundreds upon hundreds of people who were mostly transparent and quite obviously dead. A crowd was cheering. A crowd of souls. Yet were they actual people who'd lived here, or illusions created by the Gods? Leo would worry about that later.

At the center of the arena, dust swirled. Soon what was a whirl of dirt was a vortex of sand and stone, and when it vanished, a skeleton at least twice as tall as Leo stood holding a huge two-handed sword. That blade had to be the size of Evie, the level 13 Guilecaster he hoped was safe with Sara's party! Unlike the lesser skeletons they'd seen, the barbarian wore a full suit of rusted armor.

The Skeleton Barbarian extended one hand in an obvious challenge, then slapped its massive blade down on one shoulder and advanced. The spectral crowd around them hooted and hollered, and some even shouted dismissive taunts. There was no question which fighter they favored today.

Leo advanced as well. Once he and the Skeleton Barbarian were twenty paces apart, the boss adjusted its massive two-hander with languid grace and moved into a jog. Its bony feet slammed into the sandy arena as Leo increased his pace to meet it. It swung.

Despite its size, the Skeleton Barbarian moved with surprising grace. Leo dodged below the swing and avoided its first strike, but as its massive blade whooshed over him with enough speed he could feel the wind coming off it, a wave of heaviness coursed over his body.

So the Skeleton Barbarian didn't even have to hit him to afflict him with its slowing debuff? It simply had to be in proximity to him? How was that fair?

It wasn't. The Gods weren't fair. Leo had known that. He still had a job to do.

He sprang to his feet and used his superior mobility to circle to the side of the Skeleton Barbarian, which turned ponderously and stabbed again and again. His muscles ached as he pierced the Skeleton Barbarian's armor with his [Steel Spear], or tried. Despite its rusted appearance, the armor was thick. While his piercing stabs did cause its huge red Health Bar to appear, the tiny slivers Leo's strikes shaved off were nothing. It would take him ten minutes to kill this Monster like this!

As Tom launched into a rousing rendition of [-Marching Rose-], Leo felt his flagging endurance restoring itself. New Strength flooded his limbs as Tom's song counteracted the worst of the weariness imposed by proximity to the Skeleton Barbarian. That gave him just enough of a second wind to duck under the huge skeleton's next sweeping strike, and then their dance began in earnest.

Leo huffed inside his armor as he weaved, dodged, and stabbed, barely avoiding blows of the giant sword as he chipped away at the zone dungeon boss's massive Health Bar. He needed to get the tip of his spear into a joint in the armor, but the boss Monster was too tall for him to easily target its armpits, and its knees were well armored as well. Its neck was exposed but out of reach.

He experimentally retreated and watched with satisfaction as the Skeleton Barbarian lumbered mindlessly after him, putting its back to

Tom and the others. Leo decided he had Angered it to the point where the rest of his party could now join in without the Skeleton Barbarian targeting them.

"Attack!" he shouted.

Not a moment later, the Skeleton Barbarian went stiff as Erick sank an [Iron Dagger] deep into the back of one thigh. For the first time its Health Bar ashed by a noticeable amount as it took the full brunt of Erick's [-Shadow Stab-]. Then Kenneth arrived as well, battering at the skeleton with strike after strike. Leo could sense it responding to the attacks and speared it again and again.

"I'm the one you want, you bony bastard! Focus on me!"

Erick and Kenneth both stumbled back, obviously feeling the effects of the barbarian's slowing debuff. The boss begrudgingly turned its attention back to Leo, and then they danced once more. Again and again Leo called in his party, and again and again they attacked and retreated. Even with the benefit of Tom's singing, Leo barely stayed ahead of the Skeleton Barbarian's ponderous strikes... but he *did* stay ahead.

Little by little, they whittled its Health Bar down. All was going well until Leo's next step snagged his ankle on a large stone. He didn't lose his balance. He had too much Prowess for that. But he stumbled, and given how narrowly he had been avoiding the Skeleton Barbarian's strikes, as well as his fatigue, it was the opening the zone dungeon boss needed.

Its huge sword swept in sideways... and slammed into his chest. The impact didn't crack his armor—his [Steel Armor] held—but the force of the blow was so great it still felt like being hit by a runaway wagon, and it hit hard enough it actually *lifted* Leo into the air and tossed him ten paces.

He landed awkwardly but managed to roll to his feet despite his heavy armor. Only an experienced Skirmisher could accomplish such a feat. Even so, Leo gasped for each breath as agony speared his chest. That impact might have snapped a rib or two.

As he balanced and gasped, the Skeleton Barbarian stomped over to finish the job. At least it remained focus on him. He was doing his job as a Shield... but how could he avoid getting hit again?

"[-Mighty Slash-]!" Kenneth roared.

His large blade tore through the Skeleton Barbarian from behind, all but shattering its kneecap. The barbarian took a knee just out of reach of Leo, and as it ponderously attempted to turn around, Erick and Kenneth tore into it with their blades. Tom's singing grew in pitch and urgency.

Leo couldn't breathe, his chest was on fire, and his shoulder felt like it had crumbled to dust. He couldn't lift his spear to get in another strike, and his next step took him to his knees again. Then he remembered. He remembered Tom. His big brother was always watching out for him.

Leo pulled the [Healing Potion] hooked to his belt, popped the stopper with shaking fingers, and chugged it as Kenneth took the Skeleton Barbarian's full attention and Erick continued chipping away at it from behind. As the hot, sweet fluid coursed down his throat, the pain in his chest eased. His shoulder went from broken to sore. He tossed the bottle and stepped forward.

The Skeleton Barbarian, now down to less than a third of its Health Bar, chittered loudly and raised the hand not holding its two-handed sword high. It clenched its fist, and as it did so, purple energy coursed around its bony fingers.

Leo's eyes widened in horror. He was too far away to interrupt it himself, and even if he used [-Piercing Throw-], his strike wouldn't reach it in time to stop its cast.

"Interrupt!" Leo shouted desperately. "Interrupt it before—"

Thunder rumbled through the colosseum as the Skeleton Barbarian finished casting its Skill. All around them, human-sized skeletons began to claw their way out of the sand. They wore no armor and carried no weapons, but there were dozens of them. Minions. Skeletal minions.

At least six of them immediately lumbered toward Tom.

"I'll protect him!" Kenneth shouted at Leo. "Focus on the barbarian!"

As the Skeleton Barbarian once again gripped its sword with both hands, Kenneth lumbered toward the skeletons rushing toward Tom as Leo did the same. Tom backed up slowly as the skeletons approached, eyes wide, but he didn't stop playing. He didn't stop singing.

"Go!" Kenneth shouted. "Erick can't handle it alone!"

Leo tore his eyes from his big brother to find Erick valiantly slashing at the Skeleton Barbarian all alone. His knives were glancing off its armor entirely, and as it tried to cut him in half, it missed him by less than a single pace. Erick was gasping and tired. He couldn't hold the barbarian at bay.

Kenneth met the first skeleton minion and swung his huge two-handed blade. He cut the minion in half with a single blow. There were many minions now, but they were weak. Leo had to trust his party. He couldn't do everything himself... not even save his brother.

As Erick barely dodged a sideways sweep of the Skeleton Barbarian's huge blade, he did so only by diving and dropping flat. He rolled onto his back and scrambled up as the Skeleton Barbarian raised one booted foot. It slammed it down, pinning Erick to the earth. He was dead if Leo didn't intervene.

Leo tossed his spear with all his might, triggering **[-Piercing Throw-]**. He focused on his target. His **[Steel Spear]** gleamed as it rocketed across the arena, and then it hit the Skeleton Barbarian directly in the unarmored spot at the back of its neck. Bone shattered as the Skeleton Barbarian's Health Bar ashed down to almost nothing —a critical hit!—and then it fumbled its massive two-handed sword.

The blade slammed tip first into the dirt beside Erick as the barbarian stumbled sideways, releasing him. Blood coursed across Erick's chest, which Leo belatedly saw was badly injured, but Erick was no fool. He fumbled for his **[Healing Potion]** and desperately drank it down.

"**[-Windborne Recall-]**!" Leo shouted for the benefit of his party.

Leo's **[Steel Spear]** ripped itself out of the Skeleton Barbarian's back, ashing another sliver of Health Bar. As Leo charged the barbarian, he caught his spear without slowing down. Erick scrambled to his feet as the Skeleton Barbarian ponderously retrieved its sword. Then, Erick vanished in a puff of smoke.

The fight had been going on long enough for Erick's **[-Shadow Walk-]** to come off cooldown? If not for Tom's singing and buffs, they would all be exhausted by now. The Skeleton Barbarian, confused by Erick's disappearance, swung it sword blindly through the space he'd occupied. It hit nothing but air. Then Leo arrived, stabbing away as he had before. The barbarian moved much slower now.

Each stab pierced armor and drove the Skeleton Barbarian back. Still, it somehow survived, parrying strikes and enduring others.

Then Erick burst from [-Shadow Walk-] and stabbed the skeleton in the back of one knee. It dropped into a crouch, finally putting its head and neck in strike distance.

Leo took the opening. He stabbed forward with all the accuracy imbued by his experience and prowess and shoved his spear through the Skeleton Barbarian's face... and out the back of its skull. The last of its Health Bar faded to ash. With an explosion Leo felt rather than heard, the Skeleton Barbarian burst into ash as brittle bones blasted upward in all directions.

A huge glowing life crystal the size of a [Steel Helmet] dropped to the earth, followed by the Skeleton Barbarian's massive two-handed sword. Yet as the sword fell to the colosseum floor, the rust upon it melted away. A moment later the huge two-handed sword gleamed like a blade fresh from the forge, and it even had a soft glow Leo knew meant its slowing enchantment was still in effect.

The Gods had honored their bravery and skill today. They had cleansed the Skeleton Barbarian's rusty sword and offered it as a reward. With this sword, and the slowing debuff it would inflict upon both nearby Monsters and Demons, Kenneth would have one of the best pieces of equipment available to Adventurers in Evolan. Finally, a party might accept him.

Another loud crack of thunder echoed through the colosseum, and then a glowing portal about as wide as two large doors manifested in the middle of the arena. Though it was faint, Leo could see what looked to be a large cavern on the other side, as well as a sloped rocky surface leading to open sky.

That was the exit to the zone dungeon. It was open at last!

Leo turned to check on Tom and gasped when he saw the carnage. Piles of ash surrounded both Tom and Kenneth, but Tom was on his knees with Kenneth's head lying in his lap. The big man was covered in blood, his [Iron Armor] crumpled and pierced in dozens of places. Even as Tom desperately poured the last of a [Healing Potion] down Kenneth's throat, Leo knew it might not be enough.

Multiple skull and bone icons floated about Kenneth's all but ashed Health Bar. Poison debuffs. While Auracasters *could* learn a song that allowed them make their party members immune to poison, Tom did not know that song... and the poison continued to tick.

It seemed the Skeleton Barbarian's minions inflicted poison with their strikes. Why hadn't Sara mentioned that? He wouldn't be surprised if it was because the Gods had "changed things up" yet again.

Leo hurried back to Tom and Kenneth with Erick huffing at his side. They had done it. They had survived. They could escape... but would Kenneth escape with them?

As Leo dropped to his knees at Kenneth's side, the big man coughed blood. "They didn't touch him," Kenneth said hoarsely. "Not one. They didn't touch our healer."

Tom stood and started singing **[-Morning Dew-]**. It would slowly heal wounds and restore fatigue, but Leo wasn't sure if it would be enough. Those poison debuffs weren't going away.

"I told you I could protect him," Kenneth wheezed. "I'm a Shield. I shielded him."

"You did," Leo said firmly. "Now relax. You have to heal. You even got a brand-new sword out of the dungeon. Just imagine how impressed people will be when they see that!"

"Would be... nice." Kenneth's eyes fluttered close. His Health Bar ticked down.

Leo slapped him hard. "Stay awake! Hang on, man!"

Kenneth didn't respond, and Tom's singing grew more desperate. Finally, all the poison debuffs on Kenneth's Health Bar vanished simultaneously. For a moment Leo was elated that Kenneth had survived long enough for the poison to stop ticking... but then he realized Kenneth hadn't survived.

Kenneth no longer moved. He no longer breathed. His ashen features revealed the worst.

Tom's voice broke, and then his song ended. "Gods, no."

Leo rose. Kenneth had died defending Tom... but he hadn't met the Forever Death. Not yet. He looked at Erick. "Get his feet. I'll get his shoulders."

"Let me help!" Tom said urgently.

"You sing," Leo ordered. "**[-Marching Rose-]**. Strength for all of us. It's time to go home."

Tom visibly steadied himself. He played a mournful tune on his lute, then launched into a song Leo knew would be stuck in his head for days after this. Fresh Strength flooded his limbs as he slipped his hands beneath Kenneth's shoulders and lifted. Erick did the same with his feet.

Moving awkwardly with the weight of a full-grown man in battered armor, they all shambled to the portal in the middle of the colosseum. White engulfed Leo's vision, then faded. A warm wind hit him as the weight of Kenneth's body continued to test his Strength.

He heard a series of gasps and then a loud female cry. "Leo!"

It was Sara. His vision cleared as Sara, followed closely by Evie and Maria, rushed over. Leo saw several other figures as well, all dressed in white or gray robes marking them as casters of some sort. They weren't a threat. He settled Kenneth on the ground and collapsed beside him.

"Kenneth needs a **[-Resurrect-]**, but we're otherwise all alive and accounted for."

"Leo!" another woman shouted in worry.

It took Leo a moment to recognize that voice because his brain wouldn't accept that he was hearing it correctly. How could *she* be here? She didn't even know where he was!

Yet in another moment Lucy Stargazer dropped to his side and threw her arms around him. As she hugged him close, Leo swallowed in alarm. He was even more surprised when Lucy planted a warm kiss on his cheek, and then, to his shock, one directly on his lips.

He was... but she wasn't... she was a member of the Church of Celes! And she was six years older than him! And she was also incredibly attractive, and also, she'd just *kissed* him. What?

He couldn't enjoy this yet. This affection. This warmth. He had to see to his party first, and in particular, to the man who had taken multiple poisoned strikes from skeleton minions to ensure that Leo's big brother Tom escaped the Vaulted Gardens alive.

Lucy eased away and supported him with her arms. "I'm here. Just relax. You're safe now."

Sara walked over before Leo could recover. "What happened?"

Despite the lingering taste of Lucy on his lips and the warmth of her unexpected kiss, Leo focused on the horrors he'd survived. "The boss fight got out of hand, and Kenneth protected Tom."

"Damn," Sara said ruefully. "We only had one. We used it on Cyrus."

Leo's heart sank. "We only had one **[-Resurrect-]**?"

Lucy sighed. "I'm sorry, Leo."

"Most of the Spiritualists and Shamanists have already left the city to travel to Caelfall for the <Sandsea Cup>," Sara said. "But don't worry. There has to be one left somewhere. We'll find someone who can bring Kenneth back. We'll save him, I promise."

Lucy squeezed Leo once more, then stood and looked around. "Is anyone else injured?"

"No. Just Kenneth."

"Then let's get you all home." Lucy's gaze met his again, and her smile warmed his heart in a way he hadn't expected. "Thank the Gods you survived."

"How?" Leo managed. "How are you here?"

He looked past her at several other people who he now knew were younger members of the Church of Celes. Had Lucy gathered all these people to come and rescue him? How had she even known he would come out of the gardens?

"It was Glenn," Sara said. "Before he left, he found the hole in the wall that allowed Teacher to take us out of the city without being spotted. Glenn also guessed that Teacher would need somewhere remote and largely untraveled to build his base, which he believed was most likely to be hidden in the Bone Cage. There's Blazers at other areas where we might emerge, searching for us, but Glenn also thought it was possible you might come out of the Vaulted Gardens. So, here we are!"

Leo nodded dully. "Here we are."

"Glenn did all that?" Tom asked in wonder. "Is he a seer?"

"He's a Truth Seeker," Sara said. "He's getting rather good at solving mysteries."

Lucy gripped Leo's hands in both of hers and helped her up. "We're getting you all home. Sara's told us some of what happened to you, about this 'Teacher,' but we'll focus on the rest later. For now, let's find someone to resurrect Kenneth and get the rest of you some food and rest."

Now that it was evident his party was safe, Leo could focus on Lucy. "You kissed me."

Lucy smiled. "Did you mind?"

"I... didn't mind at all."

"Excellent, because I'd like to do it again soon. But not now." She turned to her younger clergy members. "Everyone, on alert! There may be more Screechers on the way out. These people are our responsibility now. We're going to get every last one of them home!"

"Yes, ma'am!" the other Lifecasters said proudly.

Sara gripped his shoulder. "We did it. We saved them."

"Not all of them," Leo said grimly. "I didn't know the Skeleton minions had poison."

Sara's eyes widened. "They've never had poison before."

"The Gods. Changing things up again."

Sara sighed heavily. "All we can do is move forward. This is a victory. Treat it as such."

Leo glanced around at the eyes staring at him in awe and gratitude—Evie, Erick, Tom, Cyrus, even Maria—and accepted what he could. He'd saved five. He'd lost one, or could if there weren't enough [-Resurrect-]s available. If there weren't... he'd done all he could.

He would worry about the rest after he'd had a good meal and a good sleep.

ACT II: A CONTEST IN THE SAND

TEN
A CONTINENT REACHED
GLENN

"Land, ho!"

To his credit, the lookout on the crow's nest of the *Surly Songbird* didn't need **[-Public Address-]** to make his voice audible. Glenn and Becka had spent the last two weeks living inside a small room in a cargo vessel as they crossed a choppy sea. Today, finally, their boat would dock at Caelfall's capital city of Aria in the level 20-26 zone of Fool's March.

Yet as much as Glenn longed to head above deck and get his first look at a foreign coast and a capital city, he had other responsibilities. Their single cabin was cramped for two people, which wouldn't have been a problem if Becka hadn't been seasick for most of the journey. Though Glenn had tended her, ensured she drank plenty of fluids, and even eased her discomfort with **[-Guardian's Heal-]**, Becka had been miserable for the past two weeks. It hurt Glenn that he couldn't do more for her.

Given Becka's rebellious stomach and constant queasiness, the small space in which they'd spent the journey felt *too* small at this point. Bringing down a bucket for Becka had saved her the effort of tromping up the narrow stairs to vomit over the side of the boat, but the smell lingered. Glenn would be happy to get some fresh air once they stepped onto dry land.

Multiple pairs of heavy boots thumped on the deck overhead as the sailors made ready for landfall. As their shouting grew and they went about their business, the dark-haired woman Glenn loved groaned as she turned onto her side. All the racket had roused her from a hard-earned slumber.

Curled up into a ball beneath their thin sheets, Becka forced her eyes open. "What time is it?"

Glenn grinned wide, hoping to cheer her up as best he could. "Time to land, apparently. You survived the journey to Aria. Congratulations! You might even get a point of Stamina out of this."

She rubbed her face and shuddered. "Don't congratulate me yet. I'm still not certain I didn't die. This could be one of the Six Hells. The vomit hell."

Glenn winced sympathetically. "I'm fairly sure there's not a vomit hell."

"There could be. Gods, I hate boats."

He squeezed her shoulder through the thin blanket. "We'll get you something to settle your stomach for the return trip."

"Or we can walk back. A **[Potion of Waterwalking]** can't be that expensive, can it? We'd get so much exercise!"

He brushed her sweaty hair back from her forehead. "Just hold on for a little longer, love. Once we dock, I'll carry you off the boat and pop you onto dry land myself."

She poked him. "Go."

Confused by her order, he frowned. "What are you talking about?"

"Go up and watch the boat pull into port. Into Aria. I know you want to see it."

"I need to stay down here with you."

"Nonsense." She forced a smile that almost felt genuine, though the sweat on her pale face betrayed her discomfort. "I'm not going to expire in the next hour, and you've been tending to me this entire trip. My hero. My savior."

"You'd do the same for me."

"Don't be so sure. I'm not certain I'd be able to handle quite so much vomit."

He laughed again, but more to change the flow of the conversation than because he found her joke amusing. "I'll stay down here with you until we land."

"Glenn, my love, you're the most wonderful man in Luxtera, but I will be fine... and this is the first time you'll be able to see a foreign shore. Go up on the dock. Enjoy the view. You'll never forgive yourself if you don't, or if you do, *I'll* never forgive you."

He had to admit, the offer was tempting. "You're certain?"

"When am I not?" She sighed and rolled over onto her other side, putting her back to him. "Now that we're close to landing, I want to get cleaned up as well, and that will be easier if I have the cabin to myself. So see? You'd be helping me too. Now go enjoy that new horizon."

He kissed her shoulder through the sheet. "You'll come up and join me?"

"Eventually. I certainly don't intend to allow you to carry me off the ship like an invalid. I'm a Junior Blazer just like you, and that is not the way a Blazer should leave a boat."

"Understood." Glenn rose. "I'll see you up there."

She waved a hand at him without turning around. "Get!"

He grinned and slid the wooden door open. As he stepped out, Becka spoke one more time.

"I'm going to make all this up to you, you know. In a tavern or even on the road. This trip was supposed to be romantic, and all I've done is hog the bed and groan."

"To be fair, even your seasick groaning is rather hot."

She tossed a pillow at him, but her weak throw meant it landed a good ways from the door. "Go, you monster!" She barely stifled her laugh as she snuggled into the sheets.

"Right. Going."

Glenn slid the door shut and then hurried down the narrow wooden hallway below decks toward the steep ladder leading above. As he passed the doors to the other travel cabins, he found more than one ajar. That suggested he wasn't the first traveler on the *Surly Songbird* to decide to catch a glimpse of the Caelfall coast. Glenn firmly gripped the sides of the ladder and tromped up.

No matter how many times he emerged onto the deck of the large boat, he never failed to be surprised by the utter lack of wind. When it was underway the boat moved *with* the wind, thanks to its full sails, which meant that the only sound was the lapping of water against the hull. The cries of gulls joined the shouts of sailors and the creaking of the deck as Glenn squinted against the bright sun.

Thanks to **[-Soul Scan-]** (which, fortunately enough, provided experience when Glenn scanned people while on the sea) Glenn knew the captain of the *Surly Songbird*, Darion Crawtack, was a level 23 Duelist. He was also twice Glenn's age and looked even older thanks to the hard life he'd lived.

Still, Darion was a friendly man who treated his crew fairly and his passengers the same, and Glenn had grown to like him over the last two weeks at sea. Darion reminded him a little of his father.

While the average Adventurer in his forties would be level 30 or higher, Glenn knew that Darion's stay in the mid 20s wasn't a result of laziness or cowardice. Given how much time Darion spent sailing instead of leveling, the fact that the captain had Evolved his Class was actually quite impressive. He had to level aggressively between long trips at sea.

Darion... like the other sailors on the *Surly Songbird*, all Adventurers like Glenn... had all chosen to honor the Gods in a different way. Unlike Adventurers who prowled the wilds of Luxtera, slaying Monsters and Demons before they could threaten commerce and Townsfolk, the crew of the *Surly Songbird* provided the invaluable service of ferrying cargo and people between Luxtera's many ports. They still leveled when they hunted between long trips, but their primary duty was sailing Luxtera's seas.

Darion had sympathized with Glenn and Becka's plight as Becka's seasickness continued to be a problem, and he had promised Glenn he would put on an extra burst of speed in hopes of shortening their journey by a day. The captain was as good as his word, and Glenn made a mental note to thank the man and to remember to pass on word of his fine service to the Blazers Guild. That could ensure the *Surly Songbird* was patronized by Blazers in the future.

Still, all those concerns fell away as Glenn got his first sight of the first zone beyond the shores of Evolan. A whole new *continent*. Caelfall was an exceedingly warm land of sandy deserts, rocky badlands, and tropical oases. Back in Wolfpine, he had never thought to see another continent until he was well past forty, and only if Becka decided she wanted to travel the world. Yet he was here, today.

Despite the many trials they had put him through since he completed his Ceremony of the Path at the tender age of sixteen, today Glenn couldn't help but feel blessed by the Gods. He wondered what sort of Monsters prowled here. With [-**Soul Scan-**], he could easily find out.

As he took in the sight of the pale-yellow sands that now stretched across the horizon beyond the sea, he marveled at how different this bright yellow sandy shore looked from the dark, muddy shores of Evolan. Though they were tiny in the distance, Glenn spotted small groups of the oddest-looking trees he had ever seen clustered along the shore. They were very strange.

Each had a segmented trunk with almost no branches to speak of, and many were slightly curved as they rose to the sun. Each was topped with what looked like a lady's sunhat made of serrated green leaves that had to be the size of a small kayak. Small lumps nestled beneath the fronds of the hat were fruit of some sort, or so one of the other passengers on the *Surly Songbird* had claimed.

He also saw a few isolated buildings that looked far too flimsy to stand up to a good storm. They looked to be made of light, thin wood and clay bricks. Still, the buildings looked old and weathered, which suggested that despite their flimsy appearance, they had weathered many a storm without issue. He would need to learn more about their construction if he had time on his journey.

The creaking of the deck announced someone coming to join Glenn in his gawking. He glanced over, expecting to find one of the friendly Townsfolk who'd commissioned a special Quest to allow them to leave the town's walls for multiple weeks to journey across the sea. He then stood at attention when he realized who had actually joined him on the foredeck.

His companion was Captain Crawtack, and he stood a bit taller than Glenn despite Glenn's impressive height. He was a lean and muscular man in loose leathers with scars that spoke of a lifetime of travel and adventure. Decades in the sea and sun had turned his skin a weathered and orangish-brown, and his oily, dark hair was unruly where it stuck out from beneath his jaunty red hat.

The captain should be at the wheel when a ship came in for a landing in a foreign port, shouldn't he? What was Darion doing down here on the foredeck? Was something amiss?

As if noticing his consternation, Darion offered an amused chuckle. "At ease, Blazer. I'm not here to berate you for being under-foot while we make our landing. I'm here to enjoy the view of land after weeks at sea. Even after so many years out here, it's still a relief to see land."

Glenn resisted the urge to correct Darion about his status—Glenn was, after all, still a *Junior* Blazer—but he instead focused on his possible mistake. "Am I? Underfoot, I mean?"

Darion clapped him hard on the back with a calloused hand, and the fact that Glenn didn't move seemed to please the man immensely. "You're fine where you are. Just don't lean over the railing. We've made it two weeks without someone falling into the sea, and I'd like that trend to continue."

"I've no intention of falling in."

Darion chuckled again. "There's rarely intent involved, lad. Though I notice your lovely lady friend hasn't joined you for the landfall. How is she this morning?"

"The same. No offense to you or your fine crew, but I think she'll be overjoyed to finally be off your boat. Before we make the return journey, we'll be certain to pick up a tonic or some other remedy for seasickness. I'm sorry if we've been trouble."

"Not at all, lad, not at all. I'm just sorry it's been so unpleasant for her. I've no problem controlling my course and my crew, but I'm afraid the choppiness of the sea remains beyond me. She's not the first to suffer from its temperamental nature, and I'm sure she won't be the last."

Glenn appreciated the man's understanding, and he couldn't help but be curious about the foreign shore. "I don't see anything resembling a city. How close are we to Aria?"

"It'll be a while yet before we see the capital. The route I took to save a day was a bit more direct, so we'll be sailing along the Yellow Coast for another hour or so. Once you've had your fill of yellow beaches and frond trees, there's not really much to see until we reach Aria."

"So those funny-looking trees on shore are called frond trees?"

"Aye. You've never seen one before?"

"I've never been to Caelfall before. So most of this is new to me."

While it was tempting to add more to his statement, Glenn didn't want to tell the captain any more about his past. He was having trouble recalling exactly where Glenn Graybreaker had grown up this morning, and he decided to change the subject to something that was less likely to blow his cover.

Glenn looked to the shore. "When we set out from Evolan I'd hoped to get on the road the day we landed, but I don't think my companion will be up for that sort of journey after all this. I think it would be best if we reserved lodgings once we landed and stayed the night."

Darion rubbed his stubbled chin. "Agreed. Best to get your land legs back and some food in her before you set out on the Safe Road. The Guardian Stones don't protect you from heatstroke."

"So can you recommend a tavern or inn in Aria that's safe and clean? Ideally a place that's not overly expensive. We've no need of luxurious amenities, just a clean bed and a room that ideally isn't infested with anything with more than two legs."

"On any other week I'd have several places to recommend, but given all the travelers in town for the **<Sandsea Cup>**, I'd imagine Aria and its reputable inns and taverns are already full to bursting with travelers. You could possibly find a cramped berth along the seedier side of the docks, but I wouldn't recommend it. Those rooms charge by the hour."

It took Glenn a moment to realize why. They certainly didn't need to reserve a room of that nature. Becka was generally quite amorous when they were alone, but seasickness was the ultimate libido killer. Glenn was determined to get Becka water, food, and rest, in that order, and being in a cramped room filled with salty air while people boned loudly next door was not ideal for sleep.

"I'll ask around." Darion grinned. "My crew's from all over, but I know several folks who are from Caelfall. They've spent more than a few weeks in Aria on leave, so perhaps one of them will have a recommendation for you. If not, I'd suggest you head for the city center and ask for lodging. They may have a register of taverns and inns that are still accepting travelers."

Glenn grimaced. "That may be best. I realize now I should have prepared better."

"I'm honestly surprised Miss Cinderflare didn't arrange your lodgings in the city. She seemed quite organized when she talked me into taking you on this passage. I even reserved an extra space in the cargo hold for that lovely Arctic Wolf of hers."

Glenn winced. "I'm still sorry about that. Sara did intend to come, but she was... called away on an unexpected mission. You know how it is with the Blazers."

Darion's brow furrowed in obvious concern. "But she's not in any danger, I hope?"

"No more than normal." Glenn continued to hide his worry about Sara and Leo so as not to raise any more questions. "I imagine she'll be just fine."

While Glenn remained certain that whoever had abducted Sara and Leo had taken them into the Bone Cage—it was the only area remote enough to hide prisoners—he hadn't been able to look for them, and he'd been out of touch for two weeks as he traveled across the sea. At least his discovery of that hole in the wall had impressed the gravity of the situation on Marion Hawkshadow and the others.

Becka's seasickness had, despite its unpleasantness, provided one unintended benefit. Caring for Becka on the long trip had kept him focused on her and not on his worry over Sara, Leo, and Ripper. He could only hope that Jenny Ambersun or Marion Hawkshadow had found them by now, and that one had sent phantom correspondence to the Aria Blazers Guild detailing their fate. He needed to know.

Darion clapped him on the shoulder again. "Feel free to stay and watch the coast as much as you'd like. I've a few more things to do before we make port. Give my regards to your lovely companion. I hope her next journey across the sea is not as unpleasant as this one."

Glenn had no doubt Darion was completely sincere. He liked this man. "I will."

The captain of the *Surly Songbird* offered a tip of his jaunty hat before stomping off across the deck. He was yelling at his sailors in moments. To be fair, Glenn supposed, it was impossible to hear much of anything across the deck of a big vessel without yelling.

In the distance, the winding shore of the Yellow Coast continued to meander alongside the passage of the boat. With the exception of small clusters of the "frond trees" Darion had mentioned, Glenn saw no sign of greenery or any water that wasn't filled with salt. The zone that surrounded Aria really was an unrelenting desert. No wonder so few leveled here.

Evolan's many pure, clean streams, both above and below ground, provided a virtually unlimited source of cool, fresh water for Adventurers hunting Monsters. Everyone who hunted in this zone would need to carry water with them, and since any objects placed in an [Unfilled Bag] dried out, they would need to carry that water the old-fashioned way.

And what of the Monsters in this zone? Did they not need water? Did they subsist on sand? What about the non-monstrous creatures, like tribbits, that populated this zone but were not worth experience? What did they drink and eat?

Glenn was still pondering these questions and more when the sound of footfalls on the deck—this time much softer—drew his gaze from the coast. He smiled at the sight of Becka walking toward him with an ease she had lacked their first few days on the boat. Now that they were mere hours from being on dry land again, she had finally gotten her sea legs. She had the worst luck with boats.

Even so, she had done a marvelous job cleaning up for their landing. She wore a blue flowing tunic that coursed over her buxom frame and a set of loose white trousers that would both reflect the constant sunlight and ensure air could circulate to keep her cool.

She'd also done her dark hair up in a complicated braid that wound around the top of her skull and down alongside one ear. She was, in Glenn's opinion, absolutely breathtaking, and he told her just that. She blushed faintly as she joined him in observing the coast.

"You'd think I was beautiful wearing a fruit sack."

"That is one fantasy that's crossed my mind."

She bumped his shoulder with hers and stared out at the Yellow Coast. "I still feel queasy, if you're concerned, but I don't think I'm going to erupt again any time soon. I will be very glad to get off this boat, though. Even walking days through an arid desert is preferable to another day on this sea."

He slipped an arm around her waist. "I'm just glad you're feeling a bit better at last. I'm sorry this journey has been so rough on you."

She lightly kissed the side of his chest as she snuggled close. "I had you to keep me company and take care of me. Without you it could have been much, much worse."

"You know I'll always take care of you, right?"

She squeezed his side. "Why wouldn't you? You just said I'm beautiful."

Glenn laughed and watched the coast meander by. "I spoke to the captain hoping for a recommendation as to where to stay, but he couldn't give me any. He suspects most of the inns and taverns will already be full with travelers on the way to the cup."

"I'd suspected such as well, which is why I packed a tent for us."

Glenn glanced at her in surprise. "Where did you have a..." He paused and smiled as he understood. "Right. **[Unfilled Bag]**."

Becka poked his side. "It's not as luxurious as one of the fine taverns in Aria's tower district, but it'll keep the sun off us and offer some privacy."

"That's nice, but what would we need privacy for?"

She sighed. "My Glenn. So innocent and chaste."

"I am that."

"I also packed some bedrolls and a small table, and some books in case we get trapped in the tent during a sandstorm."

Glenn's brow furrowed. "There's sandstorms out here?"

"Not in this zone, but they're common in Stillwatch, and it'll take us a day or two to reach Sun's Cross once we cross the zone border. Once a sandstorm starts up, your only choice is to find shelter or breathe dirt. I'd prefer not to breathe dirt."

"I'm so lucky I have you to plan all of this for us."

"You are. You really should get better at planning. Did you even bring a torch?"

"I... thought about it."

Becka chuckled quietly. "Oh, love. What would you do without me?"

"I would be very lonely while walking around in the dark." He turned her in his arm. "How long has it been since I kissed you?"

"How long has it been since I last threw up?"

He chuckled and leaned in, but she stopped him with gentle pressure on his chest.

"I'm not joking, love. I would prefer we wait until we make landfall and I can get some food and wash my mouth out. I promise, there will be kissing and more once I'm recovered."

"I waited over two years for you. I suppose I can wait another hour."

Her hands slid down his back and squeezed his rear. "I always make it worth it, don't I?"

After that, they stood together in comfortable silence on the side of the boat and watched the coastline meander by. The Adventurers sailing the *Surly Songbird* continued to shout to each other occasionally, but with the sails adjusted and the boat underway, there wasn't a whole lot for them to do. All they could focus on now was ensuring nothing went awry during their journey.

Soon after, other people joined them on the deck as well. Glenn recognized a number of Townsfolk he'd seen and sometimes spoken to on their journey, but as he'd spent most of his time in his cabin tending Becka, he hadn't really gotten to know any of them that well.

The other passengers offered nods of appreciation which he returned, but little more than that. A respectful distance remained between Townsfolk and Adventurers on the best of days, and Glenn barely knew these people.

Still, he had dutifully scanned all seventeen Townsfolk making the journey and all twenty-two sailors on the *Surly Songbird*, netting himself 195 experience from **[-Soul Scan-]**. It wasn't anything near what he'd want to acquire after two full weeks, but it wasn't nothing. Every bit helped on the way to level 15, and ahead lay the **<Sandsea Cup>**... where he would save Zack or fail forever.

Becka had, in the times she was conscious, helped him prepare mentally for what he would face once they reached Sun's Cross. The **<Sandsea Cup>** took place once every four years and rotated between the three mid-level zones of Luxtera: Evolan, Holbeck, and Stillwatch. Like all church-sanctioned events, the cup had the blessing of the Gods, and many assumed They watched it closely.

The cup took place over two weeks and drew Adventurers and Townsfolk from across the world. Those who could pay the entry fee and who arrived in time to participate in its events could enter as many or as few as they liked, provided the events they entered didn't overlap. Some events required clever Adventurers to solve complex puzzles or riddles, while others were contests of strength and guile. Some even had Adventurers fighting captured Monsters in front of an appreciative crowd.

It was a grand event, but not something the average Junior Blazer could expect to attend while training unless it happened to occur in the zone where they already resided. Fortunately, Becka's clever plotting had allowed Glenn to travel to Sun's Cross despite his status and responsibilities. While Glenn would be participating in events, he was also here for work. Blazer work.

The other element that made the **<Sandsea Cup>** unique was that the Church of Celes called Lifecasters, Spiritualists, and Shamanists in from across Luxtera. That guaranteed there were enough Adventurers with **[-Resurrect-]** on hand to ensure any accidents resulting in the death of a contestant could be undone quickly. Death during events was not common, but accidents happened.

In addition, the entire senior leadership of the Church of Celes also attended this event. They were a revered group of men and women known as the Ten Gospels. Each represented a single God. Their presence here was the only place in the next four years where Glenn would find all them in one place... and where he could use **[-Soul Scan-]** on them.

The Blazers already knew that a sect inside the church was encouraging or even forcing young Adventurers to secretly choose the Deathcaster Class, then making them serve the church as enforcers. Those who refused were imprisoned in church-run prisons until they escaped or agreed to serve the church. The only question was if the higher-ups in the church knew of this or were ignorant of it. Finding out if any of them were secretly dual-classed as Deathcasters would answer that.

Becka elbowed him gently. "You're doing it again."

Glenn pulled himself from his ruminations and glanced at her. "Doing what?"

"Brooding. You've got your brooding face on."

"I'm not brooding. I'm thinking, and plotting, and planning. Just like you suggested."

"So long as you don't forget to have fun."

He raised an eyebrow at her. "What do you mean?"

"I know why we're both here. We have not one, but two very important missions, and I intend to help you complete them both before we leave. Yet they will not occupy all of our time here, and when we are not involved in those tasks, it will be just you and me, together, unsupervised. At one of the most exciting, well-attended, and extravagant events to occur in all Luxtera."

Glenn couldn't help but grin. "So it'll be like the **<Festival of**

Isdon> back…?" He stopped himself before saying "home" and mentally adjusted. "That we visited in Grassea?"

Becka smiled coyly. "I'm not going to dive into any vats of creamed corn. But I'm certain we can find more than a bit of mischief after hours at the cup. I've heard stories from the other Blazers and people who've attended before. The parties after the daily games are legendary."

Glenn looked to the coast again. "I just wish Leo and Sara were here to enjoy this as well."

"They'll be all right. You gave the Blazers everything they need to track them down."

"I want to think so."

"I know so, Glenn. Now, hold me close while we enjoy this moment. We're visiting our first zone capital! I didn't think I'd see one of these for decades."

Glenn pulled her close and kissed the top of her head. "I'm just glad I get to see it with you."

ELEVEN
A SOULSEER FOUND

When they finally rounded a wide atoll at the end of the Yellow Coast and pulled around to the far side, Glenn stared in unabashed awe. Caelfall's capital city of Aria was a sight unlike any he'd ever seen. Unlike Lakebrooke, which was a sprawling but largely flat expanse nestled on the shore of the harbor, Aria crouched on the edge of the wide Serpent Sea like a fierce and magnificent animal.

A variety of towers formed of ancient sandstone rose from the shore to tower many stories in the air. While Glenn couldn't estimate their exact height from a distance, he suspected they had to be several times as tall as the magnificent chapel of Celes back in Lakebrooke. Each tower was topped with a puffy "cap" with a pointy top. Their colors ranged from red to brown to yellow and even a brilliant purple.

Brick and sandstone walls that looked as if they'd weathered a thousand storms wound along the shore along the water. Beyond those, a sprawl of stone and wooden buildings lay like a tattered blanket across the sand and cliffs beyond. Thin rivulets of clear blue water cut across the blanket at regular intervals, pumped up from the sea and cleansed by complicated Builder enchantments. Without the ability to convert salt water to fresh water, Glenn suspected Aria would not exist.

Becka clutched his bicep excitedly. "It's even more gorgeous than I expected. What a magnificent city! Can you imagine if you'd been chosen to serve your duty here?"

Glenn chuckled. "It would have been different."

That was an understatement. Aria alone contained more Townsfolk and Adventurers than one might find in the entirety of Evolan. There were simply so many people living here.

Had the Church of Celes delivered him to a pair of Townsfolk in *this* city, he would have joined a garrison of Town Guards that he knew, from reading, numbered over three hundred. Aria was a metropolis that dwarfed Lakebrooke, boasting a permanent population of almost ten thousand Townsfolk. It grew and shrank as couples in the city were approved to receive children by the church.

A whole legion of Cultivators and Culinarians supported the city by farming land kept fertile by the same cleansed streams that served the city proper. Every other Townsfolk class was represented here in one way or another. This was where they came to become Preceptors. This was where those who wished to complete Luxtera's Climb as Townsfolk did so.

In addition to the ten thousand or so Townsfolk who lived in Aria at any given time, high-level Adventurers coming and going on a regular basis more than doubled Aria's population. The steady flow of so much coin and life crystals ensured Merchants who opened stalls here could obtain experience at a rapid enough rate to satiate the demands of higher levels.

Most every Townsfolk who reached level 20 and gained the title of Preceptor did so while working in Aria, Eastwend, or Doveport, the capital of Aquarine. While some then returned to serve their communities, many remained in the capitals to accrue more wealth. Preceptor Fallowpeak was one who had returned, though Glenn knew he'd leveled to 20 in Eastwend, capital of Landers.

As the *Surly Songbird* turned to face toward the capital, the rippling of the sails remained the only sound on board save for the creaking of the vessel and the reassuring sound of sailors going about their work. Glenn and Becka spoke little as the grand city of Aria grew larger and larger. Their proximity assured Glenn the mighty towers across the city were at least twenty stories tall or taller.

What must the view be like from up on one of those towers? He would have to take Becka up there at least once. Seeing the city and ocean from such a vantage was likely a grand sight... and it was a sight he could savor with the woman he loved at his side.

"Everyone, attention!" Darion called from the captain's deck. "We hope you've enjoyed your view of the grand city of Aria! Now, regretfully, I must ask you to return to your cabins and wait until we've docked before coming above decks. My crew and I will need the full run of the deck to bring us into harbor without incident, and I'd hate for anyone to be caught underfoot."

Glenn squeezed Becka's waist. "That's our cue. I doubted they'd let us be up here while they docked. Shall we head back downstairs?"

Becka nodded and headed toward the steep ladder leading belowdecks. "I feel almost normal now. I wonder if I'll get seasick on dry land?"

Glenn chuckled as he walked after her. "If so, I'll start to wonder what God you annoyed."

Becka sighed. "For the time being, we're going to assume all of Them."

From belowdecks, the only cue they'd finally docked successfully in Aria was the sound of unfamiliar voices joining the chorus of familiar voices Glenn had grown used to as they sailed. Townsfolk or Adventurers on the docks of Aria were speaking to the crew of the *Surly Sailor*. Though Glenn might have imagined it, he thought he could feel the boat drifting to a halt as it moored against the dock.

Sailors shouted as they tied knots and trimmed sails. Soon after, heavy boots descended the ladder. Those boots thumped down the hall as a sailor rapped politely on the walls.

"We've just made port!" the sailor yelled down the hall. "All passengers, please make one last sweep of your cabin before you disembark! Don't leave behind anything you want to keep!"

As Becka packed up the last of her things, Glenn pulled on the gear he hadn't worn for over two weeks while the *Surly Songbird* sailed the Serpent Sea. While he didn't don his full suit of **[Steel Armor]**... that would require Becka to help him, and he'd have to take it off again once they reached wherever they were going to sleep tonight... he certainly wasn't going to leave this ship unarmed.

He pulled on the unique harness Karl Coldbreaker had made for him years ago in Wolfpine, again grateful that it was well-designed enough he could tighten and adjust the straps himself. Then, he rolled Becka—his weighted [Commoner's Mace]—from beneath their bed and slipped the weapon into its custom-made sheathe. He and the mace had been through so much, and it was a reminder of the home he wouldn't see for decades. It was a bit of Wolfpine he always had.

He was high enough level now that he was considering buying an Uncommon mace. There were Adventurer maces available that hit far harder than this, some of which might even come with powerful enchantments. He had no doubt he could find such a weapon in Aria, and if the maces here were too expensive, there would certainly be plenty of opportunities to upgrade in Sun's Cross.

Still, he would never sell this unique weapon. Once he did upgrade, this mace would have a permanent slot in his [Unfilled Bag], and the rare orichalcum Karl had worked into the weapon meant the mace could be enchanted as well. It would be the perfect weapon to enchant with a situational enchantment.

All he had to do now was figure out what enchantment would suit Becka and save up enough money to buy it. The Quest he'd created to find the hole in Lakebrooke's wall had sucked away close to the last of the fortune he'd gained from solving Lord Marshvale's murder, but he could always earn more money. He was the reason the Blazers knew about the hole. That was worth any price.

Once he had his unique weapon and its unique sheathe secured, he next checked his belt to make sure it was tight. His [Unfilled Bag] rested against his hip. He reached into the bag and couldn't help but marvel as the spectral cabinet appeared before his eyes. His pack was far more full than it had been the day he had used it to escape the Cloudy Divide with Arthur Everglow's ensouled corpse.

Glen gripped the icon for Lillian Stoutcrag's enchanted [Steel Shield] and then pulled a shield bigger than his back from a pack only a bit wider than his hand. As he strapped on the shield, he could feel his Strength passively increase thanks to [+Unyielding+], his powerful Town Guard Blessing. The rush of Strength was comforting. He flexed his fingers experimentally.

He was going to wear his shield during every waking moment from now until he locked himself into a room at night. He and Becka had been in enough scrapes that he wasn't ever going to relax when they were traveling, even if they were in the middle of a capital city or on a Safe Road. It was his job to keep her safe, and he was going to keep her safe... for, he hoped, the rest of their lives.

Once his shield was secure, he pulled another pack on over it. He carried a normal pack as well, though it sagged against his shield in a way that would have normally depressed him. They would need to carry both food and canteens on their journey, and both would dry out if placed in an **[Unfilled Bag]**.

Fortunately, Glenn's impressive Strength attribute meant they wouldn't need to rent a pack horse... not that he was even sure where they'd rent one from. He could easily carry provisions for a multi-week journey without difficulty, providing they could get it all to fit in his pack. Becka had far more items to pack than he did, and he didn't rush her. The boat wasn't going anywhere.

He was ready. He was packed. Becka was almost done as well, but she was making one last sweep of their cabin to ensure they didn't leave anything behind.

With a free moment, he decided to check his Status Sheet one last time before leaving the boat. Any good Adventurer would. It was always good to appreciate one's progress.

Name: Glenn Graybreaker
Age: 18
Level: 14
Class: Soulseer
HP: 330/330
Blood: 150/150
Experience: 101,219/112,000
Strength: 25 (35)
Divinity: 11
Vitality: 23 (33)
Wisdom: 15
Prowess: 11
Luck: 10

Gear:

- **Legendary: Class Crystal** (Locked)
- **Uncommon: [Arrow Talisman]**

- **Rare: [Blazer Pin]**
- **Common: [Fine Noble's Tunic]**
- **Common: [Fine Noble's Pants]**
- **Common: [Large Backpack]**
- **Common: [Commoner's Mace]** (Weighted / Reinforced)
- **Uncommon: [Steel Shield]** (Enchanted: Weight Reduction)
- **Uncommon: [Hiking Boots]**
- **Rare: [Unfilled Bag]**

Slotted Skills:

- **Rare: [-Guardian's Heal-]** (Town Guard / Celes)
- **Rare: [-Guardian's Smash-]** (Town Guard / Ansin)
- **<Experimental>: [-Soul Scan-]** (Soulseer / Isdon)
- **<Experimental>: [-Spirit Scan-]** (Soulseer / Isdon)
- **<Experimental>: [-Soul Singe-]** (Soulseer / Isdon)

Slotted Blessings:

- **Rare: [+Unyielding+]** (Town Guard / Kya)
- **Rare: [+Regrowth+]** (Town Guard / Kya)
- **<Experimental>: [+Intertwined Soul+]** (Soulseer / Isdon)

Known Skills:

- **Rare: [-Fight Me!-]** (Town Guard / Kya)
- **Rare: [-Public Address-]** (Town Guard / Isdon)
- **<Experimental>: [-Reveal Soul-]** (Soulseer / Isdon)
- **<Experimental>: [-Reveal Spirit-]** (Soulseer / Isdon)
- **<Experimental>: [-Soul Peer-]** (Soulseer / Isdon)
- **<Experimental>: [-Soul Scout-]** (Soulseer / Isdon)
- **Uncommon: [-Phantom Slice-]** (Duelist / Vox)

Known Blessings:

- None

Quests:

- **Level 40 (Group):** "The Soulseer's Path" (Epic)
- **Level 15 (Group):** "Resurrect Zack Silverstone" (Epic, Timed) *[1,197:05:12]*

Just over two weeks had elapsed as he and Becka made the journey across the Serpent Sea. Over 360 hours had ticked off the Quest to resurrect Glenn's best friend, and he'd only gained 195 experience. He needed almost 11,000 experience to reach level 15 and had just over a month and a half to acquire it. Winning events at the <Sandsea Cup> was his only chance... and Zack's as well.

Glenn pushed his Status Sheet away. The relentless ticking of time on his Quest to resurrect Zack was an oppressive weight he was never able to fully set down. He could only rest it on a table from time to time, focused on other, more important day-to-day tasks, before picking it up again.

Becka touched his arm. "We'll save him, love."

He loved how she could sense his emotions no matter how hard he tried to hide them. "I know."

"Good. Don't forget it." She kissed him on the cheek.

He turned to her and frowned. "You said no kissing!"

"I said you couldn't kiss *me*." She winked and squeezed his hand. "That comes later." She opened the door and stepped out. "Now, let's be off this boat and enjoy the capital. The next time I have to spend two weeks ailing in a ship's cabin will come far too soon for either of us."

They stepped out of their cabin, and then Glenn led the way down the narrow hallway to the steep ladder leading above decks. As he looked around, Glenn realized he and Becka were the last people out of the passenger area. The Townsfolk who had traveled with them must either have packed ahead of time or had less gear to equip. He hoped Captain Crawtack wasn't annoyed.

They emerged on the deck of the *Surly Songbird* to find the capital of Aria looming over them. It stretched off across the gently rising rocky slope. Aria's docks actually looked to be a bit smaller than Lakebrooke's, which was a surprise. There were a number of boats the size of the *Surly Songbird* and many smaller boats all crammed into the space.

Glenn wondered how often boats collided with one another while sailing out or sailing in. He suspected it must have happened more than once given how cramped these docks were in comparison to Lakebrooke's. Yet as he evaluated the towering rocky C in which the docks were tucked, he understood why they weren't spread out more. There simply wasn't space.

These tall rocky walls provided a wind break that meant the docks and the city beyond would be somewhat sheltered in the event any storms swept in off the Serpent Sea, which Glenn knew from reading to be a common occurrence. So it made sense why the capital hadn't expanded its docks. They had less space, but that space was more secure and safe from the weather.

Glenn glanced to the weathered dock that sat alongside the boat. It was filled with people, likely Townsfolk, going about their business or loading luggage on carts pulled by animals including horses, donkeys, and camels. Glenn had never seen a camel before (other than illustrations in books) and was fascinated by the odd-looking animals. Their humps were massive.

Most of the crew of the *Surly Songbird* were busy going about their tasks, but Glenn smiled as he saw Darion waiting for them at the gangplank. As they approached, the captain swept off his jaunty hat to reveal his slick and oiled hair. He fixed Becka with a warm grin.

"Miss Coldbreaker, you look ravishing today. I'm so sorry for the rough journey."

Becka laughed and clutched Glenn's arm. "That's kind of you to say, Captain, but I'd never hold you accountable for the whims of the sea. I'm simply grateful you got us here in one piece."

"I wish you and Mister Graybreaker a safe journey to Sun's Cross."

Glenn nodded respectfully. "And we wish you a safe journey to wherever you sail next."

They descended the gangplank to the crowded dock, and the moment Glenn touched the docks with his boots, a burst of pleasure filled his body. Discovery experience. He had now entered a new zone for the first time, and a quick look at his Status Sheet confirmed he'd been awarded 100 experience.

A good omen. He had walked for no more than a few steps before a slim, blonde-haired woman Glenn immediately recognized arrived.

She cut between two burly dockworkers and hurried toward them with a wide smile on her face.

Glenn gasped and gawked. He hadn't seen this woman in over two years! Anna Bronzelight, the only other Soulseer in all of Luxtera, was approaching. What was *she* doing here? He halted as he went through a dozen possibilities and dismissed them. Then Becka released his arm.

She rushed toward Anna. "You made it!"

Becka had done this. Becka had contacted Anna and let her know that she and Glenn were planning to attend the **<Sandsea Cup>**. Why hadn't Becka mentioned that on their journey?

As Glenn considered, he decided Becka either hadn't been certain Anna would make it or hadn't expected her to come at all. Both offered interesting questions he'd need to ask them later. For now, he was surprised how happy he was to see Anna. It had been too long.

Anna beamed at them. "I wouldn't miss this. There's no way I could let you do this alone."

Becka hugged Anna warmly. As Glenn watched the two women embrace, he wondered if he should introduce himself... or rather, re-introduce himself. He wanted to greet Anna as well, but Anna didn't know Glenn *Graybreaker*. Anyone could be watching.

Anna smiled past Becka as she stepped back to stare at him. "Who's your friend?"

Becka smiled coyly. "Take a closer look. You might be surprised."

Glenn felt a tingle in the pit of his stomach, and then he barely held back his gasp. He'd been scanned! Anna had just used **[-Soul Scan-]** on him, and he'd felt it happen! He'd never had anyone use **[-Soul Scan-]** on him, only used it on other people. Had they felt this tingle as well?

Anna's eyes widened in surprise. "Oh! That... makes sense, I suppose." Her eyes fell to the arrowhead necklace dangling from his neck. "That is a lovely piece of jewelry."

Glenn decided they should keep up appearances despite the fact there was little chance anyone from the church might be spying on them. He took a step forward and offered his hand. "Glenn Graybreaker, Junior Blazer. It's a pleasure to meet you, miss..."

"Ironstar," Anna said as she shook his hand firmly. "Also a Junior Blazer."

Glenn nodded and released her hand. So she had taken the name she'd used while a fugitive as her cover while leveling Soulseer. That made sense. Since he was hiding from the Church of Celes, Anna doing the same would make it less likely she'd be targeted while leveling as well.

Glenn smiled. "I take it you're also heading to the <**Sandsea Cup**>?"

It was obvious Anna was heading there... why else would she be here?... but if a Shadower was listening in on their conversation, Glenn wanted to keep up appearances. He was learning how to be sneaky! He wasn't on Becka's level, but he wasn't a complete novice either.

Anna smiled back. "I am. When I received Becka's phantom correspondence suggesting you'd be arriving soon, I thought it best to secure a room where you could recover from your journey."

So they would have somewhere safe to sleep after all! Glenn was immensely grateful to Anna for her help. "How'd you manage to secure a room for us?"

"It's a short hop from Holbeck to Stillwatch, so I was able to get here over a week ago and secure one of the last rooms in the capital. I've been waiting there since. The Dancing Skitterer is a modest inn without many of the amenities you might be used to, but the room has two beds and plenty of space. So if one of you wants to roll out of a bedroll on the floor..."

Becka took Glenn's arm again. "That won't be necessary."

"I thought not." Anna smiled knowingly. "Anyway, if you're not waiting for anything to be unloaded from the boat, we should head back to the Skitterer and get you two settled in. I'd love to hear more about your journey and your plans while you're here attending the cup."

Glenn nodded at what she didn't say. Phantom correspondence was far from secure, so he doubted Becka had explained their purpose here in more than the vaguest terms. He knew Anna knew about the Quest the Gods had given him to resurrect Zack, but not how much she knew about his progress. She might be displeased to hear he was still so far from completing it.

He'd explain the reasons for that when they could speak in private, safe where no one could eavesdrop and report them. For now, however, he had another matter to attend to. He needed to finally learn if Marion and Jenny had made any progress on their search for Leo and Sara. But first...

Glenn looked around once more. "Where's the rest of your party?"

Anna's lips pressed together. "They aren't available at the moment."

"Are they waiting for us back at the Skitterer?"

"They... won't be joining us for the cup. Or at all."

That surprised Glenn. "Your party let you come out here alone?"

"Let's speak more about that once we're safe in our room."

As Becka squeezed his bicep in warning, Glenn took that as his cue to relent for now. It bothered him that Anna was here without a Blazer party to escort her, but perhaps they were shadowing her from the crowd or waiting back at the tavern. He could find out later.

"I appreciate you reserving us a room," Glenn said. "But first, we need to stop by the Aria Blazers Guild. I need to let my superior know we've arrived on time and safely, and I'm hoping to hear news on two of our friends who went missing before we set sail."

Anna's eyes widened. "Who's missing?"

Glenn filled her in on the basic details of Leo and Sara's disappearance, but he made no mention of the hole in Lakebrooke's wall. He would save that disturbing information for when they were alone in a room and could talk privately. Once he finished, Anna nodded.

"Of course you'd want to check there first. I'll show you there immediately, though I'm going to wait outside while you handle your business inside. I'd prefer to avoid the guild right now."

So Anna didn't want to be seen at the Blazers Guild? As Glenn considered the reasons she might be without her party and wary about being seen at the guild, his instincts filled in the blanks. Anna was here illegally. She didn't have permission from the Blazers to attend the cup.

So had she snuck away from the Blazers? Abandoned them? Was she a fugitive once more?

Becka pressed lightly on his back. "We should get off these docks."

Becka was right, of course. If Anna was a fugitive from the Blazers, that certainly wasn't something they'd want to discuss on these docks surrounded by dozens of people. For now, they should check in with the Aria Blazers Guild and then relax in the room Anna had reserved for them.

Becka would need time to recover before they set out for Sun's Cross and, hopefully, get a good meal she could actually keep down. "Please lead the way to the Blazers Guild, Miss Ironstar," Glenn said. "And for your help and the room, we're in your debt."

"I don't think so. I still owe... Becka... far more than a room at an inn."

Glenn knew what Anna meant. He had, after all, saved her from being abducted by the Shadowers Guild agents her corrupt brother had sent to take her on behalf of the church. He wouldn't feel guilty about the coin she'd spent or the trouble she'd gone to in order to help them. He would simply be grateful for her aid. He was also curious how she'd been progressing on her own Quest.

"Would you mind if I took a look at how you've been doing?"

Anna nodded as she led them off the docks. "That would be fine."

As Glenn followed with Becka on his arm, he used **[-Soul Scan-]** on her.

Name: Anna Bronzelight
Age: 20
Level: 14
Class: Soulseer
HP: 130 / 130
Blood: 250 / 250
Experience: 102,324 / 112,000
Strength: 8
Divinity: 23
Vitality: 10 (13)
Wisdom: 20 (25)
Prowess: 8
Luck: 12

Gear:

- **Rare: [Timeworn Robes]** *(Enchanted/Vitality)*
- **Rare: [Luminal Dagger]** *(Enchanted/Blast)*

- **Rare: [Heirloom Dagger]**
- **Rare: [Silverweave Boots]**

Slotted Skills:

- **Uncommon: [-Burn-]** (Harmcaster/Xiva)
- **Uncommon: [-Freeze-]** (Harmcaster/Xiva)
- **<Experimental>: [-Reveal Spirit-]** (Soulseer/Isdon)
- **<Experimental>: [-Soul Scan-]** (Soulseer/Isdon)
- **<Experimental>: [-Mend Soul-]** (Soulseer/Isdon)

Slotted Blessings:

- **<Experimental>: [+Intertwined Soul+]** (Soulseer/Isdon)
- **<Experimental>: [+Blessed Soul+]** (Soulseer/Isdon)
- **Uncommon: [+Burning Soul+]** (Harmcaster/Xiva)

Known Skills:

- **<Experimental>: [-Soul Scout-]** (Soulseer/Isdon)
- **<Experimental>: [-Soothe Soul-]** (Soulseer/Isdon)
- **<Experimental>: [-Reveal Soul-]** (Soulseer/Isdon)
- **<Experimental>: [-Soul View-]** (Soulseer/Isdon)

Known Blessings:

- None

Quests:

- **Level 40 (Group):** "The Soulseer's Path" (Epic)

He couldn't help but wince as he compared her progress to his own. Anna was actually ahead of him in experience, though only by a hundred or so. Still, the fact that she had more experience than he did without the benefit of the large boosts he'd gained from completing investigation Quests for Brennon Shadesinger was impressive. He reminded himself she'd had a head start on leveling Soulseer, and she was able to level constantly without losing days to classroom instruction.

He was also not surprised that Anna was now using rare gear with valuable enchantments. Anna had the support of the Blazers now. They would want her to have the best equipment she could wield.

Glenn knew from speaking with his mother back in Wolfpine that it was difficult to imbue a dagger with [-Blast-], but once an Enchanter did so, a strike from the dagger could knock an enemy over with wind. That would be a dependable way for a caster to stun a melee attacker and gain distance.

Finally, he was intrigued by Anna's Skill choices. [-Mend Soul-], he remembered from viewing the Skill while in the Plaza of Selection, gave her the ability to heal her party members, just like [-Guardian's Heal-] gave him. Better yet, she had both [-Burn-] and [-Freeze-] to target Monsters and Demons from a distance. She could support her party by damaging enemies and healing the injured.

Glenn couldn't help but be a little jealous of Anna's ranged flexibility. Still... Anna likely couldn't gather the Anger of a Rock Spider Queen and then stop one of her strikes with a shield. They both had their skillsets, and Glenn reminded himself it was encouraging that Anna had progressed so quickly.

Given she still had over a year to do it, it seemed like she would easily reach level 15 and stop the calamity of Holbeck, Aquarine's 8-16 zone. She would save thousands of lives. No calamity would threaten that zone thanks to her hard work and diligence.

He closed Anna's Status Sheet just in time to avoid being run over by a burly dockworker carrying a heavy crate. There would be no more scanning until he was in a less perilous situation. He also had no idea where he was going, so he was grateful Anna obviously did.

She deftly maneuvered through a crush of people getting onto boats, getting off of boats, or moving cargo on and off boats. Aria's docks might be smaller than Lakebrooke's, but they were also more busy and crowded, at least today. Glenn suspected all this activity was at least partially related to everyone arriving for the <Sandsea Cup>.

Anna knew her business. Once they were off the main portion of the docks, Anna led them along a set of narrow and well-kept cobblestone streets. They were bordered by buildings of both stone and wood that looked as old and weathered as the towers of Aria had looked from a distance. Several of those towered over him now, and he couldn't help but stare up at them in wonder as they walked.

He would have time to sightsee later. He forced his eyes back to the road and Anna and watched for anyone who might trouble them. There was no reason anyone from the Shadowers Guild or the Church of Celes would be out here looking for them, but simply assuming they were unobserved and safe would be foolish.

Not long after, Anna stepped off the street and into the shadow of an awning by what looked to be a weapon shop. "The Aria Blazers Guild is just around the corner. I'll wait here for you to return."

"We won't be long." Glenn glanced at Becka. "Shall we go announce ourselves?"

She nodded. "Given Marion insisted we do just that once we arrived, it would be wise."

TWELVE

A BIT OF GOOD NEWS

As they rounded the corner, Glenn saw the grand Aria Blazers Guild for the first time. Even had the logo of the Blazers—a handheld torch against a shield—not been embossed in silver trim on the largest steel sign he'd ever seen, the three-story building ahead was obviously a storied structure.

This building wasn't a chapel of Celes, but it was obviously as old as one. It looked to be a sturdy building, and it was painted in the colors of the Blazers: white, blue, and yellow. He wondered how many legendary Adventurers had taken or turned in Quests here.

The walls were formed of yellow bricks that matched the color of the surrounding cliffs and, Glenn suspected, the sandy stone that was freely available in Fool's March, the level 20-26 zone in which Aria was built. Grand arched windows with white stone frames bore dark and tempered glass. These windows looked into all three levels of the Aria Blazers Guild, with a much larger window in the center of the third floor above the double doors. It also sported a fine balcony.

Glenn couldn't see past the glass, but he suspected that window held a study and library similar to that in the Lakebrooke Blazers Guild. The thought of what sort of books might be available here, in a level 20-26 zone, sent a jolt of excitement through him. After they got settled into their room at the Skitterer, there was no reason he couldn't return to the guild and ask to peruse its vast library.

At the least, he should find a bestiary for Stillwatch. He needed to know what sort of Monsters he might face if he had to leave the Safe Road. [-Soul Scan-] offered a lot of information, but there were certainly accounts from Adventurers with more experience. Their accounts could offer details that simply viewing the Status Sheet of a Monster might not provide.

Glenn only realized he'd stopped when Becka nudged him the back. He resumed walking. "Sorry. It's an impressive structure."

"Appreciate the building later, when we don't have someone waiting on us."

Glenn matched her pace. They had no sooner reached the doors before they swung open from the inside. Yet before Glenn could wonder if someone waited to greet them, a party of Adventurers wearing Blazer tabards marched out of the guild.

Glenn gripped Becka and ensured both of them stepped aside. One of the Blazers nodded his appreciation as he tromped past. Glenn stared in wonder as he looked the four of them over.

He recognized at least one set of [Midnight Mail]—the same type of armor Captain Marion Hawkshadow had worn when she descended into Grassea's Crackpaw Mine—which told him the leader of this party had to be at least level 36. A quick [-Soul Scan-] confirmed that, and the others were all in their early 30s as well.

What grand adventure was this party of high-level Blazers setting off to undertake? Nothing in this zone could give them a challenge, so perhaps they were headed down to the docks to catch a boat to a higher level zone, like Ghost Falls (Caelfall's 27-32 zone) or the Salt Flats (Caelfall's 32-36 zone). He was tempted to call after them and ask, but that would be unprofessional.

Glenn held the door for Becka, who smiled as she sauntered inside. As he joined her and let the door close behind him, he was surprised by how much the interior of the Aria Blazers Guild matched the one in Lakebrooke. The exterior was far more ornate, but perhaps the Blazers built all of their guilds in a similar manner so Blazers would know where to go regardless of where they came from.

Inside was a warm and open space. Long tables with benches allowed Blazers to sit and eat or drink, and a good number of tables were occupied. Blazer activity must be much higher thanks to the capital's proximity to the <Sandsea Cup>. Glenn wasn't surprised he didn't recognize anyone.

At the far end of the big common room was a long wooden desk similar to that staffed by Aiden Goodfellow back in Lakebrooke. The Blazers Guild administrator here was a tan-skinned, dark-haired woman who looked to be about Marion's age. She must be a veteran by now.

Glenn used **[-Soul Scan-]** on her and was unsurprised to learn she was a Preceptor Scribe. Her name was Nadia Skybough. He'd ask her to introduce herself before revealing he knew that about her.

He *was* surprised to see that Nadia was also a level 9 Harmcaster, which meant she had dual-classed into an Adventurer Class after reaching level 20 as a Townsfolk. Did she spend her weekends killing Monsters when she wasn't acting as an administrator at the Aria Blazers Guild? Did she make the long trek along the Safe Road to Stillwatch when she wasn't working here?

Again, those questions could wait. Glenn took his place in the line with Becka and was pleased as Nadia addressed each waiting Blazer efficiently and politely. The first two were simply reporting the results of Quests they'd undertaken, and while the third took a bit longer (apparently, she had neglected to fill out a form ahead of time), it wasn't long before Nadia beckoned Glenn and Becka forward.

Nadia eyed them both calmly. "Name, class, and rank?"

Had Glenn been asked to describe her he would have said she had a kind face, but her current expression was all business. "Glenn Graybreaker, level 14 Brutalist, Junior Blazer."

Becka spoke up. "Rebecka Coldbreaker, level 13 Guilecaster, also a Junior Blazer."

Nadia duly noted their arrival on a piece of parchment. "And what brings you to Aria today?"

Glenn answered that. "We're here on a special assignment from Captain Marion Hawkshadow at the Lakebrooke Blazers Guild. The captain should have sent word ahead via phantom correspondence that we'd be arriving."

"She did. I'll notify her you've arrived safely. Anything else?"

Glenn was impressed that Nadia had their expected arrival memorized. She must be very good at keeping a schedule and checking her calendar. Now, Glenn had another question.

"Any messages from Captain Hawkshadow or Jenny Ambersun? Both were involved in some business they undertook when we set

sail from Lakebrooke, and I'm hoping they'll have good news for us...
or at least an update."

Nadia eyed him a moment, then inclined her head. "Let me have a
look."

So this woman couldn't memorize *everything*. That was somehow
reassuring. Nadia ducked behind her counter.

Glenn resisted the urge to peer over it and check on her. The soft
sound of paper brushing paper suggested she was sorting through a
stack of papers, likely all the phantom correspondence that had
arrived in the last two weeks. Glenn suspected the guild here must
get a lot of it.

Nadia rose, holding a single rolled scroll sealed with a dob of wax
embossed by a Blazer's seal. "This came in about a week ago
addressed to Glenn Graybreaker."

Glenn barely resisted the urge to hop up and down in excitement.
"What does it say?"

"I haven't read it."

The scroll was, of course, sealed. "Right." Glenn winced in embar-
rassment. "Of course."

Nadia slipped the scroll across the counter. "Is there anything else
I can help you with?"

Glenn belatedly glanced behind him to find two more Blazers,
both of whom must be higher level than he was, waiting patiently for
their turn with the Guildmaster. He looked at Nadia again. "No,
that's it. Thank you so much for holding onto this for me. I really
appreciate it."

"It's my job, Graybreaker." When Nadia looked past him toward
the next person in line, she appeared as calm as ever. But Glenn could
swear he saw the hint of a smile.

He hurried with Becka to a table that wasn't entirely occupied and
sat down on the bench there. Becka scooted in beside him, and then,
after taking a breath, Glenn broke the wax seal on the scroll. He
unfurled it and leaned close to read the fine script that had come
across the sea a week ago.

He recognized this handwriting because he'd seen it before. Jenny
Ambersun had been kind enough to write him a note updating him
on Becka's progress three months after she had left Wolfpine with

Jenny and he'd stayed to become a Town Guard. His heart pounded as he read.

Glenn,

I hope your journey across the Serpent Sea was pleasant and uneventful. I'm pleased to tell you that your theory about the location of Sara and Leo was correct. We found them, and they're safe.

"Yes!" Glenn's voice echoed through the guild.

Becka giggled and nudged him. Glenn blushed brightly as he looked around and found several nearby Blazers staring at him with a mixture of annoyance and obvious amusement. He resisted the urge to hunch down on the bench and felt the need to explain himself.

"I just got good news."

"Congratulations." An older female Blazer eyed him in annoyance. "Celebrate quietly."

Glenn nodded. He took a breath and looked to the note again. Jenny's message continued.

While I cannot discuss the specifics over this correspondence, their disappearance was, as you surmised, tied to the discovery you made and reported to the guild. We also recovered a number of other Adventurers when we found Leo and Sara, some of whom we didn't even know were missing.

Other Adventurers? Did that mean Leo and Sara weren't the only Adventurers to disappear from the Old Fishing District? Glenn now found himself impossibly curious about what had occurred.

Once again, your keen instincts and investigative prowess have served the Blazers well. I'm very impressed with what you accomplished, and I believe Captain Hawkshadow is equally impressed. Finally, I wanted to let you know that both Sara and Leo insisted on following in your footsteps.

They've just departed on another boat to join you in Stillwatch, though I fear they won't arrive in time to sign up for any contests. Expect both of them a few days after the cup starts.

Glenn beamed at Becka. "Leo and Sara are coming to join us!"
Becka snorted. "I *can* read."
"Right. I know." Glenn went back to the letter.

Have a safe journey to Sun's Cross. I wish I could attend the cup, but other matters demand my attention. I do, however, have one more message to forward. Brennon sends his regards, and he wanted me to let you know he's impressed with your latest accomplishments. While he didn't say so in so many words, I get the impression he's already made his decision about you.

You're going to become a Truth Seeker, Glenn. I'm confident revealing that since it will be a matter of public knowledge soon enough. While I did not get to train you as I once wished, I'm none-theless very pleased to see how you've progressed. I hope we can speak again soon.

And Becka? You continue to make me proud as well. Keep his head on straight.

Best,
Jenny

Glenn grinned at Becka. "She seems to think I'd get into trouble without you."

"She's not wrong." Becka sighed happily. "Gods, this is a relief."

"I know. I'm so glad Jenny and the others were able to rescue them!"

"We don't know if they were rescued. Only that they were found. This *is* Leo and Sara we're talking about."

"And Ripper." Glenn rolled up the scroll and then tucked it into his **[-Unfilled Bag-]**. "Still, we've done what we came to do. We should get back to our... mutual friend... and see about that room."

Becka rose with him. "Lead the way, Truth Seeker Graybreaker."

Glenn grinned. "One day. One day soon."

He and Becka made their way out of the guild and returned to Anna. They found her waiting patiently, and Glenn quickly summarized the contents of Jenny's letter. Anna was quite pleased to hear that Leo and Sara had been recovered and would join them. Now, they had somewhere to go.

It took almost thirty minutes for them to complete the walk to an older but well-kept portion of the capital. Soon Anna took them down a road that had a number of hanging wooden signs advertising lodgings. Aria had a whole row of taverns and inns, far more than any road he'd seen in Lakebrooke, but that made sense given its size. Anna stopped in front of one in the middle of the row.

Glenn hid his grimace as he noticed the wooden sign hanging above its doors. It was obviously a large, terrifying spider, and while the spider was "dancing," that only made it, in his mind, all the more creepy. So a Skitterer was a spider, and if it spawned in this zone, a level 20+ spider.

After they left the capital's walls, Glenn wasn't going to leave the Safe Road until he was well into Stillwatch. The Rock Spider Queen he, Ashley, Becka, and Harold Stoutcrag had barely escaped in the bowels of the Water Sisters back in Evolan had been bad enough. A level 20 Skitterer would be nightmare fuel.

As they walked inside, Glenn was relieved to find that the Dancing Skitterer, despite its unnerving name, was a clean, well-kept, and sturdy-looking inn. A large common room greeted them as they walked through the doors. It was crowded despite it being the middle of the afternoon. Glenn swept his eyes across the denizens and judged them to be a mix of both Townsfolk and Adventurers.

A quick smattering of [-Soul Scan-]s as he and Becka followed Anna across the room revealed the levels in the common room ranged from as low as level 8 (Glenn saluted the bravery of someone so low coming all the way to the capital) to level 36, which meant the grizzled-looking female Adventurer he'd scanned had only four levels to the divine level cap.

That suggested this Adventurer had wandered and hunted in the wild zones beyond the capitals, where the only place to sleep and resupply were Outposts that lacked both Town Guards to defend them and the divine protection of town walls. If Glenn survived the next decade or so, he and Becka could find themselves wandering those wild lands as well. An exciting and mildly terri-fying thought.

The <Sandsea Cup> had events for all level bands, and there was no reason for a level 36 Adventurer to be here in the capital unless she, too, was going to attend. Glenn's proximity to level 15 did offer one advantage. The band of Adventurers in which Glenn would be competing would be 10-15, which would put him almost at the top of his competitive group. While Adventurers as low as level 10 could challenge him within that band, his level advantage would give him a leg up.

Anna tromped upstairs with Becka following her and Glenn following them both. The upstairs had five doors on each side, meaning this tavern only had ten rooms available for groups of guests. It made Glenn all the more grateful Anna had gotten here ahead of them and reserved somewhere for them to stay. Still, was her party looking for her? Were the Blazers?

Anna unlocked a door and ushered them inside a room that was about double the size of his room at the Iron Scabbard back in Lake-brooke. As Anna had promised, the room did have two beds, though they were narrow enough that he and Becka would have to sleep, touching, if they shared one. That would not be a problem for either of them.

Anna glanced at him. "Could you close and bolt the door?"

Glenn did so.

Anna looked at Becka. "Do you sense any company about?"

"No Shadowers I can detect." Becka's [+Shadow Sense+] Blessing allowed her to detect nearby Shadowers, at least so long as they weren't drastically higher level than she was. "We should be able to talk freely in this room, though I'd suggest we keep our voices low."

"That's good enough for me." Anna clutched her hands together in obvious worry and looked at Glenn. "I know you wouldn't be here if you didn't think we had no other options, but I need to hear you say it. You truly think winning the cup is our only chance of completing your Quest?"

Glenn nodded calmly. "I don't think it's mathematically possible to reach level 15 before the timer expires without some additional boost. You looked, didn't you?"

Anna nodded. When she scanned him, she had seen his current

experience. She knew he needed to gain almost 11,000 experience in a month and a half to meet the demands of the Gods.

Glenn fixed her with a calm gaze. "Even if we were able to level every day for the next month and a half without interruption, there's no guarantee we could get the experience we need to meet the deadline. The cup was a risky gambit, but we're largely out of options at this point. If I can win at least a few contests at the cup, the experience scrolls they offer may put me over the top."

Anna settled herself on the bed and sighed. "Thank you for trying."

"He's our friend too. We can't give up hope."

"I haven't. I just wish the Gods had given me that Quest. I wish I could do *something* other than sit on my hands while you and Becka work yourselves to the bone to bring him back."

Becka settled on the other bed. "Zack's quite special to us both."

"I know. I know you both knew him... have known him... far longer than I did. I just hate not being able to help, and..." She shuddered and took a breath. "I miss him so much. If he was truly gone I could perhaps move on, but knowing there's still a chance we could get him back and might not... it's maddening. Especially since I have no control over the result."

Glenn smiled warmly. "You're helping more than you know. You got us a room in a crowded capital when we'd otherwise be sleeping in a tent."

Anna looked at them both plaintively. "So what *can* I do to help you level?"

"Well..." Glenn looked at Becka, who shrugged. He looked at Anna again. "I guess you could start by telling us why you're here without the rest of your party."

Anna looked at the bed. "You're not going to like it."

So Glenn was right. "You slipped away from your escorts?"

She nodded.

"Do they even know you're here?"

"They know I'm safe." Anna's eyes met Glenn's again. "I wrote them a note before I left assuring them of that. They know I haven't been abducted or run off to abandon my duties. I just told them I had something I needed to handle, alone, and to expect me back in a few weeks."

Becka whistled softly. "Your commander won't be happy with you when you return. The Blazers could consider taking off without permission as desertion. They could remove you or even arrest you."

"True, but would they? Everyone knows why I need to level, and why they need to help me." She left unsaid the zone-wide calamity that would result if she failed to reach level 15 in the time the Gods had designated. "We both know I'm largely immune from prosecution."

Glenn crossed his arms as he considered. "They could still guess where you've gone, that you've come here, and forcibly return you to wherever you've been leveling. Even if they don't know you're here, we're going to encounter other Blazers once we reach Sun's Cross."

"I'll keep my hood up and my head down. My current party are all Junior Blazers bound by the same rules I am, so even if the Blazers do send someone to look for me, they won't send them. It'll be people who don't know me very well, and I've got experience at remaining hidden."

"Even so..." Glenn pondered a moment, then slipped off his arrowhead necklace. Its enchantment assured that anyone who knew Glenn Redwood would not see Glenn Redwood when they looked at him... but it wasn't locked to him alone.

Becka touched his leg. "What are you thinking?"

Glenn let the necklace hang from one hand as Anna stared at it. "Of the two of us, I'm actually less likely to be recognized in Sun's Cross. No one on this continent is going to know Glenn Redwood from Wolfpine. I doubt any of our Townsfolk could afford to come all the way up here, and the only Adventurers who I interacted with back then saw me only as a Town Guard."

"We can't know that for certain," Becka said. "The cup is tremendously popular."

"Even so, no one is *looking* for me here. People are looking for Anna. The Holbeck Blazers Guild could have sent multiple Adventurers to track her down, and they have reason to search for a tall, blonde Harmcaster. Especially if you enter contests at the cup."

Anna eyed the arrowhead necklace dangling from his fingers, then looked up at him. "So you're suggesting I wear that necklace to disguise my identity?"

"I think it might be best if you did so. Anyone who knows Anna

Bronzelight who looks at you while you're wearing this necklace will see you as someone else. Given you're currently a fugitive... again... I think it makes the most sense for you to wear it."

Anna looked at Becka. "What do you think?"

Becka tapped one finger idly on her knee. "I think it's a risk either way." She sighed. "Still... Glenn is right. Of the two of you, only one is currently being actively sought by the Blazers Guild."

"I had to come help," Anna said defensively. "It's for Zack. I couldn't *not* help."

Glenn smiled again. "I understand. If we were doing this for Becka, nothing could stop me from doing everything I could to bring her back."

Anna clenched her fists and looked down at the bed. "We were only supposed to be apart three months. He wasn't supposed to..." She sniffled again.

Glenn offered her the necklace. "We're going to complete this Quest. We're going to bring him back. And now that you're here to help, we have an even better chance of doing that."

Anna took the necklace and slipped it on. As she did so, Glenn stared in genuine surprise. Every time he looked at her, his mind struggled to resolve what he *knew* and what he *saw*.

In his head, he knew that Anna Bronzelight was sitting on a bed directly in front of him... but every time he focused on that fact, his mind rebelled. It told him he was mistaken and this was another woman who simply resembled her. That was one powerful charm!

"Anna" looked up at him in curiosity. "Is it working?"

"It is," Becka said. "I doubt anyone who knows you will recognize you now."

Anna nodded firmly. "Good. So, what's our plan for winning enough contests at the cup to complete your climb to level 15? You do have a plan, don't you?"

Glenn walked to the bed opposite Anna and motioned. Becka scooted over to give him space. As he sat down he almost slipped his arm around her out of habit, but a nudge to his ribs discouraged that.

Of course! Anna was thinking about Zack and how much she missed him, so watching him and Becka cuddle would simply make Anna feel more lonely. They would keep the public displays of affection to a minimum while Anna was with them.

Glenn leaned forward and rested his arms on his knees instead. "So far, my plan only went as far as boarding a boat to get here and then walking to Sun's Cross to enter the **<Sandsea Cup>**. So since we plan to stay the night, now is as good a time as any to strategize. Our biggest advantage will be the information we can gather before each contest, so we should figure out how best to use that."

Anna looked between them. "So, would you like my suggestions?"

"You've already done research on the cup?"

"Extensive research. I've been stuck here for a week waiting, remember?"

Becka chuckled. "And I spent two weeks retching on a boat, which left me precious little time to do the research I'd intended. So what have you learned?"

"Well, to start, I think we should pass on Monster Fighting Exhibitions."

Glenn frowned. "Why? Those seem the most straightforward."

"You're aware that contests will be going on simultaneously, aren't you? That Adventurers can't enter every contest because multiple contests occur at the same time?"

"Ah, I understand now. You're saying if we have a choice between entering a Monster Fighting Exhibition and another trial, we should pick that other trial."

"If the other contest offers a clear path to victory, yes."

"So what's the problem with the Monster Fighting Exhibitions?" Glenn glanced at Becka in curiosity, then back at Anna. "From what I read, it's just fighting a series of successive Monsters in front of a crowd. That seems like the ideal situation for someone with our talents."

Anna leaned forward. "But even if you defeat all the Monsters in the trial, you can still lose. The judges observe and comment on all of your fights and others, and the opinion of the judges can be quite subjective. You could soundly defeat everything they throw at you and still lose, in points, because another Adventurer defeated the same Monster in a flashy manner."

"She's right," Becka said. "There are Adventurers who spend years training to compete in the **<Sandsea Cup>**, and they learn all sorts of gimmicks to impress the judges. You'll see people fighting with ridiculous weapons, or in costume, or sometimes almost naked. The Monster Fighting Exhibitions are as much about showmanship and style as combat prowess."

Glenn eyed her. "You don't think I can impress the judges by fighting naked?"

Becka elbowed him. "It would impress *me*, but I'm not judging the contest."

Glenn snorted. "So what you're saying is that just walking up to Monster after Monster and smashing it to death with my mace won't impress the judges."

Anna winced sympathetically. "I'm afraid not. Even if you were to soundly defeat every Monster in the trial, you could lose to an Adventurer who did so while juggling or singing."

"So you'd suggest we focus on winning duels instead?"

"I think you should enter both singles and doubles. Those brackets are highly competitive and large, but you're almost at the top of your level band. You also likely have double or triple the Health of most Adventurers around your level. When you add that to your... advantages... you're well positioned to defeat most anyone in a sanctioned duel."

Glenn sighed. "If I'm willing to use my unique talents, you mean."

"Does that concern you?"

Becka rubbed Glenn's back. "He doesn't like cheating. Even so..."

"It's for Zack. I hate the necessity, but I understand the reasoning."

Anna nodded. "If it helps, I suspect the Gods *want* you to use your talents."

That surprised him. "What do you mean?"

"Think about all they've done to arrange this series of unique circumstances. First, the Gods offer you a Quest with an impossibly appealing reward. Next, They make that Quest almost impossible to complete. And They do all of that in the same year that the **<Sandsea Cup>** is going to occur in a zone you can reach in time to participate."

Becka nodded. "I've often thought the same. I can't help but see the grubby little fingers of the Gods pushing the scales here. They want you both involved in the cup because it's yet more information They can use in gauging the effectiveness of your Class."

Glenn considered Becka's reasoning. "It does make sense."

Anna watched him hopefully. "So does that help? Some might

consider using your talents immoral, but is it? You'd only be using Skills the Gods Themselves provided. Other Classes have unique Skills you won't be able to use, and they provide advantages as well."

"I appreciate the help in rationalizing, but I've already decided I'm going to have to be... morally flexible... if I want to succeed in this Quest. I may not like what I have to do, but I can't find fault with our reasons for doing it. We'll make dueling a priority."

"And doubles," Becka said. "Though I can't say I'm eager to engage in duels."

Glenn frowned. "I won't let anyone hurt you."

Becka smiled to reassure him. "I know that, and even if I'm injured, there will be plenty of healing on hand. I'm just not sure how much use I'll be to you in a fight against other Adventurers. My skillset is designed around distraction and infiltration, not direct combat."

He rubbed her back. "You'll do fine. It'll be just like Grassea back home."

"Except this time, we won't have to deal with the Laws of Levos."

It took Glenn a moment, but then he chuckled. "That is a bonus."

"What about quads?" Becka asked. "Could we enter those?"

"Sadly, no," Anna said. "There's only one bracket for quads, and it's 36-40. I'm not sure why, exactly, but I imagine it's simply difficult to organize a dueling bracket for that many full parties of Adventurers. Also, quads take place in the grand colosseum."

Glenn sighed. "Given the complexity of those matches and the high levels of those involved, I imagine those are the matches most everyone comes to see."

Anna smiled sympathetically. "I'm afraid so. Solos and doubles are mostly attended by duelists and friends of duelists, though the finalists do compete in the colosseum!"

"It's fine. We can't fill out a party without Sara or Leo anyway. I'm just worried that once I start winning duel after duel, *if* I win, people will wonder if I have a secret."

Becka leaned close. "Don't forget you're a Blazer. People expect us to be the elite of the elite. You and Anna can both claim you're simply good at picking up on tells."

"It's worth a try. The last person I dueled was Ash, and she never suspected I had any sort of unusual Skills, even after I beat her. So I'll just try and look confident."

"Ash?" Anna gasped. "Oh! You mean Becka's Anchorite friend?"

Becka glanced at Anna in surprise. "You remember her?"

"She's rather hard to forget."

Glenn snorted. "Ash is that. So, I think we have a start on our plans for the cup. All three of us can enroll in singles, and Becka, you and I can enroll in doubles."

"I think Anna might be a better fit," Becka said. "You should do doubles together."

Anna perked up. "You think so?"

"Anna has more offensive Skills than I do, plus a heal. Also, she has as much reason to win as we do. She's also got better gear and two levels on me."

Glenn wanted to disagree, but he considered Becka's argument before doing so. He knew how to fight alongside Becka, and he wanted to fight alongside Becka, but that might be because he simply cared so deeply for her. She wasn't wrong that Anna's Harmcaster Skills would make her more useful in a doubles duel.

"Yes," Anna said before Glenn could ask. "If you're willing, I'd like to double with you."

Glenn nodded. "That's our plan then. So, are there any other contests we can focus on? I know there's the duels and Monster Exhibitions, but are there any other contests available?"

"There is the Luminous Maze."

Glenn grinned. "That sounds interesting! What is it?"

"It's a challenge of perception and guile," Becka said. "The <Sandsea Cup> isn't all about physical contests. Otherwise, casters like me would have little reason to participate."

Anna lit up as she stared at Becka. "I think you could do very well in the Luminous Maze! You've got great instincts, and Guilecasters are uniquely equipped to see through the illusions created by other Guilecasters. I hear they're usually favored to win."

Becka's brow furrowed. "Can you enter both dueling and the Luminous Maze?"

"No, likely not. They occur at the same time, so you'll have to choose."

"Then I'll try the maze. I'm level 12 and focused on deceptive

Skills, and none of that will benefit me when up against level 15s who are here specifically to duel. You and Glenn are best equipped for dueling. I only hope we have enough moons to enter everything."

Anna patted her **[Unfilled Bag]**. "You don't need to worry about that."

Glenn realized what she meant. "We can't ask you to—"

"You *can*. I told you I wanted to help us complete your Quest, and paying the entry fees for every contest all of us can conceivably enter is how I want to help. It's not like my inheritance is good for anything else at the moment. Let me handle our finances."

While allowing Anna to spend the coin necessary to pay for their entry fees in the various contests of the **<Sandsea Cup>** went against his instincts, Glenn certainly didn't have the money to pay for all the entry fees himself. Anna was right. This was how she could help them resurrect Zack, and she wanted to help. He needed all the help he could get.

"Thank you," Glenn said. "If you're financing us, we should enter everything we can."

Anna smiled. "So it's settled. Becka tackles the Luminous Maze and any other contests that suit her talents, and you and I will enter singles individually and doubles as a team."

"That sounds like a plan to me," Becka agreed. "It's good to have you with us."

"I feel the same. Now, can I treat you two to supper?"

Glenn glanced at Becka. "Do you think you're ready to eat?"

"Oh, I'm starving." She looked at Anna again. "Do you have somewhere in mind?"

"I do, in fact. And I bet you're both going to love it."

THIRTEEN
A DAY ON THE ROAD

After a delicious (and probably expensive) meal at the fine restaurant Anna selected for them, and a relaxing and refreshing night sleeping in a bed that wasn't swaying (the first good night of sleep Becka had gotten in weeks), Glenn set out with Becka and Anna shortly after the sun rose on the city of Aria the following morning. They had checked and double-checked their provisions last night after supper, so he didn't worry about leaving anything behind.

Despite the early hour, the wide streets of Aria remained crowded. Glenn wouldn't be surprised if that was unusual and purely due to the number of people who were here to travel to the **<Sandsea Cup>**. It took them almost an hour to reach the gate leading to the Safe Road that would allow them to proceed safely through Fool's March. The Monsters and Demons in this zone ranged from level 20 to 26, but they couldn't touch anyone on the Safe Road.

Glenn was unsurprised to find the Safe Road quite crowded. In addition to people traveling on foot like him, Becka, and Anna, there were a number of mounted Adventurers, with their mounts proving both their advanced levels and their wealth. One day, after he gained a few more levels, Glenn would have a mount of his own.

There were also Merchants and other Townsfolk riding wagons pulled by beasts of burden or hauling carts of goods for sale. He suspected they would be in proximity to people for the duration of their travels. That was more than a bit comforting.

How many Quests must the local Scribes have commissioned to allow these Townsfolk to sleep outside the walls of a town without being turned to salt? Those efforts must have netted those Scribes a fair bit of experience. It made him think of his father back in Wolfpine.

What was Hal Redwood up to today? Had he leveled to 17 yet? Were he and Tania (Glenn's mother) enjoying their lives in Wolfpine even though he wasn't there?

The brief surge of melancholy came and went, replaced by satisfaction. If Captain Jeffrey Graybreaker (formerly the leader of Wolfpine's Town Guards) hadn't returned to Wolfpine to let Glenn's parents know he was still alive, he would soon.

Hal and Tania Redwood would hide that knowledge and continue to grieve in public, but inside they would no longer hurt as Glenn suspected they had for the months since the Blazers faked his death. He knew how much it would hurt him if he believed his mother or father had met the Forever Death. He'd hated the necessity of doing that to them.

Even though he knew it was a risk, it was freeing to be walking openly about as "Glenn Redwood" once more. He still wore the enchanted **[Blazer Pin]** that would allow him to present a fake Status Sheet to anyone who asked, but without the constant weight of the arrowhead pendant he'd loaned to Anna, he no longer felt like someone else.

When Becka slipped one arm through his and pressed close with a happy sigh, he glanced at her in curiosity. Anna was walking ahead of them now and looked focused on the crowd, so Glenn supposed there was no harm in a little public affection. They wouldn't make Anna pine for Zack since Anna wouldn't see it happening.

Becka kissed his arm and then smiled up at him. "I love being able to ogle you again. I think you're even more attractive now than you were back in Wolfpine."

Glenn decided to tease her. "You're only noticing that now?"

"I'm seeing *you* again. Picturing you *as* you when you're wearing that pendant is a constant effort. If I close my eyes and feel you, and listen to your voice, I know you're the Glenn I love. But when I look at you while you're wearing that pendant, my mind constantly tells me you're someone different. Handsome, certainly, but not my Glenn."

Glenn understood how difficult that must be. "I'm sorry you have to put up with that."

"It's a small price to pay to be with the man I love. But today, as we walk on a continent we've never seen with people we've never met, I get to walk with *my* Glenn once more. The man I grew up beside. So just so you know, there will be *lots* of ogling today."

"Want me to unbutton my shirt? Just a few buttons on the top?"

Becka grinned up at him. "That would be lovely."

After one more glance at Anna, whose gaze remained fixed firmly ahead, Glenn lightly kissed the top of Becka's head. "If Anna asks, I'll just say it's hot out here."

They stopped for lunch not soon after the sun reached its zenith. Both Anna and Becka pulled light tarps out of their **[Unfilled Bag]**s which they set up on the edge of the Safe Road. Those offered relief from the bright sun (it really was relentless) and allowed them to enjoy a pleasant lunch of bread, cheese, and meats, along with cool water from their canteens.

As thirsty as they all were, they rationed the water. Each of them carried several filled canteens, but it was impossible to put anything containing water in an **[Unfilled Bag]** without that water drying up. That made water a precious resource in the desert. As Glenn's eyes swept across the arid land around the Safe Road, he couldn't help but feel a little nervous.

He knew from both his reading and Anna's research that there were small stations along the Safe Road as it wound through Fool's March that offered traveling Adventurers a chance to replenish their stocks. There were several large oases not far from those stations, and local Adventurers often took Quests to escort Merchants who gathered water for sale.

Adventurers who could handle the high level Monsters in Fool's March would simply visit the oases on their own and refill their canteens. Yet because the Monsters in this zone were so dangerous for anyone of level 20 or below, those passing through it on the way to Stillwatch didn't have the freedom to visit oases on their own. Not without risking their lives.

While it felt wrong to Glenn to sell water when people literally needed it to survive, he couldn't deny that the first Merchants to come up with the scheme to open water stations along the Safe Road were clever. The only danger was that all the water stations closed down an hour before sunset. The Townsfolk working there had to enter Aria's walls before sunset.

After finishing their lunch, they tucked everything that wasn't water back into their **[Unfilled Bag]**s and resumed their journey along the winding Safe Road. Several times, Glenn caught sight of armored Adventurers engaging in battle with large Monsters he identified through **[-Soul Scan-]**. He was glad the safe stones protected him and his companions.

One of the big Monsters was a Dune Burrower, a worm the size of a carriage that was level 23. Another was a group of horse-sized lizards (Lightning Lizards) that looked to be fast and likely poisonous. They ranged from levels 21 to 23. The Adventurers fighting them looked to be holding their own, which was good, because Glenn couldn't help even if he wanted to.

The names of the Monsters out here were a bit flashier than those he remembered, but perhaps the Gods had to get more creative in naming Monsters as they populated their higher level zones. Regardless, each new Monster he scanned was ten experience toward his goal, and each passing Adventurer or Townsfolk he scanned offered experience as well. Glenn used his Skill constantly, passively soaking up experience.

They passed one water station without stopping but decided to stop at the next one when the sun hung low. They arrived shortly before it closed down, and it turned out water cost more at the end of the day. Even so, Anna paid to refill all of their canteens without hesitation. That made Glenn appreciate her deep pockets and her generosity.

Not long after, they found a relatively unoccupied stretch of Safe Road and decided to make an early camp. The sun was but a smear on the horizon, and Glenn knew they only had a few more minutes before it got dusky, then dark. They should get their camp set up and all their sleeping arrangements confirmed before it got too dark to see without torches.

He briefly opened his Status Sheet and smiled. Between scanning the Monsters he'd seen off the edge of the Safe Road and all the

Adventurers and Townsfolk they had passed today, he'd gained over 250 experience simply from using **[-Soul Scan-]**.

He suspected that number would be reduced tomorrow since he would be traveling in the same crowd, but it was still gratifying to earn as much experience as several days of hunting Monsters. Now if he could win enough events at the **<Sandsea Cup>** to earn the rest!

Glenn did one last survey of their surroundings before it got too dark to see. A safe stone sat snugly in a large stone tower about thirty paces from them, its blue glow a reassurance that no Monster or Demon could reach them here. All stood tall.

Beyond that, several wagons and a carriage were clustered together, likely a group of Merchants traveling as a team. They were far enough away that even their loud, boisterous conversation was no more distraction than a distantly babbling brook.

In the other direction, Glenn spotted several small tents that he suspected had been set up by Adventurers or groups of Adventurers like himself and his companions. Those were people making the long journey on foot to enter the **<Sandsea Cup>** and try their luck at gaining otherwise unobtainable amounts of coin, experience, and rare loot. People he would cheat with his unique Skills in order to save his best friend. It had to happen.

To the west, Glenn saw nothing but towering, windswept dunes, and to the east there was brown, rocky, scrub-covered land that looked barely capable of sustaining tribbits, let alone people or anything larger. Given they had ended up drinking almost all of the water they had set out with from Aria on the road today, he was grateful for the water stations. Even the air was dry and warm. It sapped Glenn's moisture with each breath.

As he and Becka got their bedrolls out and set them side by side, Anna walked over to them and smiled as if unsure of herself. "I feel a bit awkward asking this, but... I actually own a rather nice tent. I prefer to sleep inside my tent rather than out in the open."

Glenn frowned. "What's awkward about that?"

"I feel rather self-conscious enjoying the luxury of a fine tent when the two of you are sleeping on hard ground with only a tarp to protect you from the elements. Even so, it's really only big enough for me."

Becka smiled warmly. "Pitch your tent. Glenn and I are as used to sleeping on the road as you at this point. Also, since you're paying for everything, you deserve a little luxury."

"If you're certain." Anna watched them another moment, then inclined her head. "In that case, I'll bid you both good night."

Glenn was touched by Anna's thoughtfulness. "Have a good night!"

Anna walked back to her portion of their small camp and pulled a dry [Smokeless Torch] from her [Unfilled Bag], then lit it with a single blast of flame from her hands. Glenn supposed you never had to worry about flint and steel when you were a Harmcaster, or at least had that as your secondary Class. Then, Anna removed her large folded-up tent.

Glenn watched in bemusement as Anna staked it and raised it. It looked both complicated and luxurious. He felt a bit useless just observing her as she worked. Rolling out his and Becka's bedrolls and setting up their shelter tarp had gone quickly.

He glanced at Becka. "Should we help her?"

Becka, who was currently pressed close against his side with her arms wrapped tightly around his bicep, rapidly shook her head. "She's set up her tent by herself countless times. She might be offended if we implied we didn't think she could do so."

"Good point. Still, I am a bit... whoa!"

Becka pressed close, one hand hidden by his bedroll. "Is something the matter, love?"

"There's... um... Becka..."

"Sssh." She pressed her warm lips to his ear. "She's busy pitching her tent! She's not looking at us. No one is looking at us."

"But we uh... we shouldn't..."

"There's no one around that can see us in the dark. Also, Anna's going to be sleeping safe and sound inside her nice big tent, so she won't be watching us either. It's not even a cold night! It's almost too hot out here, so less clothing might help me sleep."

"Still, if she sees—"

"Good night, you two!" Anna called without looking at them. "Sleep well!" She crawled inside her tent and zipped it up.

Becka smiled. "She's really quite clever, that one."

As she pulled him close in the dark, Glenn couldn't help but agree with her.

Their next day on the road passed much the same as the one prior. Walking was so mundane and tedious that Glenn kept expecting something to go wrong. He almost hoped something *would* go wrong, if only so he would have something to do other than walk.

Perhaps they would come across a Merchant whose wagon had broken down, or a wounded Adventurer who needed healing, or be approached by someone whose child had run off into the sands! None of that occurred. Evidently, everyone else traveling the Safe Road was as experienced at being careful as he was.

They traveled another full day until they were almost to the edge of the border with Stillwatch, then camped one more night. While they could travel the Safe Road at night by using the guiding light of the safe stones, Glenn didn't want to risk running into any bandits along the Safe Road who might demand coin in exchange for clearing the way. He couldn't move off the road in this zone without risking a Monster attack.

The idea of bandits operating openly on a road this crowded was small, but it was also a huge opportunity for any enterprising bandits to bring in huge hauls if they managed to stop and inconvenience the right Townsfolk or Adventurers. Glenn had been keeping an eye out for Blazer pins or tabards as they passed Adventurers and seen none.

Were the Blazers already gathered in Sun's Cross for the cup? Or were they patrolling other zones that would now be greatly bereft of Adventurers to handle their Monster problems with everyone gathering to participate in or watch the **<Sandsea Cup>**? That would be something to ask Marion or Jenny about whenever he returned to Lakebrooke.

They rose and resumed their journey the next day, passing through the narrow valley connecting Fool's March and Stillwatch. Unlike the border of Grassea and Evolan, a narrow valley between two rising cliffs, the transition between Fool's March and Stillwatch was wide open. Yet any thoughts of stepping off the Safe Road were dashed once Anna explained.

Everything other than the Safe Road joining Fool's March to Stillwatch was quicksand. Anyone foolish enough to step off the road would sink and drown. Unless someone found them and fished them out, they would also meet the Forever Death. So... no leaving the road.

When the quicksand peeled away and the land around them expanded again, a tingle of experience rushed through Glenn. He recognized it as discovery experience and realized he had once again received experience for entering a new zone. He was now 100 experience closer to saving his best friend, and moreover, he was now in a level 9-16 zone... not a level 20-26.

He could handle any Monsters or Demons they encountered in Stillwatch. Glenn had never, until he traveled through Fool's March, moved through a zone where he would be helpless to fight its Monsters. Knowing anything he fought in Fool's March would pummel him based on the level difference alone had not been comforting. Was this what Townsfolk felt like all the time? He could understand why they wanted to remain safely inside a city's walls.

Once they entered Stillwatch proper, the Safe Road quickly grew even more crowded. People had come from all over to enjoy the cup, and it seemed many of them were also using the last day before the cup started to get in some last-minute adventuring.

Everywhere Glenn looked he spotted small groups of Adventurers hunting or engaging Monsters. While he dutifully used **[-Soul Scan-]** on everyone he passed, he badly wanted to join them. But he knew nothing about these Monsters, and they couldn't get distracted.

"It's like a busy day in Evolan," Becka reminded him. "Even if we had time to step off the road and go Monster hunting, it's doubtful we would find any. There's simply too many Adventurers hunting too few Monsters."

Glenn smiled sidelong at her. "You really need to stop reading my mind."

"I don't need to read your mind, love. I can read your body."

"So my body is saying it wants to go bash Monsters in the face?"

Becka offered a sly wink. "Among other things."

Glenn rolled his eyes and glanced at Anna, who was also constantly scanning her surroundings. He suspected she was doing the same thing he was, using **[-Soul Scan-]** on any Townsfolk, Adventurers, or Monsters they came across to gain the passive experience. Glenn was so used to being the only Soulseer in the party that having Anna here felt novel.

Once they were largely alone on the road, Glenn glanced at Anna.

No one would be close enough to overhear save Becka. "How much experience have you managed to gather on this journey so far?"

Anna brushed her blonde hair back from her forehead and offered him a level glance. "A little over six hundred since we set out. You?"

"The same." At least Glenn knew now he had been using his Soulseer Skill efficiently. "It's too bad events like this one don't occur more often. With this many people concentrated in the wilds outside the town walls, we could make some real progress."

She offered a smile Glenn suspected she didn't feel. "It's a nice thought."

Glenn nodded. "Every bit helps. If we can win a few contests, we can satisfy the Gods and correct the injustice that occurred back in Grassea. We *will* bring him back."

Anna squeezed his shoulder. "That's the hope."

"We know it's hard to hope," Becka said from Glenn's other side. "Just know we're not going to give up on him until we've exhausted every possibility."

Anna sighed. "Thank you. Both of you."

Glenn looked between them. "Well, I for one feel quite confident."

"As confident as Zack?" Becka asked knowingly.

"I don't think anyone could be that confident. More like fool-hardy." He looked ahead as he remembered holding his best friend as Zack literally melted in his arms, then exploded in a flash of light. "And very, very brave."

They walked most of the rest of the day in silence after that and came in sight of Sun's Cross, a walled desert city equivalent to Lake-brooke, just past noon. As Glenn looked the town over, he was surprised at how much of the city had been built up. It was obvious that the town's mayor had contracted Builders to expand the city's protective walls.

Whatever Builders had been contracted for the work had attached what looked to be the equivalent of several Wolfpines to the side of the original town wall. They and others had raised an area the size of a whole segment of Lakebrooke for the <Sandsea Cup>.

In addition to a number of small arenas and bleachers to observe them, the new area included a sizable colosseum. Would this all be demolished once the cup was over? Or would it be repurposed as a tourist attraction for Adventurers who came through this zone?

Glenn knew that the capital of Landers, Eastwend, featured a much larger colosseum in which great fights were held every few months. He had never actually seen a colosseum before. Even knowing this one was a fraction of the one in Eastwend, he was impressed. He wanted to visit it today so he could familiarize himself with its layout.

From talking with Anna over the past few days, he knew he would not be fighting in that particular colosseum... at least not yet. First, he would need to win enough preliminary matches to qualify for the small bracket of duelists who would actually engage with each other in front of a crowd. The qualifiers would winnow the wheat from the chaff.

Based on the huge number of Adventurers participating, conducting all their individual duels and events in the colosseum in front of an audience would take weeks. To avoid that, dozens upon dozens of the preliminary duels (known as qualifiers) would take place simultaneously across the city. These would be attended only by friends and family of the duelists, as well as anyone with the time and desire to scout out their competition.

In regards to one-on-one duels within the colosseum in front of a large audience, only eight Adventurers of all those who arrived here would be allowed to participate. Of those, only the top three would receive an experience scroll (the equivalent of completing a high level Quest) which they could either use on themselves or sell for a great amount of coin. That was Glenn's goal in coming here. Winning a few scrolls would help him bring back Zack.

While most Adventurers used the scroll to help themselves level, it was not unprecedented for the winners of the <Sandsea Cup>'s contests to sell their valuable experience scrolls to finance their future adventures or clear their debts. The fact that winning events in the <Sandsea Cup> awarded experience scrolls was what made it unique among leveling opportunities, and why Becka had suggested Glenn come out here and participate.

It went without saying that Glenn would use any experience scrolls he won on himself. But if Becka won her contest, she could also give her experience scroll to Glenn. Anna could do the same if she succeeded in a dueling bracket where he failed.

Everyone who chose to help him level to 15 in time to meet the Gods' ultimatum could thus contribute to leveling a single person (Glenn) as fast as possible. Given all the time they'd expended to get here, it might be the only way to save Zack.

As they approached Sun's Cross, Anna took the lead. "We should check into our lodgings before the local tavern keeper decides to sell our rooms. I paid to reserve them, but I wouldn't put it past him to resell the room if he comes to believe we won't show up."

Glenn eyed her curiously. "Wouldn't that break your contract with him? He'd lose experience for doing that."

"He could likely gain most of it back with his next contract, as well as pocketing a large additional amount of coin. He struck me as an honest man in our negotiations, but I'd prefer he not be tempted any longer than he needs to be."

Glenn nodded thoughtfully. "That does seem best. Any sign of anyone you know?"

They all knew that approaching Sun's Cross would put Anna in the most danger of being discovered by the Blazers who had been assigned to escort her, if they were here looking. They had to have guessed her destination by now. Even the power of Glenn's Guile-caster charm to disguise her identity might not be enough to fool them if they weren't careful.

Anna settled into the long line of Adventurers and Townsfolk waiting to walk past the alert-looking Town Guards stationed at either side of the south gate of Sun's Cross. "No one I recognize so far, and no sign of any Blazers. It looks like the Town Guards are the only folks checking people as they walk into the town. Hopefully, it'll stay that way."

Becka touched her shoulder. "If not, you can always give us the name of the tavern keeper and we can report to the room on your behalf."

"We'll treat that as a last resort. He might think you were lying."

Glenn looked around. "The crowds should also camouflage us. Any Blazers hoping to find Anna will be looking for a single woman in a crowd of people that rivals the population on a good night in Aria. I bet we can slip in easily!"

Someone gasped aloud from behind him. "Glenn?"

Glenn froze as if struck by the stun from [-Guardian's Smash-].

"Gods, is that you? Glenn *Redwood?*"

Like in a dream, Glenn couldn't help himself. Even as Becka grabbed his forearm hard enough it hurt, he turned, instinctively, to look behind him. That woman's exclamation had been loud enough that the people ahead glanced back to see what the commotion was.

Beaming through the huge smile on her pale and freckled face, Nora Rapidbloom took several steps closer. As she stared at him with wide blue eyes, her short red hair glistened in the bright light. "It is you! Gods, you're the last person I expected to run into here!"

Glenn could only stare in disbelief at this kind and lovely woman. The last time he had seen Nora Rapidbloom—alongside Terry Evergarden and Carmello Gainsayer, her party members—had been after the three of them verified Crackpaw Mine was filled with green poison gas. Terry had died securing the door to the mine, though Richard Deepscar had brought him back.

Nora now wore blue and white [Timeworn Robes], a considerable upgrade from the common [Moonlight Robes] she'd worn last time they'd seen each other. She must have gained at least one level in the many months since they'd last seen each other in Wolfpine... when he was still a Town Guard.

A rush of memories from over half a year ago returned. Stepping outside Wolfpine for a nightly jog. Encountering the Winnower who had disguised itself as Becka and almost dying to its attacks. Being saved by Terry, Carmello, and Nora, and enjoying a meal with them.

He remembered Nora inviting him up to her room. He remembered her gifting him her own coin as a donation to help out the friends of Rafe Slatestriker, the young man who'd met the Forever Death after Richard Deepscar expended his twenty-four hour [-Resurrect-] cooldown to bring Carmello back to life. He remembered Nora offering to share her bed, an offer he'd declined even though he'd been sorely tempted, at the time, to indulge.

As he glanced at Becka, a rush of guilt flooded him. He hadn't betrayed her that night, but he had been tempted. It didn't help that Nora was so sweet and kind.

"How are you here?" Nora asked in wide-eyed awe as Terry and Carmello, who both looked amused by Nora's befuddlement, stared at Glenn from behind her. "Did they call in other Town Guards from other towns to help in the cup? Can you... can you do that?"

Becka's hand tightened enough on his bicep that Glenn winced.

"We should discuss this in private," Becka said primly. "Let's step out of line and chat."

FOURTEEN

A REUNION WITH OLD FRIENDS

Behind Nora, Terry scoffed. "If it's all the same to you, miss, I don't plan to lose my place in line. I'm going to get inside town and get a meal."

Nora stared at him. "But, Terry, really! It's Glenn!"

Carmello grinned wide. "You can step out of line and chat with your favorite Town Guard. I'm sure you can't wait to catch up on all that he's been up to since you saw him last." He wiggled his eyebrows meaningfully. "You never did say just what happened after we all had that meal together. You certainly did seem happy the next day."

Nora blushed furiously. "You hush!" She glanced at Glenn again and winced. "I'm sorry about the two of them, as always. Still... how are you?" Nora somehow pulled her eyes from his and glanced at his two companions. "Oh! And who are your lovely friends?"

Glenn unswallowed his tongue and focused on the problem. Thanks to his foolish decision to remove his Guilecaster necklace, Nora had already recognized him and had no doubt about who he was. Terry and Carmello recognized him as well.

There was no way he could hide his identity from these three any longer, and no way he could have anticipated he would run into the only three Adventurers in all of Luxtera who might recognize him here. What he could do was minimize the damage.

He needed to find a way to explain his presence here. He needed to ensure Nora and her friends didn't speak of his past as Glenn Redwood (or as one of Wolfpine's Town Guards) to anyone else. Any talk of his past to anyone would certainly raise questions.

None of them had ever struck him as particularly pious, even Nora. He knew that if he explained that he wished to remain anonymous, she would help him do that. Beside him, Becka loudly cleared her throat. That shocked him into action.

He rested his hand on Becka's back. "Nora, it's... nice... to see you again. This is Rebecka Coldbreaker, the woman I told you about the last time we spoke at The Mead Beast. She's my... we're together."

Nora's eyes widened before she turned to Becka and smiled. "It's such a pleasure to meet you! Glenn told me about you, but he didn't mention how beautiful you were."

Terry huffed. "I said step out of line or move, you all. You're holding up the line!"

Becka gripped Nora's slim hand. "That's sweet of you to say, and you're quite lovely as well, Miss Rapidbloom. Would you mind if we stepped out of line for a moment and talked? I'm sure your companions can hold your space."

"And I'll hold ours," Anna added from behind them. "You three go on."

"Thanks!" Glenn managed. "Oh, and that's... Anna! She's another... of my friends."

Becka stepped out of line and dragged Nora by the hand. Her lips were set in a firm line. "This way, please."

Glenn, after another glance at Carmello and Terry, hurried after them. Both men looked amused by his obvious consternation, especially the sight of Becka and Nora and the possibility that they might end up fighting over him.

That was not going to happen, and this was not an amusing situation! Nora had offered him the chance to be with her, but he had turned her down. That was it.

He'd never cheated on Becka despite having numerous opportunities to do so. He'd never cheat on Becka. Though, as he thought back on a few nights with Becka and Ashley, it wasn't cheating if they were *both* involved.

Once they were out of the line, Becka beckoned Glenn close and Nora close as well. Nora seemed a bit out of sorts at Becka's request, but she didn't step away. She looked both adorably nervous and a bit curious, while Becka's features remained inscrutable.

Becka fixed Nora with a calm gaze. "How well do you know Glenn?"

Nora's blush returned with a vengeance. "Oh, I just... we met when fighting a Winnower, and he saved me when it drained my blood."

"She also donated money to help Lisa and Kain get back on their feet after Rafe met the Forever Death," Glenn told Becka. "But anonymously, so her party members wouldn't make fun of her. Which is why she had me take the coin and deliver it on her behalf."

He realized he had never discussed the events of that night with Becka other than in vague terms. For one, she hadn't asked, and there had been no reason to dig into events from so long ago. Second, Glenn hadn't been sure how to broach the fact that the Winnower (in his mind) had taken Becka's form, or that she'd attacked them while naked.

Broaching that fact with Karl Coldbreaker, Becka's father, had been awkward enough. He hadn't been sure how he could broach it with Becka herself. Fortunately, Becka smiled when Nora and Glenn finished explaining the circumstances of the last time they'd talked.

"That was very kind of you. So, what else did you two talk about that night?"

"We just spoke," Nora added quickly. "That's all we did, even after... Glenn made it clear his heart belonged with another woman. With you. He was very clear about that!"

Becka rubbed his arm. "You truly are hopeless."

He firmed his stance. "I know who I want."

Nora winced. "I'm really sorry! If I'd known he was with you, I'd have never—"

Becka touched Nora's hands again, which shocked her into silence. "It's quite all right. As we've all pointed out, there's no reason for anyone to feel guilty, and were I to meet Glenn without knowing he was attached, I'd certainly make an offer." Her features turned serious. "However, we should speak about what happens now that we've... encountered each other again. Speaking of Glenn's presence here, to others, could cause problems for us."

Nora's eyes widened. "How do you mean?"

Thank the Gods! Becka was going to come up with a suitable way to explain his presence here. Glenn had come up with nothing but a parched desert similar to that they'd walked alongside while traveling through Fool's March. He had no idea what to say to Nora.

Becka released Nora's hands and stepped back. "When you two spoke about me, did Glenn inform you I was training with the Blazers?"

Nora's expression brightened. "He did! He was so proud of you."

"Then you may be able to guess why we're here. While I'm still a Junior Blazer, that also means I fall beneath the notice of most, especially those who may be on alert for Blazers with more rank than me. Do you see why we might wish to remain anonymous?"

As Nora looked between them, her expression grew even more curious. "So you're here on a mission from the Blazers? A *secret* mission?"

"We're here on a special assignment. Moreover, it's an assignment that both I and the Blazers would prefer remain secret from those here at the cup."

Glenn looked between Becka and Nora in amazement. Not only did Nora seem utterly enraptured by Becka's story, but Becka was also telling Nora the truth... in a way. Was that safe? Becka knew what she was doing. He would trust Becka to handle this matter.

Becka continued. "Glenn is here as my protector. Again, while I cannot speak of the specifics of my mission, secrecy is, as I've already pointed out, of paramount importance."

Nora nodded eagerly. "He is very good at protecting people."

"Moreover, Glenn's not anyone most here will recognize. Had I brought a senior Blazer with me, someone might take notice. But to everyone here at the <Sandsea Cup>, Glenn is just another Adventurer here to take in the sights and contests."

Nora bit her lip. "I know Town Guards can step outside the walls of a city when granted a Quest by the mayor, but... Gods. A Quest that takes him across the world?"

"That's correct. So as you can imagine, it's an extremely important Quest. Both to the Blazers and to the people of Sun's Cross. So, Miss Rapidbloom—"

"Nora," Nora interrupted. "Please, call me Nora. If I can call you Rebecka?"

Becka smiled again. "Call me Becka. So, Nora, I would ask—"

"I won't say a thing about who Glenn is to anyone! And I'll make sure the two lunkheads in my adventuring party do the same. Carmello and Terry might play the boors, but both know when to keep their mouths shut. I will impress upon them both that any talk of... either of you... should remain between us. No one else."

"That's all we'd ask. Thank you for being so understanding."

Nora beamed at them. "I'm always happy to help the Blazers! And, of course, the Town Guards." She clasped her hands together and bowed her head. "You can always count on me."

Becka glanced at Glenn and quirked an eyebrow. "Any concerns?"

"Not a one. I know Nora enough to know she'll always keep her word, and I also know what a good person she is. I trust our secret is safe with her."

Nora sighed breathily. "Wow. You're just... you're so perfect together."

Now Becka laughed. "You're too kind."

"So... should we get back in line?"

Becka eyed Nora for another moment. "Sure. But if I may ask, what level are you?"

Glenn only then thought to check. He knew Nora had been level 14 when he'd met her in Wolfpine, but that had been over half a year ago. What level was she now?

He was awfully curious as to how she'd progressed since they saw each other last, and when they saw each other last, he hadn't had all the Skills he had now. It couldn't hurt to have a peek, could it? She wouldn't mind.

[-Soul Scan-].

Name: Nora Rapidbloom
Age: 20
Level: 15
Class: Lifecaster
HP: 80/80
Blood: 170/170
Experience: 117,466/124,000
Strength: 4

Divinity: 21
Vitality: 8
Wisdom: 17
Prowess: 13
Luck: 15

Gear:

- **Uncommon: [Timeworn Robes]**
- **Uncommon: [Padded Boots]**
- **Uncommon: [Ruby Necklace]** (Enchanted / Blood Reduction)
- **Uncommon: [Steel Knife]**
- **Rare: [Unfilled Bag]**

Slotted Skills:

- **Uncommon: [-Flash Heal-]** (Lifecaster / Celes)
- **Uncommon: [-Cleanse Body-]** (Lifecaster / Celes)
- **Uncommon: [-Cleanse Mind-]** (Lifecaster / Celes)
- **Uncommon: [-Sunlight Shard-]** (Lifecaster / Celes)
- **Uncommon: [-Soul Harden-]** (Lifecaster / Celes)

Slotted Blessings:

- **Uncommon: [+Glowing Soul+]** (Lifecaster / Celes)
- **Uncommon: [+Regeneration+]** (Lifecaster / Celes)
- **Uncommon: [+Divine Insight+]** (Lifecaster / Celes)

Known Skills:

- **Uncommon: [-Soul Cushion-]** (Lifecaster / Celes)

Known Blessings:

- None

Quests:

- None

As he'd once speculated given her slim build, Nora's Vitality was slightly lower than Becka's. Yet Nora had more Divinity than Becka and the same amount of Wisdom, though Nora was two levels higher. Nora's Luck and Prowess were also unusually high for a Lifecaster.

Why would she have so much Prowess? Her attribute was comparable to a melee class. As he considered how reckless Terry and Carmello seemed to be and speculated on how often they left Nora to defend herself, he suspected she might be very good at dodging attacks.

Nora smiled at Becka's question. "I'm level 15 now, but I'm very close to level 16. Why do you ask? Do you need someone with mending Skills?"

He glanced at Becka. "What do you think?"

Becka's eyes widened appreciably, and then she nodded. "That would be ideal."

Nora looked between them. "What? What would be ideal?"

Becka looked at Nora again. "As part of our secret mission, Glenn and my other friend... Anna... planned to enter doubles together. However, Anna and I would much prefer to enter doubles as a team of casters, and only didn't do so because Glenn needed a partner."

Nora gasped. "But I'm not a Blazer! Not like you."

"You're still a talented Lifecaster, and moreover, a person of impeccable character. Do you intend to enter the dueling brackets with your party?"

"I can't," Nora said sourly. "They've both leveled out of the 10-15 bracket. I can never manage to keep up with them, so we can't do any duels together. I'd thought perhaps to participate in the Luminous Maze and, if I'm lucky, gather some coin by offering my Lifecaster Skills to heal in the dueling preliminaries. But I'd never thought to compete in duels!"

"I'd imagine a Lifecaster like you would have her choice of partners."

"Yes, but... I don't know those people."

Glenn clapped her on the shoulder. "But you know me. I can handle the rough stuff, and with you to back me up like you did at the Crackpaw Mine, I think the two of us could go quite far. With your defense and my offense, we could make a good run at the crown."

Glenn had his own heals, of course... **[-Guardian's Heal-]**... but he couldn't use that in a duel without his healing being noticed. If observers saw a Brutalist healing himself, they'd cry foul. But with Nora present, they would just assume she was healing him.

Moreover, Nora's talent for healing and clearing debuffs was impressive. Nora had more than proven her proficiency with **[-Flash Heal-]** and **[-Cleanse Body-]** as she repeatedly healed Glenn outside Crackpaw Mine. She had healed him through a desouled Vulpor and a plague. He had no doubt she could heal him even in the chaos of a doubles duel.

Nora's features tightened. "And you're certain I wouldn't be a drag on you? I'm not a Blazer. I sometimes have a hard time keeping Terry and Carmello healthy in a fight."

As Glenn remembered how recklessly Terry and Carmello had fought the Winnower disguised as Becka outside Wolfpine, he smiled again. "I suspect that's more due to their overeager nature than any fault of yours. If you partner with me, you can rest assured I'll make your safety a priority. I always protect my party's Mender in battle."

"Gods, that would be nice! For once."

Becka stepped close to her again. "So you'll party with Glenn? For doubles?"

"Of course I will!" Then Nora frowned. "But is that... legal?"

She must be referring to Glenn's status as a Town Guard. He wasn't sure how to answer that, especially since he was cheating not just with his unique Soulseer Skills, but also with his powerful Town Guard Blessings. Again, he couldn't help but feel guilty.

"There's no rules against it," Becka assured Nora calmly. "Moreover, it's important... no, it's vital... that we do as well as we can in the dueling contests."

Nora now looked more than a bit confused. "What does winning the dueling brackets have to do with your secret Blazer mission?"

"Everything, I'm afraid. I wish I could tell you more, but... I'd simply ask you to trust me."

"Trust *us*," Glenn added. "I promise, we wouldn't ask this of you if it wasn't important."

Nora's features brightened. "I trust you. Especially you, Glenn." She glanced at Becka. "And you of course! But..."

"We hardly know each other, though I hope we'll get to know each other over the next few days. And if all goes well, I may be able to tell you more... provided you can keep a secret."

That seemed to delight Nora even more. "I can keep a secret!"

Becka smiled at her. "Then I think we've settled this matter to all our satisfaction. Shall we step back into line? It looks like our friends have made quite a bit of progress as we spoke."

"Of course. Though... I'm staying with my party. We have a room."

"I'd expect as much. I believe sign-ups open tomorrow, correct?"

"Yes. That's why we had to rush to get here."

"So could you meet us to line up for the dueling sign-ups at sunup tomorrow? We'll keep an eye out for you, and you can keep an eye out for us."

"I'll be there," Nora declared firmly.

As they walked back to line together, Glenn lightly elbowed Becka. She glanced at him and raised an eyebrow. He mouthed, *"What about supper?"*

She smiled and nodded in obvious approval.

Glenn looked at Nora. "It was lovely to see you here, but now that we've discussed what's required as far as... gossip... it would be nice to catch up on everything else you three have been up to. So how would you, Terry, and Carmello like to join us for supper?"

"Oh, I'd love that! But... you should ask them. I think they already have plans."

After they were all back in line, Glenn extended the invitation to supper to Terry and Carmello. While Terry looked a bit hesitant, Carmello's face lit up. "That sounds great, Glenn. We'd love to join you for a quick bite. Though, you understand, we can't stay long."

Anna eyed them curiously. "Do you have to retire early?"

Carmello looked wistfully toward the gates. "Some of the most legendary Entertainers in all of Luxtera will be here for this event. And I, after spending a great deal of coin and winning a lottery, have secured thirty minutes with Misty Slateswallow."

Terry chuckled. "Three times as long as you need."

Becka giggled. "Oh my. You *are* a lucky man."

Glenn glanced at her in surprise. "You know who that is?"

Becka smiled coyly. "You don't?"

Glenn swallowed hard. "I've, uh... I've heard the name mentioned."

Terry sighed heavily. "The Entertainers here for the cup are, as Carmello says, second to none. We'd love to enjoy a supper with you, but we also won't have many nights of leisure before the cup ends. So you'll understand if we excuse ourselves a bit early?"

"Of course," Anna said graciously. "And if you'll allow, the supper will be my treat."

Nora gasped. "We can't accept that!"

Carmello playfully ribbed her. "We absolutely can. We're in your debt, Miss..."

"Ironstar," Anna said. "And I'm happy to treat any friends of Glenn's to supper. As for any expenses you acquire after that, you're on your own."

"Thank you so much," Nora said fervently. "You're all so very kind."

Anna smiled indulgently. "Given you've agreed to act as Glenn's healer for duos, it seems the least I can do is offer you a meal. And hopefully get to know you better."

Becka glanced at Nora, then at Glenn. She smirked knowingly. "Oh, I bet we'll all get to know each other better tonight."

Glenn nodded eagerly. "This is perfect. I'm so glad we ran into you three."

Carmello chuckled and eyeballed Nora. "I bet you are."

Nora slugged him in the arm. "Will you stop? We're just friends!"

"And yet Glenn has so many beautiful friends."

Glenn wasn't quite sure what Carmello meant by that, so he frowned and rubbed the back of his head. "That's, uh... well. Yes. I have many talented friends."

Anna once again treated them to one of the finest restaurants in the city, and Glenn, just as he had two years ago in The Mead Beast after almost dying to a Winnower, enjoyed himself immensely. He sat on one side of a long table with Becka beside him and Anna beside her, while Carmello, Terry, and Nora sat opposite them.

Before and after they ordered the first course, Carmello remained immensely entertaining and jovial. Glenn laughed often as he realized

Carmello reminded him a little of Karl Coldbreaker, Becka's father. While they ate, Terry had many new stories with which to regale those enjoying mead and food alongside him.

Nora remained mostly quiet throughout their dinner, nibbling on bread and a salad. Yet the few times Glenn glanced at her to make sure she was having a good time, she smiled warmly in his direction. He suspected she'd grown used to letting her more boisterous party members carry the conversation, and to their credit, they certainly did.

Anna also grew more giggly and animated as the mead flowed. Glenn eventually wondered if he should ask her to slow down. Still, Anna was an adult, and the dueling and contests didn't start until two days from now. She could rest up tomorrow.

Everything was going fine until Terry finished his latest story and Carmello, who was busy stuffing his face, had nothing more to say. Nora, likely well-practiced at picking her moment, eagerly jumped into the conversation for the first time tonight.

"So, Glenn, there is one person you haven't mentioned." Nora's cheeks flushed. "How is Zack doing? Have you heard from him in the last few months?"

Glenn almost choked on his next swallow of mead. Becka clutched his thigh in warning, and at the end of the table, Anna gawked at Nora as if she'd slapped her in the face.

"Excuse me?" Anna managed.

Carmello beat the table with one fist, bouncing the supperware, and threw back his head as he laughed boisterously. "That's right! Last time we talked, you told me that silver-tongued devil was actually from Wolfpine! Please tell me he's wandering around here as well. Given how he dispatched those Glass Spiders, I'd love to see him duel."

Terry snorted. "I don't know why you think so fondly of that day. He was rude and reckless. If he's not careful, that sort of Adventurer ends up quite dead."

Anna dropped her silverware with a loud clatter.

Terry glanced at her, then frowned as he noticed her pale face. "Are you choking?"

"I... I just..." Tears glistened in Anna's eyes as she stood up.

"Please, excuse me." She popped one leg over the long bench and stalked off with her fists clenched tight.

Becka rose as well, then touched Glenn's shoulder. "Handle this. I'll go be with Anna."

Glenn swallowed and nodded. This was his matter to handle. In inviting these three to supper, he had completely forgotten they shared a common friend. He should have told them, in private, what had become of Zack Silverstone... especially with a woman who still loved Zack very much sitting at their table. He should have mentioned something.

As Becka hurried off after Anna, Terry frowned after her. "Did I somehow offend?"

Carmello elbowed Terry with a grin. "Maybe Anna's also a Silverstone fangirl. Looks like you have some competition now, Nora!"

Nora now watched him with worried eyes. "What's the matter?"

Glenn took one deep, calming breath, then swept his gaze across the three Adventurers on the other side of the table. "Zack's dead."

Their reactions ranged from visibly shocked (Carmello) to visibly chagrined (Terry), and, so far as Glenn could tell, utterly devastated (Nora). As he considered them, he remembered the day he'd watched his best friend melt in front of his eyes. He'd felt much the same.

"He... it was in Wolfpine. There was an incident."

Terry shivered. "Gods, man. I feel like the worst kind of heel. So... was Anna?"

"Yes. They were together, and for several years before it happened."

Carmello thumped the table again. "She was the girl! The one Silverstone was in so much of a hurry to get back to! Remember, Terry? The whole reason he pulled that reckless gambit in the mine was so he could get back to his woman on time."

Terry placed a hand on his big friend's arm. "This isn't the time for that sort of thing, Carm. A good Adventurer is no longer with us. It's wrong to speak ill of the fallen."

Carmello grimaced and sat back. "I wasn't speaking ill of him. But... Gods. He might have been reckless, but he was also skilled and confident. I imagined him going on to great things."

"He saved Wolfpine," Glenn said. "So... that was rather great."

Carmello nodded ruefully. "I can see a man like Zack doing that."

"But..." Nora sniffled and wiped her eyes. "Can you tell us *how* he died?"

Glenn took a moment to focus on what he could tell them. He couldn't tell them he was no longer a Town Guard because, after Zack melted after touching the Soulseer Class Crystal, Glenn had inherited the Class. He couldn't tell them that Warrick Paleheart had led a group of Shadowers to assassinate Zack and everyone with him. So what could he say?

"Terry? You remember the day we closed the Crackpaw Mine in my raid?"

"I do. A man rarely forgets a day he died."

"As you recall, we believed a Plaguemaster took over Crackpaw Mine and summoned the foul green mist you reported to Mayor Coleman. We called the Blazers to deal with it."

"I remember you saying something about that," Nora agreed hesitantly. "But we left before we could learn what happened. I always wondered what happened, but we never found the time to go back and ask around. Leveling has kept us busy for the past six months."

That explained why Nora, Terry, and Carmello had no idea Glenn Redwood, Town Guard, had "died" saving Wolfpine over half a year ago. They hadn't been back since shortly after they helped Glenn lock the door of Crackpaw Mine. Given it would likely be harder to explain how he was still alive than how he was here, Glenn supposed that was for the best.

Terry leaned forward. "So the Blazers came to Wolfpine to deal with the Plaguemaster who'd holed up in Crackpaw Mine with that elite. Vulpor, was it?"

Glenn nodded.

"And Zack? How did he come to be involved in this business?"

"He returned as well. He happened to be passing through Wolfpine about the time the Blazers showed up, and in his youth, he leveled almost exclusively in the Crackpaw Mine, often solo. He hunted there so he could level faster than he would in a party."

"Confident and skilled," Carmello agreed. "What a shame he's gone."

"But what level was he at the time?" Nora asked. "He couldn't have been much higher than 15, right?"

"He *was* level 15. Not high enough to take on a Plaguemaster, but high enough to survive in the mines. As we continued to investigate how the Plaguemaster had hidden himself in the mine, we discovered that he had opened a door deep within it that few in Wolfpine, including me, had ever seen. Zack knew where that door was."

Terry nodded sagely. "So he volunteered to guide the Blazers to the door."

Glenn smiled. "He always played the scoundrel, but deep down he was a hero as brave as any I've ever known." It felt good to speak of Zack's heroism. "So, Zack and I both joined the Blazers on their mission to take back Crackpaw Mine from that Plaguemaster. Zack led our party to the door only he knew how to find, and I helped defend him and the Blazers."

"So what happened?" Carmello asked eagerly. "How did you take out a Plaguemaster?"

"With the help of the Blazers. That's really all I can say due to... confidentiality. After that, we retook the mine and got rid of the plague."

Glenn wasn't sure what else to say in regards to Warrick Pale-heart, who had been using the alias Victor Hallowthorne, whose last interaction with Glenn was to wish him luck in exposing the church's conspiracy to enslave Deathcasters. What could he say about a man who was over a hundred years old, one who had not only dual-classed, but triple-classed, and one who had once been a Town Guard just like him? A good, just man?

"But Zack didn't make it out," Carmello said.

"He died ensuring we all made it out. Some of us, anyway. Two Blazers fell in the battle to remove the Plaguemaster as well. He had a full party of Shadowers Guild folks with him."

Nora abruptly reached across the table to clutch his hand. "That must have been so awful, Glenn."

"I survived." He took a steadying breath. "And thanks to the efforts of those Blazers and the heroism of Zack Silverstone, Wolfpine remained unharmed. The Plaguemaster was removed, the plague was dispersed, and everyone in Wolfpine and in Grassea lived as a result."

Terry nodded solemnly. "I won't say I regret every ill word I've ever spoken about the man, because that would be dishonest. What I can say is that the way he met the Forever Death is one for our history books." Terry raised his mug. "To Zack Silverstone."

Carmello raised his mug as well. When Glenn attempted to do so, he found Nora still clutching his hand. She abruptly released it.

"I'm sorry," she said again. "Is Anna going to be all right?"

"She's taking it day by day. She's a survivor."

Glenn raised his own mug, and after fumbling for hers, Nora grabbed hers as well. He, Nora, Terry, and Carmello all clinked loudly, then took a long drink. Carmello set down his mug and eyed Glenn calmly. "That was delicious. Can you thank our host for this fine meal?"

Terry scoffed. "You can't still be thinking of keeping your appointment."

"Of course I can." Carmello scowled at him. "Terry, it's Misty Slateswallow."

As Glenn stared at him, he chuckled. His laughter grew more difficult to contain as he stared at the three of them, who now watched him with more than a fair bit of trepidation. They must be wondering if he'd finally gone mad.

"Glenn?" Nora asked cautiously.

As he reined in his chuckles, Glenn wiped at one wet eye and shook his head. "It really is all right. I mean, it's Zack. If anyone would want you to enjoy a night with one of the most desired Entertainers in the world, it's Zack. In fact... he'd hate you for *not* enjoying it."

Carmello thumped his own knee and grinned. "That's right! We live for this day and the day after, not the past. If anyone understood that, it was Zack Silverstone. When I finally meet my end, on the battlefield or in bed, I'll find him and buy him a drink."

Terry sighed. "I suppose we are here to enjoy ourselves. Like many, I've often speculated that those who fall while climbing the ladder still watch and cheer us on from the beyond while enjoying the finest of food and drink. Perhaps Zack is even watching us now."

Carmello grinned. "If he *is* watching me, he'll have a rather entertaining night."

Nora gasped. "That's just... ew, Gods. Did you have to talk about it that way?"

Carmello rose. "I'm drunk and horny, and I have a beautiful woman waiting for me. Glenn, always a pleasure. Please, enjoy the rest of the night with your own girls."

"They're not…" Glenn frowned. "I'm with Becka, and just Becka."

Carmello winked at Nora and sauntered off. "Oh, I wasn't talking about Anna."

From the table, Nora glared daggers at Carmello.

The big man waved. "Have a great night, you all!"

Terry rose as well, then sketched an elegant bow. "Glenn, I'll take my leave now as well. Once again, my condolences on your loss. We'll be in town for the duration of the cup, so if you'd like to call upon us and enjoy another meal, we'll return the favor."

Glenn raised his mug. "It was great to see you too, Terry. Be safe."

"I do my best." Terry walked off and lightly thumped Nora's shoulder as he walked past. "You'll settle the tab?"

She batted his hand away. "Don't I always?"

"Anna's paying for our meal tonight," Glenn reminded them both.

Terry winked at Glenn. "Even so, I'm certain our party can contribute *something*. Now, I'm off to my next adventure!" He walked off with an eager smile on his face.

Nora rolled her eyes. "Do you ever want to *kill* your party members?"

Glenn chuckled. "That's how I often felt with Zack."

Once again, just as events had played out a half year ago in Wolf-pine, Glenn found himself alone with a sweet, lovely, and generous Nora Rapidbloom. She was now looking at him with sympathy that warmed his heart. She truly was one of the kindest people he'd ever met.

He rose, stepped around the table, and opened his arms. "It would be best if I go check on Becka and Anna. But if you'd like, before you leave, I wouldn't turn down a hug."

Nora darted close and tossed her arms around him. As they embraced—as friends—she smiled up at him. "You're a hero too, you know. I'd bet Zack would agree with me."

"I have my moments." He eased her away. "Now, good night. We'll see you bright and early tomorrow to register for doubles. With your help, I think we can excel at them."

Nora took two steps back and nodded eagerly. "I won't let you down."

"You never have."

She gasped, then shoved a hand into her **[Unfilled Bag]**. "Oh! But what can I pay for?"

"Nothing is necessary, I assure you."

"But this meal must be expensive!"

"And Anna is quite comfortable paying for it. She might not have mentioned it, but she's also a Blazer now, as is Becka, and... they... have all the resources they need to adventure safely and with fine gear. Not everyone is so lucky. So please, Nora, let tonight be our treat."

Nora reluctantly removed her hand from her bag. "I suppose that'd be all right. But... you'll apologize to Anna for us? About my boorishly insensitive friends?"

"None of you knew about Zack, and I know Terry didn't mean anything by what he said. Anna won't hold tonight against any of you. Even so, I promise I'll check up on her and make sure she's all right. That's what Becka is doing right now."

Nora smiled again. "Then... good night, Glenn. Next time I'm at a chapel, I'll offer a prayer for Zack as well. If he's listening."

Glenn remembered his last conversation with his good friend in the void of his dreams as they discussed how Soulseer worked. "I'm certain he is."

Nora waved happily and then hurried away. He turned and scanned the crowd that still filled the large tavern. He soon spotted Anna and Becka huddled in a corner, close together and speaking. Becka glanced his way. She shook her head.

She was still talking with Anna. She had the situation under control. As Glenn belatedly caught their server watching him like a Grasshawk from the bar, he realized she had just seen all five members of their party leave the table after consuming a great deal of food and mead. She must be preparing to call the guards if Glenn, too, made a run for it.

He waved at their server, smiled widely, and sat back down. She eyed him for another moment with obvious suspicion, then went back to wiping down the bar.

This was all that was required of him for the moment. It would be up to Glenn to guard the table until Becka and Anna returned. He took another long swig of mead, took one more casual glance around the tavern, and settled in for a long wait.

FIFTEEN
A CROWD WELL ARRANGED

B ecka, fortunately, was as good at comforting Anna as she was at everything else. Soon they returned to the table, and after Anna settled their bill, they all left the tavern and crossed the crowded town of Sun's Cross to their lodgings for the night. The Dancing Skitterer.

While the mood in the town was boisterous, the mood among Glenn, Becka, and Anna was far more subdued. He had been so busy drinking and enjoying himself that he'd forgotten the reason he'd come here in the first place. He did want to expose the corrupt members of the church and bring them to justice, but he was really here for Zack. To save Zack.

Could he do it? He had options in the dueling brackets, singles and doubles. He could likely also enter at least one Monster battle contest, though unless he planned to fight one naked using a frying pan, he doubted he'd impress the judges. And Becka, of course, could tackle the Luminous Maze and, with luck, place among the finalists.

They only needed to win a few events to save Zack, but what if they didn't? What would they do if they failed to place in all the events they entered? If this whole gambit failed?

They would, Glenn supposed, simply go back to leveling the old-fashioned way. He, Becka, and whoever chose to help them would remain here in Stillwatch and level as fast as they possibly could. Even a two-week trip back to Evolan would cut into their remaining time too deeply, and Glenn had noticed that far fewer Adventurers hunted here.

That was due to the parched environment. And the lack of water. And all the Monsters that inflicted poison.

Evolan was cool, covered in water, and filled with vibrant color. Stillwatch was parched, hot, dangerous, and inhospitable. As Glenn reflected on where he'd decided to level, he wondered if he had been pushing himself as hard as he should have been.

Blazers didn't shy away from tough challenges, and he now wondered if that was precisely what he'd been doing by remaining in Evolan for so long. Why compete with so many other Adventurers that he was lucky to kill six Monsters a day? Had he been afraid of traveling to a less inhospitable zone and trying his luck there?

He set his jaw as Anna led the way into the Dancing Skitterer and then up the stairs. By remaining in Evolan, he'd remained in Lakebrooke, and by remaining in Lakebrooke, he'd trained under Brennon Shadesinger. Completing investigations had gained him a huge amount of experience he would otherwise have missed out on had he left Evolan.

He had done everything he could to complete this unfair Quest bestowed by the Gods. He was still doing everything he could to save his best friend. If he failed after going to all this effort, Zack wouldn't blame him. Nor would Glenn blame himself.

And he would ensure that Anna Bronzelight, in particular, followed the same course.

Once they had settled into their room which, as Anna had promised, had two beds, Anna set her pack on the bed and then walked to the door leading to the private privy. She entered and closed it behind her. Only then did Becka tiptoe over and throw her arms around him, and Glenn gratefully hugged her tight. He rubbed her back.

"I should have told them. In private."

Becka squeezed him. "I could have told them as well."

"You didn't know them. I did. I should have thought about it, but I was too befuddled by being called Glenn Redwood again. I was an idiot to take that enchanted necklace off."

"Yet your idiocy has given me days to ogle the man I love *as* the man I love, so your decisions have benefited us both." She pulled him down for a kiss that lingered, then eased away. "Anna is just fine. The only reason she reacted as she did was the shock of hearing Zack's name from the lips of others and the considerable amount of mead she'd imbibed. His death will never stop hurting her, but she's had time to adjust. She remains strong."

Glenn hugged Becka close. "So strong. Much stronger than I'd be if I ever lost you."

"If it helps, if I lost you, I believe I could carry on."

Glenn chuckled. "You always were remarkably resilient."

She kissed his chest. "But I would forever miss you. I would think of you every day."

"I think it's best if neither of us die and we simply grow old together."

She pulled him in for another kiss, then smiled. "On that, my love, we agree."

With nothing else to do while Anna was occupying the privy, Glenn took Becka's hand and led her to their bed. They settled into it fully clothed, with their boots dangling off it, and cuddled contentedly until the door to the privy opened once more. As Anna emerged wearing a modest white nightgown with her blonde hair tied up, Glenn scooted away from Becka.

Anna raised a palm. "You don't have to do that with me. I'm not going to fall to pieces every time I see a young couple canoodling in public. You two can canoodle all you like."

Glenn blushed and settled back into bed. "Sorry about tonight's supper."

"And I'm sorry about how I reacted." Anna brushed one hand through her hair. "I hope they weren't too upset?"

"Not at all. They were worried they'd upset you."

"Tell them I'm fine next time you see them. And we'll see Nora tomorrow, yes?"

Glenn smiled. "I hope so. With a talented Lifecaster, we really could crush doubles."

"I'm eager to get started." Anna frowned. "Still, of all the luck! The only three Adventurers in all of Luxtera who know Glenn Redwood by face and name happened to get in line behind us in a crowd of hundreds as we entered Sun's Cross. The Gods test us some days."

Becka snorted. "For some of us, it's every day."

Anna padded across the room to her bed. "Still, I'm glad we have this Quest. Narrow as our chances might be, I can still hope."

"I've been thinking about that," Glenn said. "Even if we don't win enough contests to level me to 15, I think I'd like to remain here in Stillwatch after the cup. It's not a pleasant zone, but that also means the competition for Monsters isn't as fierce as in Evolan. I'm going to stay here after the cup and level where I can be sure I have plenty of targets."

Anna settled on her own bed. "Would the Blazers allow that?"

Becka tapped her lips in thought. "Normally not. But if we remind them that Evolan's people could be the victims of a calamity if Glenn doesn't level fast enough, they might be amenable to changing his zone. But what about your training with Brennon?"

"I could tackle investigation Quests here, couldn't I? In her letter, Jenny said she suspected that Marion was impressed by my part in uncovering that hole in the wall of Lakebrooke. Jenny also said she's certain Brennon is going to accept me as a Truth Seeker. Why not continue my training here as an independent investigator?"

"I imagine Stillwatch could always use more Truth Seekers," Anna agreed. "And we could level together. I haven't had as much difficulty finding Monsters in Holbeck as you've encountered in Evolan, but the competition is still there. If I mention your argument about what fertile hunting ground Stillwatch could be to the Blazers, they might allow me to stay."

"Both of you need to reach 15 as fast as possible," Becka said. "The Blazers were having you level apart so that the church couldn't snatch you both up at once if they found out, but that's far less likely all the way out here."

Glenn grinned. "I'm liking this idea more and more. So, let's keep it in our back pocket. We are still going to do everything we can to place in singles and doubles, and whatever other contests we can enter. We *will* win experience scrolls. But that isn't our only option, which means we can stress just a bit less. It's not over until my Quest timer expires."

Anna smiled from her bed. "Thank you, Glenn. That's... helpful." She swept her sheets aside and slipped her legs under them. "Now, if it's all the same to you two, I could very much use some sleep. I'm fine with a lamp lit, so don't feel obligated to bed down yet."

Becka stretched both hands to the ceiling and yawned. "I'm actually quite tired as well. We're going to need to get up early tomorrow if we want to get in line in time to sign up for the dueling brackets and other events. We should all turn in early."

Anna rolled so her back was facing them and snuggled into bed. "I do think that's best. So... good night, you two. I'm very glad we managed to find each other."

"Us too." Becka glanced at Glenn and smiled coyly. "Bed?"

He smiled back. "I need to change into something softer."

"As do I." She gripped his hands, then slipped off the bed and pulled him up after her. Without a word, she led him toward the privy. The *private* privy.

Glenn glanced back at Anna as Becka dragged him on, but her back remained to them and her shoulder rose and fell steadily. Was she... was she already asleep?

Becka opened the door to the privy and pulled him, then closed it silently. As she pressed him against the door with her soft body, he realized they weren't going to sleep yet. But really? In the privy? While Anna was in the next room?

That was wrong in every way he could think of. Which was likely why Becka was gazing up at him with such a naughty grin.

The next morning, Glenn woke before sunup with Becka draped across him and snuggled under the fine covers of their fine bed. Despite its unusual and somewhat disturbing name, the Dancing Skitterer was a lovely tavern. This bed was like a cloud.

Careful not to wake Becka, Glenn slipped out of bed, stretched, and padded to the privy to relieve himself. After he'd freshened up, he emerged to find Anna already up as well, and also fully dressed. How had she done that? Had she been waiting for him to leave the room?

Becka was still entirely passed out, but Anna barely batted an eye at her. As she rose and reached for her **[Unfilled Bag]**, she looked their way.

"I'll meet you downstairs. We should have another hour before they let people line up to sign up for events, so we should grab a quick breakfast beforehand. We could be in line for more than a few hours, and I'm not sure they let you hold a place."

Glenn nodded. "We'll see you downstairs."

Once Anna was gone, he roused Becka with a gentle nudge, a less gentle nudge, and then a hard squeeze. She grumbled and moaned before finally rolling out of bed.

Becka had never been a morning person, and despite their vow to go to bed early last night, things hadn't worked out as they wished. Or rather... they had worked out exactly as they wished. Becka was responsible for her own actions.

Still, Becka knew how important this morning was, and Glenn left her to stumble into the privy and wake up. Meanwhile, he pulled on his special mace carrier and Becka (his mace) and strapped on his shield as well. He refused to go anywhere without those, especially now. Sooner than he expected, Becka was ready, and then they joined Anna downstairs.

After a brief breakfast of warm bread and warm stew, they left the Dancing Skitterer just as the first smear of red appeared on the darkened horizon. Glenn was surprised to find the streets already quite crowded.

He supposed that was simply what life was like in a city that normally hosted two thousand and now had close to ten. The <Sandsea Cup> attracted people from across the entirety of Luxtera, and there were likely three zones' worth here now.

Once they reached the gates to the newly constructed arena grounds outside Sun's Cross proper, Glenn was unsurprised to find two Town Guards on duty at a single sturdy wooden gate. The fence around the grounds of the cup wouldn't stop a determined Adventurer, but the other Town Guards standing at attention inside it would.

Glenn suspected almost the entire garrison of Sun's Cross had turned out to run security for this event, and he felt a bit wistful as he imagined what his life might have been like if he'd ever gotten to do something like that back in Wolfpine. He had attended <Dina's Hunt> back in Grassea, but he'd done so as a boy of common age, not a full-grown Town Guard.

There was a large square built off the town that visually connected it with the grounds of the cup, and it was filled to the brim with people by the time Glenn arrived. As he spotted a few people currently breaking down tents and stuffing them into [Unfilled Bag]s, he realized they must have camped out here overnight. He should have thought of that!

Still, they couldn't fill all the brackets in a day, could they? There had to be enough events going on here to justify the massive Adventurer and Townsfolk presence. They would find spaces in the events they desired. As he, Becka, and Anna reached the back of the crowd, Glenn realized his problem. He had no idea how to find Nora.

Was she even here yet? If she was, she could be buried in the crowd milling ahead. He scanned the sea of bobbing hoods, heads, and helmets for Nora's distinctive red hair, but while he found several red-headed individuals, none were the woman he was looking for. He was still scanning the crowd when a heavy hand clapped him on the shoulder.

Glenn jumped and glanced at his unexpected guest, then grinned. "Carmello!"

Carmello stepped back and grinned. "Bright and early, just as promised."

"You're entering the dueling as well?"

"Terry and I are tackling the 16-20 doubles. But I'm not the one you're here to meet."

Someone gently touched his back. As Glenn turned to face her, he smiled with relief. "Good morning, Nora."

"Morning, Glenn!" Nora beamed at them and then looked at Becka and Anna, who had turned to confirm her presence. "I hope you haven't been waiting long."

"We just got here," Becka said. "Thank you again for agreeing to join us."

"I'm happy to be here! And... I'm so sorry about last night."

"You have nothing to apologize for," Anna said firmly. She looked at Carmello, then at Anna again. "While I wasn't entirely prepared to hear his name last night, learning you both knew Zack last night is a comfort. I'm glad you knew him. It's another reminder of all the lives he touched before... what Glenn spoke to you about."

In his head, Glenn could almost hear Zack's joke. *That's not all I touched.*

He chuckled quietly to himself. When Becka glanced quizzically at him, he shrugged and mouthed *"Tell you later."*

Carmello walked past him to look over the crowd. "That's a lot of people."

Glenn grimaced as Nora formed up on his left side and Becka pressed close on the right. Anna joined their observation as Glenn felt suddenly pensive. He glanced at Anna.

"There's six level brackets, right? And not everyone here is level 10-15! They can't possibly fill all those slots in one morning."

"That's right," Anna said confidently. "Anyone below 10 cannot compete, so the brackets range from 10-15 to 36-40. We'll find slots. Only those who arrive tomorrow will have trouble. It's going to be a wait this morning, but I don't think we'll miss out on anything."

Carmello shook his head. "I hope you're right. Regardless, I now leave the best Lifecaster I've ever partied with in your hands. Bring her back to us in one piece."

Nora slapped his arm. "When have you ever said I was the best at anything?"

"I never say it." Carmello grinned down at her. "But I think it every day."

Nora rolled her eyes. "You *are* in a good mood. Your appointment went well?"

"Misty certainly thinks it did." The big man waved. "Now have fun, folks! I'm off to sign up for myself and Terry. I think I'll snag a slot in the Demon Fighting Exhibition as well. Put that Demonslaying enchantment to good use."

Glenn's eyes widened as Carmello walked away, and then he glanced at Anna. "People actually fight Demons in the **<Sandsea Cup>**? I thought only Monsters were involved?"

Anna eyed him curiously. "Why did you think that?"

"I guess... Demons can't appear inside the town walls, right?"

"Nor can Monsters. That's why the Builders erected the grounds for the cup outside the city proper. The walls they've built hold back the Monsters and Demons of Stillwatch, but not those marked by special collars or encased in special gems."

Glenn nodded as he remembered. "Demon crystals."

"You know a bit about those, don't you?"

He shuddered as he remembered throwing himself into a group of three angry Shaitans as they converged on an exhausted Zack and an unconscious Anna. "I do, a bit. But how do they ensure the Demons don't escape once released? It's not like a fence can contain them."

"Special containment rings created by Shamanists. They're not just here to cast [-Resurrect-]s and heal people after duels. They also create rings the Demons can't escape."

Glenn thought back to the Skill Jacob Coverfall had used in the Temple of Balance back in Grassea to hold off a Devourer from the Six Hells. [-Deterrence Circle-]. That had kept Demons from entering the circle, so it made sense another circle could lock them inside.

Perhaps Shamanists had a Skill that could trap Demons. He would need to look that up later. He didn't *need* to know, but once he wondered about something this, he couldn't stop.

Becka touched his arm. "I think they might be close to making an announcement."

Glenn's attention snapped to the two Town Guards at the closed gate to the grounds of the cup. Given all the people between them and him, Glenn could only see their helmets, but as one man stepped forward, he knew what Skill the Town Guard was about to use.

[-Public Address-]. That pre-requisite to [-Arrest-] would make this Town Guard heard far and wide. Glenn had that Skill himself, though he didn't have it slotted at the moment.

The Town Guard's voice boomed over the gathered crowd. "Attention, Adventurers! If you've come to register for the events of the <Sandsea Cup>, you're in the right place! Fifteen minutes from now, we will open this gate! We would like you to line up in a fashion we've devised! We will start admitting Adventurers by the letters of their last names!"

Glenn had wondered how the Town Guards were going to form this giant and unruly crowd into an orderly line that could be admitted and sent to the sign-up tables. Was it really going to be as simple as alphabetical order? He supposed simple *was* easy to manage.

"To keep things fair, the letter of the alphabet on which we'll start was chosen at random last night!" the Town Guard bellowed. "That letter is G! So, all Adventurers with a last name starting with G, make your way to the front of the crowd! H's should follow that, and then I's, and so on! I hope most of you people know the alphabet!"

An all but deafening chorus of cheers, groans, and boos erupted from the huge crowd gathered to enter the grounds of the cup. People jostled each other as they shuffled about. Glenn acknowledged the wisdom in making this announcement fifteen minutes before the gates actually opened. That would give everyone time to get more or less in a good order.

Becka elbowed him. "Lucky you."

As Glenn eyed the huge crowd and imagined the challenges involved in keeping it organized and contained, he felt almost jealous of those Town Guards. It would be tough to organize this crowd, but oh so satisfying. He missed his own Class in that moment.

"He does have the God's own luck," Anna said ruefully. "Maybe they do have their fingers on the scales after all."

Still distracted by how difficult this all must be to organize for the Town guards, Glenn glanced at his companions. "Did I miss something?"

Becka eyed him. "I don't know. Did you, *Gray*breaker?"

Glenn gasped, and then he glanced at Nora in alarm. She still thought he was Glenn Redwood! He hadn't thought to explain that he was using a different last name because he couldn't think of any reason it would be pertinent. Now the alphabet was involved!

Nora glanced at Glenn and smiled. "Hmm? What is it?"

Becka touched his arm again. "How about I explain to her?"

Glenn nodded with relief. "Thanks."

Nora eyed Becka curiously. "Explain what?"

"There's one more interesting element of our Blazer Quest. I've told you we wished it to remain secret, and that we're traveling in disguise. For that reason, Glenn will register under a different name than his own. Rest assured, it's all above board."

Nora eyed them doubtfully. "This mission of yours gets stranger with each detail."

"Oh, trust me, I've noticed." Becka pressed her hand hard against Glenn's back. "Now, get up there. On to the front!"

Glenn balked. "But what about Nora? R will put her all the way in the back."

"You can register *for* her, silly. Only the leader of the group for doubles needs to sign up for them. That means you can register Nora and yourself for doubles first thing."

"But..." Glenn blinked. "What if we end up facing you and Anna in doubles?"

Becka patted his arm. "I promise we'll be gentle."

Glenn glanced at Nora. "I like this plan! Provided you haven't changed your mind?"

Nora winced. "I want to, but I worry. What if I let you all down?"

Glenn rested one hand on her thin shoulder. "I have complete faith in you. We took down a Winnower together, remember? And then a desouled Vulpor."

She wrinkled her nose. "You took down the Winnower. I just got a bad kiss."

"A kiss?" Becka's lips quirked. "No one told me about a kiss."

Nora backpedaled, eyes wide. "I mean the Winnower kissed me! To take my blood!"

"But didn't Glenn say the Demon resembled me at the time? Did *we* kiss?"

"It only looked like you to Glenn! To me... it looked..." She glanced at Anna, then blushed furiously.

Anna lightly cleared her throat. "Let's settle into our places in line. We only have fifteen minutes. I see no reason we shouldn't do everything we can to help the Town Guards."

"Yes!" Nora blinked rapidly. "Yes, let's do that." She looked to Glenn. "So... duos?"

He released her shoulder. "I would be honored to fight at your side."

Nora took a deep breath, then smiled again. "Me too."

SIXTEEN
A DUELIST BLOODIED

Glenn learned when he arrived that the Builders of the <Sandsea Cup> had set up a fenced-in area the size of Wolfpine for dueling to take place. It was split into dozens upon dozens of square dueling arenas. Each arena looked to be about twenty paces across and square, with five thick wooden poles planted in an X to provide limited cover from ranged attacks. They looked to have been made from trees chopped from the local woods.

The poles would not hinder his movement through the dueling square, but he could put one between him and a [-Burn-] or [-Freeze-] projectile if he timed it right. Which, as a Soulseer, he could easily do. He would know exactly when a caster completed their Skill. Again, it wasn't quite fair to the caster... but this Quest from the Gods wasn't quite fair.

Sixteen Adventurers had gathered around the dueling square to which Glenn now reported, square A4. A survey of the other fields allowed him to estimate that a similar number of Adventurers were gathered around their own assigned squares. So many 10-15 hopefuls were on the dueling field today! No wonder the qualifiers took several days.

Since Glenn had arrived, his gaze and that of the other Adventurers had remained fixed on a tall man in white robes. Their officiant. Nervous butterflies filled Glenn's stomach as he waited, but finally, as if responding to some silent call, the officiant raised a hand.

"The singles qualifiers will now begin!" As the man spoke, Glenn was vaguely aware of many other officiants saying similar things. "As you should know by now, this is a single elimination bracket! Once you lose any single duel, you're out!"

Glenn knew that fact too well. It would ratchet up the pressure on everyone participating. It was also a necessity in a contest with such a huge number of participants.

"The winner will be decided thus! The duel will end when one party falls unconscious, calls for a yield, or is unable to continue! For those of you who have never dueled before, know that if your Health falls low enough, the Gods will end your duel at once!"

That was one small comfort. Glenn knew a plethora of Spiritualists were on hand in case anyone died, to use [-Resurrect-] so they wouldn't meet the Forever Death, but even with the duel ending the moment someone fell to low Health, deaths might still occur. Someone could tumble over and hit their head or break their neck.

"Who you will duel from this group was randomly chosen last night, as was the order in which you will duel! Whichever one of you wins all three of your duels in this group will merge into a new group of people with similar success from other groups!"

Just how many level 10-15s had signed up for the singles bracket? Given nothing prevented them from signing up for singles and doubles, and the bracket qualifiers were staggered so as not to overlap, Glenn expected it would be... well, everyone with the coin.

"While you can step away after your duels, I won't recommend it, because if you're not here when I call you for your next one, you will be automatically disqualified!"

Glenn had no intention of going out like that. He planned to stay as long as he could and observe the other fighters. He had done precious little dueling in his time, so even if he wouldn't be facing the people he observed, he still needed to know common tactics.

"I will now call the first Adventurers from group A Four! Contestant Eliot L, if you are present, step onto the field! Contestant Glenn G, if you are present, step onto the field!"

So, Glenn would be the first to duel today. Even so, no one stepped onto the field. As Glenn swept his eyes across the crowd of Adventurers gathered around the field, he decided it would be up to him to act first. He wasn't going to see how far he could push the officiant.

His opponent wanted to see who he would be facing before stepping into the ring before entering himself. A power play? Or simply curiosity?

The officiant looked around impatiently. "Contestant Eliot L, step onto the field. Contestant Glenn G—"

"Here!" Glenn stepped into the dueling square. He would offer his opponent the small satisfaction of entering second. Unlike him, his opponent couldn't see his Status Sheet with the use of a Skill. He looked to the officiant. "Contestant Glenn G, present."

A dark-haired man stepped from the crowd and into the dueling square. "Contestant Eliot L, present." The man offered Glenn a sly smile. "Sorry you had to end up facing me. I'll make it quick so you'll have plenty of time to go have more fun."

Glenn offered no quip in reply. Becka had suggested he shouldn't quip. Instead, he visually sized up his opponent. It bothered him that he would be cheating today (technically) by using [-**Soul Scan-**] to anticipate his opponent's every move, but Zack needed this. Needed him.

The officiant spoke again. "Take your places in the colored squares! Glenn G, red square! Eliot L, blue square! You may commence your duel at your discretion, but neither of you can leave your square once you enter it until your duel begins."

While Glenn's opponent was noticeably muscular, Eliot had a taut athleticism that suggested speed and agility rather than raw power. He kept his black hair cut in a tail across his head, with the sides of his tan head bald. He also smiled a bit too confidently, a bit too smugly, which, to Glenn, suggested he was nervous about facing a muscular Brutalist in **[Steel Armor]**.

Eliot's own choice of armor was unusual. The man wore a dark bandana across his mouth and nose as well as **[Dusk Leather]** armor, which made no sense for an Adventurer who had registered as level 14. Glenn pondered the reasons why his opponent might choose such armor for this duel. Was it simply a matter of finances or, in this case, having none?

[Dusk Leather] armor was available to Adventurers as early as level 5, and while it was good armor for a mobile class that was just starting out (like a Duelist or a Shadower) it offered poor protection relative to the Monsters an Adventurer would face in their early teens... let alone a "Brutalist" like Glenn. Even against Glenn's weighted **[Commoner's Mace]**, that **[Dusk Leather]** would be about as useful as parchment. Perhaps his opponent intended not to get hit.

Eliot also had two **[Iron Dagger]**s sheathed on his belt. The combination of his opponent's build, armor, and weapons screamed Shadower, but the weapons didn't match the man. As Glenn considered all he'd learned as a Truth Seeker while completing large and small investigations for Brennon Shadesinger, he fixated on why these details bothered him.

A Shadower of level 14 who had acquired enough coin to pay the entrance fee for singles would almost certainly have acquired enough coin to afford a better set of armor. Eliot would have had great difficulty surviving to level 14 in level 5 armor. In addition, the **[Iron Dagger]**s on Eliot's belt (or more accurately, their leather sheathes) gleamed as if brand new. Had Eliot's daggers seen years of use, those sheathes would be more weathered.

Also, **[Iron Dagger]**s were usable as early as level 5, which suggested the ludicrous idea that Eliot had fought with these daggers for nine levels. The obvious lack of wear and tear on both the sheathes and the daggers themselves argued against that. Yet if Eliot had recently replaced his daggers, why buy iron instead of the superior steel variety?

As Glenn and his first opponent sized each other up and the officiant for their qualifier moved into position to act as referee, Glenn saw through the illusion. His opponent was not a Shadower. His opponent wanted Glenn to *think* he was facing a Shadower. The armor, the daggers, the swagger... it was like Becka's **[-Masquerade-]** Skill. A grand illusion.

The man standing across from him must have recently bought that **[Dusk Leather]** and those **[Iron Dagger]**s because the items were relatively cheap by the standards of a successful level 14. Eliot wanted to make prospective opponents think he was a Shadower and mentally prepare to fight a Shadower, then surprise them with Skills they wouldn't expect.

Yet by entering the dueling ring without armor or weapons that were appropriate to his Class, fooling Glenn into thinking he was a

Shadower wouldn't benefit Eliot. Even if Eliot was secretly a Harm-caster, he would get perhaps one good strike with **[-Burn-]** or **[-Freeze-]** before being overwhelmed by Glenn's attacks. Deception of this sense only made sense if...

Glenn felt a rush of satisfaction. There was one Class that had no need for armor or weapons. In fact, heavy armor and weapons would only impair that particular Class in battle. Eliot was an Anchorite masquerading as a Shadower.

Eliot likely intended to allow Glenn to strike him repeatedly and successfully in combat, miming pain and silently healing himself with **[-Aura Mend-]**. Meanwhile, each blow he absorbed increased his Strength by 2. Glenn would think he was winning until Eliot grew so powerful he could manhandle even a fully armored opponent into submission.

It was a clever ploy. It was also the only explanation for Eliot's choice of gear that made sense, and having now figured out his opponent's strategy for this duel, Glenn finally felt justified in validating his suspicions with his own deceptive Skill.

It wasn't *entirely* cheating if he'd figured out his opponent's plan with his own senses.

[-Soul Scan-].

Name: Eliot Longspear
Age: 20
Level: 14
Class: Anchorite
HP: 210/210
Blood: 80/80
Experience: 108,244/112,000
Strength: 20
Divinity: 10
Vitality: 21
Wisdom: 8
Prowess: 14
Luck: 6

Gear:

- **Uncommon: [Dusk Leather]**
- **Uncommon: [Leather Boots]**
- **Uncommon: [Iron Dagger]**
- **Uncommon: [Iron Dagger]**
- **Common: [Silk Bandana]**

Slotted Skills:

- **Uncommon: [-Aura Mend-]** (Anchorite / Ansin)
- **Uncommon: [-Adrenaline Rush-]** (Anchorite / Ansin)
- **Uncommon: [-Bracing Blow-]** (Anchorite / Ansin)
- **Uncommon: [-Haymaker-]** (Anchorite / Ansin)
- **Uncommon: [-Stone Punch-]** (Anchorite / Ansin)

Slotted Blessings:

- **Uncommon: [+Numb+]** (Anchorite / Ansin)
- **Uncommon: [+Fighter's Balance+]** (Anchorite / Ansin)

Known Skills:

- **Uncommon: [-Pummel-]** (Anchorite / Ansin)

Known Blessings:

- None

Quests:

- None

As the officiant who would serve as their referee called out "Contestants! Ready yourselves!" Eliot tauntingly drew both daggers. As expected.

Glenn focused on Eliot. "Duel me."

A spectral flag sent by the Gods dropped between them in the center of the field.

Eliot grinned hungrily. "I consent to this duel."

The officiant knifed one hand downward. "Fight!"

Eliot darted forward with all the speed and agility Glenn would expect from an actual Shadower. Shadowers had Skills that would allow their daggers to pierce thick armor or slide between its plates. That would make anyone who thought they were fighting a Shadower while wearing armor nervous about getting struck.

Glenn wasn't nervous about having his armor pierced. He knew Eliot had no piercing Skills. Even so, he reflexively blocked the initial flurry of dagger blows. Knife tips clattered like rain on Lillian Stoutcrag's enchanted **[Steel Shield]**. While the blows were no threat, allowing them to land would still count against him in the eyes of the officiant.

Eliot leapt forward and made a wide swipe, but Glenn easily sidestepped the blow. He found himself with a perfect opportunity to slam what seemed to be an overeager Shadower in the side with his mace. If he'd done so, Eliot would no doubt stumble off howling as if in pain.

That would be Glenn's first mistake. As he celebrated striking the first blow, Eliot would silently use **[-Aura Mend-]** to heal any damage Glenn had inflicted and gain 2 points of Strength. Now that Glenn had guessed Eliot's game, this was all blindingly obvious.

Glenn didn't strike with his mace. Instead, he simply allowed Eliot to "recover." He sidestepped around to stay within the arena as Eliot, slightly surprised that his "overreach" hadn't been exploited, and attacked again. Glenn suspected any swing he took would connect with his opponent (by his opponent's choice) and debated his options as he circled and blocked.

He knew Eliot was attempting to deceive him both through visual inspection and his Soulseer Skill, but how could he use that information? The judges might ask about his battle afterward and could become suspicious of him if he seemed to know things he could not. They wouldn't suspect him of being a Soulseer, since they had no idea Soulseers existed, but they could easily suspect him of cheating in another way. Like paying someone off.

When Eliot again intentionally overextended himself, hoping to draw another attack, Glenn obliged him by striking out with his **[Steel Mace]**... but he went for Eliot's leg instead of his thigh. The crunch of bone was audible to everyone inside and outside the circle.

No one could miss that a Shadower would have been badly impaired by the blow.

Eliot howled in what sounded like very real pain as his Health Bar appeared. He stumbled away, barely keeping his feet, and in Glenn's enhanced sight, Eliot silently activated [-Aura Mend-]. Eliot kept his feet despite a blow that by all rights should have shattered his shin, and while he made a show of limping away as if badly injured, Glenn could already tell that he had lost almost no mobility. Certainly not what one would lose to a mace strike.

The officiant should be able to see that as well.

Glenn took a step back as if surprised by what he'd just noticed. To the officiant, it would appear as if he, too, had just noticed that Eliot was still walking around despite taking a blow to the shin. A blow like that should have him either down holding his broken shin or bouncing on one leg, but he was still walking. Anyone could see that.

Glenn now had a way to explain his suspicions... but needed more. He checked Eliot's Status Sheet again and confirmed what he'd suspected. Eliot's Strength was now 22. It had increased by 2 when Glenn struck, and yet despite taking a blow that should have shattered his shin, his Health was back to full.

If not for [+Unyielding+], Glenn's Town Guard Skill that granted him 10 extra Strength so long as he carried a shield, Eliot would be almost as strong as Glenn was now. He could easily exceed Glenn's Strength after absorbing a few more blows. At that point, wrestling Glenn to the ground and forcing him into a submission hold would be a straightforward ploy.

Eliot visibly ground his teeth and danced forward with a stumble that wasn't quite convincing. An Adventurer focused on Eliot's daggers or glare might have missed it, but Glenn was focused on his feet.

When Eliot struck again, Glenn purposely swept aside his shield. Eliot was too surprised to slow, landing a strike with his [Iron Dagger] directly in Glenn's chest. The weapon sheared off Glenn's [Steel Armor] with a loud clang.

The dagger didn't come anywhere near penetrating, even though a Shadower who hoped to take down an armored opponent should have used one of his Skills to ensure his blow penetrated thick armor. More proof Eliot wasn't the Class he seemed to be.

This time, Glenn didn't hit Eliot with his mace. Instead, he *pushed* Eliot with a wide swing of his shield. He did so forcefully enough that the blow would have easily sent any Adventurer, let alone one with a broken shin, onto his ass. Eliot stumbled back and reflexively kept his feet. As he did so, Glenn heard the crowd gasp and start to murmur.

Eliot had kept his balance perfectly even after Glenn shoved him with a shield bash, despite having a "broken shin." [+**Fighter's Balance**+], his Anchorite Blessing, and instincts honed through fourteen levels of absorbing strong blows had betrayed him. Eliot's body had reacted instinctively to ensure he kept his balance... and in doing so, his ruse became clear.

Glenn lowered both his shield and his mace. "Do you want to keep tapping away at me with those daggers? Or should we start the real duel now?"

Glenn swung Becka about in a grand flourish before tossing his mace out of the ring. As Eliot gawked (and the crowd gasped), Glenn also removed his shield from his arm. He strapped it across his back. He still had it equipped, so he would continue to gain the passive bonus from [+**Unyielding**+]. Then he raised both fists.

As Eliot's grimace widened into a grin, Glenn grinned back. It was clear to both of them now that Glenn had no intention of striking Eliot with his mace any longer, which meant Eliot was no longer going to be able to bait Glenn into making him stronger. It was also clear Eliot would prefer to fight this duel hand to hand.

"You've still wearing heavy armor," Eliot pointed out. "I'm not."

"True. If you promise to wait for me, I'll take it off."

Eliot chuckled and ended any playacting. He sheathed his daggers, took a confident stance, and rolled his head about on his shoulders. "That's all right. If we're going to end the duel with wrestling, I'd prefer you have heavy [**Steel Armor**] weighing you down."

"If that's what you wish. Wrestle to pin, best two of three?"

"I'm game for that if you are. You swear to honor that?"

"I so swear."

Eliot lunged with a loud, ferocious growl Glenn suspected Ashley would have appreciated. Unfortunately for Eliot, Glenn had learned to wrestle both from Joanne Dewcrest, one of Wolfpine's most skilled Town Guards, and Ashley Bloodbraid, who could take down Monsters bare-handed, and most Adventurers as well. Thanks to his refusal to bolster Eliot's Strength by striking him repeatedly in combat, Glenn was also much stronger.

Eliot fought and wrestled well, but he wasn't Glenn's equal. Glenn pinned him soon after, let Eliot accept it, then stood up. Eliot shook it off and attacked again, and shortly after, Glenn pinned him a second time. Two out of three, just as they'd agreed.

When Glenn rolled off Eliot and rose, Eliot rose as well. He looked to the officiant and raised a hand. "I yield the contest. End the duel."

Glenn saw no reason to draw this out. "I accept." It was now obvious to everyone that Glenn was both stronger and the better wrestler.

The spectral duel flag between them vanished with a soft crack of thunder, and many in the crowd sighed with audible disappointment. They'd hoped to see two competitors pummel each other into a bloody mess. Instead, they had watched a short and abbreviated wrestling match, one that had ended before either competitor was even knocked out.

The officiant raised one hand to grab the attention of the spectators. "The yield by Eliot L is archived. The winner is contestant Glenn G. Eliot L, it falls upon you to report the results to the chief officiant."

Before Glenn could offer his hand after the duel, Eliot stepped forward and offered his hand instead. "I never stood a chance, did I? How'd you figure it out so fast?"

Glenn was pleased to see his opponent being magnanimous, especially when he had no reason to be. He shook Eliot's hand firmly and was pleased when the man did the same. As they dropped hands, Glenn took a respectful step back.

"It was your gear that first alerted me. All I knew from the referee is that you were level 14, so I found the idea of a Shadower of that level entering a duel wearing low-level armor and wielding low-level daggers suspicious. After I saw you walk off a blow that would have cracked a Shadower's leg in half, I knew something was up."

Eliot blew out a heavy breath. "I considered buying some higher level gear for this ploy. Couldn't afford to blow that much coin on a gimmick strategy like this one."

"It was still a good strategy. If I had to guess, you were hoping I'd hit you until you'd gained enough Strength to take me down? Using [-**Aura Mend-**] to heal yourself? And once you were confident you could overpower me, you'd pin me?"

"Got it in one." Eliot chuckled. "Are you a seer, Glenn G?"

"I'm a Junior Blazer. I'm also in training to become a Truth Seeker."

"Gods! No wonder you saw through my ruse so easily. Just my luck to randomly draw a Blazer Truth Seeker as my first opponent when my strategy was to deceive someone. I've always had bad luck, back as far as I can remember."

Eliot wasn't wrong. His Luck attribute was among the lowest Glenn had ever seen on a level 14 Adventurer. He wondered why the Gods had chosen to limit him in that way. He also liked Eliot already, despite this deception attempt. It had been strategic, not underhanded.

Glenn nodded to show his respect for his opponent. "Either way, you devised a novel strategy, and I enjoyed our duel. Good luck in the rest of the cup."

"You too, Blazer. If I have time, I'll come watch some of your upcoming duels. You seem like you'll be fun to watch regardless of who wins."

Eliot left the circle to report his loss to the officiant keeping track of the singles qualifiers. The officiant beckoned Glenn over. When Glenn arrived, he inclined his head.

"Congratulations on your first win."

Glenn smiled. "Thank you."

"You should know this already, but so long as you continue to win today, you'll be expected to continue to duel." The officiant spoke loudly enough that other Adventurers nearby could hear. "You're free to take refreshment between duels, and also free to either pay for healers to restore your Stamina or have your own party members do so. You can also drink any potions you like so long as those potions won't persist into your next duel."

Glenn had read the regulations for dueling in the cup thoroughly. He knew all this, but he nodded to make sure the officiant *understood* he knew all of it. "So how many duels will I be engaging today? Assuming I continue to win?"

"I like your optimism. There's sixteen Adventurers in this group, and only one of you will be moving forward. You'll need to win two more duels to be that person. If you survive, you'll join another bracket of sixteen finalists. If you keep winning in that, you'll fight six duels today."

"And that qualifies me for the semi-finals?"

"The semi-finals of the qualifiers. Not quite the same. Still, don't get ahead of yourself. Focus on this duel by duel. And remember, because we're going to repeat this whole process for doubles tomorrow, you'll have a break before you have to do singles again."

Except he wouldn't, because he was also enrolled in doubles with Nora. Now he knew why the Scribe working at the signing table had asked if he was certain he wanted to sign up for singles *and* doubles. He wouldn't have time to rest. Fortunately, he had **[+Regrowth+]**.

"I understand." Glenn nodded to show his thanks. "I'll stop asking you questions now."

The officiant smiled blandly. "We do have more duels to get through."

SEVENTEEN
A PEEK BEHIND THE CURTAIN
BECKA

Hand in hand with Glenn, Becka jogged toward the muddy staging area at the edge of the **<Sandsea Cup>** grounds. Sadly, she was among the last of the would-be "maze runners" to arrive. She had hoped to have time to evaluate the maze she'd be running from the staging area before stepping into it, but showing up just before the start had been unavoidable.

Glenn's latest duel (which she'd taken pride in watching him win) had been scheduled shortly before she was supposed to report for the qualifying round of the Luminous Maze. While Glenn had defeated his opponent, a young level 13 Skirmisher, handily and efficiently, the Luminous Maze was built on the far side of the grounds from the dueling fields. As they jogged over after Glenn won his duel, Becka had worried she would be late.

Now, as she and Glenn slowed at the edge of the crowd, Becka saw she had been foolish to be worried. A crowd of maze runners had already gathered, chatting in small groups, but their early arrival offered no benefit. Ahead, an open field sat with long fences on two sides.

There were no trees in that huge field. There were no ditches one would have to traverse to proceed. While the field did have some gentle hills, traveling up and down those would be less taxing than climbing the slopes of the Dewdrop Hills back in Grassea.

The so-called "Luminous Maze" was nothing more than an empty field about half the size of Wolfpine. The only features other than the fences and grass were a few bobbing and swaying wildflowers of various colors, red and purple and white. At the far end of the field from Becka's current position stood a line of silk ribbons held up by posts.

This couldn't be all there was to it. The Luminous Maze was not a foot race... or was it? Anna had been very clear that participants had to traverse difficult terrain, solve complex problems, and both move and think on their feet to successfully traverse the maze.

As Becka looked around at those gathered to complete the first round of the maze (there would be two rounds in total) she felt her confidence flag. Given the popularity of the dueling and Monster fighting brackets, she'd hoped for less competition in the Luminous Maze. Yet there easily had to be over a hundred adventurers here, possibly even two hundred.

Becka had learned through gossip in the common room of the Dancing Skitterer that there would be four runnings of the first leg of the Luminous Maze today, organized by last name. Once again, the alphabet had betrayed her by placing her in the first group to run.

Other 10-15 Adventurers could quiz their 10-15 friends who'd run the maze before them about what to expect, but Becka would have no such benefit. The 16-20 crowd would run the maze tomorrow, and the 21-25 crowd would run it the day after that. There were no brackets above level 25 offered for the Luminous Maze.

Becka had speculated on why there were no brackets for higher levels when she signed up. Perhaps it was simply difficult, logistically, to organize more maze running than four times over three days. Even so, she wanted there to be more to it, if only because she could glean more information if she figured out why the brackets cut off at 25.

Regardless, Becka knew only a small number of those running the maze would qualify for the next (and final) round. Even if she did solve the maze and reach the end successfully, if she was too slow, she'd still be out. She would have to be smart, quick, and clever, but she did have one significant advantage all the other maze runners did not.

She had Glenn and his unique set of Skills to give her a head start.

Glenn gripped her hand and diverted her as they reached the back of the staging area, and Becka allowed herself to be diverted. Walking with Glenn, they found a shallow hill and ascended. That let them see over the large crowd of participants (easily over a hundred) to the large group of robed individuals gathered on the far side of one of the side fences.

Becka counted at least thirty individuals and one Town Guard in full **[God Armor]**. As she glanced at Glenn in curiosity, Glenn stared at the distant group of robed figures as well. His narrowed eyes suggested he was using **[-Soul Scan-]** to obtain their Classes, levels, and Skills. His lips moved silently as he read pages she couldn't see.

A moment later, he met her curious gaze. "Mindbenders, Guile-casters, and Arctists."

Becka nodded thoughtfully. "How many of each?"

"Of the eighteen Mindbenders gathered below, three of those are Preceptors. The others range from level 24 to level 38. Then there's twelve Guilecasters ranging from 14 to 20, and six Arctists ranging from 20 to 29. That's an awful lot of people to create a single maze."

Becka snorted. "That many Mindbenders could change a lot of minds."

Glenn eyed her with worry. "Will you have to consent to a duel? Multiple duels?"

"I don't think so. Suspending the Law of Consent between that many Adventurers and close to two hundred maze runners would take the entire day. It's simply not possible, logistically, so they must have slotted Skills they can use without violating the Law of Consent."

Glenn smiled in obvious relief. "What about Monsters? Demons? Will you face those?"

"There was no mention of Monsters or Demons as an obstacle in the maze. This was widely advertised as a challenge of wits, not combat. That said, none of the Class below need to attack a person directly to confuse or misdirect them. They can alter the environment."

"How do you mean?"

"An illusion need not be harmful to be effective. Mindbenders and Guilecasters can create all sorts of illusions, and Arctists can create ambient ice, snow, and rain. If you combined enough illusions with enough foul weather, you could create quite the maze." Becka tapped her lips. "And now we know why there's no brackets above 25."

Glenn smiled with the satisfaction of having solved a problem that vexed him before. "Anyone above 25 with a high Divinity attribute might see through the illusions and simply walk to the finish line." He sighed. "Doing this feels so wrong."

Becka couldn't help but giggle. "Just like last night."

"Quiet, you."

"So, love, what else can you tell me about my opponents today? Start with the Guilecasters and what Skills they have slotted. Anything you can tell me could help."

"Right. I'll try not to repeat any, but if I do, I'll trust you'll forgive me."

She squeezed his meaty bicep. "I'll try."

"[-Create Fog-], [-Mask Other-], [-Transpose-], [-Phantom Mirror-], [-Phantom Entity-], and [-Throw Voice-]." He looked at her again. "Do you know what all of those do?"

Becka nodded thoughtfully. Using the Skills Glenn had just called out, the Guilecasters gathered to create the Luminous Maze could create a dense fog, create lifelike illusions of Monsters or even people, project their voices across the empty field while disguising those voices as someone else, make objects look like other objects, and mirror the terrain.

It was as she'd surmised. All of the Skills in question targeted the environment, not the person, and none would touch the maze runners directly. That would allow the Guilecasters to fill that empty field with dozens of lifelike visual and audible illusions without violating the Law of Consent. She would have her work cut out for her if she wanted to find her way through that.

Becka looked to Glenn again. "Mindbender Skills now."

Glenn took a breath. "[-False Ground-], [-False Light-], [-Skew Perspective-], [-Mind Barrier-], [-Silence-], [-Shadow Trap-], [-Mirror Box-], and [-Phantom Monster-]."

Becka shuddered as she considered those and what they suggested might happen. "I know what a lot of those do, but I'm unfamiliar with [-Phantom Monster-] and [-False Light-]."

Glenn focused again. "[-Phantom Monster-] says 'Create a physical copy of any Monster whose life crystal you possess. The Monster can physically engage your enemies and absorb strikes for one minute. This Skill consumes 80 Blood and the life crystal of the slain Monster. Ten-minute cooldown.'"

"That's a bit intimidating. Even so, the Monster can't attack me without violating the Law of Consent, since a Mindbender is controlling it. So, at best, the illusion could bar my path. It can't hurt me in the maze, but it could physically stop me from advancing for one minute."

"I guess so." Glenn now sounded worried again.

Becka rubbed his arm to reassure him. "What about [-False Light-]?"

Glenn once again read the description of the Skill directly from the Status Sheet of whatever Mindbender he'd focused upon. "Alter the ambient light level in a radius of fifty paces around the targeted area for five minutes. All who enter the affected area will see the area as if lit at the level you choose. 10 Blood, five-minute cooldown."

"So it can be used indefinitely so long as the Mindbender has 10 Blood to renew it at the end of its duration." Becka shook her head. "They could make that entire field dark as night in as many directions as they like. How many Mindbenders have that Skill slotted?"

A booming voice cut across the crowd. "Attention, maze group one! We now call you to line up by order of level! Level 10s in the front, level 15s in the back! You have five minutes to assemble before you will be tasked to enter the Luminous Maze! May the Gods smile on you!"

Becka hissed. "Drat, we're already out of time."

As she moved down the hill, Glenn grabbed her arm. "I'll walk with you."

"You need to leave now if you want to get back to the dueling fields and claim your next victim. You've given me more than enough of a head start to challenge this." She spun to kiss him lightly on the lips, then patted his hand on her arm. "Now let me go."

Glenn reluctantly released her. As he watched her with nervous worry in his eyes, Becka smiled her best smile... for him. "I'm going to be just fine, love. You're the one who could get his head caved in if you're thinking about me instead of your opponent. Go! Win!"

Glenn's warm smile returned. "You can do this."

"And after I do, we'll celebrate again tonight. The wrong way." Becka shooed him with a motion of her hand and turned to head down into the crowd. "Now run! Fight well!"

Glenn took off at a much faster pace than he had kept on the way over here. He would have no trouble making his next singles duel and, Becka hoped, trouncing another opponent. Now, Becka had to cut her way into the dense crowd and take her place.

A few steps later, Becka was deep in a throng of eager and anxious maze runners. As she expertly slipped through openings and moved closer to the front, she couldn't help but feel vaguely guilty for having gained all the information Glenn had provided. No one here knew the Classes of those gathered to create this maze or their slotted Skills.

The vast majority of these contestants likely had no idea that Mindbenders, Guilecasters, and Arctists were about to make their lives very strange. Even so, the feeling passed quickly. There was no reason the other maze runners couldn't have learned about the maze from people who'd run it in prior years. Gossip would spread.

Becka had every reason to request additional information. She had a friend to bring back from the dead. Zack deserved her best effort... and even a little more.

The crowd was still arranging itself more or less in the proper order when the Town Guard once more bellowed across it using [-Public Address-]. His voice carried over the crowd without issue. Everyone went silent and listened.

"Attention, maze group one! When we call for you to assemble, all level 10 Adventurers must line up on the starting line! Anyone who moves into the maze before the start is called will immediately be disqualified!"

Becka continued forward until she was roughly in the middle of the crowd. As she moved into position, she glanced at a tall, beefy fellow who was obviously a Brutalist. He had big muscles and a strong chin, but he wasn't Glenn.

Becka politely tapped his arm. "Excuse me. Might I ask your level?"

The Brutalist glanced at her, then grinned wide as his gaze coursed shamelessly up and down her body. "Gods, you're gorgeous! What's your name, miss?"

"Taken."

"That's a weird..." The Brutalist caught on. "Oh, right. Sorry." He winced. "I'm level 12."

"Wonderful." Becka smiled politely. "It's good to know I'm in the right place."

The Brutalist shifted awkwardly and focused on the Town Guard. Becka slipped a pace or two ahead. Two large men blocked her way, but she expertly skirted around them and gained a few more places in the crowd.

Soon she arrived behind a blonde-haired woman in mage robes who looked to be about her age. Becka politely tapped her on the shoulder. "Hello, I'm level 12. You?"

The woman glanced back at her and frowned as if annoyed. "11. Now *sssh!*"

Becka stepped back. She decided not to press her luck any further.

Around her, people continued to exchange levels and greetings and exchange positions based on the results. Despite the fact that they were all competing today, everyone who was running the maze in group one seemed excited to do so and largely polite. Once the maze started, though, Becka suspected it would be every Adventurer for themselves.

The question was, why arrange the crowd from level 10 to level 15?

Becka supposed it was simply a way to make the contest more fair. A level 10 had two less Skills and one less Blessing than a level 15, so to prevent those at the top of the bracket from dominating the maze, giving the lower levels a head start seemed fair enough. At level 12, she would be starting in the middle of the pack. She was glad for Glenn's tips.

Soon enough, the Town Guard's Skill-enhanced voice boomed over the crowd. "We will now present the rules of the Luminous Maze! Today, maze group one has one hundred and forty-two contestants! Of those, only thirty-five of you will be advancing to the final leg of the maze! That means three out of four of you should make other plans!"

The guard's pronouncement was followed by shifting in the crowd and a good bit of nervous laughter. For her part, Becka had not expected the cutoff to be so shear. Worse, as she scanned the crowd of level 10 and level 11 Adventurers ahead of her, she gave up before she was done counting. All those people would enter the maze before her.

What must the level 14s and 15s feel like? They would likely be panicking at the thought of having thirty-six lower levels complete the maze before they entered it. That would make them nervous and reckless, which, while it wasn't exactly fair, would otherwise work to her advantage. Still, given that everyone had paid a five-moon entry fee, there must be more.

"When we call for the start, all level 10 Adventurers should immediately enter the maze! One minute later, we'll call for level 11, then level 12 a minute after that, and so on! Again, if you enter the maze before your level group is called, you will be disqualified!"

As grumbling began to arise from the back ranks of the gathered Adventurers, specifically those of level 13 and higher, the Town Guard clanged his [Guardian's Mace] against his [Guardian's Shield] so loudly that Becka involuntarily covered her ears. That shut the crowd up. Would the level 10s really get a five-minute head start?

"Here is how the thirty-five Adventurers to advance to the second and final leg will be selected! Only the first seven level 10 Adventurers to reach the far side of this field will advance to tomorrow's Luminous Maze! All other level 10s will be eliminated! That means only the first seven people to complete the maze in each level group will advance to the next round!"

Sounds of relief erupted from the back ranks as Becka nodded to herself. Each level of Adventurers would be competing solely with themselves. That meant the head start the level 10s would get would not be a head start at all.

Even if every level 10 and level 11 Adventurer reached the far side of the maze before her, Becka could still qualify for tomorrow's Luminous Maze so long as she was one of the first seven level 12s to complete the maze.

That selection process was both fair and efficient. The more she learned about the Luminous Maze and how it was conducted, the more Becka grew excited to take part in it. Perhaps, if she chose to evolve her Class to Mindbender at level 20 and gained a few levels beyond that, she could one day be one of those gathered to *create* the maze.

The Town Guard bellowed again. "One last point of order! If you at any point are touched by an officiant of the maze, you are disqualified! These officiants will only touch you if you have already failed in some respect that would eliminate you from competition!"

So the moment someone fell in a pit or stepped into a trap, the trap wouldn't harm them. But it would be a cue from an officiant to tell them they'd been eliminated. Becka wondered if the maze officiants might be Shadowers. They could easily hide themselves.

The Town Guard continued. "Moreover, if at any point you believe you cannot complete the maze, take a knee at your current location and raise your right hand above your head! The officiants will immediately disqualify you. However, you will no longer be targeted by any aspects of the maze! Kneel at your position until an officiant guides you to the side!"

So the Luminous Maze would be challenging—or terrifying—enough that people who attempted to complete it might become so frustrated, turned around, or terrified they would rather take a knee than continue. Just what did these casters have in store for them today? Given the breath of illusionary Skills at play, Becka might encounter horrors in there.

Yet she doubted any horror or setback would be sufficient to deter her from doing all she could to win an experience scroll that could help save Zack.

"The call to enter the maze will come in one minute!" the guard bellowed. "Prepare yourselves, and may the Gods be with you today!"

Becka spent the next minute conducting deep breathing exercises. Zack needed her to do this, Anna needed her to do this, and Glenn was confident she could do this. She would not let any of them down. She might not be the strongest in their party, or have the strongest Skills, but she *was* clever. Today, she would prove it.

"Level 10s, enter the maze!" the Town Guard yelled.

Ahead of her, a larger number of people than Becka expected rushed across the white line painted at the front of the grassy field. Most had taken only a few steps before they reeled, stumbled, and spun about. As the entire crowd of would-be maze runners advanced in unison so the level 11s could line up at the starting line, the level 10s stumbled and yelled.

There was a great deal of shrieking and shouting, and a number of people started swatting at the air. Several people stumbled and went down. One young Adventurer even took a knee and raised her hand in the air. She was visibly hyperventilating with her eyes shut.

That Adventurer had surrendered almost immediately after entering the Luminous Maze, and had given up after paying a five-moon entry fee! Just what were those Mindbenders throwing at them beyond that line? Why couldn't Becka see it from here?"

Soon after, the level 10s began advancing… or some of them. At least half were heading toward one of the two fences on the side of the maze rather than the finish line. Five were actually stumbling back. One stumbled across the starting line from the opposite side, and they had no sooner stared at the level 11s in shock before the Town Guard yelled.

"Anyone who exits the maze on the wrong side is eliminated! You're out!"

After cursing and stomping one foot, the unlucky level 10 stormed off. The fact that he had gotten so completely turned around in under a minute was genuinely disturbing. Becka was fast growing to suspect today's maze run would be more challenging than she'd hoped.

Everyone waited in breathless wonder as the level 10s who were still largely proceeding forward stumbled across the field. Some of them simply vanished, and some stopped moving forward at all. Again, Becka paid close attention. She imagined some might be trying to climb invisible walls... or perhaps cliffs? She recalled the Mind-bender Skill [-Mind Barrier-].

Sooner than she expected, the Town Guard bellowed. "Level 11s! Enter the maze!"

As the level 11s charged into the empty, grassy field and Becka and all her fellow level 12s hurried up to the starting line to take their places, the reactions of the level 11s was similar to that of the level 10s. None of the level 11s took a knee as that one young Adventurer had done, but many swatted angrily at the air or cursed and stumbled about.

And still, despite standing right at the edge of the starting line, Becka saw nothing but a wide, sunny, grassy field... filled with dozens of flailing, cursing Adventurers. Once more she took deep breaths and worked to calm her pounding heart. She had to be ready for anything.

"Level 12s! Enter the maze!"

As Becka surged across the starting line, she stepped into a literal monsoon.

EIGHTEEN
A LUMINOUS MAZE

B ecka stumbled as so many others had stumbled. Cold, wet wind tore at her face, her hair, and her clothing. She raised one hand to shield her face against dagger-like droplets and, rather than being overwhelmed, marveled at the wind and rain.

Mud sucked at her boots with every step, and dead and spindly trees dotted the bleak landscape. Mindbenders and Guilecasters could make her *see* such things, but how could they make her *feel* them? This mud sucking at her boots? This rain pounding her hand and face? This wind that felt like it could tear her clothes right off her body if it grew much stronger?

The sky was so dark it looked close to night, so **[-False Light-]** must be in play. As for the rain battering her face and clothing, it *must* be real. The Law of Consent would not prevent someone from splattering harmless water all over her, so perhaps this was why the Arctists were here. They were using their ice and water Skills to create this storm.

This didn't explain why she hadn't been able to see this squall before she stepped over the line. As Becka continued gamely forward and considered, however, the answer came to her. What she saw now was not the illusion. The illusion had been the grassy field.

Now she grasped it! Mindbenders could not make mud suck at her boots or make rain from nothing, but they could hide both from people who could neither see nor touch it. On the far side of the starting line, all they would need to do was create an illusion of a fair and open field. What actually waited for maze runners... the meat of the maze... would be invisible.

This revelation stopped her in her tracks. Now that she knew the Mindbenders had altered what she saw from the near side of the finish line, everything she had seen before was suspect. The finish line might even be in a completely different place than it had appeared.

There could be hidden pits to trap her, snares to bind her feet, even stationary hazards like [-Shadow Trap-] that had been placed in the field hours ago. [-Shadow Trap-] would blind her for a good minute if she stepped into it, and it was one of the few Skills that the Law of Consent allowed to target her. That was because she would *choose* to walk into it.

As someone cried out to her right, her gaze snapped in that direction. She spotted a young male Adventurer she didn't recognize with their head down and their hands raised. As they walked forward, blinded by the rain, Becka saw too late what waited for them.

A river. There was a frothing, raging river crossing the field. The Adventurer was walking right for its shoreline, but he couldn't see it with his eyes squinted and his hands raised.

Becka instinctively stumbled in his direction. "Stop!" Her voice was barely audible across the storm. "Stop, wait!"

The Adventurer either didn't hear her or didn't trust her voice. When he attempted to ford the river, he slipped and dropped *beneath* it. Becka knew now that was no simple river.

It must be part of a pit, and now that Adventurer was trapped within it. He would not complete the Luminous Maze. An officiant might be leading him away right now.

As she looked around for other Adventurers, she spotted a few shadowy forms ahead and to her sides, but not nearly as many people as had entered the maze. The Mindbenders must be selectively hiding people from her and other contestants. How?

Becka remembered that Glenn had mentioned some of those running the maze had slotted the Skill [-Phantom Mirror-]. That could create a straight reflective wall that would essentially mirror any terrain it overlooked. Were [-Phantom Mirror-]s present to her left and right, they would hide other Adventurers... and [-Mask Other-] could hide herself.

It seemed clear the only way forward was across the river that had swallowed that Adventurer. So how could she avoid his fate? Becka set aside what she could see and feel and focused on how she would build such a trap. She had seen the Adventurer stumble and fall below the river, so how would she design a trap with those effects?

The river had to be an illusion. It would be impossible for water to froth and rage so vigorously without washing out the land beyond the field set aside for the Luminous Maze. The river also coursed mostly parallel to the starting line, at least so far as Becka could see. Why have it course straight across when a winding river would be more frightening?

Even if the Mindbenders could hide the maze and its specifics, they couldn't dig pits big enough to swallow a full person with illusions. Yet the Builders who had erected the grounds for this cup could bend earth as easily as one molded clay. As Becka continued forward to the edge of the river, she imagined what must wait ahead. A trench. A simple trench.

Moreover, there would be paths where one could cross the trench... to make the maze possible... but such paths were impossible to see. A glimpse of movement allowed her to spot another Adventurer stumbling across the river like she was walking across a balance beam. A huge gust of wind overbalanced her, and into the "water" she toppled. Into the trench.

So the challenge here was four-fold. First, one had to recognize that the river was an illusion. Next, one had to determine it hid a trench. Then, one had to find a way to safely cross that trench... perhaps a narrow beam like the one that Adventurer had attempted to cross. And finally, one had to cross that narrow beam while being pelted by physical wind and rain.

If only she had more Prowess! Leo could cross a balance beam in his sleep. Still, she had to take this one step at a time, and the first step would be finding where to cross.

Could she simply dip her boot into the water until she found hard ground? No. The Mindbenders would anticipate maze runners trying something like that, and the trench might be greased and sloped once she got too close. She would fall down and slide into it.

She considered pulling a few objects from her **[Unfilled Bag]** and tossing them ahead of her. If they dropped away, she would know a pit waited ahead, but she had too few items to do that for long. The answer came to her quickly. She raised one hand and focused.

[-Shadow Bolt-].

At the mere cost of 20 Blood (she had plenty of Blood to spare) she blasted the river with inky black magic. She knew what happened when **[-Shadow Bolt-]** struck a hard surface from extensive practice. It would flash bright purple and then fade.

No flash followed her **[-Shadow Bolt-]**. It had passed through the illusionary river and hit somewhere below. As she'd suspected. Had she continued forward like that young Adventurer, she would now be in the pit and out of the running.

Becka blasted bolt after bolt along the river. The fourth bolt exploded in purple light, which assured her whatever was hidden beneath the river was solid. She hurried over to stand in front of that portion, then remembered the Adventurer tumbling off that balance beam.

She wasn't a Skirmisher, and her balance wasn't great on the best of days. She was also terrified of heights, and what if, while she was crossing that river, a Mindbender suddenly suspended the river and showed her how high up she was? She could freeze.

Crossing this river would not be dignified. It would not be fun. But Becka knew, now, how to do it safely. She dropped to her hands and knees, ignoring the fact that this would make her clothing quite muddy, and crawled forward. She secured the way forward with her hands.

Soon she shut her eyes as well. She did not want any visual surprises to alter her path, nor did she want to be misled should the Mindbenders use **[-Skew Perspective-]**. She trusted her hands and found what felt like a muddy wooden platform. It was only as big as her body.

But it was wood, and sturdy wood! Reluctantly, Becka dropped onto her front and wriggled forward like a snake. Rain hammered her flesh and wind tore at her hair and clothes, but with her entire body now resting on the ground, she couldn't be moved.

Using her hands to guide her, Becka wriggled forward. She soon found that the wooden platform narrowed to a wooden beam. Pressing her body hard against it and clutching the sides with her arms, Becka inched her way across with her eyes closed.

The wooden beam eventually widened back out into a platform, and then became mud once more. Only once Becka was certain she had crossed it did she open her eyes. She grinned as she stared at what looked like a series of spiked wooden walls ahead.

She stood in triumph. She was wet, cold, and covered in mud, but she had successfully navigated the first barrier of the Luminous Maze. Behind her, a woman shouted in shock before suddenly going silent. A level 13 had just fallen into the trench.

The rain was still coming down around her, but far less hard. The bulk of the squall seemed focused behind her, which suggested the Arctists maintaining it could not cover a large area. And now that she had bested the "water" challenge, they would focus on others.

As Becka walked forward cautiously, slipping her boots forward rather than taking large steps, she examined the line of spiked walls ahead. She suspected these walls, like the trench, were physical structures. The Mindbenders had hidden these walls as they had everything else.

She reached the first wall not long after. It looked to stretch from one end of the muddy field to the other, but she could trust nothing she saw. She raised her hand and fired another **[-Shadow Bolt-]** at the wall. It burst into purple just like it should.

Having verified the wall was solid, she touched it. It was firm, flat wood. Touching the wall would not harm her, though as she examined the many nasty-looking wooden spikes atop it, she suspected those were no illusion either. An Adventurer could try to go over those... but they could be cut badly, or worse, fall into something on the other side.

Again, the spiky wall skirted the Law of Consent. The Builders had merely created spikes. It would be her *choice* to climb over them, risking punctures and cuts. The more she saw of this Luminous Maze, the more Becka was impressed by its crafty design.

Yet if the maze designers did not intend her to go over the wall, she must be expected to find a way through it. The simplest way would be if they'd built the wall in segments with openings through which she could pass. Mindbender illusions would hide those.

Becka felt along the wall slowly, running her palms across the wood. Another man cried out nearby, after which his scream was cut off. Another victim of the Luminous Maze, and in particular, of this part of it. So to what trap had he fallen victim?

Becka's palm abruptly snapped forward, and she pulled it back just in time. She had found an opening in the wall. As tempting as it was to simply dash through it... she was, after all, competing with dozens of other level 12s... she again paused out of caution.

That scream she had heard was troubling. She couldn't be the first to decide there were hidden openings in the wall. That meant that the moment she found an opening, she would eagerly dash through... and meet a trap.

If she pushed her hands through the illusionary wall segment, something might grab her. How to proceed? If only she'd brought some sort of long stick! She made a note to gather sticks and other sacrificial objects and put them in her [Unfilled Bag] if she survived this round.

Becka ground her boot tip into the mud before the opening in the wall. The mark would not last long, but it would last. She then hurried down the wall until she found another opening, marked it, and found a third. Another Adventurer stumbled out of thin air.

They almost collided before Becka leapt back. She blinked in surprise. It was the big Brutalist she'd seen earlier, the one who'd told her she was gorgeous! While she appreciated the compliment, she hadn't wanted to give him any impression he had a chance.

He gawked at her. "Where did you come from?"

"Same as you, I imagine." She pointed. "There are holes in the wall."

"Yeah, I noticed that. But I saw someone go through one, and they screamed."

Becka frowned thoughtfully. "Yet if the holes aren't the way through, what is?"

The Brutalist smiled. "Hey, want to work together? With your brains and my brawn—"

"No thank you," Becka interrupted. "I don't mean to be rude, but I'll be faster on my own. I do wish you luck." She took two steps sideways until he vanished.

She had just passed through another [-Phantom Mirror-]. She was certain of that now. The Guilecasters had used numerous [-Phantom

Mirrors-] perpendicular to the starting line, splitting the space into many slices that would limit who could see who.

Becka continued sidling sideways, marveling as more Adventurers, many of whom were feeling their way along the wall like her, popped into and out of existence. She paused when she spotted a tall female Adventurer brace herself before the wall. She dived forward.

She passed through the invisible wall, but she did not cry out. She was onto something! Becka hurried toward the space the female Adventurer had passed through and eagerly examined it. Nothing different, so it wasn't the space. It was the matter of travel.

That Adventurer had dived through the space rather than walking through it. Perhaps the trap was set to catch someone who blundered through with their head held high. If she dived through it instead, she might remain low enough or move fast enough to avoid the trap.

Time continued to be against her. She had as much information as she felt she could reasonably gather. Becka moved to the position the Adventurer had last occupied, braced herself as that woman had, and dived as far as she could directly forward.

Something big whooshed over her head with a rush of wind, and then she landed in a heap on the other side of the wall. She'd avoided the trap... whatever the trap might be. As she glanced backward, she saw a gasping, muddy Becka staring back.

Another **[-Phantom Mirror-]**, this one concealing the wall she'd just passed and whatever trap lie in wait. As she looked herself over, she grimaced. She was an absolute mess, with her hair matted with water and her clothes covered in mud.

She pressed forward. Two more walls awaited her, but now she knew the trick to bypass them. She felt along until she found an opening and dived through twice more.

The last time she dived and rolled to her feet. As she looked back, just before a **[-Phantom Mirror-]** blocked her perceptions, she saw the trap. It was a simple spinning pole that would strike anyone who walked upright, padded to avoid injury.

Anyone who walked through would be smacked in the head by the pole. They would then fall backward, and perhaps a trapdoor dropped them into a trench where they would be met by an officiant and ushered out of the maze. By diving forward, Becka had both leapt over the sensitive portion of the floor and avoided the spinning pole.

Wheels within wheels. As she pressed forward again, she took a diagonal path instead of a straight one. Once again, she passed through [-Phantom Mirror-] after [-Phantom Mirror-] until she spotted a fellow Adventurer. They ran, screaming, directly at her, as if they were being chased by some sort of Monster. Yet there was no Monster to be seen!

Becka smoothly stepped aside. The Adventurer vanished as she passed back through the long [-Phantom Mirror-], but their screams continued beyond. She stretched out her hand and watched as the tips of her fingers vanished.

She traced the line of the mirror as she would a wall, using it to guide her forward. As she did so, she could swear she was walking either left or right. She strongly resisted the urge to correct her direction of movement. This was [-Skew Perspective-] hard at work.

A [-Phantom Mirror-] could only be projected in a straight line. While the Mindbender illusions might make it seem she was turning left or right, the length of the mirror acted as her guideline. She followed it with one hand inside until the ground ahead bubbled and spewed.

As Becka watched in alarm, a muddy Antlion clambered out of the dirt. It spread its arms and stomped its feet, then clicked its mandibles and roared. Becka raised her fist and unleashed [-Shadow Bolt-]. As the Antlion screeched and lurched toward her, [-Shadow Bolt-] passed through it without affect.

Becka confidently strode forward. The Antlion charged until it was a pace away and them burst into smoke which passed by her. The Mindbender had seen her shoot her bolt and, with his ruse exposed, moved his attentions elsewhere... Becka hoped.

She suspected that the closer she got to the finish line, the more direct attention from the Mindbenders she would receive. That was not comforting... but she was making progress! She suspected she had already completed more of the maze than most.

Her next obstacle soon presented itself. It was a tall hill with a steep grade, and this hill was quite muddy. Becka stepped through the nearest [-Phantom Mirror-] and spotted two Adventurers yelling and cursing as they slid back down.

So what might be the last challenge of the Luminous Maze was the simplest and most effective. Climbing a steep and muddy hill was difficult on a good day. After coming this far, damp from rain and covered in mud, it would be even more difficult.

Becka stepped back into her own portion of the maze and considered the muddy slope ahead. She couldn't scale it as she might another hill. Her boots would slide down uselessly. Yet there had to be some way to scale it. There had to be some way to complete the maze.

Becka walked forward as fast as she dared. No illusions presented themselves. She gamely attempted to climb the hill and immediately slid back down, now covered in even more mud. No surprises there. Was she done? How could anyone climb this hill?

A tool. There had to be some sort of tool or trick hidden in the maze. As she remembered another Skill Glenn had mentioned her opponents had slotted—**[-False Ground-]**—she dropped at the base of the hill and fumbled about with her hands.

She saw nothing but mud and sticks, but she was patient and careful with her hands. She felt along the muddy ground until her hand slapped down on something cool and metal. Grinning, Becka felt her way further, then recovered two metal poles.

As she lifted them from nothing, she recognized them. Pitons! They were exactly what she needed to climb a hill! She now suspected that while the surface of the hill was mud, it must be solid underneath. Builders could create a hill with solid dirt and drape mud across it.

Holding the pitons close, Becka walked to the hill and then swung with all her might. The piton penetrated the mud and stuck hard. Grinning, she stepped forward and pulled herself up a few steps by gripping the piton, then swung with the other. It, too, stuck.

Now it was simply a matter of hauling herself up. Unfortunately, Becka had never gained a great deal of upper body strength. If only Glenn were here! He would make short work of this obstacle... but then again, he might also have tumbled into that first trench.

Becka ground her teeth, held strong to the higher piton, and wrenched the lower one loose. She found that so long as she placed the tips of her boots deep into the mud and didn't try to move them, they didn't slide down. She lifted the lower piton and swung.

Huffing and wincing as she clutched the pitons, Becka slowly and painfully climbed the muddy hill. She saw no other Adventurers, and wouldn't be surprised if the Guilecasters had moved [-**Phantom Mirror-**]s even closer to her to isolate her. They wouldn't want the other maze runners seeing her climbing with pitons and start looking for those.

Though it felt like it took all the Stamina she possessed, Becka finally slapped a piton into the ground atop the hill. Another came after it, and then she dragged herself forward with a groan. She rolled onto the top of the hill, which was muddy but firm, and collapsed.

She wanted to lie here and recover, but she was so close to the end... and she had to finish in the top seven. She pushed up, shuddered, and soldiered forward. The finish line waited just ahead. Was it another illusion? Could she trust it? She was too tired to test it.

As she stumbled across the finish line, people in gray robes materialized out of thin air. Officiants and Lifecasters! One raised his hand and cast a Skill, and then Becka gasped as new energy flooded her. [-**Reinvigorate-**]. She certainly welcomed that.

"Congratulations," the Lifecaster said. "You've completed the Luminous Maze."

Becka nodded gratefully. "What number am I? Of those who've completed it?"

"You are finalist number ten."

Becka's burgeoning hopes crashed back to the ground. She had needed to finish in the top seven among level 12s, and instead she had missed her goal by three. If only she had been faster! Even so... she had completed the maze when most had not.

Zack wouldn't be disappointed with her. Neither would Glenn. She had given this her best effort, and she would take comfort in knowing she *had* completed the maze.

The Lifecaster tilted his head as he watched her, then frowned as if he'd realized something. "You're number ten out of all participants, miss. You're the tenth person to complete the maze of everyone who started it, including the other level groups."

Becka gasped. "So that means... I'm in the top seven among level 12s?"

"You're the first level 12 to complete the maze, miss. That means you've qualified for the final round." The Lifecaster smiled warmly. "Congratulations. You won't be needed for the rest of the day, but be here bright and early three days from now. If you'd like to get cleaned up and change your clothes, you can speak to the officiant near the registration building."

Becka grinned widely. If she was number ten to complete the maze but two groups had started before her, that meant she had actually passed up many of the level 10s and 11s who'd started before her. That was a wonderful feeling. She had not just won, but excelled!

Even so, her experience had been harrowing. If this was only the first leg, what would they be throwing at her three days from now? And could she win against a crowd who had all completed the first leg of the maze as quickly as she had?

She supposed there was only one way to find out.

NINETEEN
A DUET OF HOT AND COLD

GLENN

As he walked out onto the dueling fields early on the second day of the <Sandsea Cup>, Glenn smiled to himself as he remembered Becka's excited recounting of her experience in yesterday's Luminous Maze. He had loved hearing about her adventures there, and he had actually been a bit jealous he hadn't entered it himself. Still, dueling was his strong suit.

Glenn had won all six of his duels yesterday, ending his day in the qualifiers as the last of not one, but two groups of sixteen competitors. That meant he would continue to duel in the single bracket tomorrow as he advanced relentlessly toward the quarter-finals.

After hearing how difficult the maze had been over supper, Glenn was even more impressed with the woman he loved. His Soulseer Skills couldn't penetrate illusions, and he didn't have Becka's clever mind to guess what sort of traps lie in wait for him. The Luminous Maze was, in many ways, the perfect challenge for her.

As for him, defeating other Adventurers in duels was his challenge. As he glanced at the red-headed woman walking confidently at his side, she offered a warm smile. Nora Rapidbloom was his partner now, and today they would enter their first doubles duel.

Glenn suspected he could go quite far with Nora to support and heal him. He had never leveled beside a Lifecaster, and the thought of having her shields and healing magic to bolster his defenses was exciting. Having Nora with him was like having a walking, magical shield!

Every duel in which he participated grew his confidence. Dozens of Adventurers were already out. Even if some of those he had faced yesterday were competing today with their friends, he had already beaten them once. It would be even easier to beat them again.

He missed Becka. He wished she was here, but she and Anna were scheduled to take on doubles in another group of brackets. Becka's journey through the Luminous Maze would not take place for three more days. Glenn hoped to be there to watch her.

When they reached their designated dueling square, which today was B6, Glenn found a huge crowd of Adventurers assembled and eventually counted twenty-six. That wasn't surprising, since he and Nora had arrived fifteen minutes early. They made twenty-eight, and he knew thirty-two Adventurers were expected. Sixteen teams of two.

Who dueled who within each group of duelists was randomly assigned the night before the duels and not announced in advance. The only hard rule was that all contestants must complete their duels in half a day. Most duels only lasted a few minutes, so this was fine.

From Glenn's experience in singles, he knew the number of Adventurers present across a dueling field varied throughout the day. Some tried to stay and watch every duel so they would learn more about their opponents, while others would leave as soon as they won to rest up so they would be ready for their next challenge. And obviously, as the day wore on, less and less Adventurers were present, since most had already been eliminated.

Glenn did not expect that he and Nora would be chosen to duel first... the chances of that happening again were eight to one against... but he had to be ready for that. They took their position in an open spot and waited patiently. Eventually, three more people arrived, which brought the total number to thirty-one. Someone was missing.

The officiant soon stepped forward. "Contestant Jared L! Jared L, are you here?"

The crowd of Adventurers around Glenn and Nora looked about expectantly, but no one stepped forward. This hadn't happened yesterday. What would the officiant do if one person on one team didn't show up on time? Would they be disqualified?

"Jared L! You have one minute to appear, or you and your partner will forfeit!"

A young woman wearing [**Timeworn Robes**] stepped forward. "He's coming! I promise! He just had to buy some potions before we got started today!"

The officiant scowled at her. "Agnes M?"

Agnes winced. "Yes, that's me."

"You both knew when we were scheduled to start the doubles bracket. If your partner is not here in one minute, you will not be able to participate in—"

"Coming!" a man bellowed from afar. "I'm coming, I'm coming!"

Glenn glanced toward the shouting person and saw another man, also wearing [**Timeworn Robes**], sprinting across the dueling field. He was breathing hard and stumbling, so he must have run a long way. When he arrived, he dropped his palms to his knees.

The officiant eyed him with obvious annoyance. "Jared L?"

"That's me!" Jared wheezed and raised his hand. "I'm here!"

The officiant sniffed. "See that you are more prompt in the future."

"Yes, sir! I will be, sir!"

Nora lightly touched his arm and leaned up on tiptoes to whisper in his ear. "They're both level 15. The minimum level requirement for [**Timeworn Robes**] is level 15."

Glenn had known that, but he was still pleased that Nora had told him. She couldn't know that he could simply learn each opponent's level by using [-**Soul Scan-**], so her offering this point of data was both useful and clever. She would make a good partner.

He lightly bumped her shoulder with his. "Good to know."

Her smile grew as a blush shaded her features. "Happy to help!"

The officiant repeated the same spiel he had yesterday, explaining how duels would be conducted, that each duel would be single elimination, and so on. Some Adventurers barely listened—those must have dueled in singles yesterday—while others paid rapt attention. Glenn mentally noted who fell into each group. Some already had experience.

"We will now announce the first duel for the day! Contests Agnes M and Jared L, step onto the dueling field! You will be red team!"

Glenn huffed ruefully. No wonder the officiant had been so anxious about Jared L's absence. If he had not arrived when he had, the team scheduled to face him would have earned a bye. Glenn knew if the other team didn't show up, their opponents won automatically.

"Contestants Glenn G and Nora R, step onto the dueling field! You will be blue team!"

Glenn could scarcely believe his luck. He'd been chosen first to duel yesterday for singles, and now again for doubles. What was the probability of that happening? Yesterday it had been one of eight, and today it was also one out of eight, so was that... one in sixty-four?

No time for math! Glenn focused his gaze on Agnes and used [-Soul Scan-]. He rapidly noted a range of attributes that made sense for a level 15 and her class: Harmcaster. She had slotted [-Burn-], [-Freeze-], [-Stone Skin-], [-Freezing Slick-], and [-Inferno-].

"Glenn?" Nora gave him a gentle nudge.

Glenn snapped from his reading and marched forward. The officiant was now giving him the evil eye, which made him worry he'd almost gotten them disqualified. He made a mental note to not use [-Soul Scan-] on his opponents until after he was in the dueling square. The duel couldn't start until he gave consent, so there was no reason to delay stepping inside.

Nora hurried alongside him as they entered the dueling square, which they had to walk through to reach the two faint blue squares marked on the other side. As they walked, Glenn glanced over his shoulder and checked Agnes's Blessings. [+Burning Soul+], [+Gusting Soul+], and [+Freezing Soul+]. All Blessings lowered the Blood required to cast Skills.

Once they had taken their place in the blue squares, approximately three paces apart, Glenn used [-Soul Scan-] on Jared. He was also a Harmcaster with attributes similar to Agnes's. His slotted Skills were [-Freeze-], [-Blast-], [-Stone Skin-], [-Freezing Slick-], and [-Freezing Cube-], and his Blessings were [+Freezing Soul+], [+Gusting Soul+], and [+Double Cast+].

That last Blessing was a concern. [+Double Cast+] was a controversial Blessing because many considered it closer to a Skill than a Blessing and believed the Gods had erred in its design. A Harmcaster with [+Double Cast+] could instantly refresh all the cooldowns on their slotted Skills once every twelve hours. When used correctly, it was very powerful.

Even so, it was also situational, and once Jared used it, he wouldn't be able to use it again for the rest of the day. That meant he would only get to use [+Double Cast+] in one of his (possible) six duels. It would be a Skill of last resort... but what a last resort!

Glenn had another concern. [-Freezing Slick-] was a rarely used Harmcaster Skill with little real utility other than inside confined spaces. The fact that both Harmcasters had it slotted suggested they had plans to use it today. That could prove quite troublesome.

"Contestants! Begin your duel when you are both ready!"

Across the field, Agnes called out. "Duel my party!"

The distinction in wording was important. Had she only said "Duel me!" she would have been challenging Glenn or Nora alone. By asking for a party duel, she was asking on behalf of her and her partner. Glenn could only accept using the same wording.

Instead of doing so, however, Glenn looked to the officiant. "Time!"

The officiant narrowed his eyes. "You call for a time out?"

"Yes, sir!"

Agnes stomped a boot. "Can he do that?"

Glenn could. He knew the officiants for the qualifiers didn't mention that participants could call a time out because they were hoping to proceed through the initial batch of duels quickly. Glenn had learned about this rule from historical duel accounts.

The officiant sighed. "Contestant Glenn G, you have a five-minute time out."

Each duelist or group only got two timeouts per day, but could call them before any duel to strategize. Knowing when to call a timeout was crucial in high level dueling. In Glenn's case, he now knew he was facing two Harmcasters at the top of his bracket with a fearsome array of ranged Skills... as a Brutalist. He needed to devise a plan with Nora.

He beckoned her to follow and walked backward until he'd placed one of the large poles at the corner of the X of five between him and their opponents. He pulled Nora as close as he dared, almost close enough to kiss, but not because he was feeling amorous. He could not risk that their opponents could read lips.

Nora watched him, wide-eyed. "What is it?"

"I think they're both Harmcasters, which means we might already be in trouble."

She gasped. "How can you tell?"

"It's the way they carry themselves," Glenn lied. "Also, Agnes said Jared was late because he was purchasing potions. Given how quickly Harmcasters burn through Blood, I suspect they had to buy extra Blood potions to be ready for multiple duels today."

"All casters burn Blood though."

"But not at the rate a Harmcaster does. Both Lifecasters and Guile-casters are more Blood efficient, and Lifecasters also regenerate Blood faster. And if we are facing two Harmcasters, Nora, that puts us at a big disadvantage. Or me, in particular."

Nora grimaced. "And me, since I'm slotted to heal you."

During their strategizing last night, Glenn and Nora had agreed she would not slot **[-Sunlight Shard-]**... her only offensive Skill... in favor of stacking more defense. Nora had slotted **[-Flash Heal-]**, **[-Cleanse Body-], [-Cleanse Mind-]**, **[-Soul Cushion-]**, and **[-Soul Harden-]**.

[-Soul Cushion-] was the pre-requisite to **[-Soul Harden-]**, and both served the same purpose: creating a buffer of invisible Health points that would absorb attacks directed at the person Nora buffed. In theory the Skills were redundant, but as they did not share a cooldown, a Lifecaster could stack them. That meant Nora could create one Health shield of 50 Health and another of 100 Health at the cost of 10 and 20 Blood, respectively.

Nora leaned even closer. "So how do we beat two Harmcasters? Do you have any ideas?"

"Well, I do know a few Harmcaster tricks. Are you familiar with **[-Freezing Slick-]**?"

"I've never heard of that one."

"It's not commonly used since it's so situational, and it really only works in very narrow environments. But a Harmcaster can use it to create a sheer and icy surface on the ground for five paces from where they cast it, and it only costs 5 Blood. It also has a ten-second cooldown."

"That's fast!"

"I know, and when I thought about it, I realized it's perfect for duels like this one. The entire square is only twenty paces across, so they could use it to coat the whole thing in slippery ice. That would make it near impossible for me to make any forward progress without slipping and falling."

"At which point they could simply batter you with spells or duck behind one of the pillars if we tried to attack them back at range." Nora hissed through her teeth. "That'll be hard to beat."

"Four minutes!" the officiant called.

Glenn ignored him. "That's why I called time. I need to ask you some questions about your Skills." He hoped she wouldn't ask why he was so certain of the enemy's plan. "First, I suspect they'll spray down the entire dueling square, other than their part of it, with [-Freezing Slick-]. They probably have Skills like [-Burst-] and maybe even [-Tornado-] to blow me backward if I try to advance."

"And if you fall and get hit by those, you'll slide away on the ice."

"Right. Meanwhile, so long as I'm not making forward progress, they'll batter me with [-Burn-], [-Freeze-], or other cheap and powerful Skills. Eventually I'll drop, and then they'll come for you."

"And I can't take one Harmcaster alone, let alone both."

"But I have an idea to get past their ice, if they use it. First, when you cast [-Soul Cushion-] and [-Soul Harden-], is it directional? Like a shield? Or does it go all around me, like a bubble?"

She eyed him dubiously. "You really don't know?"

"I've never leveled beside a Harmcaster."

"Oh!" She winced. "Because you're a Town Guard, you're rarely outside the walls."

Glenn smiled as she created the exact lie he needed. "That's right."

"It's a bubble. It covers you on all sides, and any damage you take on any side of you will deduct Health points until the bubble pops, for lack of a better term."

"Okay. Next question. Can you cast either of those Skills on an inanimate object?

"On... like, a rock?"

"Sure. Could you cast [-Soul Cushion-] on a rock?"

"Three minutes!" the officiant yelled.

Nora's eyes went distant. Glenn realized she was checking her own Status Sheet and, likely, reading the description of [-Soul Cushion-] and [-Soul Harden-]. He used [-Soul Scan-] on her and did the same. He could have done that first, but then she might wonder how he knew about her Skills.

Nora's gaze returned. "They both say surround your target. So... yes. I guess my target could be anything, though I've never actually cast either Skill on anything but a party member."

"Great. So when this duel starts, I'm going to run behind the leftmost pillar. You run behind the one on the right. I suspect the Harmcasters will do the same, then start spraying down the dueling square with [-Freezing Slick-]. I'll throw down my shield, and then you cast [-Soul Cushion-] on it."

She eyed him dubiously. "On your shield?"

"That's right. I'm going to use my shield like a boat, but it's too flat for that as it is now. But if you surround it with [-Soul Cushion-], it should simply glide along the ice."

"So you..." She gasped. "How are you going to make it move?"

"My mace. I'm going to use it like a paddle after I start my slide."

She eyed him dubiously. "Are you pulling my leg?"

"I'm not! It could work. And if it doesn't, I'll just grab my shield and try to make my way to them on my own power. Still, I don't think that'll be possible if they're constantly hitting me with [-Burst-]."

"This is a strange plan, Glenn. You're certain this is how you want to tackle them?"

"I know it sounds a bit unorthodox, but let's try it. At worst, we get a good story out of this."

"But you said winning these dueling contests was important to your mission."

She was right. How to explain? "We should have said participating. Becka can exaggerate sometimes. So, will you do it?"

"Two minutes!" the officiant yelled irritably.

"Yes." Nora thumped his arm. "I trust you. If you think it's a good idea, I'm on board."

"Great." Glenn grinned wide. "So, to be clear, we only do this if they coat the dueling square using [-Freezing Slick-]. Otherwise, I'll just charge like a Rock Troll. In that case, hit me with [-Soul Cushion-] and [-Soul Harden-] and then take cover. I'll call for help when I need heals."

Nora nodded vigorously. "I've got you."

"One minute!" The officiant yelled.

Glenn looked in his direction. "We're ready!" He walked back to his blue square as Nora did the same. As they settled in, he once more faced Agnes and Jared.

Agnes looked more than a bit annoyed. "Are you two done making out?"

"We're done talking. Sorry for the wait." He took a breath. "Duel my party."

A spectral flag dropped out of the sky and landed midway between them.

Agnes huffed. "We accept your duel."

As the flag turned solid, Agnes and Jared sprinted out of their squares just as Glenn had expected... and just as he had told Nora they might. Agnes joined Glenn in darting for the southern pillar on the X, while Jared dashed for the northern one. Nora darted there as well.

Glenn looked at Agnes as he dashed. She was likely the leader of the duo. **[-Soul Scan-]**.

Agnes's Status Sheet appeared as Glenn slammed his back into the tall pole. He was pleased to see he could still see it even *through* the pole. Neither Agnes or Jared called out—they would be fools to call their Skills aloud—but Glenn saw a brown bar flash into being and then complete.

[-Freezing Slick-].

The sound of crackling ice told him Agnes and Jared had activated that Skill at the same time and were even now spraying the dueling field with a thin layer of incredibly slick ice. Ice created in such a manner would be as slick as oil and difficult to traverse. In the field, a Harmcaster could use **[-Freezing Slick-]** to trip up or halt the charge of a charging Monster... with mixed results.

As Nora peeked around her own pillar, she gasped as Glenn's nigh-prophetic suspicions were confirmed. Glenn threw down his **[Steel Shield]** and pointed at it. He didn't say a word.

Nora pivoted to face him and swept both hands around each other, then thrust them out. A barely perceptible oval appeared around Glenn's shield. She could cast her Skills on inanimate objects! She had just covered his shield in a **[-Soul Cushion-]** bubble with 50 Health points.

Glenn dropped Becka into his hands and dashed out of cover. As he picked up his shield, he was pleased to find that his hands grasped the bubble around the shield rather than the shield itself. It might look flat, but it was now a long, narrow oval with two sides, like a coin with its edges squished.

His skin tingled as Nora cast her second Skill: **[-Soul Harden-]**. That would create a shield of 100 Health points around him, which could absorb one or two casts from the Harmcasters. As he rushed toward them, he was unsurprised to see over half the dueling field already glittering with solid ice. It had progressed past the central X. Agnes and Jared each crouched behind a pillar beyond that.

Above Agnes, a brown bar appeared and rapidly ticked forward. **[-Burn-]**.

The moment before Glenn's foot would step onto the incredibly slick and smooth sheet of ice, he dived forward with all his Strength and tucked his shield beneath his chest. He hit the ice and went prone as a burst of flame roared over his head, followed by a bolt of ice. Neither struck.

When Glenn's now-oval shield hit the ice, he sledded forward with his legs trailing but providing little drag. Gasps of shock rose from around the field as Glenn rocketed across the ice sheet. He was now using his shield as a sled, and it was working!

Still, the Harmcasters reacted as he'd expected. Bursts of flame and chunks of ice battered him and were absorbed harmlessly by **[-Soul Harden-]**. Better yet, the spells were dissipated completely by Nora's buff, which meant the impacts didn't slow his momentum!

He whipped violently as Jared hit him with **[-Burst-]**, sending him sideways, but he was ready for that. He slammed Becka into the ice and used his mace as an anchor to swing himself around and fly forward again. At that point, he was almost at Agnes. She gawked at him like he'd gone insane.

Agnes screamed and launched another **[-Burn-]** at his face. It hit him full-on and then vanished at the same time as his **[-Soul Harden-]** bubble, doing no damage at all. Glenn rolled off the icy sheet, grabbed his shield, and leapt to his feet with his mace raised.

Agnes hadn't coated the ice beneath her own feet, but she could only back up so far until she reached the edge of the dueling field. If she stepped out, she'd be disqualified. Somehow, in the most unpredictable and likely maddening method possible, Glenn had reached her.

He tackled her before she could cast another spell. They went down with him on top, and he straddled her and raised his mace as a threat. Yet he waited before he struck.

He couldn't just bash her skull in with his mace. She could still yield, and a single hit from his mace could shatter her head. He'd never risk killing her by mistake.

She glared up at him. "Jared! Now!"

Glenn glanced at Jared and used [-Soul Scan-]. A casting bar for [-Freezing Cube-] appeared above Jared's head, and Glenn knew he had shocked these two enough that they were attempting to lock him in a cube of ice. That would give them a minute to attack Nora, alone.

Glenn rolled while simultaneously pushing Agnes between him and Jared as a shield. A block of ice the size of a person encased Agnes, and Glenn shoved her off him and sighed with relief. He hadn't known if he could use Agnes's body to block Jared's Skill.

With Agnes now out of the fight for a full minute, Glenn lumbered to his feet and charged the second Harmcaster. Another casting bar appeared above Jared's head. [+Double Cast+]. With this duel deteriorating rapidly, Jared had resorted to activating his Blessing with a twelve-hour cooldown.

The bar completed, and Glenn knew he would never reach Jared in time. He changed direction as he hit more ice and [-Freezing Cube-] once more appeared above Jared's head. He dived behind a pillar... only to be encased in a block of ice. Devilspit! He'd been certain he could avoid that.

The ice abruptly shattered, dropping Glenn to the field. He sputtered and stumbled up, then glanced at Nora to see her giving him an eager thumb's up. Only then did he remember that he was dueling with a Lifecaster as his partner.

Nora had slotted [-Cleanse Body-], and apparently [-Cleanse Body-] could remove [-Freezing Cube-]! Fighting with a Lifecaster at his side offered *so* many benefits. Glenn once more charged Jared and howled like a maniac. He unleashed a maniacal howl for intimidating effect.

Faced with a charging Brutalist, Jared had a split-second decision to make. If he kept his head and kept his cool, he'd have just enough time to cast **[-Burst-]**. That would slow Glenn or knock him on his rear. That would give Jared time to reposition. That was what a calm, collected man would do.

Yet Jared had just seen Glenn skate across a seemingly impenetrable ice slick like some sort of armored penguin. He had tried to **[-Freezing Cube-]** Glenn once and hit his partner, and then when he had again used **[-Freezing Cube-]** on Glenn, Nora had removed it. Somehow, Glenn had anticipated his every move.

Eyes wide, Jared cast **[-Stone Skin-]** instead of **[-Burst-]**.

Glenn grinned and swung with all his might. **[-Stone Skin-]** would turn Jared's skin as hard as iron for ten seconds, but the Skill had a five-minute cooldown. It could only be used once per battle. And even with his skin hard as iron, Glenn's mace still hit him hard enough to ash his Health Bar by a third.

More gasps followed as Glenn struck again and again. One half. One-third. He feathered his last strike so as to knock Jared off his feet. As he fell backward, his Health Bar dropped almost to nothing... and the officiant called out.

"Jared L is eliminated!"

That was Glenn's cue to cease swinging. He likely couldn't hit Jared again due to the Law of Consent, but he wasn't going to test that. With one Harmcaster down, he walked over to where Agnes, features furious, remained frozen in her partner's block of ice. He waited by her with his mace.

Nora *eep*ed somewhere nearby. As Glenn glanced at her in worry, she fell right on her rear on the ice. She was fine, just inconvenienced. Even so, she couldn't make any progress across that ice slick while walking, so she crawled toward him on hands and knees.

As seconds ticked away, Glenn locked eyes with Agnes. Nora reached him just before the ice dissipated, then grabbed his shield to balance himself. As the ice melted, Glenn charged.

"Yield!" Agnes shouted. "End this duel!"

Glenn lowered his mace instead of striking her. "I consent to end this duel."

The duel flag vanished as the officiant called out. "The winners of this duo duel are Glenn G and Nora R, by KO and yield!"

Instead of offering her hand or walking away, Agnes spit on the ice. "You cheater!"

Her accusation hit Glenn harder because she was right. Yet before he could respond, Nora stepped forward and shoved Agnes. "How dare you!"

Glenn stared at Nora in shock. Agnes merely sneered. "Don't try and deny it, you hussy. Your boyfriend cheated! That's what you were up to during the timeout!"

"He's not my boyfriend!" Nora yelled. "And he doesn't cheat! Glenn is..." She paused and stepped back. "He is one of the bravest and most honest men I've ever met."

Nora might as well have punched him in the gut. Her faith in his good nature hurt more because it felt undeserved. He *had* cheated using his unique Skills, and by doing so, he had robbed Agnes and Jared of a win they had every right to. Their strategy had been clever and effective.

Agnes glared. "How did he know what Skills were going to use? No one could know!"

Nora glared back. "He knew because Jared yelled about potions when he arrived."

"That doesn't tell him anything!"

"Enough!" The officiant had taken the field before Glenn noticed. "Agnes M, are you officially lodging an accusation of cheating? Keep in mind, if it's not upheld, you will not only be forbidden from participating in more events, you'll be disqualified from any events you've already won."

Agnes glared at the officiant, then at Glenn. "How did you know?"

He firmed his stance. "Know what?"

"How did you know we would use [-Freezing Slick-]? You were instantly ready with that... shield toboggan. There's no way you could have planned to use that ahead of time!"

Glenn had to lie convincingly. As Nora looked at him with faith in her eyes, he felt even more worried. What could he tell Agnes to convince her he had anticipated her ploy through simple deduction? He was a Truth Seeker, but he wasn't a seer... so far as anyone knew.

As his mind rapidly scrambled for anything that could inform what he should say, the words of the officiant played back in his head. *"You will not only be forbidden from participating in more events. You'll be disqualified from events you've already won."*

The second part of the officiant's statement was an odd addition. How would the officiant know that Agnes had already won another contest at the **<Sandsea Cup>**? Unless he had seen her win a contest at the **<Sandsea Cup>**? Which she could have if she won a singles duel yesterday?

Glenn decided to make the leap. "I knew because I've seen that trick before, Agnes."

Her retort caught in her throat. As she stood with one finger outstretched, speechless, he knew he had her. He had been careful in how he phrased his statement... had she informed him she had not dueled yesterday, he could simply have said he saw another Harmcaster pull the same trick... but it seemed his instincts had been right. It felt wrong to win this way, but he did have to win.

She lowered her finger, defeated. "I don't remember you."

"I don't see why you would. We never dueled, but I watched many duels yesterday."

She kicked the ground. "Fine. You win." She huffed and marched toward Jared, who was sitting and catching his breath near a Lifecaster in white robes. "Good luck, Glenn and Nora."

Glenn barely prevented himself from responding with *"You too!"* He would have been genuine in his statement, wishing her luck in other brackets, but in her foul mood, Agnes would certainly have taken it the wrong way. He had narrowly avoided being called out for cheating... which, no matter how he justified it, he was doing. He didn't know whether to feel relieved or guilty about his win.

Nora thumped him on the arm. "Ignore her. She's a sore loser and a grump besides. Your strategy was brilliant. Bizarre, but brilliant!"

He forced a smile for her benefit. "Thanks."

"Gods, that was so much fun!" Nora clenched her fists. "My heart's *still* pumping, and all I did was use a few Skills and then hide behind a pillar. That was such a rush!"

Glenn chuckled, unable to continue to feel dejected as he evaluated her cheerful mood. "Hopefully our next duel won't be as complicated. I can't imagine that combination is one we'll encounter too often in doubles, but at least now we know how to face a pair of Harmcasters."

Nora giggled. "Shield toboggan!"

The officiant called out again. "We will wait five minutes for the ice from the last duel to melt!" He called the name of the next four duelists, which was Glenn's cue to leave the field.

Nora came with him, then stopped close at his side. "So... now we get a break?"

"We have a little under an hour before our next duel, yes. I'm going to stay and watch as many as I can, but you can take a break if you like."

"No. I'll watch too. It's good to know what our prospective opponents can do, and I might also learn tricks that'll help me keep Terry and Carm from falling in the field. They still give me grief over every time they've died."

Glenn resisted the urge to hug her. He liked her quite a bit, but only as a friend. He never wanted to make her think otherwise. "I doubt those deaths were your fault."

She huffed. "I wish you could make *them* believe that!"

TWENTY

A TRIP TO THE SIX HELLS

A s Becka approached the isolated area of Sun's Cross where she, beneath the watchful eyes of those tasked to officiate, would tackle the second and final leg of the Luminous Maze, she arrived with a weight on her shoulders. She and Anna had been eliminated from doubles yesterday by a ruthlessly quick pair of Skirmishers, and Anna had been eliminated from singles by a powerful Harmcaster who wore **[Ring-Mail Armor]**. Only Glenn and Nora remained in the fight, with Glenn continuing to dominate singles and he and Nora crushing doubles as well.

Becka remained quite proud of them. Having now gotten to know Nora over the past few days, Becka genuinely liked and respected her, and she was a fantastic Lifecaster. With Glenn to ensure their opponents never got near her, Nora ensured no one could ever take him down.

Today was Becka's last chance to make a difference. To help Glenn help Zack and, as well, protect the people of Evolan. If Becka didn't complete the Luminous Maze, she wouldn't have anything to contribute toward Glenn's climb toward level 15. She couldn't help him save Zack. So despite her trepidation about what waited ahead, she would put in her best effort. Nothing would stop her.

There was one comfort in her quest. The Luminous Maze had multiple winners. The first three Adventurers to complete the maze in each of its level brackets would be awarded an experience scroll worth 2,500 experience, with the first in each level group awarded a scroll worth 5,000 experience.

Those experience scrolls were the reward Becka sought, not for herself, but for Glenn. Tomorrow, Glenn would face seven other finalists in the 10-15 bracket of singles, and he and Nora would battle in the 10-15 bracket of doubles as well. All fights would take place in the colosseum beneath the bright sun of Stillwatch. Yet even if Glenn won both singles and doubles, taking first place, each win would net him an experience scroll worth 3,000 experience. Not enough.

Even both scrolls would not level him to 15, so if Becka didn't come through for him (and Zack) today, Glenn would go into tomorrow's duels knowing that even if he somehow won, he would still lose.

She refused to put Glenn in that situation. So as she looked around at the other two hundred or so entrants gathered for the finale of the Luminous Maze, she resolved to defeat all of them.

Or all but three. If they could get Glenn close enough to level 15, he could likely gain that amount of experience in time to resurrect Zack. It was no longer an impossible goal... but they had now made all the mistakes they could make. From this moment on, everything had to go perfect.

As nice as it would have been to have Glenn with her today, she had insisted he take the day off to rest and recover. Between singles and doubles, he had spent six straight days dueling eight hours a day. He needed to be rested and ready to face his duels tomorrow.

Becka knew from her last experience that even if Glenn had come to cheer her on, the Mindbenders and Guilecasters whose Skills formed the Luminous Maze would make it impossible to follow her progress. The maze was more for contestants than spectators, though large crowds did turn out to see what they could see. Finally, if she failed today... she didn't want Glenn to witness that.

The Town Guard once again explained the rules, but everyone had already organized themselves by level groups before he began speaking. Every one of these over one hundred participants had completed the first leg of the Luminous Maze, which meant every one of them was clever and skilled. There would be no clumsy Brutalists or terrified Lifecasters to cushion her climb today.

The Town Guard's repetition of the rules ended quickly. As he announced the start of the second Luminous maze, level 10s poured across the starting line... and vanished. A **[-Phantom Mirror-]** showed the level 11s alone.

The casters behind the Luminous Maze were making it more difficult in every way possible. Now, Becka couldn't even see what the 10s and 11s were encountering before she stepped through that **[-Phantom Mirror-]**. Perhaps that would be for the best. She would have no preconceptions.

The Town Guard's next bellow sent her blood racing. "Level 12s! Enter the maze!"

Becka breathed deep, stepped through the mirror, and gasped as her whole world went black as night. Wind roared on all sides of her —conjured by Arctists, no doubt—and this darkness must be due to **[-False Light-]**. A wave of nausea rose inside her when she realized she could just barely see ground beyond the dark, and that ground was spinning like a top. **[-Skew Perspective-]** at work.

Becka dropped to her knees and breathed to manage her nausea. Soon enough the darkness faded back to light and the endless spinning stopped, but neither of those changes offered her much comfort. Because, as Becka looked around, gaping in alarm, she realized she was in hell.

Or, more specifically, she sat now in one of the Six Hells. As she looked around in astonishment, she recognized this realm, from the books she'd read on the subject, as the Rock Hell. It was exactly as she had seen it described in every Adventurer account of the place.

The Mindbenders had recreated the Rock Hell in such detail and with such conviction that she could not imagine it as anything else. The world they had made was terrifying... but also beautiful in its complexity. One day, she would love to craft an illusion as complex and convincing as this one.

Becka now stood in the center of a barren, floating island holding jagged hills of glass-sharp stone and crisscrossed with rivers of molten lava. Off the edges of the island was sky and void, and thick clouds of ash and smoke roiled around the edges of the island like a sea. She floated above the clouds.

Becka had never been to the Rock Hell, of course. Few had, save for level-capped Adventurers exploring each of the Six Hells in raid groups as they conquered Monsters and Demons that could wipe legions of low-level Adventurers. Only the strongest could survive in the Six Hells.

Yet Becka recognized this setting because of all the journals she'd read that talked about the Six Hells, particularly accounts published by level-capped Adventurers. While some Adventurers were repulsed by the idea of entire realms created by Demons, Becka had found the idea fascinating. Given her general disdain for the Gods, she had always wondered how *other* deities might handle things.

In the case of whatever Demons had created the Rock Hell, they had decided that their ideal world was one without water or trees or vegetation of any kind. Becka knew, rationally, that she still stood in a huge field in Luxtera that Builders had spent the last four days restructuring from scratch to support the final leg of the Luminous Maze. Yet she *felt* as if she were somewhere far more dangerous.

Shadows flickered in and out all around her, likely the other Adventurers in the level 12 bracket proceeding cautiously across the island. Mindbenders must be hiding them from her. Becka needed to get moving. Yet as she rose, she realized she had no idea what direction she now faced.

The darkness and spinning during her arrival had completely turned her about. With the illusion of seemingly infinite space on all sides, she had no way of telling in what direction the finish line waited. Worse, if she took a step in the wrong direction, she could stumble over the starting line.

If she exited the maze on the wrong side, she would be immediately disqualified. She was surprised that none of the level 10s or level 11s had stumbled back out before she entered, but then she remembered that today she was competing only with Adventurers who had completed the first leg of the Luminous Maze. None of those people would fall for such a simple trick.

So how had those before her figured out what direction to go?

Other than the gentle whistle of the constant Stillwatch wind (Becka's only reminder that she was still standing in Luxtera) the only other sound was the bubbling of distant lava rivers. She looked up for any trace of the sun and found nothing. How could she orient herself without the sun?

Simple enough. Becka raised her palm and focused straight ahead. **[-Shadow Blast-]**.

Her bolt of inky black energy rocketed forward and vanished. So there it was. Her blast had gone through the invisible [-Phantom Mirror-]. Becka was just about to walk in the opposite direction before she paused again. What were the chances of her choosing the right direction on the first try?

She pivoted completely about and raised her palm, then sent another [-Shadow Blast-]. It too vanished like the first, and Becka cursed softly. The Law of Consent prevented anyone from targeting her directly... but could they hide her [-Shadow Blast-]s? They were not, after all, alive.

As another gust of warm wind teased her hair, Becka cursed herself for not being quicker on her feet. After living a full week in Stillwatch, she had learned that the warm wind off the mountains always blew in from the west. She also knew she had entered the Luminous Maze on the south side. And while Arctists could create wind and make it blow very hard, that wind was always cold. Not warm.

She closed her eyes and rotated her body until she was certain the gentle wind was hitting her, and teasing her hair, from her left side. Left would be west, which would put south (and the starting line) behind her. That meant if she walked forward at this point, she would be going north... and out.

Five cautious steps assured her she had solved the first challenge. She increased her pace across the hard and uneven ground, but only to a walk. She needed to be cautious of any hidden traps which, given the difficulty of this final leg, would likely be everywhere.

Still, she saw no other Adventurers, and she would very much like to know how they were hiding everyone from everyone else. She encountered her next obstacle not long after. A wide river of molten lava coursed between her and the north. Even from here, she could *feel* its heat.

Mindbenders and Guilecasters couldn't make her feel heat without violating the Law of Consent, and Arctists dealt with wind and ice, not flame. So had the Luminous Maze staff added Infernists to their roster of casters? She knew they could physically heat up rock and stone, and that, again, would not be a direct attack. It would get around the Law of Consent because she would *choose* to walk on it.

She couldn't simply step onto the river of lava. Even if the lava would not kill her, doing so felt like it would violate the rules of the Luminous Maze. A Shadower officiant could step out and grab her arm, then disqualify her for "dying." There had to be some other way to cross this river... but how?

Perhaps the answer was hidden in her environment, like the pitons she'd uncovered near the end of the last leg of the Luminous Maze. Becka dropped to her hands and knees beside the river and lava and felt around carefully, but encountered nothing but hard rock. Not even sand.

No wonder there were four days between the first and second legs of the Luminous Maze. It had likely taken the Builders who constructed this maze four days to rearrange so much of it and turn what had once been a grassy field into hard rock. After crawling about long enough that her knees ached, Becka rose and dusted off her hands. She must be falling further and further behind!

She could not ford the river without being disqualified. It was far too wide to leap even if she could sprint as fast as Ripper. There was one Skill that might allow an Adventurer like Leo to ford this river... [-Featherstep-], a staple of Skirmishers... but the maze designers couldn't have built this obstacle around a single Skill only available to one Class. What was she missing?

Regardless, what she was doing right now was wasting time. She couldn't proceed forward, so she chose to walk west along the river of lava. Perhaps she would find a point of crossing if she followed the river closely enough. Perhaps it only continued endlessly due to Mindbender illusions.

Becka walked along the side of the lava river until she reached the edge of the floating island of rock. The lava fell off the side of it and into a void of upside-down sky, in a lavafall, and as Becka slipped the toe of her boot off that rocky edge, she saw and felt nothing but void. If she leapt off this cliff, she would likely survive the fall to the "ground," but would be disqualified from the Luminous Maze.

Should she double back? Run to the other end of the lava river? How had she encountered no one else despite sharing this field with hundreds of other Adventurers?

She was spiraling. She needed to be calm. So despite everything inside her telling her to hurry, she instead settled with her knees spread and her palms resting atop them.

She closed her eyes and breathed deeply in and out, practicing one of the many meditation exercises Jenny had taught her to use when she was grappling with a problem she couldn't solve. A worried mind was a desperate mind. In her head, she could almost hear Jenny speaking.

"When there's an obstacle in your mind that you can't solve, don't hammer yourself against it. Instead, find a way to discover that the obstacle does not exist. There is nothing to force your way through because your path forward has always been clear. Or... that's what I tell myself."

Becka breathed and considered all she had seen so far. Sooner than she expected, an inkling of an idea came for her. The Luminous Maze creators could have made the final leg of this maze look like anything, any place in Luxtera. Why the Six Hells? And why the Rock Hell, specifically?

What if the clue to solving the obstacle was hidden in the lore of the Rock Hell itself? Becka had read so many stories about the Six Hells, as many as she could find, but had not considered that reading useful until now. What if, instead of treating this maze like a Builder's construct, she treated her environment as the Rock Hell itself? If she took this place at face value, what changed?

Becka opened her eyes and gasped. She had forgotten one fact about the Rock Hell that now seemed blindingly obvious in hindsight. It was a series of rocky islands floating in a great sky... but there was more than *one* level of islands. If she couldn't cross this island... what about the one below it?

She hopped up and hurried once again to the rocky edge of the island which "floated" in the void. Below her coal black clouds roiled, but they couldn't be more than a single story below her. Like a fool, she had immediately assumed that because this was a field made to look like the Rock Hell, and it had been built on the ground level, she couldn't go beneath it. But what if she could?

Becka dropped to hands and knees once more and crawled along the island's edge. Soon, she found a steep but manageable slope... or rather, a chute. It was all but invisible unless one looked directly down on it from above. Her heart soared as she realized she had found the way through.

Now, how to traverse it? Becka was now certain there was another level of passable terrain hidden beneath the roiling coal clouds... or the illusion of them. With time ticking away, she settled on flipping onto her stomach and simply sliding herself backward. She lowered herself into the chute bit by bit, which had the added advantage of keeping her eyes on the island. Not the void.

The rock below her grew steeper and steeper. Soon she was to the point where she knew going any further down would cause it to slope to the point she would lose traction and slip into the void. She had always been terrified of heights, and her body and mind screamed at her that she now dangled thousands of paces in the air. She had to go back up! Or... she had to have faith in her conclusions.

Becka dropped. Her stomach flipped and she barely suppressed a shriek before her boot tips slammed onto something hard that halted her slide. She froze there for a moment, disbelieving, then unfroze her paralyzed body and glanced down. Below her, beneath her boot tips, she saw it.

The top rung of a wooden ladder.

Becka almost shouted for joy. Instead, she looked straight ahead and anchored herself by pushing her hands into the chute on either side. She carefully stepped down to find the next rung, then the next. Soon she could grab the rungs with her hands, and then she descended what she now knew was a sturdy wooden ladder constructed by a Builder. Coal black clouds soon consumed her.

It was too dark to see, so Becka simply kept climbing down. Not long after, the ladder ended. She stepped off onto solid rock, and when she opened her eyes again, she smiled.

She was still in hell, but not the Rock Hell. She now stood in one of the endless fields of pink and purple grass in the Shade Hell, which was one of the more pleasant ones. The ladder she had climbed now stretched up what had become a pillar of slick white calcite. The same tower presented differently.

Becka set off confidently through the thick purple grass of the Shade Hell. As she traced her hands through it and it lightly brushed across her skin, she knew it must be real grass Builders had bodily transplanted to this lower area of the maze. They were simply making it look purple.

She didn't make it far before her progress was balked by another large calcite cliff. As she made her way around it, she mentally connected this towering cliff to the rocky islands she'd seen in the

Rock Hell. This Builder construct was a rocky island above and a calcite tower below, so was it possible there was more than one way to cross the Luminous Maze?

Perhaps a Skirmisher *could* use [-Featherstep-] to ford the lava river and even move from island to island. A Harmcaster might be able to use [-Freezing Slick-] to freeze the lava long enough to run across it. It made sense, in retrospect, that the designers of the Luminous Maze couldn't force maze runners to go any particular way. They could only present obstacles for runners to solve and allow those runners to use whatever methods were available to them to proceed.

Becka's obstacle now was this towering wall of calcite. As she hurried around it, proceeding northeast (she hoped), she looked for another ladder or other way up. She found none.

When she finally made it around the tower, she was confronted with a fence of interlocking purple crystal growths that looked incredibly sharp. One touch of a tip assured her it was quite real, and quite physical. In the Shade Hell, these crystalline fences were known as Shade Crystals.

A chunk of this purple crystal was required for all sorts of powerful enchantments, and because only a party of eight level 40s could easily enter the Shade Hell and acquire it, it was also more valuable than gold. As exciting as that might be, Becka knew this to be another physically accurate Builder prop.

Could she simply blast her way through the fence? She launched a [-Shadow Bolt-] at the crystals and was disappointed when it fizzled out. Whatever these crystals were made of in the real world, it was not something she could so easily blast away, just like in the Shade Hell.

Come to think of it, could a Harmcaster use [-Inferno-] to destroy an obstacle? None had done so in the first leg of the Luminous Maze. Or they had, and Becka hadn't seen them do it due to Mindbender illusions. Regardless, she didn't have any Skills powerful enough to destroy this fence.

It felt like every time she began to proceed forward, she found herself stumbling back. People would be completing the maze soon, and she suspected at least one level 10 and possibly a level 11 had already done so. A level 12 would soon join them, and then any chance to help Glenn would be gone.

Becka racked her brain for what she'd read about the Shade Hell. These Shade Crystal fences were all over it, and in the actual Hell, Adventurers would hack them apart with [Arcane Pickaxe]s built by Preceptor Blacksmiths and blessed by Preceptor Enchanters. She didn't have an [Arcane Pickaxe] handy, however, and hiding a facsimile beneath [-False Ground-] would be too obvious.

Or would it? Anyone who had done yesterday's maze and had searched the side of the lava river above would easily draw the conclusion that the Mindbenders wouldn't use the same puzzle twice. But wasn't the assumption they wouldn't repeat puzzles a puzzle in and of itself? A mind trick?

Becka dropped to her hands and knees and felt around near the fence until her hand landed on the hilt of something invisible. She gasped in shock and delight as she lifted up and pulled a sparkling white pickaxe from the illusionary ground. She laughed at the absurdity of this simple ploy.

How many Adventurers had missed this pick because it was too obvious? Because they overthought the puzzle? She had focused so hard on finding a complex solution, the simple solution had eluded her. She walked forward and struck the crystalline fence of Shade Crystals with the pickaxe.

A section of the fence disintegrated before her eyes, and as she fumbled forward with one hand, she felt no trace of it. There was likely a real person swinging open a gate in the physical fence. Becka walked forward confidently and kept doing so until her world again went black.

She had walked into another field of [-False Light-]. She waited patiently and barely twitched as someone plucked her pickaxe from her hand, likely to put it back where she had found it so the next Adventurer to come through here could make the same discovery.

Her patience was rewarded when the light returned, though this time, she had again been transported. As she looked around at a ground formed of blue and white and towering hills of ice, she realized she was now in the Freezing Hell. The maze builders definitely had a theme going today!

When the wind picked up, it was cold enough Becka hugged

herself reflexively. Those Arctists were certainly enjoying themselves now! As Becka evaluated her surroundings, she suspected the snow flurries in the air were as real as the wind. Arctists could make those with their Skills.

She advanced and nearly slipped and went down. This slick ice wasn't illusionary! She had once read that even the most hardened Adventurers rarely visited the Freezing Hell because it was so difficult to do something as simple as walk around. Crampons were a hard requirement to cross these slick icy plains without slipping and falling, and Becka did not have any of those.

After the third time she slipped and fell on her rear, Becka huffed and resigned herself. It now seemed obvious that the Arctists had resorted to the Harmcaster Skill **[-Freezing Slick-]** and used it to coat this part of the maze. As she remembered Glenn telling her about his "shield toboggan" duel, she couldn't help but chuckle. If only she had seen that! And if only she had a shield!

Still, Glenn showed her the way. Becka alternated between crawling on her hands and knees, scooting forward on her bottom, or sliding sideways along the slick surface. As humiliating as this might be, it was also a way to move forward without continuing to risk twisting her ankle or breaking her arm.

This ice was frigid. Her hands and body ached wherever she touched it. Still, no matter how uncomfortable this maze became, Becka would continue on. Glenn and Zack needed her to be strong.

She continued until the ice grew less slick, then stumbled to her feet. The ice here was visibly harder and less wet, and as Becka ran her hands over it, she realized it was really rock. Chilled rock.

There were limits to what Arctists could accomplish, and only so much area they could cover with **[-Freezing Slick-]**. So now, with the slippery part of the maze over, the Mindbenders had taken over once more. What new challenge did they have in store for her?

As Becka cautiously moved forward, a mist appeared in front of her and steadily thickened. Soon enough she was in a fog so thick she could barely see her hand in front of her face. Another illusion, but an effective one. As the ground behind her shifted, she knew **[-Skew Perspective-]** was at work as well.

So the Guilecasters had used **[-Create Fog-]**. She should have known this was coming. She could also wander in circles for hours or until the maze finished thanks to [-Skew Perspective-], and that was one error she could not afford to make. Once again, she stood still and closed her eyes.

She couldn't trust her eyes, but she could trust her other senses. She focused on those. A warm breeze still blew from her left side—from the west—which assured her she was continuing to move north and closer to the finish line. She also felt heat from the burning sun hidden overhead.

In the end, it was once again the wind that saved her... and her hair. She pushed both hands out in front of her and took cautious steps, paying close attention to how the wind blew and which direction it drew her bangs across her forehead. She might not be moving directly north, but the warm wind was the one thing she knew would move in a consistent direction and which the Mindbenders couldn't alter.

Her hands smacked into a wall. She opened her eyes again to find a sheer mirror that stretched to the horizon on each side and rose higher than she could see. She gawked up at the incredible illusion.

She was now in an approximation of the Wind Hell. Adventurer accounts said an endless fog surrounded the Wind Hell, and once one found one's way in, it was very difficult to find one's way out without assistance. There were also many mirrors like this in the Wind Hell, seamless and clean.

She saw herself in the infinite mirror, watching herself from a pace away. As her reflection smiled coyly, Becka felt a chill as she realized she *hadn't* smiled. That wasn't her reflection.

Her copy in the mirror spoke in her own voice. "You've finally made it all the way here, too late. If only you'd been faster, Rebecka dear. Four level 12s have already crossed the finish line, and we've been watching you flail about since they arrived. It really is amusing. You really thought—"

"Shush now." Becka frowned. "You've just used [-Masquerade-] to become me, which tells me I'm far enough ahead of the others that I can receive personalized attention from an officiant of the Luminous Maze. That suggests I have in no way been eliminated. So how close am I to the end?"

Mirror Becka laughed in a way that she had to, grudgingly, admit was rather diabolical. "I wanted to speak to you before you departed.

You see, Rebecka dear, I am one of the creators of this maze, and I have but one question for you before you leave and return to your old life."

"No. I have a question for you first. Why the Six Hells?"

Other Becka arched her eyebrow. "How do you mean?"

"It's a fantastic illusion, and I'm not exaggerating when I say it's been genuinely thrilling to experience this level of... artistry. Most Adventurers, however, are terrified by the idea of the Six Hells. Is that why you chose this theme for the Luminous Maze? Did you wish to terrify us?"

Other Becka tut-tutted. "You do not seem terrified."

"I'm not. I've always found the Six Hells fascinating, but I am disappointed you didn't choose to reproduce the Spike Hell."

Other Becka sniffed as if offended. "Too many moving parts and too much danger of runners accidentally impaling themselves on the props in a panic. I argued we should try, but I was overruled."

Becka chuckled as she imagined the chaos. "I can see how that might be a concern. So, is it fair for you to speak to me? An officiant speaking to a runner? Or are you the final challenge?"

Other Becka smiled mischievously. "What challenge would that be?"

"In Benjamin Ravendust's account of his journey through the Wind Hell, he mentioned encountering a mirror as tall as the sky and a Demon inside it that took his form. It asked him one question. Had he not answered it, he is certain he would have died."

"You *are* well read!" Other Becka sounded pleased. "Very well. I will ask you one question. However, be aware that if you get this question wrong, you may not be able to complete the maze."

Becka nodded at the inevitable. At least the maze was almost over, and the fact that she was now receiving personalized attention suggested she was among the top few. "What's the question?"

Other Becka smiled malevolently. "Duel me?"

A spectral duel flag dropped between them, directly on top of the mirror, and Becka froze in shock. So far, every challenge she had faced had been physical obstacles supported by visible illusions. None of those obstacles thus far had required the Law of Consent be violated, and all had skirted around the law by simply being present in the maze and forcing her to proceed through them.

Yet this challenge was different. People rarely if ever dueled Mind-benders because so many of their Skills were horrifying when used against a person. A Mindbender could use [-Waking Nightmare-] to lock the other duelist in a horrific dream, or [-Beguile-] to force them to obey their every whim for five minutes. There were likely other Skills that were equally as terrifying.

The question being asked was a difficult one. Was Becka willing to duel a high-level Mindbender to complete the Luminous Maze while knowing all the horrors that could entail? She knew the Mindbender wouldn't kill her and might not even physically injure her... the maze officiants would never allow that... but some scars went deeper than the physical. Scars of the mind could often not be cured.

She wanted to help Glenn. She wanted to save Zack. But was she willing to risk her own mind and her own sanity to do so? Would anyone be willing to risk their mind to win a game?

Most wouldn't. And as Becka realized that the vast majority of Adventurers who reached this point and were asked this question would say "No," she also knew how she could avoid being elimi-nated. There was only one answer she could give "herself" if she wanted to complete this maze. She had to show the maze officiants she wanted this... even if it forced her to live in a waking nightmare.

Becka took a breath. "I accept this duel."

The flag solidified. A moment after that, Becka gasped as her arms and legs betrayed her. Her vision turned an odd shade of purple as Other Becka raised one hand and wiggled several fingers like a puppeteer operating its puppet. Which Becka was now. The Mind-bender has used [-Beguile-]!

Other Becka winked. "It was a pleasure, Rebecka Coldbreaker. Now dance."

The infinite mirror faded as Becka's legs walked her through it. She was now a passenger in her own body, and she was so terrified she could barely think. Yet she did think... she had to think... and a moment later, she gasped as a bright blue plain appeared ahead.

She now stood on ground made of glowing white lines and shim-mering blue squares. The grid extended endlessly in all directions, though she knew it couldn't in reality. It didn't match the descriptions of any of the Six Hells, so this must be something else. A floor of mirrored plates?

Also, for the first time since she'd entered the maze, she saw another Adventurer. A blonde Harmcaster wearing **[Timeworn Robes]** stood in the middle of one of the bright blue squares ahead. When she saw Becka, she gasped and thrust out one hand in warning.

"Careful! Only some of these squares will hold weight! Others collapse as soon as you put both feet on them, and it's hard to tell which is which!"

Becka would have appreciated the warning had her body not still been walking itself forward. She strode out across the grid of blue squares as the Harmcaster gasped.

"Stop! You'll fall if you touch the wrong square! If we work together, we can find the pattern!"

Becka's boots moved of her own accord, and soon she was not just jogging across the squares. She was skipping. As it became increasingly clear the Mindbender now puppeting her body did not intend to harm her, she grew to appreciate the way the other Adventurer moved her limbs. She had never been a particular graceful dancer, but she felt like she could *fly*.

The tips of her boots and heels danced seemingly at random from square to square, but none of the squares collapsed. Behind her, she heard the Harmcaster cry out before her cry was abruptly cut off. Becka knew without looking back that she had attempted to step onto another square that collapsed.

As Becka continued to dance across the endless plain of squares with firm and confident steps, she finally realized what the Mindbender she had encountered was doing. She was puppeting Becka's body using **[-Beguile-]**... but she was only doing that to guide Becka to the *correct* squares.

She'd answered the question correctly! The Harmcaster she'd just seen must have refused to duel the officiant, fearing the repercussions. The other woman had deprived herself of the opportunity to be personally puppeted across the plain of collapsing blue squares. She could still win... but not easily.

One last dance step brought her to a line of solid blue, and then Becka's limbs became her own again. The control was lifted, and then a voice spoke inside her head.

"I consent to end this duel."

Becka smiled. "I consent to end this duel."

That was it. There were no more challenges to best. As Becka stepped across the finish line, the images of the endless blue room faded to reveal a bright blue sky, a blazing sun, and a group of Lifecasters, Mindbenders, Guilecasters, and Arctists gathered by six different Adventurers.

As a group, they clapped for her. Some cheered and several hollered. As Becka stared around in increasing disbelief, she couldn't believe it. She dared not believe it. This had to be the last illusion in the maze. This was some sort of trick.

One of the Mindbenders pulled back her hood. As she walked forward, Becka realized who this Mindbender was. Herself.

The woman passed her face over Becka's face... on her own face...and wiped away the illusion created by **[-Masquerade-]**. That revealed a dark-haired woman perhaps the age of Glenn's mother, Tania. She had a twinkle in her eye as she gazed proudly at Becka.

"You are the first person to complete the Luminous Maze in the level 12 group." The woman inclined her head. "Congratulations, Rebecca. We all enjoyed watching you win."

Becka felt like she might faint. She didn't. Instead, as she looked around at the appreciative smiles of those gathered, Adventurers and officiants, she smiled instead.

"Please. Call me Becka."

"Becka!" someone shouted happily.

Her heart soared at the sound of Glenn's voice. She turned in time to see the man she loved rushing toward her, grinning like a madman. Anna was with him, but Becka gasped again as she saw who else they'd brought along. Ripper. Leo. Sara.

Ripper bounded ahead of Glenn and charged so fast Becka was worried he would leap on her and pin her. Instead, Ripper skidded to a halt just in front of her, whined, and turned his white-furred head sideways. Becka laughed as she eagerly scratched his cheeks and ears, and his tail thumped.

Glenn arrived first, throwing his arms around her and hugging her tight. Anna, Leo, and Sara all arrived next, and Becka enjoyed a series of hugs and heartfelt congratulations before one of the officiants politely ushered them away from the finish line of the maze. Others would be coming.

As Becka leaned drunkenly against Glenn, safe in his arms and surrounded by some of her best friends, she felt as if her steps weighed nothing at all. They hadn't saved Zack yet. The 5,000 experience she could now gift Glenn toward level 15 would only take him halfway to his goal.

But if he won both dueling brackets tomorrow... solo and doubles... he would be able to reach level 15. He would be able to give Zack his life back, and Anna, through her tears, was as aware of that as Glenn and everyone else. They were so close to completing the Gods' impossible Quest.

And tomorrow, Glenn would finally fight in the grand colosseum.

ACT III: A CONSPIRACY'S END

TWENTY-ONE

A SUSPECT'S SCENT
GLENN

As he walked the crowded streets of Sun's Cross with Becka snuggled close up against him and friends all around, Glenn couldn't have been in better spirits. He had always known Becka was capable of winning the Luminous Maze—she was clever and strong and brave—but he had also known that a dozen factors out of her control could prevent her from doing so.

None of those factors had stopped her. No challenge she faced had been enough. The woman he loved had won one of the most difficult contests in the **<Sandsea Cup>**, and in doing so, she had gained an experience scroll worth months of hard leveling.

He couldn't be more happy. He couldn't be more proud of her. And he also couldn't wait to hear the story behind what had happened to Leo and Sara after they vanished from Lakebrooke through the hole in the wall. They had arrived shortly before he set off to wait for Becka at the finish line of the Luminous Maze and had assured him the story must wait.

Yet they were now together. Safe and together. And so after everyone tromped up to the room Anna had reserved for them in the Dancing Skitterer and locked the door, and after Becka verified with **[+Shadow Sense+]** that no Shadowers were hiding in the room with them to eavesdrop, Ripper thumped down in the middle of the room and Leo began his tale.

As Glenn listened in increasing alarm, he learned of how Leo and

Sara had been taken, and of how "Teacher" had led them to the Bone Cage just as he'd surmised their abductor might. He heard of the discovery they made below, Adventurers who had abandoned Luxtera's Climb who Teacher forced to fight. He heard of their narrow escape from the Goblin horde and Teacher's brave sacrifice to secure their escape, and then the challenge that followed.

A trip through the Vaulted Gardens.

Glenn had never tackled the Vaulted Gardens. He had never been desperate enough to subject his party members to a challenge that could lead to them meeting the Forever Death. Even so, he listened in rapt attention as Leo relayed his journey through the gardens, and Sara provided some details about hers. If only he'd been there to help them!

Finally, as Leo concluded his story with their arrival on the public side of the Vaulted Gardens, he looked at Sara. "You tell them about the scripture now. We've already decided we're going to take up Teacher's cause, so we may need their help."

Becka leaned forward and brushed her hair back from her face. "His cause?"

Sara took a deep breath and then, calmly and quietly, told the story of what Teacher had shown her the first day she arrived. The scripture she had touched and opened with her own hands. The voice of the God who had spoken in her head. The voice of Ralun.

Once she finished, no one spoke. Glenn reeled as he struggled to accept what Sara had told him. All of it sounded like madness, but Sara was not mad. She was one of the most level-headed Adventurers he'd ever met, and she would not make something like this up.

Anna whistled softly. "It's baffling. I can't help but wonder if it was some sort of trick. The idea that something like that could be suppressed so completely..."

"It was a Scripture of Ralun," Sara said calmly. "I have no doubt of that, and I've grown more certain of the voice in my head every day since. It was Ralun. Ralun spoke to me."

Becka sighed softly. "I wish I could have seen it. I bet there's all sorts of knowledge about the Gods and our paths that are lost to us in the modern day."

Leo glanced at Becka. "I thought you disliked the Gods and their games."

"Oh, I do." Becka smiled. "But the more you know about how your enemy thinks, the better you will be prepared to deal with them."

Sara eyed them cautiously. "So you believe me?"

"I do." Becka held Sara's gaze. "I've never known you to exaggerate or embellish your experiences in the past, and you've proven repeatedly that you have good instincts. So yes, I believe you did find and read an actual Scripture of Ralun." Becka frowned. "I also find it quite plausible the Gods would penalize us for refusing Luxtera's Climb."

Glenn didn't like the idea of people being penalized for breaking a rule they didn't know existed. "You really think the Gods would refuse an afterlife to people because of that?"

Becka eyed him. "Have you forgotten what they almost did to Wolfpine?"

Glenn winced. He certainly had not.

Becka continued. "According to what Sara has read, Ralun clearly informed us what would happen if we abandoned Luxtera's Climb. The church has simply suppressed that information, as they tend to do. So in this case, the blame lies with the church."

"*Some* in the church suppressed the rule," Leo corrected. "Don't forget the organization includes good people as well, people who have no idea of the truth a select few have hidden."

Becka nodded. "I don't blame everyone in the church. I always found Richard Deepscar pleasant enough, and I also wouldn't dare impugn Lucy's motives, especially now that you two have decided to date."

Leo blushed bright and glanced at the bed. "It's not about her."

Becka smiled his way. "I am happy for you both, by the way."

Leo kept his eyes on the bed. "Thanks."

Glenn decided they'd debated this topic enough for one day. "Either way, I'm just glad to have you both here, and I'm very glad you were able to escape this 'Teacher.' Even if he genuinely believed those who'd abandoned Luxtera's Climb were in danger, and he wanted to fix that, abducting people and forcing them to fight Monsters is not the answer."

Becka lightly elbowed him on the bed. "Then what is?"

"I'll think about it and get back to you."

Anna shuddered. "Well, after all that, I could use a meal. A big meal."

"That's right!" Sara brightened and smiled. "Becka, we should celebrate your accomplishment today. I've never known anyone who tackled the Luminous Maze and won, so I wouldn't be surprised if you become a bit of a celebrity over the next few days. Everyone is going to want to meet the winners of the Luminous Maze, especially the lovely ones."

Becka snorted. "Please don't butter me up further. I might grow intolerable."

Glenn laughed and squeezed her. "I could eat. Gods, could I eat. We're halfway there, aren't we? Halfway to returning Zack to the world of the living."

Leo shook his head. "The world we live in gets stranger every day."

Anna rose. "We can consider all these dangers and oddities another time. For now, let's enjoy a fine meal as... a party... and relax until the duels tomorrow."

Sara rose. "Thank you, Anna. Also, it's good to see you again. I still feel..." She winced.

Anna walked around Ripper and gave Sara a hug. Sara looked a bit surprised, then hugged Anna back. The two women smiled as they embraced.

Anna stepped back. "I do not blame you for what happened to Zack."

"I know. I blame me for what happened to Zack."

Glenn rose and frowned. "Don't ever. It's like we talked about during those first few days in the forest before we found Ripper. Blame the Shadowers. Blame Warrick Paleheart."

Leo shuddered. "I can't believe that man is still out there. And he really told you that he owed you a favor? That you could call on him and he would just... help you out?"

Glenn shrugged. "That's what he said."

"And you *believe* him?"

"Mad as he might be, he seemed earnest enough."

Anna glowered. "Well, I'm never going to forgive him."

Glenn raised a hand. "I haven't forgiven Warrick for what he did to Zack. I simply feel like I understand him a bit better now. Understanding your enemy is how you beat him."

"Or how you avoid being killed," Becka reminded him.

Anna ushered them toward the door. "No more talk of killing. Food! Mead!"

Ripper hopped to his feet and trotted gamely toward the door. Sara smiled and walked after him. "Listen to the woman, Glenn. Tonight, we're just going to be normal Adventurers."

They left Anna's room and headed downstairs as a group. As they walked back into the streets of Sun's Cross, Glenn found them even more crowded with people. With the Luminous Maze over and dueling suspended, the only contests still going would be Monster Battles. It was tempting to go and watch those, but he would enjoy a meal with his friends instead.

At his side, Ripper growled deep and low in his throat.

Everyone stopped in the street. Glenn knew that growl. Ripper had detected something that worried him, and he was letting his pack know.

Ripper stood now with his nose pointing in the direction of the distant colosseum with his ears tilted back and his dark, wet nose twitching as he sniffed. His lips curled back to reveal the tips of his terrifying teeth. He looked like he'd scented prey.

Sara whistled softly, and then Ripper and everyone else moved off the road and out of traffic. There, Sara knelt at Ripper's side and stroked her fingers up and down his spine as she spoke soothingly and quietly. "What is it? A Desouled?"

A desouled body was the only thing Glenn could think of that might set Ripper off like this. They stood now inside the walls of Sun's Cross (technically), which meant the Gods would prevent all Monsters and Demons from penetrating the arena grounds. He tried to imagine why a Deathcaster would risk having a desouled corpse out in the open like this.

This wasn't Wolfpine. The arena grounds outside Sun's Cross were filled with powerful Adventurers, some of which, like Mammoth Cloudcrusher, had long ago reached the divine level cap.

Even a powerful Deathcaster who attempted to do harm to others in a crowd of people this large would quickly be overwhelmed, and that was before the Town Guards got involved. So why was Ripper alarmed? What did he smell?

"You're certain?" Sara asked softly.

Ripper snorted, sneezed, and glanced at Sara with remarkably intelligent eyes. Glenn had no doubt the wolf understood their language now. Ripper was a very smart wolf.

Sara stroked Ripper's head and ears affectionately, and the huge white wolf happily panted at Sara's touch. She rose and beckoned them close.

Glenn was both curious and excited to learn what Ripper had discovered. He hadn't planned to do any Blazer work today, but despite his sympathy for Deathcasters who had committed no crimes, he wouldn't shirk his responsibility to stop one who might.

Sara eyed them calmly. "Ripper just caught the scent of Teacher. Teacher is somewhere on the grounds of the **<Sandsea Cup>**, or at the least he passed through this area recently."

Leo gasped at the same time as Becka, but it was Leo who spoke first. "But... I watched him die!"

Becka touched his arm. "You saw rocks collapse inside a tunnel that separated you from him. You did not see him die. As someone who spent the day with illusions, that's obvious."

"He was facing down an entire Goblin horde, alone!"

"A horde he could have summoned or controlled as part of his training regimen for you." Becka scowled as she considered. "It's possible he intentionally trapped you outside the entrance to the Vaulted Gardens to force you and the others to resume Luxtera's Climb."

Glenn looked around warily. "How close?" The idea of a Death-caster as powerful as Teacher made him nervous. He might need Mammoth's help to arrest this one.

"He's not here," Sara said. "Not close. But Ripper's certain he's passed this way recently. He's also confident he can follow Teacher's scent to wherever he is now."

Becka's brow furrowed. "Even in this crowd? There's hundreds of people in the streets."

Ripper looked straight at Becka and offered a low, offended whine. Despite the gravity of the situation, Glenn couldn't help but smile. Ripper *definitely* understood human speech.

Becka seemed to recognize Ripper's protest as well. "I'm just asking."

"It's him," Sara said. "Ripper never forgets a scent."

Glenn looked at Sara and Leo. "You also said this man bested you and Leo two on one. In that case, I doubt even the five of us could arrest him if it comes to a fight. Not if he's sufficiently high level and he has powerful Desouled at his command."

Sara tapped her lips in thought. "He can't summon his Desouled openly without drawing attention, especially not in a crowd with this many powerful folks. If we can call the arrest close enough and get some [Lawgiver Cuffs] on him fast enough, he may not be able to react." She glanced at Becka. "Just like you did with that high level Shadower in Evolan."

"That only worked because he wasn't expecting it. It might not work with a man who seems as cautious and intelligent as this one. Also, if we fail to arrest him the first time we try, he'll know we're onto him. He could flee before we could try again."

"Or start a rampage that could get multiple people hurt or killed," Leo said grimly. "I don't like our options, but we can't just ignore his presence here. Whether his intentions were good or not, he still abducted people against their will. He needs to answer for that crime."

As one, the three of them looked at Glenn. It was all too easy to understand why. They were looking to him for leadership, again. Even Anna was waiting expectantly.

"It's really my call?"

Becka offered a comforting smile. "It has to be. Leo and Sara were both abducted by this man, so they can't be trusted to make an unbiased decision as to whether we should pursue him." She glanced at the two of them. "I hope you don't mind me saying that."

"No, you're right," Leo agreed. "I want to arrest him, but I'm not sure we can. Safely." He looked at Sara. "Should we notify the church? Given all the high level Spiritualists and Shamanists here to watch over duels, they should have enough strength to arrest him."

Becka shook her head. "If Teacher does have a genuine Scripture of Ralun, the people leading its suppression in the church are unlikely to let him keep it. So if we forward news of Teacher's presence to the church and they arrest him, we may lose our chance to prove the

Scripture of Ralun exists and that the church is unfairly targeting Deathcasters."

Sara winced. "They could toss Teacher into a cell where we couldn't speak to him. I know what he did to us was wrong, but I do believe his concern for us and the others was genuine. If we could simply speak to him again in a neutral setting, we could learn a great deal."

Leo snorted. "Or he could kill us so his secret wouldn't be revealed."

"I don't think he'd do that," Sara reminded everyone, but then she sighed "Still... I can't say for certain he'd negotiate with us. As you all have pointed out, he might also split the difference and vanish again. He's obviously remained free for quite some time."

Glenn looked at Anna. "What do you think we should do?"

Anna's eyes widened. "I'm just a spectator here! I know nothing about this man or what he's done. I'll help you however I can, but I'm not about to make a call like this."

Becka looked at Glenn. "I can make an unbiased decision, but I'm only one vote. So this is up to you, Glenn. Do we report Teacher's presence to the Town Guards? The high-level Blazers? Or do we try to arrest him ourselves and interrogate him in private?"

Glenn considered the possibilities the others had offered and the options they presented. As much as he expected the decision to be difficult, however, as he considered everything they knew, he found the path forward clearer than he expected. They couldn't be certain they could arrest Teacher on their own, but they also couldn't let him escape.

Thanks to his unique Skills as a Soulseer, they didn't *need* to confront Teacher. Not yet. The first step was finding and identifying him. Then they could plan their next move.

"Have Ripper track him to wherever he is now. Once we're close, I'll use [-Soul Scan-] on everyone in the area until I find him. If anyone has Deathcaster Skills on their Status Sheet, we'll know we have our culprit. We'll also have Teacher's real name and level, so we can find him later even if he leaves the area."

"And what do we do if we do find him?" Leo asked.

"We notify the Blazers. Specifically, we go and tell Mammoth once we're certain we have the right culprit. Then, we all arrest Teacher together."

Becka smiled. "I don't know many who could get the best of Mammoth Cloudcrusher. Though I agree we shouldn't bother him without verifying our target."

"That's my thinking. Scout first, without letting our target know we've identified them, then return with high level help and attempt an arrest." He looked at Sara. "You've made it clear that while Teacher was likely part of the Church of Celes at one point, he's not with them anymore." He looked to Leo. "You also mentioned he has respect for the Blazers."

"He said that," Leo agreed doubtfully. "I thought he was simply buttering us up."

"That's possible, but I still think this is the best play. Identify him in case he leaves or escapes, enlist Mammoth and others to arrest him quietly and away from any church observers, and then see what he's willing to tell us about this Scripture of Ralun."

Becka raised her hand. "I agree with Glenn."

One after the other, Sara and Leo raised their hands as well. Even Anna raised her hand, then offered a warm smile.

Glenn chuckled as he looked around at his friends. "So, it's unanimous." He looked at Ripper. "It's on you now, brother. I know you can track him down."

Ripper snorted loudly and dismissively, yet despite his seeming distaste for Glenn's words of encouragement, his tail wagged more than a bit before it stopped. Ripper lowered his nose to the ground and sniffed, then raised his head and sauntered forward.

"Follow us," Sara advised.

With Ripper covertly sniffing the ground every so often to ensure he didn't lose the trail of their quarry, Glenn and the others followed Sara and Ripper across the <Sandsea Cup> grounds. They passed crowds of people spectating random duels and others resting, chatting, or eating. The smells must be overwhelming to Ripper, yet the wolf continued on confidently.

It soon became evident they were headed for the new Sun's Cross colosseum. So far as Glenn knew, there were no active duels or exhibitions going on right now, so with luck, the colosseum would be more lightly populated than on previous days. Ripper led them confidently onto the main road leading to the colosseum and forward. Soon, they reached the south gate.

A single Town Guard stood on duty there. He stepped forward to block their path. Why would a Town Guard be preventing people from entering the colosseum? Glenn scanned him reflexively and identified him as Steven Tallhorn, level 14.

Tallhorn raised his hand. "The colosseum is currently closed for a private event. Only people working with the event staff are allowed inside."

So that was the issue. The colosseum was currently closed to anyone but those working as part of the <Sandsea Cup>. That suggested Teacher worked for that group as well.

Before the others could say anything, Glenn stepped forward. "We're not here to watch the exhibitions. I'm here to speak to someone already in the colosseum. We agreed to meet here for a private consultation related to an ongoing Blazer investigation."

Tallhorn's eyes might have narrowed behind the holes in his full-face helmet. It was hard to tell. "Could I ask your name, citizen?"

"Glenn Graybreaker, Junior Blazer and Truth Seeker in training."

"And given the magnitude of your claim, can I see your Status Sheet to prove it?"

Glenn showed the man his Status Sheet. His enchantment continued to ensure Tallhorn would see nothing that would surprise him. He would see only what Glenn wanted.

"And who are you here to speak to, Truth Seeker Graybreaker?"

The fact that Tallhorn had acknowledged Glenn's title without questioning it was encouraging. "As I stated, I'm meeting a person of interest inside the colosseum to discuss a sensitive matter. To protect the integrity of my investigation and to safeguard the identities of those involved, they would prefer to remain anonymous."

"And your companions?" Tallhorn looked around. "Are they Blazers as well?"

Glenn nodded and looked around. "Go ahead and introduce yourselves."

Leo, Sara, Becka, and Anna all introduced themselves in turn, including their status as Blazers and their ranks. Tallhorn swept his gaze across them once more, then looked to Glenn once more. "You're the only Truth Seeker in this party, correct?"

Glenn hid his disappointment. He suspected he knew where this was going. "Correct."

"So is it necessary for your fellow Blazers to be present while you speak to your contact inside the colosseum? If all you're doing is meeting with them to speak?"

Glenn knew he would be safer if he asked that everyone be allowed to accompany him, but given the colosseum was closed and security seemed tight, he suspected asking Tallhorn to admit five people (and one wolf) who weren't supposed to be there was pushing it. Also, what if Teacher recognized Sara and Leo?

"It's not necessary," Glenn admitted. "I will, however, need my wolf."

Tallhorn looked at Ripper as if seeing him for the first time. "Why?"

"To keep my contact honest." Glenn smiled what he hoped was his most charming smile. "I've never met this contact before, and I'm somewhat worried they may hesitate to be honest with me. I'm not all that intimidating, but Ripper here can be quite intimidating."

Ripper growled and bared his teeth, glaring at the Town Guard. Even so, his tail wagged before he caught it. It was amusing to know Ripper could be so easily won over with flattery, but it probably helped that Glenn meant every word. Ripper could sense that.

Tallhorn observed Glenn for longer than he expected, but Glenn didn't resent that. Having stood a watch himself for years, he knew that the guard was mentally weighing his duty to Kya and his commander against the need of a fellow citizen. When your God would turn you to salt for defying the smallest decree, caution was warranted.

Tallhorn took a step back. "I recognize the urgency of your mission, but I also need to verify your story before I can admit you. Who in the Blazers can verify what you've told me?"

"If you want the source, send phantom correspondence to the Lakebrooke Blazers Guild addressed to Brennon Shadesinger. He's my mentor in the Blazers."

Tallhorn relaxed. "Even all the way out here, we've heard of Brennon Shadesinger."

Glenn chuckled. "Most everyone has."

Tallhorn returned to the side of the gate. "You and your wolf may enter the colosseum. I'll have to ask that the rest of your party remains outside."

Glenn turned to his friends. "I can handle this. Don't you worry."

Becka smiled. "What gave you the idea any of us were worried?" She leaned close and gave him a quick peck on the lips, then slipped close to his ear.

"Nicely done, love. Scan him and get out. Don't take any risks."

Glenn squeezed her in response, then stepped back and evaluated Sara, Leo, and Anna. "I don't think this conversation will take long. Can you all wait for us out here?"

Sara nodded and looked to Ripper. "Ripper, follow Glenn."

"And be careful," Anna added. "We don't want to have to bring you back too."

Ripper panted happily and padded forward. Glenn looked at Tall-horn once more to confirm they were free to pass, then walked through the gate into the colosseum.

Moving into the shade beneath the seats above was a relief. Even though Glenn knew it was simply his perception, it felt like the sun out here was hotter than the one in Evolan.

Glenn led Ripper forward confidently until they turned a corner in the hallway, then stopped and looked at the wolf. "Lead the way, brother."

Ripper stepped past him, sniffed the air, and confidently set off down the hall. It wasn't long before they encountered a pair of Life-casters who looked to be a bit older than Glenn coming the opposite direction. Both eyed Ripper in surprise and Glenn with obvious curiosity.

Ripper ignored them both, which meant they weren't Teacher. Glenn nodded politely and slipped past them before either could attempt to engage in conversation.

Not long after, Ripper turned at a four-way crossing and headed in the direction of the central arena. That was where they encountered a thick, closed door. Ripper sniffed at it, then stepped back and looked at Glenn expectantly.

He couldn't easily open doors. Glenn reached for the handle and found it locked. He hesitated but a moment before squeezing and turning with every point of his Strength.

He winced as a quiet *crack* sounded from inside the lock. He didn't like destroying the property of others, but he didn't have a key to this door. He needed to find his prey. With its lock damaged, the door opened without issue. Glenn stepped through with Ripper on his heels.

He emerged onto the edge of the main arena floor to find it more crowded than he expected. Workers... likely Townsfolk making some extra coin... were in the process of erecting makeshift wooden walls and barricades for some sort of event. Watching over them were nicely dressed Townsfolk who might be Builders supervising the work. Was Teacher one of those?

There were also a few men and women in clean white robes. Church members. Glenn focused on each in turn and used **[-Soul Scan-]** repeatedly. The first two people he scanned were both Spiritualists with no unusual Skills, but the third, a man, made him catch his breath.

His target was a man who looked to be in his late 50s or 60s, which meant he could be even older in reality. Due to their healing and regenerative Skills and Blessings, many Lifecasters lived to be older than the average Adventurer. Glenn scanned his Status Sheet with a mixture of dismay and satisfaction at finally having a plausible suspect.

His name was Duncan Steelwright, a Preceptor Spiritualist, and he was dual classed as a Deathcaster. Or, specifically, a Necromaster. He was a level 28 Necromaster.

Glenn glanced down at Ripper and spoke quietly. "Is that him?"

Ripper fixed his gaze on the man Glenn had scanned. His ears twitched before he swallowed, and then he looked up at Glenn with obvious confidence. Along with his intrusive **[-Soul Scan-]**, that was all the confirmation Glenn needed that he'd found his quarry.

Fortunately, no one out on the arena floor seemed all that interested in yet another person who'd stepped out beneath the sun. Glenn felt fortunate that there were enough people working in the arena that his arrival went largely unnoticed. He whistled softly to Ripper and went back the way he came, once more stepping into the cooler shade.

Duncan was here in the guise of a Preceptor Spiritualist on hand to use **[-Resurrect-]** to bring back any Adventurers who were accidentally killed during the **<Sandsea Cup>**. He was secretly a Necromaster, and he was also the man who'd abducted Leo and Sara, as well as six others, and forced them to fight Monsters. Glenn had found Teacher.

It was also all the more clear to him that attempting an arrest with just him and his party would be a poor idea. They needed help... but if they could convince Mammoth Cloudcrusher to aid them, Glenn doubted they would have any problem getting Duncan into cuffs. Then, finally, they could all get the answers they craved about this man, his belief that the Gods would punish those who strayed from Luxtera's Climb, and his Scripture of Ralun.

As much as he loved books, Glenn wasn't all that excited about reading that one.

TWENTY-TWO
A TEACHER ARRESTED

With his friends waiting outside the busy tavern with Ripper, Glenn slipped into the crowd huddled beneath the cool shade of the large common contestant's tent in the center of the small town erected for the <Sandsea Cup>. The wooden benches and tables, which stretched for twice the length of the Lakebrooke Blazer's Guild, were all but filled to capacity with folks enjoying a midday meal and some cold mead.

Even four days into the cup, the Adventurers participating or observing after they'd been knocked out of their latest contest rivaled a busy day in Lakebrooke. As Glenn firmly but politely navigated the crowd, using his broad shoulders and height to ensure most of those who barred their way went around them, he realized that it was unlikely he would see a combination of Adventurers like this under any other set of circumstances.

Adventurers as low as level 6 sat at the same table with folks who had reached the divine level cap and everyone in between. Their gear ranged from low-level robes and worn **[Dusk Leather]** to shimmering **[Midnight Mail]** that gleamed like glass while somehow also soaking up all the light that touched it. The hubbub in the tent was deafening.

Given the crush of people in the tent, moving forward quickly without trampling someone was impossible. Every moment Glenn delayed was a moment where Duncan Steelwright—Teacher—could leave the colosseum and slip away, but at least Ripper had his scent...

and Glenn had his true identity. Whether they caught him today or a month from now, Duncan Steelwright would answer for his actions, justified or not.

Fortunately, the area the Blazers present at the cup had claimed for themselves was not difficult to locate. Someone had hauled in a tall pole and hung a Blazer banner from it. It clearly marked that section of the tent as off-limits to those who were not Blazers.

While the idea of excluding non-Blazers bothered Glenn in principle, he had to admit it did make sense for security purposes. Blazers could talk freely about whatever investigations or tasks they'd recently undertaken without worry of being overheard. Members of the Shadowers Guild would be particularly eager to eavesdrop.

As Glenn reached the edge of the Blazer section, several people in gleaming armor glanced up at him with a mixture of curiosity and amusement. Glenn tapped the enchanted [Blazer Pin] on his collar. That satisfied the folks on the outer perimeter.

Even in a crowd this large, a man the size of Mammoth Cloud-crusher was not hard to locate. He towered head and shoulders over most people. Mammoth lounged atop a table with his broad back resting against one of the support posts with a frothy mug in hand. The other Blazers had given him a respectful amount of space.

As Glenn made his way forward, Mammoth languidly glanced his way. Their eyes met, and the huge man nodded incrementally as Glenn approached. Two Blazers who looked to be almost as high level as Mammoth glanced Glenn's way as well. Glenn realized then they'd volunteered to keep any Blazers awed by the man's reputation or level at arm's length.

Mammoth briefly inclined his head to his escorts (not that he needed escorts) and then raised his mug to Glenn as Glenn finally moved close enough to speak. The Blazers at the table with Mammoth would overhear everything they discussed, of course, but if Mammoth trusted these people to sit with him, Glenn would trust them too. He was among friends here.

Unlike the day they had first met outside Grassea's Temple of Balance, Mammoth Cloudcrusher did not wear his helmet or [Crystalline Armor]. He wore a simple [Commoner's Tunic] and pants and boots not unlike those he had lent Glenn after he left his duties as a Town Guard. Glenn had made one of those boots into a dog bowl.

What Mammoth did wear, equipment wise, was a glittering **[Crystalline Shield]** with a rainbow aura. Glenn didn't know what the rainbow aura did, but it must be a powerful enchantment. Mammoth, like Glenn, was careful not to go around in public without a shield.

Mammoth's weathered features hadn't changed since the last time Glenn spoke with him as they overlooked Grassea and he learned Glenn Redwood was dead. His dark hair was a bit shorter now, little more than fuzz on his huge, round head, and while his face and scalp remained crisscrossed with white scars, a brand new puffy red one ran along his ear.

What had this man been up to in the last half a year? What world-ending challenges had Mammoth Cloudcrusher faced? While it felt a bit wrong to do so, Glenn now realized he had the chance to finally learn every detail about his childhood hero. Mammoth wouldn't mind.

[-Soul Scan-].

Name: Mammoth Cloudcrusher
Age: 68
Level: 40
Class: Cleaver
HP: 910/910
Blood: 420/420
Experience: 472,500/472,500 (319,244/322,000)
(176,000/176,000)
Strength: 69 (79)
Divinity: 40 (50)
Vitality: 91 (101)
Wisdom: 32 (42)
Prowess: 28
Luck: 18

Mammoth Cloudcrusher was now dual-classed... or tri-classed. That was not at all surprising, given that a man like Mammoth wouldn't rest on his laurels even after leveling Town Guard to 20, leveling Brutalist to 20, and Cleaver to 40. So what new Class had he chosen?

A quick survey of his plethora of Skills and Blessings told Glenn

Mammoth's third Class was an Anchorite, and he had already Evolved the Class into Deathstriker. Was he following in the footsteps of Glory Heartseeker, learning from her as he tackled Luxtera's Climb for the third time? Or did he simply enjoy crushing Monsters and Demons with his bare hands?

As Glenn mentally compared Mammoth Cloudcrusher's Status Sheet with what he remembered of Warrick Paleheart's—that man's Status Sheet remained seared in his mind—he was shocked at how much more Strength and Vitality Mammoth possessed than Warrick despite being over 30 years younger. Mammoth only had two capped Classes, not three.

Then again, as Glenn thought back, he could see why this might be the case. Warrick had mastered Town Guard, certainly, but then he had capped Spiritualist and Plaguemaster, both Classes that focused on Divinity and Wisdom. Warrick greatly outclassed Mammoth in those attributes, so it made sense Mammoth, who had mastered Cleaver (and was now working on Deathstriker) would be superior in terms of Strength and Vitality.

In a one-on-one duel, Warrick Paleheart would have the edge on Mammoth Cloudcrusher at range, but Mammoth would pummel him in melee. And if Glory Heartseeker, Mammoth's party member, was present? The two of them could take Warrick down and capture him with ease. It was comforting to know such strength was available.

And today, that strength could be Glenn's.

Mammoth sipped his mug, then raised it in salute. "How goes your day, Glenn?"

"Honestly? Better than I expected."

"You wouldn't visit if you didn't have something on your mind. What is it?"

Glenn winced. "Am I that obvious?"

"You're driven by the job, Graybreaker. That I appreciate. Now, how can I help you?"

"Do you recall that unpleasant business in Evolan just before I left to hop on a boat out to here? Involving the abductions?"

"Aye. What of it?"

"I've found the man who abducted our people and others. He's here, at the cup, but he's far too powerful for me and my party of

Junior Blazers to successfully arrest. So, if you weren't too busy, I was hoping—"

"You need muscle," Mammoth interrupted with an amused smirk.

"I do." Glenn smiled. "We could very much use some muscle."

One of the two Blazers tasked with keeping random people from begging for Mammoth Cloudcrusher's autograph leaned forward. "Want our help as well?"

Mammoth stretched his huge arms. "You two can relax. I could use some exercise."

Mammoth rolled his head around his huge shoulders and smacked his lips. Muscles rippled in his godly physique. One day, Glenn hoped, he could obtain the levels and accomplishments that Mammoth Cloudcrusher had obtained. One day.

Mammoth set down his mug and then settled his large booted feet on the earth. As he rose to his full height, Glenn once again found himself looking up at a man who stood taller than him by more than two heads. It was rare for Glenn to look *up* at people.

"You know where he is now?" Mammoth asked.

"I know where he was forty minutes ago. If he's left that area since, I'm confident Sara's wolf can track him to wherever he is now."

Mammoth reached a hand into the **[Unfilled Bag]** attached to his large belt and drew out a pair of gleaming silver **[Lawgiver Cuffs]**. "Well then, Truth Seeker Graybreaker. My strong arm is yours. Point me to your quarry and I'll see what we can do."

Glenn smiled warmly. "Thank you. I really appreciate you taking the time."

Mammoth's chuckle was like distant thunder. "I've got nothing much more interesting to do at the moment. Now, let's go."

Glenn led the way out of the crowded tent. This time, people gave way, but he wasn't foolish enough to think people had suddenly decided to make way for Glenn Graybreaker. They were making way for the man who followed and towered over him. Glenn could understand.

They successfully escaped the crush of the tent to find the rest of Glenn's party waiting with Ripper. The big Arctic Wolf's ears flattened as he stared up at the huge man walking behind Glenn. Ripper's tail slipped between his legs. Even Ripper was intimidated by a level 40 Adventurer, but the wolf relaxed as Mammoth smiled, took a knee, and offered his hand.

After a curious look at Sara, who nodded and stroked his ear, Ripper padded forward and sniffed Mammoth's huge and calloused hand. Mammoth then scratched Ripper under his chin. The big white wolf relaxed and was soon panting happily.

"You're a strong one," Mammoth said approvingly. "Nice to meet you, Ripper."

Ripper's ears rose as his tail wagged incrementally. He sneezed, then turned and walked back to stand proudly by Sara's heel. Glenn could swear the wolf was preening.

Mammoth rose once more and looked around. "Shall we?"

"It's an honor to meet you, sir," Leo said.

Mammoth offered a faint smile in response. "I imagine it is." He eyed Anna. "And you'd be the other one. Of you and Glenn, you're cuter."

Anna blushed brightly. "Uh... thank you? I think."

Glenn cleared his throat. "This way. We last saw our quarry at the colosseum."

Glenn set off toward the large and recently built structure with his friends and Mammoth trailing behind. The walk back felt quicker than the walk to the tent, even though Glenn knew the distance hadn't changed. When he reached the Colosseum, he saw no sign of the Town Guard who'd greeted them before. Folks were also moving freely in and out.

"I guess it's open again," Becka said.

"Aye," Mammoth agreed. "It's about time for the Monster Derby."

Leo blinked. "Monster... derby?"

Sara glanced back at Mammoth. "I don't recall seeing that event on the schedule."

"It's not on the official schedule since it's not a sanctioned event. It's a private contest organized by wealthy Merchants from all over the realms, and it's invitation only. Spectators are allowed to watch, but not everyone knows about it."

Glenn couldn't help but be intrigued. "What kind of event is it?"

"Contestants ride powerful Monsters around the colosseum on a big track. The Adventurer who manages to avoid falling off the longest wins."

"They ride *Monsters*?" Sara's brow furrowed. "Are these Monsters Hunter pets?"

"No."

"So what happens if the Adventurer falls off?" Leo asked cautiously.

Mammoth smiled. "Then the riding turns into a fight."

Glenn looked ahead as they reached the entry to the arena. "That sounds horrifically dangerous. And if this event isn't sanctioned by the cup officials, does that mean there aren't any Spiritualists on hand to cast [-Resurrect-] if someone dies?"

"The Merchants who run the event and manage the betting do recruit some to handle any accidents, but they generally recruit Spiritualists who aren't part of the Church of Celes. Independents. The church leadership isn't too keen on the event."

"So that explains what Teacher..." Sara trailed off, then corrected herself. "What Preceptor Steelwright is doing here. He's a Spiritualist with the ability to [-Resurrect-] anyone who dies during the Monster Derby, but he's not a member of the Church of Celes."

"At least anymore," Leo reminded them. "I imagine he was excommunicated when he left the church, especially if he stole a Scripture of Ralun."

Mammoth grinned. "That will make this easier. I don't think arresting a member of the Church of Celes in front of all these witnesses would sit well with the other hundred church members who are present at the cup."

"We'll try to avoid arresting him publicly," Glenn said. "Once we're inside, perhaps we can find a way to lure him away from the crowds and any witnesses." He looked at Becka, Leo, Anna, and Sara. "This is where we part ways until it's over. You'll watch the exits?"

Leo, Sara, and Ripper couldn't approach Duncan without him recognizing them, and there were too many exits to the colosseum for them to watch without Anna and Becka's help. Even if Duncan believed they wouldn't recognize *him*, seeing the people he had abducted would certainly put his guard up. They needed him relaxed before they announced the arrest.

Glenn and Mammoth would be entering via the south entrance, and Becka, Sara, Anna, and Leo would cover the east, north, and west. Short of a hidden tunnel leading out, Duncan couldn't leave without being seen.

"We'll watch the other entrances," Leo agreed. "I wish we could go in there with you."

"He won't get past us," Becka said confidently. "Or, at least, he won't get away."

Glenn frowned at her. "No dying this time."

She scoffed. "I've died *once*."

"I'm just saying. Be careful, please."

Becka offered her warmest smile. "I always am."

"That goes for the rest of you as well. Don't try to arrest Duncan if he flees. Just follow him as best you can, and don't hesitate to call for a Town Guard if you think he's going to pull out a Desouled. Better we lose our chance to interrogate him in private than allow an innocent to be harmed because we hesitated to act."

"And you'll be careful as well," Sara said.

Glenn pointed a thumb over his shoulder at the large level-capped Blazer supporting them. "I have an escort. Just be ready to track Duncan if he runs." He looked to the shadowed archway leading into the colosseum. "Let's go."

Mammoth cracked his knuckles loudly enough they likely heard it fifty paces away. As Glenn led his childhood hero into the colosseum to arrest a powerful Deathcaster who was hiding perhaps the only Scripture of Ralun not hidden away deep beneath a church, he found himself reflecting on how much his life had changed in the past few years. He'd always hoped for grand adventures... but he'd never expected the stakes to rise so quickly.

The air inside the shaded tunnels that wound through the colosseum was much cooler than the air outside, a welcome relief. Glenn led Mammoth down the same path he'd taken when he was last here. When he turned the corner to proceed down the hall toward the door leading to the floor of the arena, however, he found two men standing at the door (which stood open) with one in the process of replacing the lock.

Glenn slowed momentarily, then resumed his confident pace. As he approached the door and the men, one looked up. His gaze passed dismissively over Glenn before he spotted Mammoth walking behind Glenn, and then his eyes widened noticeably.

"Is there... what's the problem?"

Glenn used [-Soul Scan-] on both men to ensure neither was a threat. These men were Devin Grassley, a Culinarian, and Jared Gale-cleft, a Scribe. Level wise, both were in their early teens, as one would expect from Townsfolk in an 8-16 level zone. They must be moon-lighting as hired help at the colosseum to make some extra coin, which made sense.

"Problem with your door?" Glenn asked calmly.

The second man, Jared, recovered enough from his shock to scowl in annoyance. "Some fool snapped the lock. Now Preceptor Lastleaf has us stuck down here replacing it in case some Monster makes a run into the tunnels." He visibly gathered his courage and asked what both men must be wondering. "Who are you, and why are you here?"

So Preceptor Lastleaf was one of the people who'd organized this event, or at least one of the wealthy Merchants involved. Glenn filed that fact away despite having no use for it at the moment. He never knew when some new fact might come in handy.

Glenn smiled placidly. "We're Blazers, and we're here on Blazer business."

The first man, Devin, frowned. "What type of business?"

"I can't share that information. I can tell you that we can't delay. So if you'd be so kind as to step aside..."

"Fine." Devin abandoned his attempts to pull the broken lock out of the door frame and stepped aside. "Though I don't know that you'll find anyone out on the arena floor right now. Everyone's already up in the stands or in the medical area."

That must be where Duncan Steelwright was. "And where's that? The medical area?"

"Head up to the spectator level and look for the tent-covered area right up against the wall next to the expensive seats," Jared said. "Now, can we finish our job before they unleash those Monsters into the arena? I don't want to be anywhere near here when that happens."

Glenn inclined his head. "Of course. Thanks for the help and the information."

"Sure," Devin said doubtfully. "Good luck."

Glenn led Mammoth back the way they'd come and then down

another hall until he found a stairway leading up. After a decent climb, they emerged onto the top level of the colosseum. There, rings of wooden benches would allow rowdy spectators to watch the excitement below.

Glenn swept his eyes across the rings until he found the tarp-covered area Jared had told him to look for. He led Mammoth down the stairs in that direction. They weren't alone.

Both Townsfolk and Adventurers who had either heard about the Monster Derby or been invited by the Merchants who'd organized it to participate in betting were already staking their claim to benches on the lower tiers. It would be difficult to arrest Duncan in front of all these witnesses without drawing attention.

As Glenn approached the shaded medical area, he spotted six figures wearing nice robes of various types, including a man wearing rare **[Moonlight Robes]** that were only available to high-level Casters. He recognized Duncan Steelwright from earlier. As Glenn approached with Mammoth sauntering behind him, Duncan casually glanced their way.

Glenn had just enough time to turn his gaze to the arena. He kept it there as they approached the medical area, hoping Duncan would assume he and Mammoth were simply two more Adventurers who'd come to bet on the Monster Derby.

He didn't need Duncan bolting for the exit before they could take him in quietly. As they approached, a plan for getting Duncan away from the others formed in his mind. He would have to lie, but he was getting better at doing that.

Once they reached the medical area, Glenn swept his eyes across the six people gathered in turn. All were watching him expectantly, but none seemed inclined to engage in conversation. Several were watching Mammoth with nervous looks in their eyes.

Glenn waved. "Sorry to bother you so early in the afternoon. I was hoping to speak to Duncan Steelwright. Is he here?"

Several of those gathered involuntarily glanced at Duncan, which was all the excuse Glenn needed to do the same. Anyone could guess the man's identity based on the reactions of the others. Rather than denying it, Duncan simply smiled a benign smile.

"I'm Duncan." He eyed them curiously. "How can I help you today, Blazers?"

Now to see if he could get the man away from witnesses. Glenn made himself look suitably forlorn. "We were hoping to engage your services. We've had an... accident... during a Blazer training exercise, and we need you to perform a **[-Resurrect-]**."

Duncan winced in obvious sympathy. "I wish I could help, but I've already signed a contract to reserve my **[-Resurrect-]** for any accidental deaths that might occur during today's private event. I can't help you without violating my contract with my employer."

Of all the times for Duncan to choose the moral route! Glenn grimaced. "This is for the Blazers. Can't you make an exception?"

"I wish I could." Duncan eyed him. "Out of curiosity, who gave you my name?"

Glenn mentally scrambled. "Town Guard Tallhorn."

"You spoke to a Town Guard about me?"

"I spoke to a Town Guard to ask if he knew anyone who could offer an emergency **[-Resurrect-]**. No one from the Church of Celes is available right now, but he mentioned that you and several other Lifecasters had been hired for a private event."

Duncan smiled easily. "I wonder who told him that?"

"I can do it!" another man piped up from Duncan's side. This one looked barely old enough to have acquired **[-Resurrect-]**. He stood. "I'm always glad to help the Blazers!"

Glenn barely held back his grimace as he used **[-Soul Scan-]** to verify the man's identity. Nathan Wildsprout, level 31 Spiritualist. Nathan wasn't lying about his qualifications... but he also wasn't the man Glenn was here to arrest.

It hadn't occurred to him until now that Duncan could just refuse his request and that another of those Spiritualists gathered might unwittingly answer it. Becka was so much better at fooling people! If only she was here to handle this.

Still, Glenn focused on what he knew and moved recklessly toward his next course of action. "Didn't you sign a contract with Preceptor Lastleaf as well?"

Nathan grinned proudly. "I'm only here as a backup! I doubt we'll need all six **[-Resurrect-]**s unless the event today goes very poorly."

A Glenn Graybreaker who was here to find a Spiritualist to provide an emergency **[-Resurrect-]** would be pleased at this news and not hesitate to recruit Nathan to bring his fellow Blazer back to life. As Glenn casually glanced at Duncan again, he couldn't fail to see the measured curiosity in the man's eyes.

Duncan was watching him for a clue to his intentions. One of the man's calloused hands also rested on the top flap of his **[Unfilled Bag]**. He was ready to bolt.

What if Duncan pulled a Desouled out of that bag in the middle of the arena? What type of damage could it do before Glenn stopped it? His mind raced with possibilities and dangers until he found one last ploy that was as risky as it was brilliant. He hoped.

Glenn nodded and motioned for Nathan to rise. "Thank you. That'd be very helpful."

As Nathan rose and moved to join Glenn, Duncan and the other Spiritualist in the medical area had to stand up to allow him to squeeze by on the narrow bench. As Nathan was passing in front of Duncan, Glenn produced his gleaming **[Lawgiver Cuffs]**. He stepped into the medical area. The eyes of everyone present widened, but especially Nathan's.

Glenn raised the cuffs and stepped toward Nathan and, by necessity, Duncan. "Don't move, Nathan. Keep your hands where I can see them."

"What?" Nathan asked in alarm.

Glenn offered his most disappointed frown. "I apologize for the deception, but you're under arrest for violating a Gods-blessed contract with Preceptor Lastleaf."

"But I..." Nathan stared as Glenn approached. "But you asked me to help a Blazer!"

"And you signed a contract that you would only use your **[-Resurrect-]** for the purposes of Preceptor Lastleaf's private event. A Gods-blessed contract."

Nathan's face contorted in anger. "So this was all a trick? You tricked me?" He huffed and pointed. "This is entrapment!"

Glenn truly felt bad for using the man like this, but he was now standing within tackling range of Duncan Steelwright with the man trapped between him and the back of the seating ring behind him. Glenn kept his gaze and visible focus on Nathan instead.

Glenn jerked a thumb at Duncan. "You could have said no, just like this man here. Now, give me your hands." He popped open one cuff. "You can speak with Preceptor Lastleaf yourself and explain your actions."

Nathan backed up. "No, I don't think I will!"

Duncan turned to face the man. "Nathan—"

"You're under arrest," Glenn snapped... but he looked at the back of Duncan's head instead of at Nathan. He made to snap his **[Law-giver Cuffs]** onto Duncan's wrist.

The man casually batted Glenn aside with a wave of his hand and vaulted for the exit.

Chaos unfolded as the other four Spiritualists trapped between the seats behind and the seats ahead panicked. Glenn slammed into them and tumbled down a row as Nathan tumbled backward and Duncan vaulted for safety. He almost made it.

Mammoth Cloudcrusher took four long steps that were frightfully fast for a man his size. He snatched a hold of Duncan's **[Moonlight Robes]** and bodily yanked him back.

Duncan spun and launched a chop from one hand into Mammoth's shoulder, but it landed without effect. As the two men wrestled with neither gaining the upper hand, Glenn understood just how strong Duncan secretly was.

Even so, Mammoth had his prey pinned in place for the moment. Glenn managed to disentangle himself from the Spiritualist he'd almost flattened, pulled out his **[Lawgiver Cuffs]**, and stumbled over. Duncan once more attempted to wrench his hands free and run or reach into his **[Unfilled Bag]**, but Mammoth had his wrists locked in a vice.

Glenn slapped one side of his **[Lawgiver Cuffs]** on Duncan's wrist, then snapped it shut. The moment he did so, Duncan relaxed in Mammoth's vicelike grip. Mammoth released his other wrist, and Glenn snapped the other cuff around it.

Just like that, with Mammoth's help, Glenn had captured the dangerous secret Deathcaster who abducted Leo, Sara, and six others and forced them to fight Monsters against their will deep beneath the Bone Cage.

As Nathan scrambled to his feet, he looked around wildly. "But... he said no?"

Glenn fixed Nathan with a calm gaze. "I apologize for the deception. We were never here to arrest you. We were here for Duncan. I just needed you as a distraction."

Duncan said nothing. Now that he was bound with Glenn's **[Lawgiver Cuffs]**, he could neither use his Skills or resist Glenn's orders. He was, for all intents and purposes, helpless.

"But what did Duncan do?" Nathan asked in confusion.

Glenn frowned. "That's Blazer business. It doesn't involve anyone else here. You all can go about your business as you'd planned."

Mammoth crossed his arms and glanced at Glenn. "What now?"

Glenn locked eyes with Duncan, who seemed oddly calm despite having just been captured by two Blazers who he must suspect knew all about his crimes. Despite the situation, Duncan looked almost serene. Glenn saw no trace of worry or anger. That worried *him*.

He couldn't jump at shadows. It was possible Duncan was simply very good at hiding his emotions... or possibly insane. Either way, Duncan was no longer a threat, and he both had crimes to answer for and information Glenn needed.

"Now," Glenn said, "we go somewhere quiet and have a polite conversation."

TWENTY-THREE

A DIVINE GAMBLE

With Glenn in the lead, Duncan marching behind him, and Mammoth bringing up the rear, Glenn led the way out of the colosseum and to the first archway they'd used to enter. He saw no sign of Leo, but he didn't expect to. Leo would have seen him emerging with Duncan in cuffs and have left to gather the others. They would wait for his signal to emerge.

Glenn led Duncan and Mammoth out of the path of foot traffic. After he did so, Duncan looked between them. "You're Blazers."

"Good eyes," Mammoth said.

If Duncan noticed Mammoth's sarcasm, he chose not to make a point of it. "From what I know about Blazers, you can't simply arrest anyone you like. You must have cause for arresting a person. So what cause do you have to arrest me?"

Glenn eyed him. "I think you know."

"I don't. I've never met either of you in my life, and I was given to understand by Preceptor Lastleaf that there was nothing illegal about his private event. If there is something legally amiss in our contract, I certainly wasn't aware of it."

Glenn considered how best to interrogate this man. He focused on all his conversations with his Blazer mentor, Brennon Shadesinger, about the best way to get a suspect to open up to you. How to gain their trust.

He'd had plenty of experience interrogating people back in Lakebrooke, but Duncan might be the toughest suspect he'd ever interviewed. This man would not be easily intimidated. Glenn also suspected he would be unlikely to confess no matter how hard Glenn pressed him on it. The price for a confession would be too great.

So should he start by directly accusing Duncan of abducting Leo, Sara, and six others from Lakebrooke and locking them in an underground cave where he forced them to fight Monsters? Duncan had no reason to admit to his crime, and the only proof Glenn had was Ripper's nose... which was not admissible in court. Moreover, if Glenn started there, Duncan might refuse to say anything and simply remain silent.

Glenn knew Duncan was secretly a Deathcaster, but couldn't explain how he'd learned that without revealing he was also a Soulseer. He wasn't ready to reveal that secret to Duncan or anyone who didn't know it yet. Being able to see anyone's Status Sheet helped him find his quarry, but he couldn't testify about what he'd seen in court.

After a moment's reflection, Glenn decided to see what information he could gather from Duncan that he didn't have. He knew Duncan was a Deathcaster, and they suspected Duncan was a former and now excommunicated member of the Church of Celes. Finally, Duncan couldn't know that Glenn knew any of that, which gave Glenn an advantage.

Sara claimed Duncan possessed a Scripture of Ralun, a holy book that, according to current church doctrine, should not exist. Sara had also said she believed Duncan's quest to save Adventurers who had given up Luxtera's Climb was sincere... at least in his own mind. Whether Duncan was right or not, he *believed* Adventurers who abandoned Luxtera's Climb would not enjoy the pleasant afterlife reserved for those who tackled it with eagerness.

So Glenn would approach his interrogation of Duncan by attempting to lower his guard and his defenses. Duncan, if he was like any other suspects Glenn had interrogated, must fear the worst. He must fear that Glenn knew he was both a secret Deathcaster and guilty of abducting people from Lakebrooke. If he thought otherwise, he might be more inclined to talk.

Glenn imagined a crime that Duncan might be relieved to be accused of, given the alternative. "We received a report from a reliable source that you were also present at an illegal tournament that took place outside Stillwatch last night."

"I was not," Duncan said calmly. "I haven't left Stillwatch since I arrived."

As he spoke, Duncan subtly relaxed. His shoulders widened a hair and his fingers unclenched. Both were signs of a man who had been worried the worst was going to happen and was now secretly relieved it had not. Glenn's approach was working well so far.

"My sources say otherwise. As you may or may not know, all unsanctioned dueling tournaments are disallowed in the zone where the <Sandsea Cup> is taking place, during the cup. Any unexpected deaths could put [-Resurrect-]s on cooldown that could be needed for sanctioned contests in the cup."

"I'm aware of the rules against unsanctioned dueling in the zone during the <Sandsea Cup>," Duncan assured him placidly. "I understood Preceptor Lastleaf's event to be sanctioned by the cup officials. I have not violated any rules. If someone told you I have, I humbly suggest that they made a mistake."

"You deny being present at an illegal underground duel two nights ago?"

"I do. Preceptor Lastleaf's event is the only place I've volunteered my services."

Now that Duncan believed Glenn believed he was guilty of a crime of which he was innocent, Duncan had less incentive to lie. In fact, Duncan would now be incentivized to tell the truth as much as possible. Even if Glenn didn't yet know Duncan was a secret Deathcaster or had abducted people in Lakebrooke, Glenn might figure it out if he dug further.

Duncan had every reason, now, to be as honest as possible with Glenn and the Blazers. Duncan's goal would be to prove himself innocent of a crime he was, in fact, innocent of, then leave before the Blazers "discovered" the crimes he had actually committed. Now Glenn could ask questions while disguising his intent in asking them.

"How long have you been in Caelfall?"

"I arrived just under three weeks ago on the *Flowing Corsair*."

If Duncan was telling the truth—which circumstances and Duncan's goals suggested he would—that meant he had arrived in Caelfall a few days after "Teacher" supposedly died in a rock slide beneath the Bone Steppes. Had Teacher—or Duncan—returned to Lakebrooke that same night and set sail on a chartered vessel, he could have arrived about the time Duncan had.

So far, the timeline matched. Duncan could have been present in Lakebrooke and could have abducted Leo and Sara while still having time to leave them outside the entry to the Vaulted Gardens and sail to Caelfall. Now to nail Duncan's claims down.

"Can anyone who sailed here on that ship verify when you arrived?"

"Captain Crossfellow. I've sailed with him before, and while we don't know each other well, we are casual acquaintances. I'm not sure if he's still at harbor in Aria, but if you speak to him, I'm certain he'll verify when we arrived in Aria."

"And did you then travel directly to Stillwatch?"

"No, I spent a night in Aria. Then I followed the Safe Road from Aria up to Sun's Cross and arrived for the **<Sandsea Cup>** six days ago. I haven't left this area since."

"Where are you staying now?"

"At the Rowdy Runner."

"And can anyone there verify you have booked a room there?"

"The tavern keeper." Duncan provided her name. "She can also verify that I've had meals sent to my room every night since I arrived. You said you have testimony I was present at an illegal dueling tournament recently. You said that tournament took place at night?"

Glenn looked at Mammoth as if visually confirming something. For his part, Mammoth simply looked amused by the whole situation. Perhaps the man enjoyed watching Glenn string along a suspect. Glenn didn't exactly enjoy it... but at least it was going well.

"It did," Glenn admitted, as if he wasn't comfortable doing so.

"Then I couldn't have been there," Duncan said confidently. "The tavern keeper can verify I requested my supper just past sundown and returned my dishes later that night, every night since I've arrived. I don't go out much. She also doesn't allow people in or out past curfew, so I could not have left the Runner afterward."

"You could have snuck out," Mammoth offered. He looked to be enjoying himself.

Duncan smiled blandly. "I'm not a common age boy any more, my friends. I've neither the inclination or the physique to climb out of windows or clamber down gutters. Even had I done so, my room faces a busy street that is still busy even at night. Someone would have spotted a strange man climbing out of his window and reported me."

Glenn made himself look uncomfortable. He imagined how he'd feel if he had accidentally nabbed the wrong suspect and did what he could to wear that worry on his face. He was certain he'd never be as good at deceiving people as Becka, but he *was* learning.

Glenn added a hint of annoyance in his tone. "Where did you sail here from, then?"

"Why do you need to know that?"

"Why don't you want to tell me? Are you hiding something?"

"No, of course not. I sailed here from Lakebrooke. Captain Crossfellow can verify that fact as well."

"And what do you do in Lakebrooke?" Glenn looked him up and down. "You're at least level 30. What business would you have in an 8-16 zone?"

Duncan's brow furrowed. "This interrogation is moving rather far afield from its target."

Glenn made himself look even more annoyed... if that was possible. "Just answer my questions, please. If you're truly innocent, you'd want to cooperate. Wouldn't you?"

Duncan sighed a put-upon sigh. "I'm not proud of this, but without the steady work provided by the Church of Celes, I must work independently from time to time. Lakebrooke is like any other zone. There are any number of Adventurers leveling there at any given time, and when one dies, if there is no Spiritualist with [-Resurrect-] on cooldown available to bring them back to life, I intercede... for a fee."

Glenn scoffed. "So you charge desperate Adventurers to save their friends."

"As does the church," Duncan reminded him mildly. "All I ask in return for my services is the cost of the reagents and a small tip. I also gain experience from using [-Resurrect-] regardless of the level of the person I bring back, as you well know."

Glenn paused his questioning as if thinking deeply about what to ask next. "So, if I understand you correctly, what you claim is this. You've been here in Stillwatch for six days, but you've never left your room at night. You arrived in Caelfall three weeks ago on Captain Crossfellow's vessel and were in Lakebrooke before that. As an independent."

"Correct. You should be able to verify all of this by speaking with the people I've mentioned. I could not have been at this illegal dueling tournament."

Glenn visibly pretended to consider his next question long enough to assure Duncan he was going to get off the hook. "So why did you leave the church in the first place and become independent? Did you do something they didn't like?"

"What leads you to believe I was ever part of the church?"

"You're a Spiritualist. Don't all Spiritualists join the church?"

"I still don't see what this has to do with this accusation about being present at an illegal fighting tournament two nights ago. An accusation you could disprove after one conversation with the tavern keeper at my inn."

"You didn't answer my question."

"And I don't see any reason why I should. I've offered you proof I was not present at the event of which I am accused of breaking the law. All you need do is verify it, and you will see you have the wrong person. The rest of my life is not your business."

"So you dislike the church. Is it their policies that bother you?"

Duncan said nothing.

"Do you have a grievance against the Church of Celes, Duncan? Is that why you refuse to work inside sanctioned channels?"

Duncan crossed his arms. "I don't care to discuss this anymore with you, Blazer, and you've offered no reason why I should. If you think I'm guilty of this crime, then place me in a cell until you've verified my innocence. Otherwise, release me."

Glenn looked to Mammoth again for "help." The big man just shrugged, still wearing a half-amused smirk. He was obviously enjoying watching Glenn play his games but had no interest in joining him, at least in this deception. It was time to turn up the heat.

Glenn turned his gaze to Duncan. "Then I have just one more question for you."

As he spoke, he raised one hand high. That was the signal he'd told the others to watch for. Duncan noticed the odd gesture, but he obviously had no idea what it meant.

Behind Duncan, Leo, Sara, Becka, and Ripper walked into view around the curve of the colosseum. They quietly approached from behind Duncan's back.

Duncan didn't glance behind him, choosing to stare at Glenn instead. He wore a put-upon frown. "I have to say, this is all quite unreasonable."

Glenn pointed behind him. "Do you know any of those people?"

Duncan casually glanced over his shoulder. The man stiffened visibly before he caught himself, and worse, he knew he had stiffened. He knew Glenn had seen that.

"Have you ever met anyone named Tom Brightbow?" Glenn added calmly.

As Duncan turned to face him again, his face looked like it was made of stone. Even so, he could not fully hide the trace of panic in his eyes. Glenn had him.

"What about Maria Rainfeather? Cyrus Hillmane? Evie Green-feather? Oh! What about Erick Crestwing? Have you ever met him before?"

Duncan said nothing. Glenn could see the gears whirring in the man's mind as he tried to figure out how Glenn knew these people. How Glenn knew he was connected to them.

All Duncan knew was Glenn was a Blazer Truth Seeker... and the ways Truth Seekers worked kept criminals awake at night. Some even claimed they could read minds, though Glenn knew that to simply be a matter of research, observation, and deduction. The skills Brennon Shadesinger's tutelage had helped him hone to a fine edge.

Glenn allowed himself a faint smile. "One of the Blazers behind you is Leopold Argentshade. The other is Sara Cinderflare. She's the one with the massive white wolf."

"I've never met them," Duncan said calmly. "Nor do I recognize those names."

As Leo, Sara, Ripper, Becka, and Anna stopped less than ten paces behind Duncan, Ripper bared his teeth and growled loudly. His opinion of Duncan—Teacher—couldn't be more clear. Sara stroked her fingers down the back of Ripper's head to calm him, then spoke.

"Teacher, you can't fool us any longer." Sara walked around Duncan to stand beside Glenn, forcing the man to look at her. "We know who you are now. I know why you did what you did back in

Lakebrooke... why you abducted us... but you must have known that once you released us, we would eventually track you down. We're Blazers."

Duncan eyed her calmly. "I'm sorry, young lady, but I don't believe we've met."

"Then you didn't show me a forbidden tome deep beneath the Bone Cage? A tome that some now claim does not exist?"

Some of the color left Duncan's face at Sara's words. "I don't know what you mean."

Leo stepped forward and scowled. "Cyrus died, you know. So did Kenneth! Both died on our trip through the Vaulted Gardens, the trip you forced us to make. If not for a very lucky set of circumstances, both would have met the Forever Death. That's on you."

Duncan looked to Glenn again. "I don't know what led you to make these wild accusations about me, who these people are, or anything about the events to which you refer. I can, however, assure you that you are mistaken. I'm not the man you think I am."

"Ripper knows otherwise, Teacher," Sara said. "He never forgets a smell."

"Then I would suggest your wolf is mistaken as well."

Ripper growled derisively at that.

Glenn walked close to Duncan and stared him down. He could tell the pressure on this man was building by watching his breathing. With all his cards on the table and Duncan on the defensive, it was time to close the trap. He would force a confession... or else.

"I imagine the Church of Celes would have no trouble figuring out who you are. I also imagine they'd be very interested to learn you have possession of a tome they and the church leadership claim does not exist."

Duncan's jaw clenched.

"So tell me this... Teacher. Most of the leaders of the Church of Celes are here in Stillwatch right now for this event. Some have served sixty years or more, and if you were as highly placed in the church as I and Sara believe you to be, one or more of the current church clergy must know you. Do they know you still have a Scripture of Ralun?"

Duncan's features went entirely flat.

"Do they know who you are? Can they identify you? And if they do identify you... and if they do search your [**Unfilled Bag**], and your room, and we speak to the tavern keeper and the captain and anyone else you've spent time with over the past few months... what do you think they'll find? Is there a chance they could find something you wish to keep hidden?"

Duncan narrowed his eyes. "You don't want to involve the church in this."

"I'm not thrilled about the idea. But I'll do what I must to ensure you never abduct anyone again, and that you pay for the crimes you have committed."

Duncan didn't defend or justify himself. Glenn suspected the man wanted to, to justify his actions by pointing out he was only trying to save their souls, but he was too savvy to be baited into doing so. Yet he was definitely sweating now.

This interrogation was moving in the right direction. Glenn now knew Duncan would do just about anything to avoid being turned over to the church authorities. If he accepted that Duncan did have a Scripture of Ralun in his possession—a tome that otherwise existed under lock in key in the deepest vaults of the most secure churches in the land—Duncan would be desperate not to lose it. And the church, to keep their secret, would be desperate to get it back.

"Here's the rub, though," Glenn added. With the consequences of resistance clear and his target desperate for any escape, it was time to offer Duncan a way out. "I have my own issues with the church. I'd prefer not to involve them if I can avoid doing so."

Duncan watched him warily. "Is that so?"

"So while I *could* turn you and all your belongings over to the church, that isn't your only option right now. You could, instead, turn yourself over to the Blazers. Voluntarily. Confess your crimes and explain why you did what you did. We can make you a key individual."

"I told you, I haven't done anything."

Glenn made his tone earnest now. "You abducted the people I've mentioned to save them, didn't you? You truly believe that the church has us all fooled. You know, from reading the tome only you possess, the tome you shared with Sara, that any Adventurer who abandons Luxtera's Climb will be doomed to an unpleasant afterlife. What was the saying?" He looked to Sara for confirmation. "After death they may wander forever, blinded by the light."

Sara grimaced and nodded. As Duncan looked askance at her, Glenn saw the hint of betrayal that crossed his features. Yet there was something else in Duncan's eyes now as well. Justifiable anger at an injustice he perceived as unforgivable... and, perhaps, hope?

Glenn calmly made his case. "If what you say is true, and the Gospels who lead the church have hidden this fact from the world, then the church is in the wrong here, not you. That means you were right to leave the church and take the scripture. It means you were, if not right, at least well-meaning when you abducted Leo and Sara and Maria and all those others."

Duncan's jaw gradually unclenched.

"The church leaders endangered them, didn't they? They endangered their souls by hiding that their refusal to resume Luxtera's Climb could lead to them ending up in an afterlife nothing like the one they'd expect. You wanted to save them, to save others, but you're only one man. You have no one to amplify your message. No one but us."

"You?" Duncan asked doubtfully.

"Yes. Me... and the Blazers. You know who we are and what we represent. We enforce the laws, true, but our first and most important calling is to protect Adventurers and Townsfolk. A threat to Adventurers like the one you claim... a threat so serious it endangers their immortal souls... is a threat the Blazers would eagerly confront."

"Even the Blazers can't stand against the church."

"But what if I told you we're standing against them already? What if I told you we know secrets about the church and the Gospels that already have us investigating their leadership and questioning their methods? What if I told you all we lack is proof?"

Becka chose that moment to touch his shoulder. "Are you sure you want to take this route? If we tell him what we know about the church, there's no going back."

As she spoke, Becka squeezed his shoulder in a way she could be certain Duncan wouldn't notice. She had stepped onto the stage brilliantly, assuming the part of the cautious ally who didn't fully trust Duncan while Glenn was growing increasingly more likely to do so.

Glenn smiled at Becka. "I think he can help us. If he's willing to tell us the truth."

"And what do you know about the Church of Celes and their methods?" Duncan asked.

He was hooked. Glenn could tell he was hooked. Given all this man must have experienced over the past few decades—leaving his church, leaving his friends, tackling the huge task (as he saw it) of saving Adventurers who abandoned Luxtera's Climb on their own—Duncan must have spent the last few decades being very lonely. Fighting alone.

Glenn knew a bit about how that felt. He knew the weight on his chest and the pit in his belly from when he'd learned he'd have to forever leave behind Wolfpine, and his parents, and his friends, to assume an identity that wasn't his and complete a difficult timed Quest offered by the Gods themselves. A Quest that, if he failed, could lead to hundreds of deaths.

Glenn knew what it felt like to have the whole world weighing down upon his shoulders, at least a little. He knew what it must feel like to be desperate for acknowledgement and help. Duncan must be feeling that burden. He must be desperate for someone to believe him.

He glanced at Becka again. "I need to speak with him alone."

"Are you sure that's wise?" Leo asked.

"No. All of you, give us some space and keep an eye out for anyone who might eavesdrop. That includes you, Mammoth." Glenn smiled. "If you don't mind."

Mammoth chuckled. "If it's all the same to you, now that we've got the excitement out of the way, I'd rather get back to my cups and my revelry. Unless you think you'll need my help to arrest another high-level individual?"

"I suppose the difficult part is over with. Thank you. You've been a huge help."

"I am huge." Mammoth waved and walked off. "Have fun with your interrogation!"

As the big man strode off, Leo, Sara, Becka, and Anna all took up positions where they could intercept anyone who might try to stop Glenn's interrogation of Duncan. It was just the two of them now. An intimate discussion between two people.

"We don't have proof of the church's deeds," Glenn said. "At least not proof we can present in court without allowing those truly responsible to slip free of culpability."

Duncan looked again at those who'd assembled so they could speak in private. He looked at Glenn. "But you've heard rumors."

"I have. I've heard that high-ranking members of the Church of Celes have secretly dual-classed as Deathcasters. I've heard that they've invited other members of the church to do so as well. I've heard that they even force Deathcasters to use Desouled to enforce the will of the church in a way that gets around the Law of Consent."

Duncan's eyes narrowed. "It is forbidden for any Adventurer to choose the Class of Deathcaster, and all who do so will be arrested and tried."

"So they can serve the church," Glenn said. "So the church will control the only Class in all of Luxtera that can control Desouled, which are the only creatures capable of arresting or even attacking others without their consent. Is that why you left the church, Duncan? Did you disagree with their methods? Did you think they were wrong?"

Still Duncan said nothing, but Glenn could tell it took effort to remain silent.

"And then there's your Scripture of Ralun. Since Sara told me about your forbidden book, I've been asking myself why the Church of Celes would hide the existence of Ralun's own words. They must be aware that should anyone ever learn that they suppressed the words of the Gods, they would tell everyone. They would lose all credibility among the populace if the populace ever learned they were *hiding* Ralun's words. So why risk doing so?"

Still Duncan didn't speak. Yet Glenn could see the hope blossoming behind his eyes, the desperate need for acceptance and understanding. The desire to *confess*.

"As I considered why the church leadership would go to so much trouble to hide the Scriptures of Ralun from the world despite the difficulty and danger in doing so, I've come to one possible conclusion. The scriptures must explicitly state that Deathcaster is *not* a forbidden Class. That is one of the only reasons I can think of why the church would suppress them. If Ralun's own words countermanded their decree. Is that true?"

Duncan's eyes widened imperceptibly as Glenn spoke. It was all Glenn needed to know he had uncovered the truth. The Scriptures of Ralun contradicted the words of the current church leadership, and if he was right, Duncan had one of those forbidden tomes in his possession right now. Duncan had evidence that could end the church's conspiracy!

The approach Marion Hawkshadow and the other Blazer leadership had taken to root out secret Deathcasters in the church had seemed reasonable on its surface. He and Anna would scan the senior leadership of the Church of Celes and others until they had a full accounting of all secret Deathcasters within the church. Once they had a complete list of everyone involved, the Blazers could arrest them all at the same time.

Yet completing that plan would take years. Perhaps longer. People like Russell Stillwound would continue to languish in secret church prisons, and people like Harold Stoutcrag would continue to wander in isolation and loneliness. Worse, if Duncan was right, Adventurers who died after abandoning Luxtera's Climb would suffer a fate worth than death.

As Glenn considered their suffering, he realized he wasn't content to wait for the plan of Marion and the others to bear fruit. With Duncan's testimony and the words of Ralun Himself, Glenn had all the evidence he needed to expose the corruption in the leadership of the church. Once that was done, the conspiracy would fall.

People like Lucy Skygazer were the reason Glenn believed this. Lucy was, without doubt, a good person, loyal and devout and brave. He had to believe that the majority of the church, the rank-and-file who loved and adored Celes, were just like Lucy. If Glenn was to reveal the truth about their leadership, they would demand new leadership. They would demand *justice*.

If he found a way to prove the church's leaders were corrupt, the church would investigate and correct itself with no pressure from the Blazers. Marion would likely disagree with him if he suggested this course of action, but he had to trust his instincts... and the goodness of people who'd devoted their lives to helping others. The true core of the church.

Glenn focused on Duncan again. "If what I believe is true... and from watching you as we spoke today, I highly suspect it is... then this need not be the end of your quest to save others. It need not end with your arrest by the church and permanent suppression of the truth you hope to spread. You and I, with the help of the Blazers, can bring the truth to light together."

Duncan watched him without expression. Now it was Glenn who chose not to speak. Instead, with his offer on the table and his quarry desperate for any escape, it was time to let Duncan choose his own path. He had nudged the man as far as he could.

"Let's say anything you've speculated about is true," Duncan said finally. "Theoretically."

Glenn smiled. "Theoretically."

"How would you do what you describe?"

Glenn took a breath as a desperate but plausible plan came together in his mind as if he'd spent hours forming it. "I'd start by winning a bracket of the <Sandsea Cup>. I'm currently a finalist in both the singles and doubles brackets. All I need to do is win one of those."

Duncan's eyes narrowed. "How would you winning a dueling bracket change anything?"

"Think about who will be here tomorrow. All ten Gospels. The entire leadership of the Church of Celes is present at this cup, and they will be present at the awards ceremony."

Duncan visibly considered that.

"And who else will be present at the award ceremony? Besides them?"

"Everyone who attended the cup, I imagine."

"That's right." Glenn smiled as Duncan saw the same plan he did. "So if I win singles or doubles tomorrow, at the end of the day, I'll be invited up on the grand stage. To celebrate my victory, I'll be allowed a brief speech to thank my family and friends and the cup officials."

Duncan's eyes gleamed at the thought. "And what would your speech contain?"

"Before that, let's consider who will *hear* my speech. I will speak in front of hundreds of clergy members who would be scandalized and angered to learn that their leadership lied to them. Thousands of Adventurers and Townsfolk might feel the same."

"That does sound... promising."

"Now imagine if my speech revealed certain secrets the current church leadership wished to remain hidden. Imagine I revealed the secrets the church hopes to hide in front of thousands of witnesses. That would make my words difficult to suppress, wouldn't they?"

Duncan scowled. "But you have no proof."

"We have your tome. The Scripture of Ralun. We could show people that."

"No one would believe that any of the Gospels were secretly Deathcasters, and you certainly couldn't get them to show their Status Sheets to everyone. They would call you a liar, and what then? Even if your Blazers believed you, the church's rank-and-file might not." Duncan stared him down. "What if you start a war you can't stop?"

So Duncan had thought about this too, just like Marion. The fact that Duncan remained concerned about the well-being of others further convinced Glenn that he and this man could make an alliance that could bring down the Deathcaster conspiracy. All it would take is for the two of them to trust each other... which would require Glenn to trust this man.

"As it happens, I can prove the senior leadership are Death-casters."

Duncan eyed him curiously. "How?"

Glenn looked at Duncan again. *[-Soul Scan-].*

Duncan's Status Sheet—his real Status Sheet—displayed before Glenn's eyes. Glenn skimmed it once more, then spoke again. "133,044 of 140,000."

Duncan's eyes widened. "What?"

"That's how much experience you're at when you level as a Deathcaster."

"How can you—"

"58 Strength," Glenn added. "54 Vitality. 49 Skill."

Duncan stared in disbelief. "How did you learn that?"

"That's not all." Glenn calmly read off the other features of Duncan's Status Sheet, the sheet only he could see, including his Slotted Skills and Known Skills. He was halfway through Known Blessings when Duncan raised a hand for him to stop.

Glenn obliged him. He waited for the question he knew must be coming.

"How? How can you see my Status Sheet?"

Now, for the final act of trust. The final act that, he hoped, would bind this man's own crusade to his. They might have different methods for doing so, but Glenn now felt confident both he and Duncan wanted to end the conspiracy that had consumed the leadership of the Church of Celes. Both of them wanted to help people... and they could, together.

Calmly, Glenn reached to the enchanted **[Blazer Pin]** on his collar, the one that allowed him to display a fake Status Sheet to whoever asked, and removed it. Then, he revealed his Status Sheet to Duncan. His real Status Sheet with his unique class.

"Soulseer," Duncan whispered. He looked at Glenn again. "What does it do?"

"Have a look. Start with **[-Soul Scan-]**."

Duncan's eyes peered as he read text they could both see. "So, that's how."

"That's right."

"And that's how you identified me. Despite us never having met before."

"No, that truly was Ripper. Like Sara said, he never forgets a smell."

Duncan sighed. "It didn't occur to me to disguise my scent in a town of this many people. I accounted for human senses, but not those of a wolf."

"So you did abduct those people. You did force them to fight in your arena."

"Given all you've shown me you're capable of, both in terms of your Gods-given Skills and your impressive powers of deduction, I suppose there's little benefit to denying that now. I also wasn't lying about what would happen to their immortal souls if they didn't get back on the ladder. I was trying to *save* them."

"And you have the Scripture of Ralun you showed Sara in your possession."

"I do."

Duncan now believed they shared the same goal. He believed... and wanted to help. Glenn was excited that both an alliance and a victory might be possible now.

"Then our plan may work. Here's how it would play out. After I win one bracket or the other, I'll wait until I'm called upon to give my speech. When I'm given the attention of the entirety of the arena, I'll tell everyone what the church tried to hide."

"Which is..."

"Some among the leadership are secretly Deathcasters. They are also forcing other Deathcasters to work for the church upon pain of imprisonment."

"And what then?"

"You attend as my guest. You produce the Scripture of Ralun in front of everyone in the colosseum. You read the words of Ralun Himself, the passages that prove that Deathcaster should not be a forbidden Class. Those words... your words... proves the Gospels are lying."

"The Gospels will order their clerics to take that tome from me and arrest us both for heresy. Even if they decide to intercede on your behalf, the Blazers will still be forced to start a war they may not be able to win, and as for me? They might simply kill me."

"Not if I prove my words by calling out the church leaders," Glenn said. "When the members of the church arrest me, I'll call out the specifics of their Status Sheets just as I've called out yours. I'll show that I can see Status Sheets without their consent."

Duncan whistled softly. "You'll prove they're Deathcasters by proving you can see their Status Sheets even when they don't allow it. They'd never see that coming."

"No. They would not."

"But won't this make you even more of a target for them? You'll be revealing, in front of the church leadership, that you can expose them."

"It would be a problem if I revealed it in private. But if I confront them in public, with thousands of witnesses, they can't just arrest me. They certainly can't harm me, not unless they pull Desouled out of their **[Unfilled Bag].** At which point everyone will see who they are."

Duncan shook his head. "You're a rather reckless man for a Blazer."

"I'm not just a Blazer. I'm also a Town Guard, a Soulseer, and a Truth Seeker. To honor all of those duties in more, I believe this is my best chance to correct an injustice greater than any I've ever encountered. We will have no better chance to make this right.

Duncan finally smiled. "The way you say that, you almost make *me* believe it."

TWENTY-FOUR
A DUEL IN THE FINALS

The day of the finals for singles and doubles in the 10-15 bracket arrived like any other. Glenn had classified Duncan Steelwright as a key individual under his authority as a Truth Seeker, and while he doubted he had the rank to do that if anyone looked into it, no Blazers here right now seemed inclined to do so. The rules of the <Sandsea Cup> again worked to his advantage.

Dueling in the colosseum didn't last one day. It would last six days, with each glorious day devoted to a single bracket. The first bracket to fight was 10-15, but the next five days would feature 16-20, 21-25, and 26-30. After that would be 31-35 and 36-40 (including quads) which would be the highlight of the contest. Yet, fortunately for Glenn, the awards ceremonies occurred each night.

That meant if he won today, he would be able to make his speech. The speech that would either doom him to a church prison or ensure Deathcasters could never again be abused by a few overzealous traitors within the church. One way or the other, his journey through the cup would end today.

Duncan remained with Sara, Leo, and Ripper in their private room at the Dancing Skitterer. If all went well and Glenn won the quarter-finals, semi-finals, and finals in either the singles or doubles bracket, Sara and Leo would escort Duncan to the colosseum shortly before the start of the awards ceremony. Becka, as the winner of the Luminous Maze, already had her invitation.

This evening, each winner of events in the **<Sandsea Cup>** would make their speeches and receive their prizes: experience scrolls. The event would be well attended, and the crush of people arriving at the last minute would make it unlikely anyone would spot Duncan. Glenn needed to win singles or doubles in order to make his speech and reveal the dirty truth to the entirety of Sun's Cross.

Despite coming up with his plan, Glenn remained nervous. He didn't simply need to win multiple duels today. He would also show the people who had hired Warrick Paleheart to murder him that he was still alive and leveling a forbidden Class. They would then attempt to murder him again, not out of malice or spite, but to "protect the realm" from future Soulseers.

Worse yet, he would be acting on behalf of the Blazers without clearance to do so using authority he did not have. He was unilaterally choosing to openly challenge the church leadership in front of thousands of people and hope against hope that the church's rank-and-file would back him over their leaders. If he mucked this up, the Blazers could be drawn into a war with the church.

Or, more likely, they would disavow him and his actions to avoid that same war.

Nora bumped her shoulder into his. "We'll be fine, Glenn. I've never had more fun than I have fighting beside you. Three more duels to go, and we'll be winners! I've never done anything like this!"

Glenn forced a smile. "When you say it like that, it doesn't seem that hard."

There were only three possible outcomes today. The first would be that he failed to win both the singles and doubles brackets, which could doom Zack to the Forever Death and doom him to the drudgery of Marion Hawkshadow's long-term plan. He couldn't bear to think about that.

The second possibility would be that he won one bracket or the other but failed to convince the church's rank-and-file to turn against their leaders. In that case he would likely be taken into custody either by the church's forces or the Town Guards of Sun's Cross. The Blazer leadership would disavow all knowledge of his actions, and he would end his life in a camp like Russell Stillwound.

The final possibility was that he would win one or both brackets and that his victory speech tonight would convince everyone present that the leaders of the church were corrupt, Deathcasters should not be a forbidden Class, and the Scripture of Ralun and all Ralun's words were real. That was the possibility Glenn fixed inside his mind. Believing anything else was counterproductive.

Glenn wasn't the only Adventurer still in the running that stood both in the singles and doubles brackets. He had done his research on every Adventurer who had made it to the finals, and a man named Kaden Tallstrider was currently his biggest worry. Glenn remained uncertain how he would deal with the man even if he knew everything he'd do ahead of time.

A Harmcaster as strong as Kaden... who fought in **[Ring-Mail Armor]**... was uncommon but not unprecedented. He was known as a "battle mage," though his strategy was unorthodox and unusual. To be effective as a battle mage, an Adventurer had to somehow increase Strength, Divinity, Vitality, and Wisdom all at the same time. That was difficult to do for the best Adventurers.

While casters could not wear most forms of heavy armor—the Gods did not allow it—**[Ring-Mail Armor]**, which was available to unclassed individuals, was one exception. It offered no passive bonus in Blood like robes, but it did offer protection from glancing blades. Kaden wore it well.

Yet while Kaden remained Glenn's biggest worry, the rest of those remaining in the singles and doubles brackets were almost as impressive. Only the best of the best had lasted this long, and while Glenn would otherwise have felt honored to be among their number, knowing he had used **[-Soul Scan-]** to grant himself an unfair advantage made his victories feel... tainted.

Still, accepting the stain on his personal sense of honor was a small price to pay for resurrecting his best friend, and now he had an even bigger goal in mind. Freeing the Deathcasters the church leadership was hiding in secret prisons and ending an injustice that had gone on for far too long. While too many people had thought "the ends justify the means" over the years... in this case, they did.

Glenn hoped.

Today's dueling would be part of a full day of entertainment. They would alternate between singles and doubles matches in the 10-15 bracket and then conclude the day with Monster Battles in the same. This meant there would be six matches in both the singles and doubles brackets. Glenn would be fighting, at most, three matches in each: a quarterfinal, a semifinal, and a final to win it all.

Fighting in that many duels back to back would exhaust even the most hardened Adventurer, and Glenn, like Kaden, was competing in two brackets at once. He would be fighting double the duels others were, and often doing so without rest in between.

Fortunately, Anna once again had his back... and Zack's. As she joined him, Nora, and Becka in their private staging pen of the colosseum, just off the arena floor, she patted her **[Unfilled Bag]**. "I've got enough **[Health Potion]**s, **[Blood Potion]**s, and **[Endurance Potion]**s to keep a whole party running through a zone dungeon. So don't hold back out there, either of you."

Nora smiled warmly at Anna. "You're far too generous."

"I only wish I could do more. If only I hadn't been so careless!"

Glenn squeezed her shoulder. "You're the only reason we can afford to enter all these contests, and the Skirmishers who took out you and Becka are in the finals with us. We'll get your revenge. As for these potions, well... I'll simply say thanks. I'll pay you back with any money I win from the cup."

"Just win. You know why."

"We do," Becka assured her.

Nora eyed them curiously. "Secret Blazer mission?"

Glenn nodded.

"So do I ever get to hear what your secret mission is?"

Glenn smiled at her. "At the awards ceremony today, if all goes right, I'll tell you everything."

Nora grinned wide. "All the more reason we have to win!"

Glenn looked to the colosseum and swept his eyes across the sizable crowd that had already gathered in the stands. Hundreds more were visibly streaming in as the Town Guards tasked with keeping people from stampeding did their work outside. It still boggled his mind somewhat to see this many people in one place. Worse, and soon... all of their eyes would be on him.

Becka touched his chin. "Just focus on the battle, love. The crowd is unimportant."

Glenn smiled. The path ahead was intimidating, but he would

walk it beside the woman he loved. He had to believe that with Becka's help, not even a challenge this great could defeat them.

As nervous as he was while waiting for the first duel to start, Glenn didn't waste energy. When the brackets were announced (with who would face who chosen at random) he breathed a sigh of relief. While he would, again, be fighting in the first solo quarterfinal duel, a duel would get his blood pumping and calm his nerves. Better yet, he would not be facing Kaden in his first match.

He'd be facing Ila Grassclaw, one of two Skirmishers who had made quite the impression on the crowd as she tore through the solo bracket and, with her partner, the doubles bracket as well. Ila was one of the two Skirmishers who had knocked Anna and Becka out of doubles.

Ila was no doubt a formidable opponent and one who would be difficult to beat, but Glenn *could* beat her. He was certain of that, because he had seen her fight and heard accounts from others. He knew enough about her that his knowledge and **[-Soul Scan-]** would give him an edge.

In his experience, Skirmishers generally went along three paths when making their climb toward twenty. The least common was to focus on durability and survivability, fighting in heavy armor with a spear and shield. It was the least common path taken not because it was ineffective, but because those who desired to fight in that way were better off choosing Brutalist.

The most common path was the path Leo had chosen, and it was the most common because it was also the safest and most effective. Leo used his maneuverability and a Skirmisher's many Skills enhancing movement to great effect, but also wore heavy armor and used a long spear to fight the enemy at a distance. That let him freely shift between the roles of Shield and Knife as the situation demanded it and allowed him to counter both armored and agile Monsters.

A Skirmisher who followed the balanced path had only one weakness—a lack of Skills to deal with Demons—but those wealthy enough to purchase a Demonslaying enchantment for their weapon, like Leo, could easily make up for that deficiency. Leo was proof that path was a good one.

The last path a Skirmisher could take wasn't as rare as the armored defensive variant, though it was less common than the balanced path. Those were Skirmishers who focused on pure speed and agility, trading the heavy armor and long spears favored by others in their class for the ability to move, attack, and re-position with skill approaching a Duelist.

The fact that anyone who wanted to fight that way would often simply choose Duelist was why this path in Skirmishers was somewhat uncommon. Ila's choice to follow the path of agility, as a result, was why she had become so popular and favored in the brackets. Her fighting style was reckless, flashy, exciting, and uncommon. She was far more interesting than a dull, slow Brutalist.

The greatest danger to Glenn would be if their duel concluded with neither of them being knocked out. In that case, the judges would decide the winner based on the fervor with which both combatants fought and award points for style, precision, and skill. Glenn wasn't unaware that in a match of style and precision, Ila would be far more favored to win... so he would simply end their duel by KO before it could come to a judge's decision.

When the officiant chosen as referee for the first match of the finals of the singles bracket called him to report, Glenn strode into the center of the colosseum. As he walked out beneath the still-rising sun and in front of thousands of people, the roar almost threw him off-balance. That many people cheering at the same time was deafening. He hoped his ears would recover.

Yet the roar of the crowd wasn't the only thing different about dueling in the grand colosseum in front of thousands. As Glenn stepped onto the sand, a booming voice he'd never heard before echoed over the colosseum. It was [-Be Heard-], a Politician Skill.

"We're just about ready for our first singles quarter-final, folks, and we're going to hit the ground running! Give it up for our first two quarter-finalists in the 10-15 bracket, Glenn Graybreaker... also a Blazer, here all the way from Evolan... and Ila Grassclaw, a wandering warrior with *many* fans!"

It seemed Mayor Whitley, the current mayor of Sun's Cross, was going to personally comment on today's duels. That would make things more interesting. And annoying.

Ila strode out of the pit on the other side of the arena, dark hair trailing as she fixed him with a mocking smirk. Glenn noticed—objectively—that she was a good-looking woman, with a muscular and athletic frame not dissimilar to Ashley Bloodbraid. Ila's skimpy armor made no secret of that.

Rather than a single spear, Ila carried a pair of enchanted **[Magesteel Pike]**s. While each could be wielded with one hand and lacked the range of a spear, they still counted as spears, which meant both would work with all of her Skirmisher Skills. She was trading reach for speed.

One pike burned bright red: enchanted with **[-Burn-]**. The other was blue and left a trail of mist in its wake: enchanted with **[-Freeze-]**. As Ila strode into the large circle that would mark their dueling space, the roar of the crowd somehow grew even louder. Glenn heard catcalls and what might be offers of marriage as well, but he did his best to tune those out.

As he stepped to the edge of the dueling field on one side, Ila did on the other. He looked past her confident smirk and into her soul. *[-Soul Scan-]*.

Name: Ila Grassclaw
Age: 19
Level: 15
Class: Skirmisher
HP: 160/160
Blood: 120/120
Experience: 121,263/124,000
Strength: 18
Divinity: 13
Vitality: 16
Wisdom: 12
Prowess: 24
Luck: 15

Ila's Vitality was lower than he'd expect for a melee class, likely because she had spent her entire climb learning never to be struck in combat. Her Strength was more than respectable, however, and her Prowess was comparable to an Evolved Class. With that combination of speed, agility, and those enchanted **[Magesteel Pikes]**s, she would be a very dangerous opponent.

Like her weapons, Ila's Slotted Skills and Blessings suggested she planned to focus almost entirely on offense. **[-Featherstep-]** would allow Ila to step into the skies and attack him from above if he tried to protect himself with his shield, and like Leo, she could also chain **[-Piercing Throw-]** with **[-Windborne Recall-]** to launch those enchanted spears at him from any direction.

A woman so focused on defeating her opponents likely wouldn't hesitate to blow all her cooldowns in her first match of the day even if it left her with less options later. After all, if she lost to Glenn in her first match, she wouldn't have any options at all. Glenn, by comparison, would need to fight strategically and conserve his strength so as not to be tired for his doubles match with Nora.

As Glenn took one more look over Ila's slotted Skills and Blessings, he fixed an attack plan in his mind. He knew how he could win. Now, he had to execute.

He expected the officiant to tell them to step into their squares. Instead, Mayor Whitley's voice echoed across the colosseum. It seemed he intended to make a speech before singles began.

"And here we are, folks, watching the final matches of the glorious **<Sandsea Cup>**! An event that could only occur here thanks to the endless lobbying of me, your devoted mayor!"

The crowd cheered... sort of.

"Today you will witness feats of martial strength and prowess more impressive than any across the entirety of Luxtera! The best of the best fight here in Sun's Cross, folks, and they can't wait to entertain you today! We'll see bravery, ruthlessness, and blood. Lots of blood!"

The crowd roared their deafening approval of Whitley's speech, and Glenn winced when he realized Whitley wasn't about to stop there. It seemed the mayor intended to milk this event for all it was worth. Given the huge size of this crowd, Glenn suspected Whitley might level because of it.

"Now, let's set the stage for our grand play! We're starting with the singles dueling quarter-finals, and our first two warriors have each defeated over a hundred Adventurers to be here! They may only be level 15, but they've proven that their skill in battle is unsurpassed! Let's have another warm round of applause for Skirmisher Ila Glassclaw and Brutalist Glenn Graybreaker!"

The crowd erupted in another round of deafening cheering and chanting. Overwhelmed, Glenn glanced at where Becka, Nora, and Anna all waited. Becka began jumping up and down and cheering wildly. Her obvious mockery of the crowd set him at ease. They were, after all, simply having fun.

Whitley continued. "In all her many duels before today, Ila has wowed the crowd with her speed, bravery, and aggression. Not to mention she's easy on the eyes!"

Catcalls and cheers rose from the colosseum crowd at that. Before Glenn could frown at them on her behalf, Ila raised both hands and danced in the field, eagerly pumping up the crowd. Glenn kept his frown to himself. If Ila wanted to trade on her good looks, that was her business.

"And her opponent? Glenn Graybreaker came up out of nowhere, folks, but he's smashed and slammed through the competition like a Rock Troll through a paper wall! Not to mention his legendary match where he used his shield as a toboggan. This is one Brutalist who's strong *and* clever!"

Glenn barely held back his wince at hearing such praise heaped upon him, especially in front of this crowd of thousands. Did Mayor Whitley really have to build them both up like this? What if he lost? Losing in anonymity would be bad enough, but losing after all this build up would be embarrassing.

"Now, with the stage set and the actors ready to play their parts, are you ready for some dueling, Sun's Cross?"

The crowd roared again.

"I didn't quite hear that! Are you ready to watch some dueling, Sun's Cross?"

This time, the roar from the crowd felt like it shook the ground. No, that was the colosseum shaking. Because everyone sitting in those stands was now stomping their boots in unison on the wood and stone. Glenn hoped the whole thing wouldn't collapse on them. It sounded like it might.

"That's the enthusiasm I wanted to hear!" Whitley roared. "Now! Let them fight!"

Whitley wasn't an outright ass like Coleman, but Glenn could do with a bit less talking. Still, he supposed this sort of buildup made the dueling more fun for the crowd. This was a show as well.

"Glenn G!" the officiant called. "Are you ready?"

"Yes. Ready."

"Ila G! Are you ready?"

"I am!" Ila brushed one hand through her long hair and spun once more to wave at the crowd. "You folks haven't seen anything yet! And don't forget, I'm *available!*"

The roar the crowd offered in response left Glenn's ears ringing in his helmet.

The officiant wisely stepped off the field. "Step into your squares, then duel when ready."

Glenn stepped into the blue square on the dueling field. Ila stepped into the red. They were old hands at this dance at this point, and the dueling field was set up as it always was, clear of all obstacles save for five thick pillars forming the points of an X. Ila nodded his way, and Glenn nodded back.

"Ila Glassclaw, duel me."

A spectral flag dropped between them."

Ila grinned dangerously. "I accept."

The flag solidified, and she *lunged.*

Even prepared as he was for her speed and agility, Glenn was still shocked at how fast Ila closed the distance. She crossed the field in what felt like a breath. He barely got his **[Steel Shield]** up in time to stop two well-timed thrusts from each of her glowing pikes.

Whitley chortled. "Look at her speed, folks! She's like a Trap Viper from the sand!"

Despite successfully blocking Ila's strikes, the **[-Burn-]** enchantment on one seared his arm through his shield, while the **[-Freeze-]** enchantment that followed cooled and slowed his muscles. Glenn's Health Bar also inched down incrementally, ashing despite the fact that he'd blocked both strikes. Some damage from the enchantments on Ila's weapons could soak *through* his armor.

Glenn followed up Ila's opening with a swing of his own, one that came heavy enough it would have likely crushed her skimpy armor if he'd scored a direct hit. Yet Ila was out of reach before his strike was even halfway to its zenith. She danced around him and attacked again and again.

Whitley, of course, just had to comment. "It might already be over for Graybreaker, folks! He looks like a stunned turtle out there!"

Glenn ignored Whitley and focused on defense. He accepted the mingled stings of flame and ice that passed through his shield and armor and into his body. Whatever damage got through was tolerable and more than survivable given his enormous pool of health. If these were the only strikes she could manage throughout the duel, she wouldn't drop him... but she would still win on points.

"This barrage is almost embarrassing to watch!" Whitley shouted. "What happened to the ruthless Brutalist who cracked a set of **[Steel Armor]** with one swing? Is he tired?"

Perhaps Glenn could be. He circled Ila instead of giving ground and also huffed loudly, making himself sound exhausted. Then, he did what he knew Ila must be waiting for.

After barely blocking her next set of coordinated strikes, he stumbled backward as if exhausted. He allowed his shield to drop just enough to give her a clear view of his helmet and head... if she chose to strike at them. And Ila, flush with adrenaline, reacted exactly as he'd expected.

Thanks to the fact that he'd used **[-Soul Scan-]** on her at the start of the match, the words **[-Piercing Blow-]** appeared in front of her just before she activated her Skirmisher Skill. It would allow either her flaming or icy pike to stab right through his helmet, into his face, and into his head. That would end the duel and might even kill him.

His death wouldn't be permanent. A Spiritualist was on standby just in case one of them died. Still, Ila would knock him out in a single blow and further bolster her reputation as a fierce fighter. The moment she tossed her glowing red pike, Glenn snapped his shield back into position.

It shouldn't have been possible for him to correct so easily had he truly stumbled, but his balance had been perfect since he executed the maneuver. Even so, Ila's burning pike still pierced his shield, his skin, his flesh, and his bone... but didn't pierce further. It lodged in his arm and shield.

Whitley roared in delight. "A spear through his arm and he's not even slowed! Graybreaker's not just a turtle. He's a Rock Troll!"

Glenn knew something about **[-Piercing Blow-]** that many did not. While it did allow any spear or pike a Skirmisher tossed to pierce almost any armor, it could only pierce *one* layer of armor. Instead of taking a spear through his helmet (and head) Glenn had taken it through his shield and arm instead.

The pain of a spear through his arm was excruciating, and Glenn's Health Bar ashed by a full one-eighth. Even so, he remained above two-thirds thanks to his massive Health bar. More importantly, he had deprived Ila of one of her two pikes... because one pike was embedded in his arm.

Glenn pushed away the pain and lurched after Ila. He couldn't use [-Guardian's Heal-] to heal his arm because everyone would see his Health Bar rise and wonder why. Ila dodged his next strike with ease and attempted to go back on the offensive, but she seemed unaccustomed to fighting with only one pike. Her balance, her flow, her rhythm... everything to which she was accustomed was now off.

"He's got Ila on the back foot now, folks! She's fighting with one arm tied behind her back! Can Graybreaker turn this around? Was his defensive posturing a ploy?"

Glenn grinned dangerously. This was the downside of spending your entire climb focused on a single style of fighting, in this case, dual pikes. You could master that particular style and become all but unstoppable when using it, but once you were forced to fight with a different weapon or in a different way, you found yourself unsure how to do so and couldn't react instinctively.

A brown bar appeared above Ila's head. "[-Windborne Recall-]."

He'd been expecting Ila to call back her pike. Ripping it out of his arm would do more damage to him and also return her to full effectiveness. Just before she completed the Skill, Glenn gripped the hilt of her spear and held tight. It bucked in his hand like a wild thing, then went limp.

He'd successfully kept her from retrieving her spear! The way her eyes widened told him she couldn't believe what he'd done, and the rage on her features told him he'd infuriated her. Disbelief and rage were not a good combination if one wanted to keep one's head. Ila must be so frustrated.

"I can't believe it!" Whitley shouted. "Graybreaker just denied [-Windborne Recall-]!"

Whitley knew his Skills; Ila, with the only Skill that would allow her to retrieve her spear on cooldown, attacked. As Glenn easily blocked all follow-up strikes from her single spear, Ila screamed at him. Desperation filled her eyes, and desperation would make her reckless. As she dived beneath his next swing and went in for a blow at his side, Glenn was, once more, expecting that.

Ila's icy pike crackled as it glanced off his **[Steel Armor]** and froze his skin, shaving more points off his Health Bar, but not enough. He swept his shield arm around and clocked her right in the side of her chest with its hard edge before she could withdraw. That sent her reeling.

Whitley roared with the crowd. "She's seeing stars after that, folks! I heard that hit up here!"

Glenn's shield bash sliced Ila's Health Bar in half. Dazed and wobbly, Ila barely kept her feet, but just barely. As she stumbled backward, she looked truly disoriented.

Glenn brought his mace around in a great arc that came in low, lower than Ila could duck. She didn't quite escape his range, and his mace struck her unarmored calf. Bone split and blood soared. Ila screamed and collapsed with a broken leg. Her Health Bar ashed down to less than a fourth.

"Oooooooh!" Whitley's roar joined cries of delight and anger from the crowd. "Two big hits from Graybreaker and our beautiful Skirmisher's got a broken wing! Can anyone *stop* this monster?"

As Glenn stepped forward and raised his mace to deliver the blow that would finish her, he saw that Ila could not continue the fight. He'd taken away her weapon, her balance, and her leg. Her ability to fight was focused entirely around her mobility, and she had none of that now.

He stepped back and looked to the officiant. "I call for a yield."

The crowd in the arena had gone deathly silent. In that silence, the officiant's voice was impossibly loud. "Glenn G calls for a yield. Ila G? Do you yield this duel?"

Ila spit blood, but not in Glenn's direction. "Damn you!"

Glenn eyed her calmly. "I don't want to make this any more painful than it has to be, and I don't want to risk killing you. Your leg's broken and you're down a spear. Your fought well, but our duel's over."

Ila glared daggers at him. "I can't... I suppose I don't have a choice."

The roar of the crowd rose again, with many chanting "Smash her!"

Glenn glanced toward the crowd. He visibly conveyed his disapproval by shaking his helmeted head like he was disappointed with every last one them. Shocking them both, many of them went silent.

He looked back to Ila. "You yield, then?"

Ila shuddered, glared at Glenn, and then sighed. "I yield."

The officiant raised a hand. "Glenn G is the victor. Glenn G advances to the semi-finals!

"And that's your first duel, folks!" Whitley shouted. "What a tale! The striking Trap Viper falls victim to the crafty Rock Troll! Glenn Graybreaker is our first semi-finalist in the singles bracket, but there's three more to be crowned! Now, get ready for the opening round of doubles!"

The roar from the crowd returned in force. While the jeers and boos were audible, the cheers and congratulations all but drowned them out. It was curious how quickly the loyalty of the crowd changed. As Ila clutched her broken leg and grimaced, a Lifecaster in white robes approached.

He raised one hand and immediately cast [-Flash Heal-] on Ila several times. With each heal, Ila's Health Bar rose. Her broken bone receded until it vanished entirely back into her skin.

Meanwhile, Glenn took a firm grip on Ila's still-glowing [Magesteel Pike]. When he ripped it out of his arm and his shield, the pain and nausea that flooded him almost dropped him. He would never get used to ripping objects out of his own body, no matter how many times he did it.

Fortunately, the Lifecaster turned his heals on Glenn after that. The soothing cool of healing Skills sealed his wounds and eased his aches and pains. When his Health Bar once again disappeared, Glenn breathed a sigh of relief. Yet when he offered his hand to Ila, she batted it away.

She hopped up and glared. "I *needed* this, you giant lunkhead."

Glenn pictured Zack's knowing smirk. "So do I."

"Glenn G, you may return to the staging pit," the officiant said. "Ila G? Please report to the aid station for a full examination before you depart the arena."

Glenn walked back to the staging pit without another word. He couldn't help but feel guilty about taking the chance to win the singles bracket from Ila Grassclaw. She might have reasons as desperate as his to win this contest... but he had to put his reasons ahead of hers.

When he returned to the staging pit, Nora hopped up and down and happily slapped him on the back, while Becka kissed him right on the lips. After those two were done with him, Anna offered a **[Vitality Potion]**, but Glenn waved it off. "I'm not exhausted. Not yet."

Anna eyed him doubtfully. "You just took a spear through the arm."

"I've had worse. I am a bit worried about my shield, though." He presented it to them and pointed to a hole big enough to stick his finger through. "That's going to be a problem if I have to block any ranged enemy Skills, like **[-Burn-]**. I'll always take some damage through the hole."

Anna reached into her **[Unfilled Bag]** with both hands and then, without fanfare, pulled out a second gleaming and unblemished **[Magesteel Pavise]**. "Here." She wobbled as she set it down.

Glenn stared at the huge shield, which was almost as tall as he was, and then at Anna. Not only would it block blows from any height, but the material from which it was formed meant it would be highly resistant to ranged Skills as well. That shield must have cost a great deal of coin.

His gaze snapped back to Anna. "How did you know I'd need an extra shield?"

"I didn't know you wouldn't."

Glenn set aside Lillian Stoutcrag's **[Steel Shield]**—he could get it repaired later—and took up the new shield Anna offered. It was well-balanced and well-built. "I'll give it back to you in one piece."

"So long as it keeps you in one piece, Glenn, I'll be content."

"You've done very well," Becka said. "We should have time to focus before—"

Outside, a loud horn interrupted her. As they all turned to listen, Mayor Whitley announced the brackets for the doubles. The first pair to fight in doubles today would be Liam N and Hendrick W. And the pair they would be facing? Glenn G and Nora R.

Becka huffed angrily. "It's like the Gods Themselves conspire to tire you out!"

Glenn grinned and shrugged. "Maybe. After this battle, I'll have six full duels to rest."

Nora clutched his arm. "You should drink a **[Vitality Potion]**."

"I'm fine, remember?" He turned on her. "Remember who I am."

After a moment, Nora nodded. "I remember."

"Now." He clapped her on the shoulder. "Let's hear what Whitley has to say about us."

TWENTY-FIVE
A TRAGIC ACCIDENT

After a harrowing doubles duel against a Duelist and Shadower team that was the first time Glenn couldn't stop Nora from being struck in battle, Glenn and Nora narrowly won their quarter-final duel in doubles. Nora was dropped after the Duelist and the Shadower conspired to attack and outpace Glenn, but their ruthless focus on Nora hurt them dearly.

When Nora, who they'd attacked relentlessly, finally went down from a **[Steel Knife]** in her back, Glenn saw red. The next minute passed in a blur of blades, clubs, and swings, but with Nora out of the fight, the Duelist and Shadower had no choice but to face him directly rather than dancing around out of reach. And once they came within reach, Glenn showed them what a monster he really was.

The doubles duel ended with both men on the other team unconscious and Glenn stumbling around with a sliver of Health. A few more swings and it would have been the end of him, but he'd survived. He and Nora would move onto the semifinals of doubles... once Nora recovered.

After they were back in the staging pit and Nora was resting after being healed, sucking down a potion, Glenn winced and watched her. "I'm sorry about that. I couldn't keep up with them."

Nora spit up a bit of potion, then giggled and wiped her face. She set it aside and touched his knee. "Please, I level with Terry and Carm. Don't get me wrong, that hurt, but I've taken more than my fair share of blows in battle. You don't have to treat me like I'm some delicate flower."

Becka sat down on Nora's other side. "You are nothing of the sort. I can't believe you survived a as long as you did with both of them after you. I'd have dropped in the first few blows."

"You don't have [-Soul Cushion-] and [-Soul Harden-]. But... thank you."

"We've got six more duels to sit through," Glenn said. "Just rest and relax."

Another solo duel followed, where Kaden Tallhorn, the armored Harmcaster, defeated a fast but ultimately outclassed Duelist. The Duelist could easily have sliced through any normal Harmcaster, but Kaden's armor made that much more difficult. Glenn's disappointment grew.

Of the two, he'd far rather fight a lightning-fast Duelist who would pummel him with melee strikes than face a Harmcaster who was armored like a Brutalist. Most Harmcasters couldn't easily move in heavy armor due to their lower Strength attributes, and without robes, Kaden was giving up a good bit of extra Blood. Even so, he made up for that with the powerful strikes from his [Commoner's Club].

After Kaden's win, the doubles semifinals resumed. Glenn was relieved when the two-Skirmisher team that had knocked Becka and Anna out of doubles (which included Ila Grassclaw) went down when facing a duo of Rangers and their fearsome pets, a huge Moss Beast (Glenn hadn't even known you could take a Moss Beast as a pet) and an Antlion wearing a jester's costume. What an odd choice.

Based on the bracketing, Glenn knew he and Nora would face those two Rangers next. With the addition of their pets, they had a full party versus the duo they faced, and while that didn't seem fair to Glenn, there were no rules against it. Fortunately, Glenn knew how to fight Moss Beasts and Antlions.

Four more duels followed over the next hour, and then the semifinals bracket for solos and doubles in the 10-15 bracket were set. Only four Adventurers (or pairs of Adventurers) remained in singles. Kaden Tallhorn defeated a Harmcaster specializing in fire Skills, and then Kaden and his partner, a level 14 Shadower named Cullen Twoblades, defeated a pair of level 15 Shadowers.

After that match, Kaden and Cullen grew even more intimidating. Soon, it was time for Glenn's semifinal singles battle to begin. And his opponent? Once again, Mayor Whitley stoked the crowd.

"It's time for the last semifinal of the single bracket, folks! After this, one of these two will move on to face Kaden Tallhorn, who some are now calling the Bronze Mage. Now, in the blue square, we've got the spear-grabbing, shield-surfing, relentless Rock Troll Brutalist, Glenn Graybreaker! Let's hear it for him!"

As he stepped back out onto the field, Glenn was shocked as the crowd erupted. Were they... cheering for him? Hesitantly, he waved, and the cheers only grew. He looked to the dueling field and easily spotted his opponent. Given the lack of competitors, it was no surprise.

Whitley then introduced Glenn's opponent. "And facing him, a towering mountain of muscle that could give even the Rock Troll pause! A man so strong he broke a pillar of the arena when he tossed a fully armored Skirmisher into it like a sack of wheat! Let's put your hands together for Bart Hartstone, also known as the Avalanche!"

Ahead walked the towering mass of muscle Mayor Whitley had just announced, an Anchorite who looked to be close to the same size as Mammoth Cloudcrusher. As Glenn trudged out onto the field, he used **[-Soul Scan-].** He grimaced as he evaluated Bart once more.

Name: Bart Hartstone
Age: 21
Level: 15
Class: Anchorite
HP: 280/280
Blood: 150/150
Experience: 117,424/124,000
Strength: 29
Divinity: 8
Vitality: 28
Wisdom: 15
Prowess: 9
Luck: 11

Even with the unfair advantage provided by Glenn's Town Guard

Blessing, **[+Unyielding+]**, Bart had almost as much Strength as Glenn did and close to as much Vitality. Without the +10 to those attributes provided by Glenn's shield, Bart would be both stronger and tougher. Worse, Glenn knew that every time he hit Bart, unless he feathered his strikes, Bart's Strength would go up by 2.

Glenn couldn't smash his way through 280 Health Points without raising Bart's Strength to an obscene amount, and while Bart's Blood was low for his level, he still had enough Blood to use **[-Aura Mend-]** five times. So after absorbing five big blows, Bart would still be at full Health but now walking around with 39 Strength, or close to 50 if he used his Blood to activate **[-Adrenaline Rush-]**.

For the first time since he'd started in the dueling brackets, Glenn was facing an opponent who was not only stronger than he was, but just as tough. He'd grown comfortable simply rolling over his opponents like a Rock Troll, but Bart could not be rolled over. He was too big.

Could Glenn challenge Bart to wrestling? The man stood a good head above Glenn, and the muscles on his shirtless body made him look like he could crack an Antlion in half. Wrestling involved skill and leverage, certainly, but a good part of it was still raw Strength. Bart had that.

So if he couldn't beat Bart into the ground without turning him into an overpowered monster, and he couldn't wrestle Bart into submission because the man could easily do the same to him, what were his options? The only ranged Skill he had was **[-Soul Singe-]**, and that would tickle the man.

The answer came to Glenn as he stepped into the blue square and remembered the time he'd dueled *another* Anchorite on the Safe Road to Evolan. It wouldn't be easy, but it was the only chance he had. He would just have to watch for his opening and take it when it came.

Whitley continued blathering on. "It's a clash of titans today, folks, the two biggest men in the field colliding like a hammer and an anvil. Who will break first? Who will shatter beneath the strain?"

The officiant called out. "Contestant Glenn G! Are you ready?"

"Yes."

"Contestant Bart H! Are you ready?"

Bart simply growled his assent.

"Duel when ready!" the officiant announced.

The crowd went silent as Glenn and Bart stared each other down. Bart rolled his bald head around on his massive shoulders, then reached out with one hand. He beckoned mockingly.

"It's time to lose." His voice was like stones grinding upon stones. "Duel me, Graybreaker."

The dueling flag dropped.

Glenn nodded. "I accept this duel." They stomped toward each other like two huge waves about to crash together on the sea.

Glenn ducked Bart's first attempt to grapple him and slammed him in the side with his mace, but he feathered the strike. It barely ticked Bart's Health Bar, but it also wouldn't be a blow hard enough to grant him any additional Strength. Glenn soon found that, even in armor, he was fast enough to barely avoid Bart's clumsy punches and lunges. Yet he couldn't strike back without penalty.

Whitley called out. "What's going on? It's like Graybreaker's afraid he'll hurt Bart's feelings! Has the mighty Rock Troll lost his will to fight? Or is he terrified he'll fall beneath the *Avalanche?*"

Gods, Whitley was annoying! Glenn continued striking, dodging, and blocking as Bart became increasingly incensed by Glenn's refusal to engage him. The fact that Bart was growing frustrated was good. Glenn needed him frustrated. Finally, Glenn's silent taunting accomplished its goal.

A brown bar appeared announcing Bart had just activated [-Adrenaline Rush-]. For the next two minutes, Bart's speed, Strength, and Prowess would be massively enhanced. He would also be seeing literal red as adrenaline filled him, which would make him reckless. Too reckless.

With [-Adrenaline Rush-] active, Bart was almost too fast to avoid. The first time Glenn was too slow and took a fierce punch to the side of his [Steel Armor], he huffed. He could swear he heard his armor *dented*. He blocked Bart's follow-up blow with his massive [Magesteel Pavise] only to have a dent show up on that as well. He'd just gotten this shield, and now Bart was pummeling it!

Yet his tall shield was the key to his strategy. Glenn slapped the side of Bart's shoulder and head again and again with Becka, never hitting hard enough to increase Bart's Strength. He blocked blow after blow with his shield as he danced circles around his opponent. Circles with a purpose.

Bart snarled. "Fight me, coward! Stop dancing and fight!"

"It looks like Graybreaker's completely lost his nerve!" Whitley shouted. "The Avalanche is so powerful even the Rock Troll can't face him! He's on the run!"

Glenn was running... sort of. Bart lunged and grunted, and Glenn ducked and weaved. Finally, he took a blow directly to the chest, by design, and it hit him hard enough to send him flying.

As the edge of the dueling field approached, Glenn worried he'd pushed his luck too far. Bart also followed up after his strike, charging like a bull. Glenn landed and braced for the impact.

Glenn yelled at the top of his lungs. "You can't get through my shield, you big ox! Give up! You're outclassed!" With the motions hidden behind his towering shield, he unsnapped the straps holding it onto his forearm.

Bart howled as he sped forward. Just as Glenn had hoped, Bart grabbed Glenn's giant shield in frustration. The huge man tore at the shield with all his might, hoping to drag Glenn along with it and then pummel him into submission. Instead of resisting, Glenn *tossed* his shield... with Bart holding on.

Bart howled in triumph as the shield came free, but didn't notice the direction he was moving. Glenn spun his body about with Bart's momentum, sending the man flying away clutching his **[Magesteel Pavise]**... and completely out of the dueling field. Bart was now disqualified.

"I don't believe it!" Whitley shouted. "The Avalanche came down on Graybreaker so hard he fell out of the ring! Graybreaker played him like a lute! Graybreaker's our second finalist!"

The crowd roared in either approval or disapproval. Glenn couldn't be sure which. What he could be sure of, as Bart threw down his shield, was that the big man didn't agree with the judges. As Bart huffed and snorted, Glenn knew the man was still seeing red. He backed up as Bart charged.

Glenn was vaguely aware of officiants rushing in and saw the glimmer of a Town Guard's **[God Armor]**, and then he was fighting for his life... or consciousness. Bart swung wildly and rapidly, entirely out of control, and Glenn, without his shield, had no choice but to duck and dodge. Yet he was tired from his contest... the duel hadn't ended, so **[+Regrowth+]** hadn't kicked in... and slow.

One of Bart's meaty hands connected with his **[Steel Helmet]**, and then the world spun. Glenn slammed into a pillar hard enough he momentarily blacked out. When he came to, he was on his back with his helmet missing and Bart was sitting on top of him. Crushing Glenn's neck.

Then two Town Guards arrived and bodily lifted a still-thrashing Bart off Glenn. The man writhed and howled until a Town Guard slapped a pair of **[Lawgiver Cuffs]** around his wrists, at which point he collapsed in their arms. He could no longer fight or punch, so all he could do now was roar.

Another Town Guard grabbed the dueling flag still floating in the arena and snapped it in half. Glenn remembered doing much the same when patrolling with Scott Rosewillow, his old partner back in Wolfpine. Dots danced before his eyes, and then the warmth of **[-Flash Heal-]** arrived.

Becka dropped to his side and helped him up, then Nora and Anna arrived and did the same. As the three of them helped a shaky Glenn to his feet, the Town Guards now led a visibly dejected Bart away in cuffs. He would be spending the night in jail, or possibly more than one night.

"Well, that was..." Mayor Whitley was momentarily silent, which was a shock in and of its own. "Not sanctioned, but certainly exciting. And look at that, folks! Graybreaker's back on his feet thanks to his trio of lovely companions! Let's hear it for our second singles finalist!"

The crowd's roar nearly sent Glenn stumbling. His friends supported him as he picked up his **[Magesteel Pavise]** and then helped him back to the staging pit. As **[+Regrowth+]** did its work, his Strength returned and his lungs re-opened. He was lucky Bart hadn't popped his head off.

Whitley shouted outside. "Our final stage is set, folks! Our two singles finalists are Glenn Graybreaker and Kaden Tallhorn! We'll see Kaden again next, but for now, give it up for the Rock Troll!"

The crowd cheered their lungs out.

Glenn took a potion from Anna and sipped as he recovered, and had a bit of luck. Kaden's team was called to doubles next, so Glenn didn't have to fight another duel back to back. Kaden and Cullen easily dispatched the two-Shadower team, which set them on a collision course with Nora and Glenn.

Glenn was also disappointed to see even two Shadowers couldn't bring Kaden down. Was that really simple **[Ring-Mail Armor]**? It seemed as durable as Mammoth Cloudcrusher's **[Crystalline Mail]**, and Kaden seemed far too durable for a Harmcaster. Leveling against type had served him well.

Today Glenn would face Kaden in the solo bracket and once again in doubles. He would have to fight an armored Harmcaster not once, but twice. Worse, in their doubles match, he suspected Cullen Twoblades, Kaden's Shadower friend, would remain in **[-Shadow Walk-]** until he could ambush Nora.

That left Glenn with no good options. One would be to stay right beside Nora to guard her while Cullen circled invisibly, pinning him down. That would leave Kaden to bombard them from afar with impunity.

Or, Glenn could go after Kaden and leave Nora to be devastated by Cullen. If he couldn't knock out Kaden quickly enough, he'd then face a two-on-one situation like that he'd faced in his and Nora's first doubles duel. Except this time, against the two opponents, he might not win.

Still, before he could tackle Kaden again, he and Nora had their last semifinal match to win. They would face the two-Ranger team (and their pets) that had rolled over Ila Grassclaw and her friend, who had, in turned, rolled over Becka and Anna. Glenn couldn't help that adding pets was a bit unfair.

As he and Nora marched out to the field, the Rangers jogged out as well with their huge Moss Beast and slightly smaller Antlion loping along in tow. Glenn realized then that he didn't know if Ranger pets could die in duels. He suspected they couldn't and would simply fall unconscious if their health was knocked low enough. Once again, Mayor Whitley just had to chime in.

"We're at the last semifinal match of the doubles, folks, and it's going to be a real one. The hulking Glenn Graybreaker and the lovely Nora Rapidbloom now face not two, but four opponents! Can they survive the tag team of Fungus and Aunty, pets of Jesse Calehorn and Reese Stonemason?"

As Glenn walked forward, he used **[-Soul Scan-]** on Jesse, Reese, the Antlion, and the Moss Beast. He was surprised to learn that both the Antlion and the Moss Beast had real names and a Prowess attribute, just like Ripper. The Moss Beast was named "Fungus," while the Antlion in the jester costume was, humorously enough, named "Aunty." Just as Mayor Whitley said.

The names, Prowess, and higher-than-normal Divinity attributes of both Monsters proved that when a Ranger adopted a Monster, as Sara had adopted Ripper, the Monster became "unique." Did Fungus and Aunty also have Ripper's growing intelligence?

That was a mystery for another day. Glenn didn't have to get to know those Monsters today, just get past them to their masters. And with [-Soul Scan-], he would know every Skill these Monsters used before they used it. The Monster also couldn't complain if he used [-Guardian's Smash-], since they couldn't tell the officiant it lasted five seconds longer than a Brutalist's [-Mighty Smash-].

Before he entered the dueling field alongside Nora, he beckoned her close. "I want to come up with a clever strategy, but there really isn't one. I'll charge and use my shield to block as many arrows as I can, and you stay on my heels and use as cover. If they try to flank us, follow me to either side of the field. We'll use the side of the dueling square to ensure they can't pincer us."

She nodded eagerly. "Do you want me to buff you this time?"

"No. Save [-Soul Cushion-] and [-Soul Harden-] to protect yourself. I have armor and more than enough Health Points to weather multiple arrows, and you can heal me through the rest."

"What about the Monsters? They'll never let us reach their masters."

"Of the two, I'm guessing the Antlion is weaker." Glenn wasn't guessing, but he would ensure Nora thought he was. "So I'm just going to hit it straight on. If the Antlion moves aside, I'll charge the Rangers, and if it doesn't, I'll have a Monster cushion. Just be sure and keep up."

Nora thumped his chest armor, then winced and shook her head. "Let's do it!"

They stepped into the blue squares, and after the flag dropped, the fight was on. Glenn raised his massive shield and charged the Rangers, and Jesse and Reese, as expected, split up to pincer them. Meanwhile, Fungus and Aunty charged forward to run interference.

Aunty had less Strength than Fungus, so Glenn targeted Aunty first. He slammed straight into the Antlion and barreled ahead. Whitley, as always, provided his running commentary.

"Reese and Jesse open with a classic circle C! Fungus is closing and Aunty... ooh! The Rock Troll hit him like a boulder!"

Aunty, as expected, grappled Glenn and battered his armor and helmet. Aunty also dug his legs into the grassy field. That would have worked had Glenn not tossed his arms around Aunty in a bear hug, shield and all, and lifted the Antlion off all four feet. He had *just* enough Strength to do that.

Whitley whooped excitedly. "Look at that! Graybreaker's carrying that Antlion around like a giant baby! I can't believe I'm seeing this, folks!"

Nora cried out behind him, suggesting at least one of the arrows from Jesse had made it through her shield. The heavy thumping of Fungus's feet told him the Moss Beast was closing from behind as well, and Reese, ever nimble, was darting toward Glenn's side of the ring. Reese would circle and shoot.

Glenn decided on a risk. *[-Soul Singe-]*. For the first time since he'd entered the brackets, he used his ranged Soulseer Skill on Reese. It would only shave off 2 Health Points a second, but the itching and burning might distract her enough she'd make a wrong move.

"Look at that Moss Beast charge, folks! Rapidbloom better watch out!"

Behind them, Nora shrieked as Fungus caught up with her. It slammed its joined fists down on top of her. It didn't quite break through her [-Soul Harden-] bubble, but it dropped her to her knees and killed her momentum. Meanwhile, Aunty was close to tipping Glenn over. He was dizzy from its strikes.

"Oh, Rapidbloom's gonna' feel that one in the morning!" Whitley crowed.

Then they got lucky. Reese stumbled, probably reeling from [-Soul Singe-]. Glenn, still carrying Aunty ahead of him as a body shield, caught up and flung the Antlion away.

Reese tried to get up, but she was too slow. Three brutal swings of his mace later, the Ranger dropped with a sliver of Health Points and collapsed. Aunty shrieked and rushed over to guard his downed

Ranger but didn't attack. Taking out a Ranger also disqualified her pet from battle.

"Reese and Aunty are out, folks! That means... look at Fungus! He's tossing Rapidbloom around like his personal plaything! He's shaking her like a ragdoll!"

Behind him, Nora shrieked as Fungus yanked her once more into the air. Even as Glenn sprinted back to save her, Fungus pulled Nora's arms out painfully to each side. That left her utterly defenseless as Jesse riddled Nora's shield bubble with arrow after arrow, each stopping closer to its mark.

As Glenn arrived, he swung at Fungus's leg. At the same moment, one of Jesse's gleaming arrows struck Nora in the head. Nora's Health Bar, which had been at half due to Fungus's rough treatment, instantly faded to a sliver of red. She was out.

As Fungus stumbled with Glenn's strike, he tossed an unconscious Nora with force. And as Nora's limp and spinning body flew across the arena, she hit a pillar with her head. Her neck bent in a way it shouldn't bend, with a sickening crack, and then her body dropped.

As Nora hit the field, her Health Bar charred completely black... and vanished. As the crowd collectively sucked in its breath, Glenn realized, to his horror, what had happened. Nora was dead. The momentum and impact of hitting that pillar had just killed her!

That arrow through Nora's head had been a critical hit, but the Gods had protected Nora from death. When they did so, her duel ended. But after Glenn struck Fungus, the Moss Beast accidentally lost his grip and tossed Nora... and then, simply through existing momentum, Nora hit that pole.

The Moss Beast had not intended to kill Nora. Jesse hadn't intended to kill Nora. The Moss Beast had simply lost its balance when Glenn smashed its legs and sent Nora flying through the air on accident. Which was why the Law of Consent hadn't saved Nora from death.

As Fungus leapt between Glenn and Jesse, Glenn wanted to sweep Nora up in his arms and scream. Instead, he used **[-Guardian's Smash-]** to stun Fungus for ten seconds (a Moss Beast, after all, couldn't report him) and then sprinted past the Monster toward Jesse. She unleashed arrow after arrow as he charged, but his shield and armor blocked them all.

Glenn was almost on top of Jesse when she tossed down her bow. "I yield!"

Glenn had never imagined striking an opponent after they surrendered. Before today, he wouldn't even have been tempted to do so. Yet as he stumbled to a halt with his mace raised and a now-unarmed Jesse cowering with her hands raised, he almost swung anyway.

Nora was dead. She'd died brutally. One swing would crack Jesse's head like Fungus had cracked Nora's head, and she would be down and out of the fight... but he knew Jesse hadn't meant to kill Nora. It was just an accident, and horrible as this was, a **[-Resurrect-]** waited nearby.

Glenn forced his mace down and away. "I accept your yield."

After a long silence, Whitley's booming voice returned. "And it's over, folks! The Rock Troll and Rapidbloom have won the day! Lifecasters are on the field. After a **[-Resurrect-]**, she'll be right as rain!"

Jesse lowered her hands and stared at him with what looked to be real sympathy. "I'm sorry, Glenn. You have to believe me. Fungus didn't mean to kill her, nor did I!"

Glenn ground his teeth. "I know." He inclined his head politely. "It was an accident, and it's as much on me as you. Good duel. Both of you. You fought well, and... I need to see her."

Whitley shouted again. "All dueling will be suspended for ten minutes while the officiants make sure Miss Rapidbloom is able to continue. We'll be back soon, folks! Now's a good time to stretch your legs, or pick up another delicious bucket of our sumptuous skitterer legs!"

By the time Glenn reached Nora, multiple Lifecasters and an officiant had already surrounded her body. As one man gingerly eased the arrow out of her head... it had gone in above her left eye and come out the back of her head... a second cast glowing Skill after glowing Skill on her.

With the arrow out, soon Nora's body was whole again. Her neck was unsnapped and the hole that arrow had put through her head was closed. Her body was as it had been before she died, and it remained ensouled, but she was still dead. In twelve hours, her soul would depart.

"Step back!" a Spiritualist in white robes ordered.

Someone took his arm. Glenn glanced over to see Becka clutching him with worried eyes. He pulled her close and hugged her as they watched the Spiritualist work. Nora would be fine. He had to remind himself that despite this accident, she would be just fine.

The Spiritualist chanted and moved her glowing hands in a wide circle several times, and then a massive blast of light burst from Nora's chest. **[-Resurrect-]** had been cast. With a gasp, Nora burst back to life... and promptly passed out.

Becka pressed against him. "She's alive. Thank the Gods."

Glenn hugged her. "That was horrible. I never want to see anything like that again."

The Spiritualist walked over. "Would you like one of us to carry her back to your pit?"

Glenn parted himself from Becka. "No. I've got her."

As gently as possible, Glenn picked up Nora's limp body and carried her back to their staging pit on the side of the arena. Anna stood wringing her hands, and then, with a gasp, she reached into her **[Unfilled Bag]**. She pulled out a fluffy comforter and laid it across a bench.

Glenn was grateful for her forethought. He settled Nora on the comforter and then stepped back, measuring his breathing. That had been too close. He had gotten so wrapped up in the fun and challenge of dueling that he had forgotten just how dangerous it could be.

Anna gently brushed Nora's hair away from her eyes. "I can't believe that arrow went through her head. Thank the Gods for **[-Resurrect-]**." She looked up. "Will they disqualify you now?"

Glenn frowned. "How do you mean?"

"Coming back from a **[-Resurrect-]** takes time, and if you die to head trauma, it's even more difficult. It's going to be hours before she's awake, let alone capable of fighting in a duel."

Glenn ground his teeth. "Gods, you're right. I didn't even think about that until now." He looked at Becka, who winced, then back at Nora. "Just when things were going so well."

He considered heading back into the field to ask the officiant what would happen next. But he saw the people out in the colosseum already hard at work setting up for the next duel... which would be his duel, with Kaden Tallhorn... and decided to wait with Nora. He'd know his next move soon enough.

A few minutes later, a tall male officiant approached their staging pit. "Graybreaker? Can you come speak with me, please?"

Glenn walked to the edge of the pit. "Yes, sir. I'm here."

"How is Miss Rapidbloom?"

"Breathing steadily, but I don't think she's going to wake up in the next five minutes, let alone the next hour. What happens now? Can we reschedule the final doubles duel for tonight?"

The officiant shook his head. "Sadly, all brackets must move forward on the existing schedule. If you think you can no longer continue in doubles, you can let us know. We'll award you both second place in doubles. That's one experience scroll for each of you, each worth 1500 experience."

Glenn considered. "What if I wanted to fight the doubles duel alone?"

Becka touched his arm. "Careful, Glenn."

The officiant grimaced. "You can't fight alone. You can only compete in doubles with a partner. I can ask for another ten-minute delay, but unless your partner can be ready to fight after that, your best option may be to forfeit and take second place. No one will be less impressed."

This wasn't right. Glenn stared into the officiant's eyes. "There has to be some other option. Is there... can I ask someone else to join my doubles team? Like a substitute?"

The officiant idly tapped his chin. "It's not entirely out of the question, but I'd need to discuss the possibility with the other judges. You would also need to substitute someone who can be here in the next ten to fifteen minutes. We can't wait any longer than that."

Glenn mentally considered how long it would take for Anna or Becka to get back to the Dancing Skitterer, in these crowds, tell Leo and Sara they needed one of them to join in the dueling as a substitute, and get back here in time to duel. It could easily be close to an hour.

As his eyes looked to the field again, he realized he already knew the path he would take. He turned to Becka. "I need you on my doubles team. I want you as our sub."

Her eyes widened. "I'm a poor duelist. Anna should sub for you."

Anna stepped forward and nodded. "If you need me, I'll do it."

Glenn offered Anna a sympathetic glance. "I know you want to help Zack, but I think Becka's our best option given who we're up against. She's smart, and clever, and she has something both of us don't." He leaned close to Becka and lowered his voice. "**[+Shadow Sense+]**."

Becka considered that. "I'm only level 12."

"And Cullen's only level 14. With your Divinity, you could probably make up the difference."

Anna touched Becka's other arm. "He's right. Now that I think about it, you are the best choice. If Nora or I were dueling alongside Glenn, Cullen could hide indefinitely to either tie Glenn to us or take us out once Glenn went after Kaden. But you will feel Cullen even in **[-Shadow Walk-]**."

"But I..." Becka firmed her stance. "All right. If you both think I can do it, I'll sub."

Glenn hugged her tight, then turned to the officiant. "I think it's obvious to everyone that Nora can't continue after her accident, but I also imagine you will have a lot of disappointed spectators if they don't get to see a finals match in the doubles bracket. Mayor Whitley might be annoyed."

The officiant raised an eyebrow. "So you'd like Rebecka Coldbreaker as your sub?"

"Yes. Also, don't forget, she won the Luminous Maze. Please remind the judges of that. Imagine how excited the crowd might be to see the winner of the Luminous Maze take the field alongside the Rock Troll. If that's the last duel of the day, the climax, you could have a real winner on your hands."

The officiant smiled subtly. "I'll take your arguments to the other judges. In the meantime..."

Mayor Whitley's voice once more bellowed through the colosseum. "Thanks for all your patience, folks! I just spoke with the Lifecasters on the field, and I'm relieved to tell you all Miss Rapidbloom is alive and recovering without injury! Now, at long last, it's time for singles finals!"

"I think you're needed outside," the officiant said.

Anna thumped his back. "Go get him. Take him down and claim your win. Remember, Kaden is all that stands between us and... well... everything we're after here today."

Glenn nodded grimly. "I suppose it is time we finally had a chat."

TWENTY-SIX

A CHEATER PROSPERS

As Glenn strode back onto the dueling field, he found his final opponent in the singles bracket, Kaden Tallhorn, standing impassively on the far side of the dueling square. As Glenn looked the other man over with fresh eyes, he couldn't help but feel a bit intimidated. Kaden wasn't a tower of muscle like Bart had been, but he was easily as muscular as Glenn.

Moreover, Kaden could cast ranged Skills. Glenn could as well, with [-Soul Singe-], but it did a tiny amount of damage. And while Kaden's [Ring-Mail Armor] wouldn't do much against a blow from a club, he also carried both a [Bronze Training Shield] and a [Commoner's Club]. From how the club crackled, Glenn knew it must also be imbued with orichalcum... and enchanted with [-Volt-].

The Gods restricted casters from wearing heavy armor, wielding heavy melee weapons, and using shields in battle. That had to be why Kaden had chosen a shield, armor, and a weapon available to unclassed Adventurers. Once imbued with orichalcum, these items could be enchanted... though almost no one would ever do that due to the expense.

Even a [Commoner's Mace] wielded with Strength could damage a Monster in a pinch, and adding a [-Volt-] enchantment on that mace would ensure each strike did a set amount of damage to the target regardless of how hard the mace was swung. If Kaden won the bracket today, Glenn wondered how many young Harmcasters might try to emulate him.

Mayor Whitley started his standard spiel. "Hundreds of eager Adventurers entered the 10-15 singles bracket, folks, and now we're down to the final two. In the blue square, we have Glenn Gray-breaker! The Rock Troll! And from speaking with those who know him, including one of his many lovely companions, I can tell you that underneath that armor he's handsome as they come!"

The crowd went wild at Mayor Whitley's words, and a whole lot of cheering sounded like it was female cheering. Inside his **[Steel Helmet]**, Glenn couldn't help but grind his teeth. He really wanted to shove Mayor Whitley off a stage at some point. The man just wouldn't let well enough alone!

"And in the red square we have Kaden Tallhorn, the Bronze Mage! A Harmcaster that fights like a Brutalist, and is twice as deadly as both! He'll freeze or zap you at range before pummeling you into pudding up close! He's dominated every duel he's entered! Can anyone stop him?"

Again, the crowd cheered raucously. As they did so, Glenn tightened his grip on his mace and forced himself to focus on the battle ahead. The duel he would soon *win*.

Today was Glenn's day, the day he earned his place on the victory stage, revealed the church's Deathcaster conspiracy to everyone, removed the corrupt church leaders from power, and completed a Quest that would resurrect his best friend. No pressure at all, really.

He used **[-Soul Scan-]**.

Name: Kaden Tallhorn
Age: 21
Level: 15
Class: Harmcaster
HP: 210/210
Blood: 190/190
Experience: 123,988/124,000
Strength: 16 (21)
Divinity: 13 (18)
Vitality: 16 (21)
Wisdom: 14 (19)

Prowess: 8
Luck: 15

Gear:

- **Uncommon: [Bronze Training Helmet]** (Enchanted: Mystic Reinforcement)
- **Uncommon: [Ring-Mail Armor]** (Enchanted: Mystic Reinforcement)
- **Uncommon: [Timeworn Trousers]** (Enchanted: Blood Reduction)
- **Common: [Commoner's Mace]** (Enchanted: Volt)
- **Common: [Bronze Training Shield]** (Enchanted: Mystic Reinforcement)
- **Uncommon: [Infused Boots]** (Enchanted: Blood Reduction)
- **Rare: [Unfilled Bag]**

Slotted Skills:

- **Uncommon: [-Blast-]** (Harmcaster/Idros)
- **Uncommon: [-Tornado-]** (Harmcaster/Idros)
- **Uncommon: [-Volt-]** (Harmcaster/Idros)
- **Uncommon: [-Lightning-]** (Harmcaster/Idros)
- **Uncommon: [-Freeze-]** (Harmcaster/Idros)

Slotted Blessings:

- **Uncommon: [+Gusting Soul+]** (Harmcaster/Idros)
- **Uncommon: [+Freezing Soul+]** (Harmcaster/Idros)
- **Uncommon: [+Lightning Soul+]** (Harmcaster/Idros)

Known Skills:

- **Uncommon: [-Freezing Slick-]** (Harmcaster/Idros)

Known Blessings:

- None

Quests:

- **Level 15:** Win an event in the **<Sandsea Cup>** (Anonymous)

Glenn was glad he was wearing a full-face helmet, because his jaw dropped when he finished reading Kaden's Status Sheet. He had read Kaden's Status Sheet before, of course, but none of his gear had been enchanted and he certainly hadn't possessed five extra attribute points in four attributes. Kaden was... Kaden was cheating! And not cheating like Glenn!

The extra five points added to Kaden's attributes were the give-away. **[Strength Potion]**s increased one's Strength by 5 for six hours, and **[Divinity Potion]**s increased one's Divinity by 5 for six hours, and so on. But it was *illegal* to use any potion buffs in the **<Sandsea Cup>**.

Attribute-enhancement potions were expensive, and allowing some Adventurers to use them in the dueling brackets would force others to either fight without the benefits of potions or go into debt to purchase them. Even worse, because the officiants had failed to detect that Kaden was using potion buffs, there was no way Glenn could accuse Kaden of cheating.

Glenn had no way of knowing Kaden was cheating without **[-Soul Scan-]**, and he couldn't very well reveal *that* without eliciting a number of other questions. Questions about his now scarily famous "shield toboggan" duel with Agnes. Someone would certainly ask when *else* he had used **[-Soul Scan-]** to read his dueling opponent's attributes and slotted Skills.

Everyone would know after he exposed the leaders of the Church of Celes, of course. But by that time, Glenn would have already activated the experience scrolls awarded to him for winning the brackets. So while many would be angry, he would still be able to bring Zack back from beyond.

How could the Lifecaster assigned to view Kaden's Status Sheet before the dueling started have missed that he had an extra five points of Strength, Divinity, Vitality, and Wisdom? Glenn, like every other contestant, had showed his Status Sheet to a Lifecaster when he arrived. Still... his enchanted **[Blazer Pin]** hid his true Status Sheet. What if one of Kaden's items did the same?

Kaden could have an enchantment allowing him to produce a fake Status Sheet that looked just like his real Status Sheet. It would hide the extra attribute points bestowed by his potions. Enchanting an item specifically to emulate his non-buffed attributes for the <Sandsea Cup> would be very expensive, but Glenn knew it was doable. Both the Blazers and multiple Deathcasters had done it.

Finally, he looked at the Quest Kaden carried.

Level 15: Win the Sandsea Cup *(Anonymous)*

Glenn knew firsthand how much it cost to make a Quest anonymous because he had paid for an anonymous Quest himself. He'd changed the Quest completed by Everett Commoncloud to reveal the hole in the wall of Lakebrooke.

In addition, every single piece of Garret's gear was enchanted. He knew from conversations with his mother that both Blood Reduction and Mystic Reinforcement were rare and prohibitively expensive. No level 15 could afford so many of those!

A Blood Reduction enchantment reduced the amount of Blood consumed by all Skills, so it was coveted by any Class that used Skills which consumed Blood. It also required the Enchanter to be level 16 or higher and consumed reagents from zones in the 20-30 range. And Mystic Reinforcement, which drastically increased the protection offered by a piece of armor, could only be added by a Preceptor Enchanter who consumed an ultra-rare mythril ingot in the process.

Even the price to get one enchantment done was too expensive for a level 15 to afford, let alone five of them. Someone *very* wealthy had bankrolled Kaden's entry into the <Sandsea Cup>. In addition to commissioning that expensive Quest, they had given him high-level enchanted gear, a supply of expensive attribute-enhancement potions, and an enchantment to present a fake Status Sheet.

Under other circumstances, Glenn would have felt even more nervous about facing an opponent that was so well-equipped who was also buffed by powerful potions. But in Kaden's case, he was shocked to realize he actually felt relieved.

Since he'd arrived, he'd worried Kaden was better than him somehow. Stronger. Smarter. Faster. A better duelist.

Yet that wasn't the case at all. Kaden, despite what Glenn had feared, was not an unstoppable wall of armor and Harmcaster Skills. He was, in fact, quite mortal beneath it all, and the only reason he'd been so effective in all his duels so far was because of his equipment and his illegal potions.

Perhaps Glenn Graybreaker was finally going to have himself a real fight.

"The Rock Troll and the Bronze Mage have each defeated so many in battle, and now, in front of you, the best crowd in all of Luxtera, they face each other. Who will stand? Who will fall? It's time for the two most powerful low-level duelists in Sun's Cross to collide, folks. Let's hear those cheers!"

The crowd cheered and thumped the stands with their boots. As they did so, Kaden spoke words Glenn couldn't hear over the noise of the cheering crowd. A spectral duel flag fell midway between them. Other than the five pillars, he had no cover to protect him from Kaden's ranged Skills.

But he did have a [Magesteel Pavise], which was naturally resistant to magic attacks. And he did have the Strength and Vitality of a Town Guard, thanks to [+Unyielding+]. And he did have the ability to see his opponent's Status Sheet thanks to [-Soul Scan-].

All in all, the odds were about even. "I accept," Glenn said.

His words weren't audible. The crowd drowned them out. But the duel flag solidified, and the moment it did so, Glenn charged for the central pillar.

A brown casting bar appeared above Kaden's head and completed in less than a second, and then a bolt of ice slammed into Glenn's shield. [-Freeze-]. The ice did no damage thanks to his [Magesteel Pavise], but damage wasn't the point. [-Freeze-] slowed any target it hit, and Glenn's steps grew heavy.

Every step he took now felt like he was running underwater. No matter how hard he pushed forward, he slowed. From his square, Kaden calmly tossed [-Volt-] after [-Volt-] after [-Volt-]. Unlike [-Burn-] and [-Freeze-], which had at least some small amount of travel time, [-Volt-] was instant.

Worse, [-Volt-] had one distinct advantage over other Harmcaster

Skills in regards to dueling armored opponents. It did bonus damage if the target was wearing metal armor, and Glenn's armor was made of steel. Another **[-Freeze-]** hit him the moment the slowing effect from the first was about to wear off, and then another **[-Volt-]**.

By the time Glenn made it to the cover of the central pillar, he was stumbling and gasping for breath. He tasted blood in his mouth. His body felt burned all over, and every pore tingled with pain. As he belatedly checked his Status Sheet, he was dismayed at the results.

HP: 230/330

He was already hurting. While **[-Volt-]** only knocked off 20 Health Points under normal circumstances, Glenn was taking bonus damage from each strike thanks to his armor. While the damage from the **[-Freeze-]** strikes had been completely absorbed by his shield, he was still slowed.

In the time it had taken him to reach the middle of the dueling field and find cover behind its central pillar, Kaden Tallhorn had knocked off almost a third of his Health Points. He also had his Blood Reduction enchantments, plus **[+Freezing Soul+]** and **[+Lighting Soul+]** to ensure he had the Blood to hammer Glenn again and again. He had likely burned half the Blood he would without those.

"Look at those hits!" Whitley shouted. "Without even taking one step, the Bronze Mage just blasted the Rock Troll down to two-thirds health! But while it looks like this might be the end for Graybreaker, folks, don't count him out. He could still pull this out! Let's hear those cheers!"

Unfortunately, the deafening cheering of the crowd made it impossible for Glenn to listen for the clanking of armor that would suggest Kaden was repositioning. Under any other circumstance, he could have used **[-Guardian's Heal-]**s to return himself to full Health. He couldn't heal himself now. Hundreds would see him getting healed, and then they would *know* he was cheating.

He peeked around the corner and was instantly blasted in the face with **[-Volt-]**. As he ducked back behind the pillar, he winced as Kaden's ranged Skill shaved another 25 Health Points away. He hadn't even struck the man once in combat, and now he was starting to wonder if he could.

What was truly frustrating was that Glenn had *seen* Kaden do this to others. He had seen this strategy every time he watched Kaden duel, and yet somehow, he had been foolish enough to think that *he* would easily counter it. It had looked so easy to defeat Kaden when he wasn't on the field.

Whitley's voice bellowed again. "Is Graybreaker finally out of tricks? Remember, all duels are timed! Let's hope he has a plan other than 'hide behind the pillar,' or this will be a boring final match!"

Whitley was right. Glenn couldn't hide behind this pillar forever. If a duel lasted a full five minutes without a KO or yield, the duel would be called by the officiants. The judges would choose the victor based on who had been the most aggressive or efficient, and right now, that was Kaden.

Glenn had no choice. He had to move, and he finally had an idea as to how he might break Kaden's concentration. He unsnapped his shield from his arm, then strapped it onto his back. He would still have the bonus in Strength and Vitality from [+**Unyielding**+], but he needed to be able to move his full upper body without the constriction of holding a heavy shield in one arm.

He rolled around the corner of the pillar and spotted Kaden hiding past the rightmost pillar on the outside of the X next to the red square. The man raised his hand as Glenn charged forward at his fastest pace. A blast of ice smacked him in the chest: [-**Freeze**-]. His steps again grew heavy.

Glenn charged forward as Kaden stepped out and launched [-**Volt**-]. He was down to half health now, and he still had at least fifteen paces to cover. Another [-**Volt**-] landed, but he was almost close enough. Ten paces would be close enough for what he intended.

Ahead, a brown cast bar appeared above Kaden's head. [-**Blast**-]. He was about to hit Glenn in the chest with his wind Skill, knocking Glenn away far enough that he could then continue to strike him with impunity. Glenn had known Kaden would try that... which was why he no longer carried his shield.

Before the cast bar on [-**Blast**-] could complete, Glenn unleashed his last, desperate ploy. As he had practiced on many slow days in Wolfpine back when he was a Town Guard, Glenn *threw* Becka (his weighted mace) with all his Strength.

As his mace spun end over end toward Kaden Tallhorn, it was

easy to imagine the man's eyes widening in surprise. The faceplate of Kaden's **[Bronze Training Helmet]** crumpled like a copper mug in the hands of Mammoth Cloudcrusher. It collapsed inward and, likely, crushed Kaden's nose.

The cast bar for **[-Blast-]** vanished. As Becka rebounded off Kaden's crushed helmet and thumped onto the field, Kaden stumbled while flailing with both hands. No more **[-Volt-]** spells arrived. Still fighting through the slowing effects of Kaden's last **[-Freeze-]**, Glenn stomped toward his opponent.

Five paces. Three. He was just hauling back to punch Kaden and knock him out of the dueling field when the man blindly threw out both hands. A brown cast bar appeared.

[-Tornado-].

Glenn howled as a huge mass of wind hit him just before he landed the punch that would have sent Kaden out of the field. That wind lifted him off the ground as easily as Fungus had lifted Nora. As wind pummeled him, he flailed helplessly in midair above the dueling field. He was now trapped in the center of a localized tornado. Harmcasters used this Skill for crowd control.

As Glenn watched in helpless fury, dangling and flailing, Kaden grabbed and ripped off his ruined helmet. It must now be impossible to see out of due to its smashed front visor. As Glenn got his first look at his furious opponent—dark eyes, dark hair, and one very crushed nose—Kaden spit blood.

Then he tossed his hands forward and fired a **[-Blast-]** into his **[-Tornado-]**.

The two Skills combined to great effect. An explosion sent Glenn hurtled backward across the dueling field. He slammed into the central pillar hard enough it knocked the breath out of him.

The moment he dropped onto his rear, another **[-Freeze-]** hit him in the chest. And then, one **[-Volt-]** strike after another hammered him and his armor. Again and again and again.

Glenn's body seized up. White flashes consumed his vision as pain became his world. The roaring of the crowd faded to nothing. When he next became aware, Glenn swallowed blood and realized he sat in a crumbled heap against the central pillar. Each breath rattled in his throat.

Across the dueling field, Kaden fell to his knees. He was breathing like he'd just finished a marathon, but he raised one fist in victory. That was when Glenn noticed their duel flag was gone. A moment later, the crowd went wild. Mayor Whitley announced the end of Glenn's hopes.

"What a contest! What an upset! The Rock Troll proved his valor and guile time and again, but in the end, even he was no match for the Bronze Mage. The singles bracket is over, folks, and we have our victor! Kaden Tallhorn! Kaden Tallhorn wins the 10-15 singles bracket!"

A rush of warm, soothing energy flooded Glenn's body. The blood pooled in his mouth didn't go away, but the agonizing combination of freezing muscles, tingling bones, and burning flesh began to fade. The cup's Lifecasters were using [-Flash Heal-], and they had to use a lot of [-Flash Heal-]s.

Becka dropped to his side and threw her arms around him, but she couldn't lift him alone. He was too heavy, and his body didn't work. Anna arrived next. They helped Glenn stumble to his feet, and then Anna and Becka, grunting with effort, helped him stumble back to the staging pit.

As he allowed them to guide him, Glenn couldn't help but feel like he'd failed them and Zack. Kaden Tallhorn had cheated, certainly. He had expensive gear and expensive enchantments and every attribute-enhancing potion available to level 15 Adventurers.

Even so... this defeat felt like karmic justice for all Glenn's victories over Adventurers who didn't have [+Unyielding+], [+Regrowth+], and [-Soul Scan-] to aid them in battle. Those Adventurers had faced as many disadvantages as they dueled Glenn as Glenn had faced when dueling Kaden, if not more. None of them had Town Guard Blessings or the Skills of a Soulseer.

How could Glenn blame Kaden for taking advantage of unsavory bonuses when he had done the same? He had told himself over and over he was doing this for Zack, to save Zack, but in his focus on *saving* Zack, had he allowed his moral compass to drift? Had he truly *cheated* to win?

He had cheated. As thrilled as he had been by all his victories, and as much as he recognized his tactical thinking and battle instincts had served him well, he had still won so many duels only because he had information he could never have had otherwise. Because he was a Soulseer.

Perhaps this was what the Gods had wished to prove by luring him to the <Sandsea Cup>. They had wanted to learn if Isdon's new Class was broken... at least in regards to dueling. Glenn now knew this Class was broken as well as anyone. He shouldn't be dueling unless people knew.

Whitley's voice boomed. "We've got an usual situation on our hands, folks! We have two duelists in the finals of the <Sandsea Cup> who are fighting in both singles and doubles! The Rock Troll may have lost his first battle with the Bronze Mage, but there's a rematch coming! We're going to take an additional ten-minute break, and then we'll be right back with the final doubles match!"

Becka helped him settle on a bench. He collapsed against her and huffed quietly. He was going to have to go right back out in that field again soon, and he couldn't afford to lose again.

Glenn spit out another fleck of blood, then worked his jaw. "Gods, that was awful."

Becka leaned close. "I saw. It looked awful. I'm just glad you're safe."

"I didn't win the singles bracket."

"That's all right. Remember, you'll still get an experience scroll for taking second place, and we also have the scroll from the Luminous Maze. I'll be making a victory speech."

He nodded tiredly. "So long as I can be up there with you. As your... boyfriend, I suppose."

"I imagine a few words from the Rock Troll might be allowed. We also have doubles ahead."

Ignoring his aching neck, Glenn glanced behind him to find Nora still sleeping peacefully. Her chest rose and fell evenly, and had he not known an arrow had gone straight through her head recently, he would have thought she had just laid down for a nap. He looked at Becka again.

"Just so you know, Kaden is cheating."

As Becka raised an eyebrow, Anna gasped from his other side. "Cheating how?" She focused on the crowd as if looking for Kaden, to scan him, but he'd already returned to his own pit.

"He's using attribute-enhancement potions. But even without

those, I think he still would have pummeled me as he just did. The way he's geared up and slotted, he's like... the anti-Glenn."

Anna glared at the field. "We need to report him to the officiants."

"How? The Lifecaster who examined him didn't catch it. I think Kaden is using an enchantment we're both familiar with to ensure people can't see his real Status Sheet."

Anna gasped. "Oh, no."

"That's right. I know he's using potions, but I can't say *how* I know. You know?"

As Anna settled again at his side, glaring at the arena, she bared her teeth. "It's not fair. This was for Zack. We were doing all this for Zack, and now we're going to lose to someone who is paying his way to victory? How could any level 15 afford such luxuries?"

Glenn glanced at Nora, who continued sleeping peacefully. They could talk freely here. "We haven't lost. Not yet. There's still doubles, and now I know how Kaden fights. I just need some time to strategize, revise my tactics, and we can take him down in doubles."

Becka patted his armored knee. "That's the Glenn I know. Always optimistic."

"I'm sorry I dragged you into dueling. I know you hate it."

"I don't hate it so much when I'm with you."

"But even so? There's no one else I'd want to face this battle with."

Becka's lips quirked. "Nora could heal you, and Anna could toss all sorts of flames."

"Yet you're the one I always fight for. You're the reason that no matter how many defeats I suffer or times I fail, I can go on. I go on so I'll never disappoint you."

"Hush now." She kissed him gently. "They'll be time enough for that sort of thing later."

An officiant approached their staging pit. "Duelist Graybreaker?"

Glenn nodded tiredly. "That's me."

"I have the official call from the judges. Because of the unique circumstances involved in the injury to your current partner, and Rebecka Coldbreaker's popularity due to her victory over the Luminous Maze, they will allow Rebecka to act as a substitute for Nora Rapidbloom. If you're willing, you can fight in the last doubles match together. The two of you can finish the doubles bracket out."

Becka sighed. "So that's it then. We're facing the Bronze Mage and his shadow friend.

Glenn poked her. "At least he'll be tossing **[-Volt-]** spells at someone else this time."

Becka gasped and thumped his shoulder. "So much for my loyal protector!"

From behind them, someone cleared his throat. "Glenn?"

Glenn achingly twisted around to look, then nearly fell off his bench. "Brennon?"

TWENTY-SEVEN

A REMATCH FOR THE CROWD

From behind him, Glenn's mentor in the Blazers and his trainer in the way of truth seeking smiled a warm smile. "I'm sorry to bother you during your duels, but I was hoping we could speak."

Brennon Shadesinger remained a tall and handsome man, with a strong chin and close-cut blond hair. Today he was dressed for battle, wearing his rare, colorful, and powerful **[Robe of Mysteries]**. He also looked tired, and Brennon Shadesinger never looked tired.

Glenn rose, winced as his knees creaked, then turned and groaned. "Sorry if I'm a bit slow. I took a beating out there. How can I help, sir?"

"It's a minor thing, really. I was hoping you could answer a few questions about your duel."

"Of course. What do you need, sir?"

Brennon glanced at Anna. "Just so you know, the others are very concerned about you."

Anna stiffened. "Who?"

"Your party. I didn't tell them you were here, but they are here looking for you. So is Nadia, though she's not very happy to be pulled all the way from the guild office in Aria. You should have checked with your superiors before coming here to the **<Sandsea Cup>**. They might have approved it."

Anna glared and wrung her hands. "I had good reasons."

"Of that, I have no doubt."

Glenn stepped forward. "If that's what this is about—"

"It's tangential." Brennon raised a hand. "I'm actually here about an entirely different matter. After a complicated investigation, I'm now certain a wealthy Preceptor, or several wealthy Preceptors working together, have launched a conspiracy to rig the dueling brackets of the **<Sandsea Cup>**."

As the irony of Brennon's statement washed over him, Glenn couldn't help but chuckle. Still, he knew Brennon well enough to know he was right. "What evidence have you gathered so far?"

"I've uncovered anonymous transactions and the names of three local Merchants who acted as go-betweens to hide the source. I'm now certain someone very powerful and very wealthy has recruited at least one Adventurer in every bracket below 30. They provided them all the resources they need to win, including, possibly, illegal attribute-enhancing potions. The only thing I don't know is who that is."

Glenn nodded numbly. "That's an interesting theory. So... why would someone do that?"

Brennon simply watched him indulgently.

Glenn slapped his palm to his forehead. "It's the betting. Of course it's about the betting. If you could correctly place bets on who will win every bracket in the **<Sandsea Cup>**, you could make a fortune. So proving the brackets are rigged is why you're here?"

"That is one of my reasons." Brennon looked past Glenn. "Based on the duel I just observed, I also believe you may have encountered the Adventurer who the cabal I'm after selected to win this bracket. Kaden cast enough **[-Volt-]** spells he's obviously equipped with Blood Reduction enchantments, but few level 15 Harmcasters could afford those."

Becka nudged Glenn. "His power level did seem a bit ridiculous, didn't it?"

Should Glenn tell Brennon that Kaden was using attribute-enhancement potions? How could he tell Brennon? Did Brennon already know?

His mentor smiled. "So, Glenn, I really only need to ask you one question. Based on your observations of Kaden Tallhorn in your duel just now, do you believe it possible he's using attribute-enhancement potions as well? You fought him most recently, so I'd value your opinion."

Glenn debated but a moment. "It is... possible, yes. That he was enhanced."

"And do you base that on comparing how well he fought to others you've fought with similar Skills and levels? Or are you basing that on what you saw when you looked at his Status Sheet?"

Becka gasped, and Glenn's eyes widened before he could catch himself. Brennon had trained him to hide his feelings, but not well enough to hide this. As he stared at his mentor, a man who had trained him and who he'd trusted for months, he knew denying his Class was foolhardy.

"How long have you known?"

"Since about a month after the events in Grassea's Temple of Balance. Until now, I've found no reason to involve Luxtera's newest Class in my investigations, and I certainly can't do so in any official capacity. But I do know of it, and I do know who you are." He looked at Anna. "And you."

She shook her head in disbelief. "Who *are* you?"

Glenn chuckled. "He's... well, he's insightful. And yes, I saw his Status Sheet before our duel. He's using four attribute-enhancing potions, and I suspect he has an enchanted item that presents a fake Status Sheet that prevents anyone who looks at his Status Sheet from seeing that."

Brennon inclined his head. "That's very useful. Good luck in your doubles duel, Glenn."

Glenn blinked. "You aren't going to arrest Kaden for cheating?"

"Not yet. Now that I've verified the identity of at least one of the Adventurers the cabal chose to win this bracket, I have another link I can tug on and follow to those behind this."

"But what about stopping these people? The singles have already been decided."

"But bets have not been dispensed. The next step in my investigation will be to report my suspicions to the Preceptor Merchants financing the <Sandsea Cup> and have all betting payments frozen until I conclude my investigation. It won't make the officiants popular, but by paying close attention to which Preceptors complain and how, I believe I can find the culprits."

"The people who put all this in motion. The people who rigged the dueling brackets."

"That is correct."

Glenn nodded. "I'm glad I could help."

"And I'm sorry I can't help more. I know it's going to be difficult going up against Kaden again in the doubles bracket, but if it helps, I believe the conspiracy has only chosen one Adventurer in each bracket to minimize their chances of discovery. I don't think Cullen Twoblades is enhanced."

From behind Glenn, Mayor Whitley bellowed. "It's almost time, folks! Find those seats and get ready for the finale of today's dueling double feature! It's the last doubles match of the day, and we've got a last-minute substitution I think will take everyone by surprise. Hold onto your seats!"

Brennon snapped his fingers. "I forgot one other thing." He reached into his **[Unfilled Bag]**. "While I wasn't certain Kaden was the Adventurer chosen by the conspiracy, I did have a strong suspicion he was involved. For that reason, I wanted to ensure whoever faced him had a fair chance."

As Glenn watched in increasingly wide-eyed disbelief, Brennon pulled a full suit of **[Magesteel Armor]** out of his **[Unfilled Bag]**, followed by a second set of the same. Then he produced a huge two-handed **[Magesteel Mace]**... it was as big as Glenn's **[Guardian's Mace]** from his time as a Town Guard... and set that in the staging pit as well. The mace glowed a soft blue.

Glenn swallowed and stared at the unexpected boon in equipment and gear. "What is that?"

"Two sets of **[Magesteel Armor]** enchanted with Volt Reduction. The **[Magesteel Mace]** is also enchanted with **[-Freeze-]**, so if you hit your target, it should slow them significantly. While arresting Kaden Tallhorn for cheating would complicate my investigation, I don't think I'll suffer should he simply lose one bracket. In fact, that may help me. So, Glenn, I hope you and Becka find this gear of use."

[Magesteel Armor] was one of the only types of heavy armor a caster could wear, since it combined elements of robes and armor. It was also, just like most rare items, ridiculously expensive. Two sets must have easily set Brennon back 100 moons. And that mace... another 50?

Before anyone else could say anything, Anna rushed forward and threw her arms around Brennon. She hugged him tight, then stepped away with a huge smile on her face.

"Thank you. Thank you for helping us. You can't imagine how important winning doubles is to... all of us."

Brennon smiled. "I might have some idea." He gave Glenn a pointed look. "I'll let you two get changed into your new gear. I don't have time to stick around and watch the doubles finals, but I already have some strong suspicions about who's going to win this bracket."

With Anna's help, Glenn and Becka changed into their new **[Magesteel Armor]**. They had some privacy in the staging pit, but Glenn was so eager to have his rematch with Kaden Tallhorn that he would have changed in front of the colosseum crowd if it was necessary. He could actually win this!

Moreover, Becka would now be far better protected in this expensive armor than she would have been in her **[Shadow Robes]** which, while offering a passive bonus to Blood, would not protect her from Cullen Twoblades' **[Steel Knife]**s. Cullen could still cut her, but he'd need to burn his armor penetration Skills to do so, and also aim his strikes instead of simply slashing wildly.

The best aspect of this new armor, of course, was its expensive enchantment: Volt Reduction. On its own, **[Magesteel Armor]** was already resistant to ranged Skills, cutting the damage by one third. Volt Reduction would cut the damage from Kaden's **[-Volt-]** spells in half by an additional amount, which combined was... more than half. Glenn couldn't do the exact math in his head.

What mattered is, in regards to Kaden's lightning attacks, this armor had effectively doubled both his and Becka's Health Points. They would also be much more resistant to the chance that an electric strike might paralyze them. Strikes would still hurt, but less than half as much.

An officiant reached their staging pit. "Contestant Graybreaker? You're needed on the field."

Glenn raised a hand. "Time."

The officiant blinked. "You're taking a time out? Now?"

"I am. We need to do a bit more preparation before our next duel, so let Mayor Whitley know we'll be delayed. We'll be out before five minutes passes, I assure you."

The officiant frowned. "You had best be. The judges will be very cross if they authorized a substitute for you and then you're disqualified for being late." He stepped away and jogged, probably to let the judges know there would be another delay.

Several minutes later, he and Becka were both armored up. This armor fit both of them perfectly despite having previously been a uniform size. Just like all God-blessed Uncommon gear, the gear would resize itself to the wearer once worn... and Becka's armor looked *very* good on her.

Brennon hadn't provided helmets, and Glenn would rather go helmetless than wear his **[Steel Helmet]** in the next duel. It would simply cause him to take more damage from **[-Volt-]**. While he wasn't excited about fighting without a helmet, physical attacks wouldn't be a factor once they defeated Cullen.

Glenn strapped his new **[Magesteel Shield]** onto his back—he wouldn't be using it to block, but he still wanted the advantage from **[+Unyielding+]**—and then picked up the enchanted, two-handed **[Magesteel Mace]**. It was heavy. Heavy for him. He *liked* that it was heavy, because while he knew he could easily swing it about, he also knew anything he hit with this mace would fly a good ways.

He was looking forward to making Kaden Tallhorn fly a good long ways.

Glenn glanced at Becka. "You good?"

She nodded and brushed back her long hair. "Still getting used to this armor, but good."

"You can handle this duel. I know you can. Now, let's give the crowd the surprise they've been patiently waiting to see for the last fifteen minutes."

Becka's smile made her even more beautiful. "I do want to see Kaden's expression."

The moment Glenn and Becka marched out of their staging pit, the crowd in the colosseum went silent at the sight of their dramatic change of wardrobe. Then the crowd went wild, cheering and hollering and (for some of them) booing at the fact that Glenn had been busy since his last duel. Someone, it seemed, was betting heavily on Kaden's team to win.

There was no doubt that Brennon Shadesinger's donation of gear and weapons had come at the best possible time. Some in the crowd would likely cry foul when it became known Glenn and his new doubles partner had somehow acquired armor that was perfectly crafted to counter one of their remaining opponents. For Glenn's part, he simply needed this win... and the experience scroll.

Mayor Whitley's voice once more boomed across the colosseum. "Would you look at that! I'm not sure I believe my eyes, folks, but it looks like Graybreaker tossed the Gods a prayer for help while recovering from the drubbing Kaden gave him in the singles finals. The Gods answered!"

The booing grew louder then, but enough cheers countered it that Glenn knew he hadn't yet lost the crowd. It felt good to have some people out there genuinely cheering for him. He knew Terry Evergarden and Carmello Gainsayer were out there as well, and the only reason they hadn't sprinted to his staging pit to check on Nora was because the Town Guards would arrest them.

"But guess what, folks? The Rock Troll's wardrobe change isn't the only surprise we have for you! The judges have debated long and hard, and everyone agreed that after all these doubles duels, we didn't want to let the doubles bracket go out with a forfeit. We want to end it with a fight!"

The crowd roared its overwhelming approval.

"Nora Rapidbloom is still recovering, and after her accident, she will be unable to continue as Glenn's partner. But it turns out that Nora's not the only comely Adventurer in Glenn's orbit, and the judges have agreed to allow another beautiful mystery woman to join Glenn for his last doubles match!"

Glenn huffed. "Why does everyone keep harping on your looks?"

"I'm sure many of you have already recognized her, folks, but that lovely lady at the Rock Troll's side? That is none other than the 10-15 Adventurer who won first place in the level 12 bracket of the Luminous Maze. The coal-haired enchantress! The luminous shadow goddess! Let's give a big, Sun's Cross welcome to our newest doubles duelist... Rebecka *Cold*breaker!"

Now the crowd went absolutely nuts, and Glenn glanced at Becka in surprise. She seemed surprised by the fervor in the crowd as well. As they reached the edge of the dueling field, Glenn was shocked to see Becka smile and wave like a noble. The crowd went mad.

Glenn looked around, tentatively raised his hand, and immediately dropped it. No. He wasn't feeling that. He'd let Becka handle inspiring the crowd.

"Marry me, Rebecka!" a bold man shouted from the stands.

Glenn spun and scowled in that direction. "Back off! She's mine!"

He only realized he'd bellowed that statement at the top of his strong lungs when the crowd in that direction momentarily went silent. Then they cheered wildly again, and he spotted several Adventurers happily ribbing a now sullen-looking Brutalist. The blond man looked upset.

Though Glenn couldn't hear Becka's laughter over the crowd, the way she smiled at him as she thumped his arm was a delight. Then they both turned to face the dueling field again and found that Kaden Tallhorn (minus his **[Bronze Training Helmet]**, which Glenn had utterly destroyed in singles) and Cullen Twoblades had taken the field.

Glenn scanned Cullen out of necessity.

Name: Cullen Twoblades
Age: 21
Level: 14
Class: Shadower
HP: 120 / 120
Blood: 100 / 100
Experience: 119,422 / 124,000
Strength: 13
Divinity: 11
Vitality: 12
Wisdom: 10
Prowess: 16
Luck: 16 (21)

Glenn was relieved to find Brennon was right. Cullen was not cheating, at least not with potions, and his gear, while suitable for a level 14 Shadower, all fell within the finances that might be available to a talented Shadower who did regular jobs for the Shadowers Guild. Those could be lucrative.

Cullen had slotted **[-Shadow Walk-]**, of course, but he'd also slotted himself for both crowd control and heavy damage. **[-Disarm-]**,

[-Daze-], [-Shadow Stab-], and [-Brain Strike-] offered Cullen an excellent kit of abilities to stun or delay enemies, or take them down before they could react.

Fortunately, Becka's new [Magesteel] armor would allow her to survive a direct hit from [-Shadow Stab-]... at least one. Glenn, of course, didn't intend to let Cullen get anywhere near her, but it was comforting to know they had that cushion. What surprised him was Cullen's third Blessing.

[+Gambler's Luck+] was available to any Shadower who chose a Blessing, but it had one important caveat... the Shadower first had to have a minimum Luck attribute of 15. Many Shadowers never took it since their Luck wasn't that high by level 15, and they wanted a Void-strider or Timestrider Blessing at level 20 when they evolved. Yet Cullen had it... and it complicated things.

Glenn didn't know exactly how Luck would influence a duel. He just knew that the more luck a person had, the more likely they were to escape defeat when it seemed inevitable. Cullen wasn't cheating—[+Gambler's Luck+] added 5 Luck passively, just like the Soulseer Blessing [+Lucky Soul+]—but he had been blessed during Luxtera's Climb.

Cullen's only enchantment was a [-Freeze-] on one of his [Steel Knife]s. His other gear had no enchantments, which again suggested he was self-financed. Either the people who had fitted out Kaden hadn't approached him or he'd refused their help. Glenn filed this information away.

As Kaden and Cullen stepped into the red squares, Glenn beckoned Becka close. "Keep me between you and Kaden like a pillar. We'll advance on him together and let him exhaust himself casting [-Volt-]. The moment you feel any tingles, shout out the direction and dive."

"Understood." Becka shuddered. "I really don't want to get stabbed in the back."

"Also, if you can, try and land some [-Shadow Blast-]s on Kaden. He doesn't have a helmet any longer. If we're lucky enough to blind him, he won't be able to target us with [-Volt-]."

An officiant called out. "Step onto the field, blue team!"

Glenn stepped forward and entered one blue square. Becka entered the other. They faced down their opponents. While Kaden scowled and involuntarily rubbed his now-healed nose, Cullen eyed them both with obvious amusement... and sketched a mocking bow.

Whitley called out again. "The stage for doubles is set! The Bronze Mage and his elusive friend now face down a newly armored Rock Troll and a sultry shadow goddess! A woman who conquered the Luminous Maze has a trick or ten up her sleeves, so watch out, folks!"

"Get on with it!" Cullen yelled to no one in particular. "I want my scroll!"

Glenn chuckled. He wondered if Cullen was annoyed because Mayor Whitley hadn't given him a ridiculous nickname. Calling Cullen "Kaden's elusive friend" wasn't very flattering.

Glenn took a breath. "Duel my party!" he bellowed across the field.

A spectral flag dropped.

Kaden and Cullen exchanged a glance, and then Cullen vanished in a puff of smoke. Kaden turned back to Glenn and bared his teeth. "We accept!"

"Go!" Glenn charged.

Becka huffed directly behind him as a [-Freeze-] smacked Glenn at once, but he was shocked and pleased to find he didn't slow down as much as he had before. His new [Magesteel Armor] was mitigating the slowing effect from [-Freeze-], cutting it at least in half.

This would actually work in his favor, as Becka couldn't sprint quite as fast as him. This slow would balance them out.

"Look at him move!" Whitley yelled. "Glenn shrugged off that ice like it was a cold shower!"

[-Volt-] after [-Volt-] spell splashed into Glenn's armor, but while each burned, the pain was a fraction of what it had been before. He had no doubt that each spell was doing half the damage it had before, or even less since it could no longer take advantage of the bonus damage from steel.

Glenn reached the central pillar with Becka on his heels in half the time he had before, but this time, he didn't take cover. He dashed right past it and barreled on, taking more [-Volt-]s to the face.

"What a difference! What an upset! Graybreaker's chomping lightning and asking for seconds!"

As Whitley finished, Glenn checked his Health Bar. 342/390. In this armor, those [-Volt-]s were barely hurting him, and Kaden would need to do far better than this to make a dent.

Kaden took off at a respectable run, sprinting not sideways as Glenn would expect but at an angle to allow him to run almost parallel to their charge. He was trying to get a line on Becka, who he must suspect had far less Health. Glenn altered his course to keep himself between Kaden and Becka, and as he did so, tightened his grip on his huge new [Magesteel Mace].

"The Bronze Mage is on the run, folks! Can he keep his distance and recover?"

"Left!" Becka screamed as she dived right.

Glenn had been waiting for [+Shadow Sense+]. As his next foot landed, he swung his new [Magesteel Mace] in a sweeping arc that covered five paces of open air. A heavy thump followed.

Cullen Twoblades rolled away with a third of his Health Bar missing, then flipped to his feet with a scowl. Most importantly, Cullen's [-Shadow Walk-] was now on cooldown! Glenn debated as to how to proceed before remembering how much he believed in Becka.

"Take Kaden!" He vaulted over her and charged Cullen.

Becka cried out as a [-Volt-] slammed into her, but the sound of her responding with [-Shadow Bolt-] told him she had cast her Skill despite taking a [-Volt-] to the face. All her training with the Blazers had hardened her for this. Becka could more than handle Kaden at range.

Whitley chortled. "The Bronze Mage and the sultry sorceress are toe to toe! I think this buxom beauty wants revenge for her man!"

Glenn used [-Soul Scan-] on Cullen. As Glenn charged Cullen with a howl, Cullen darted aside as if trying to evade, but then darted back with speed and agility Glenn could only admire. The man's enchanted [Steel Knife] sliced upward.

A brown casting bar for [-Disarm-] appeared. Just before Cullen's knife impacted his hands, Glenn voluntarily released his mace. The knife hit his hands and his mace went flying... but because his hands didn't tingle, he knew [-Disarm-] had failed.

He'd had other Blazers use [-Disarm-] on him in duels before, in training, and the tingle it left behind made it impossible to wield a weapon for half a minute. But you couldn't disarm an unarmed opponent, and he could pick up his mace any time he liked. Cullen couldn't know that.

As Cullen followed up with several lightning-fast stabs, Glenn saw the brown cast bar filling for **[-Brain Strike-]**. Becka was still fighting Kaden one and one, and he didn't have time to be stunned for twenty seconds. He hit Cullen with **[-Soul Singe-]**, and the burst of unexpected damage threw Cullen off-balance just enough his other knife whiffed over Glenn's head. **[-Brain Strike-]** failed.

Glenn lowered his weight and slammed into Cullen's middle. He lifted the slimmer man off the ground and slammed him into a pillar like it was an anvil. Cullen wheezed with his breath knocked out of him, and as his Health Bar dropped to one-third, Glenn knew he'd cracked some ribs.

"Graybreaker just crushed Cullen like a grape!" Whitley yelled. "We felt that one in the stands!"

Behind him, another **[-Shadow Bolt-]** fired, but Glenn didn't hear any more **[-Volt-]**s. Had Becka gotten lucky and blinded Kaden with a strike?

Finally, Whitley's blather provided useful information. "Kaden's on the ropes, folks! Rebecka blinded him with that last strike! How can he toss out spells if he can't see?"

As Cullen bounced off the pillar and thumped onto his stomach, Glenn snatched up his **[Magesteel Mace]**. He hefted it and swung down without asking for a yield, which would take time. As he hit Cullen's back, an invisible force cushioned his blow enough that he could tell the difference.

Cullen's Health Bar went to a sliver. He was out. Glenn spun and charged Kaden.

"Cullen's down, and Rebecka's still pummeling Kaden with bolt after bolt! It's two on one folks, and the Rock Troll's back for vengeance! Kaden better hope he knows how to use that shield!"

Ahead, Glenn spotted Kaden stumbling along the edge of the field, one hand desperately wiping at his face. A black cloud buzzed there, blocking his sight. **[-Shadow Bolt-]** had a chance to blind its target, and because **[-Volt-]** and **[-Burst-]** required line of sight, Kaden couldn't cast them.

Becka was down to below half health after her ranged exchange with Kaden, but Kaden looked about the same. His fortified **[Ring-**

Mail Armor] did nothing to mitigate Becka's **[-Shadow Bolts-]**. As Glenn thundered toward Kaden, he knew Kaden could hear his armor clanking over the crowd.

A brown cast bar appeared. **[-Tornado-]**. This time, Glenn was ready for it.

He dived into Becka and knocked them both aside as a storm of swirling air burst into being... directly to their left. Becka landed and rolled as Glenn came to his feet, readied his mace, and charged Kaden from the other side. Kaden tracked him and channeled one last spell.

[-Lightning-].

Glenn dived aside as Kaden's blind-fired burst of lightning crackled past his ear. Had it struck him, he would have been stunned for a full six seconds and taken a good amount of damage besides. Yet with his partner gone, his vision blocked, and his spells silenced, Kaden was now nothing more than a big armored training dummy.

A training dummy Glenn walloped so hard that Kaden's Health Bar dropped to a sliver as he literally *flew* out of the arena with the impact.

Kaden thumped, rolled, and went still as Nora, but Glenn was relieved to see that small sliver of Health remained. Kaden was unconscious, not dead. It was over. They had won doubles!

Glenn threw down his mace and roared, then turned just in time to see Becka running toward him. Her face was scuffed and one of her bangs was still smoking, but the rest of her dark hair trailed in the sun. Armor and all, she leapt into his arms.

Glenn caught her and kissed her in front of the entirety of Sun's Cross. He kissed her as desperately as he had the night they'd kissed in front of all of Wolfpine after the guards selected him as a Town Guard. His world became warmth and joy as the crowd cheered so loudly they made him deaf.

He couldn't hear Whitley's final commentary, and he didn't care. Brennon was one part of this victory, but Becka was the real reason they had won this doubles duel. At level 12, she had run circles around two Adventurers three levels higher than her. She was skilled, gorgeous, and kind.

That was the moment Glenn Redwood knew he would marry her.

TWENTY-EIGHT

A SPEECH FOR THE AGES

A fter doubles concluded, the rest of Glenn's day passed in a blur of congratulations, meetings, and tours. Glenn, with Becka and Nora in tow, found himself being led by eager and friendly **<Sandsea Cup>** officiants from meeting to meeting to meeting. Nora had recovered enough to hear what had happened after her death, and rather than be upset, she was overjoyed to hear they had won.

Becka also promised Nora that the experience scroll for winning the doubles bracket would be hers as well. Between Glenn's semifinal experience scroll (1,500), his doubles final scroll (3,000), and Becka's first place in the Luminous Maze (5,000) they wouldn't level Glenn to 15… but they would get him so close he could taste it. He could level simply by scanning the crowds with **[-Soul Scan-]** as they filtered out of Sun's Cross to go home. Once on the Safe Road, they'd give experience.

The Gods were going to resurrect Zack Silverstone, and Glenn couldn't wait to hug (and then tease) his best friend. Even so, as he watched tears streaking down Anna's face… happy tears… he knew his joy at this development couldn't quite match hers. Zack, like him, was a very lucky man.

Though Nora had tried to beg off going on the victory tour with them, Glenn insisted. The two of them had climbed all the way to the finals of doubles together, and without her heals, he'd never have made it. Becka had won their last match, but Nora had won all the others. The only thing that made their tour a bit awkward was that Kaden, as the winner of the singles bracket, was made to join them.

Still, after a few awkward stares, Kaden and Glenn ignored each other, and Becka and Nora seemed perfectly comfortable doing the same. As a group of four, they were paraded out in the arena once more, where they bowed before the raucous cheering of the crowd. Then an officiant presented official medals of gold (for Glenn, Nora, and Kaden) and one additional silver medal for Glenn.

First he met the wealthy financiers of the **<Sandsea Cup>**, Preceptor Merchants all, and Glenn wondered which of them had fixed the betting brackets. None looked particularly annoyed that Glenn had beaten Kaden in the doubles bracket, but he suspected Kaden winning there had been simply a bonus for them. Kaden had "won" the bracket that counted, and these merchants were even more rich.

Next, Glenn, Becka, and Kaden were introduced to the Preceptor Spiritualist who was in charge of organizing healing and resurrection for every duel in the **<Sandsea Cup>**. Upon scanning him, Glenn was relieved to learn he was not a secret Deathcaster. He seemed like a nice man.

From there, Glenn and his friends were whisked through a gallery of important and wealthy officials who all wanted to congratulate him, Nora, Becka, and Kaden for one thing or another. Glenn was a bit annoyed by how eagerly Kaden accepted the kudos and congratulations, but then again, Kaden wasn't the only one who'd cheated. At least Glenn had a good reason for doing so!

Finally, just when Glenn was certain the glad-handing would never end, they were ushered into a private dining room where they were served a fine meal (and dessert) while the officiants organized the closing ceremonies for the day. There were many such days of celebration ahead.

While Glenn had now accomplished all he set out to accomplish, the cup would go on. Tomorrow, the dueling and other contests for the 16-20 bracket would take place, and if Glenn wasn't passed out in bed with Becka, he might even come watch. There was also, of course, the chance that he would be in a church prison tomorrow. He'd find out soon enough.

Just before the time to step out on the grand stage erected in the center of the colosseum arrived, Sara, Ripper, and Leo arrived with Duncan Steelwright as their guest. Each winner of a bracket or event in the **<Sandsea Cup>** was allowed to have two guests on stage when they received their experience scroll and made their short speech, so Glenn and Becka's choices had been easy.

Glenn had requested Sara and Ripper, and Becka had requested Leo and Duncan. As Duncan arrived, Glenn stepped close and spoke quietly. "Do you have what we discussed?"

"I do." Duncan watched him with fresh respect. "I honestly didn't think you were going to win either dueling bracket there for a good while. Where did you acquire that armor?"

"A good friend." Glenn hesitated, then thumped Duncan's arm. "I hope, if all goes as we hope it will tonight, I'll be able to count you as a friend as well. Or, at least, not as an enemy."

"If you accomplish what you say, I'll have no reason to oppose you."

Sara stepped to Duncan's side. "That's wonderful to hear... Teacher."

Leo simply grumbled something and idly patted Ripper's head.

An officiant entered the room. "They're ready for you. Please, follow me."

As Glenn glanced at Kaden, he found the man alone. As they all fell into line to head back out onto the colosseum floor, Glenn found himself curious enough to ask. "No guests?"

Kaden shrugged noncommittally. "No one who wanted to come."

That was a bit sad. Still, Kaden was going to receive a 5,000 experience scroll for "winning" the singles bracket, and likely a fair amount of experience from his anonymous Quest as well. He'd also receive a financial reward for his victory and leave the cup with gear well above his level. The only thing he wouldn't leave with would be his helmet... though, Glenn supposed, a Blacksmith could repair it.

As Glenn stepped out once more onto the sandy surface of the huge colosseum, he saw that the crowd had thinned out. The stands were still crowded, but a good third of the audience must have left to enjoy good food, good drink, good friends, or a good Entertainer. That was unfortunate, since he was going to expose a Deathcaster conspiracy tonight, but hopefully word would get around.

He was really doing this. He was really going to stand on that hastily constructed stage and reveal that he was a Soulseer to an entire colosseum of people. After keeping his Class hidden since he gained it, what he was about to do felt very much like a dream. He would no longer have to hide.

Which still didn't mean he wouldn't spend the rest of his life in a church prison.

The stage was already crowded when Glenn emerged with everyone else. He saw six more Adventurers who had won various events, likely the Monster battle and Demon battle exhibitions that had taken place while he was getting glad-handed by the cup's officiants. As he'd hoped, everyone important was also on the stage, and not just Mayor Whitley of Sun's Cross.

Six male and four female Preceptors in fine robes, all of whom looked hale and hearty despite their advancing age, were seated in the rows of seats on the stage. Because of the tremendous reliance on Lifecasters, Spiritualists, and Shamanists to heal and even resurrect Adventurers during the <Sandsea Cup>, there was no greater concentration of clergy than here at this event. These were their leaders.

These ten elected members of the Church of Celes were collectively known as the Ten Gospels. Each of them was charged with representing the interests of one of the Ten Gods of Luxtera. The Gods were even said to speak through their Gospel on occasion, though Glenn suspected that was just a tale.

There was even a Gospel charged to represent Ralun, though that woman never spoke in public. Instead, she wore a silken bandana marked with the symbols of Ralun and Celes, a sun and moon. Glenn didn't know if Ralun's Gospel had always worn that bandana. If Duncan was right, she hadn't.

Most of the time, the Ten Gospels could never be found together. They spent their time moving between the churches in Eastwend, Doveport, and Aria, preaching to both their own people and others and doing good works. The <Sandsea Cup> was one of the few places where they could all be found together, as the Church of Celes hosted grand mixers for its clergy and staff here as well.

The presence of the Ten Gospels at this cup was how Becka had sold Marion Hawkshadow on giving Glenn special permission to sail across the sea and enter it. There would be no better opportunity to scan the Ten Gospels while they were all in one place and determine if they, like others, were secret Deathcasters. Becka had figured that out long before he did.

Glenn's mission, of course, was simply to scan the Gospels and memorize the names of any who were secret Deathcasters. He was not to expose them, and if he did, he suspected Marion would either kill him or pin a medal on him. Even if his plan succeeded, he wasn't sure which one he'd receive.

Glenn scanned all ten of them, one after one, and found the results as he expected. Six of the ten Gospels were secretly dual-classed as Deathcasters, Necromasters, or Plaguemasters, though, shockingly enough, the Gospel of Ralun was not. Nor was the Gospel of Celes.

So now he knew. Six of the ten Gospels had decided that Death-caster should be a Class used and controlled by the Church of Celes, and they had spent the past fifty years or more arranging things to fit their goals. They had even suppressed the words of Ralun himself, the Scripture of Ralun, because it would contradict their words. Deathcaster was not a forbidden Class.

As Glenn marched up the wooden steps onto the stage and glanced at the stands filled with hundreds or even, possibly, more than a thousand people, he felt good about his plan. This wasn't everyone at the cup, but the news would spread like fire after he delivered it.

In a few hours, everyone in Sun's Cross would know the truth about Soulseer and the Deathcaster conspiracy. As days followed, the news would spread across Luxtera. No matter what happened after he left this stage, the secrets of the church and the Blazers would come out today.

The officiant ushered Glenn to his seat, and Glenn was amused to see a seat had even been set aside for Ripper. He was, after all, Glenn's guest. After he and Sara stared at each other for a moment, silently consulting, Glenn simply lifted the chair and folded it, then set it aside. Sara sat down and patted the blank space of stage beside her. Ripper settled in and sat with impressive dignity.

Glenn took his seat beside Sara, with Becka to his left, Nora to the left of her, Duncan to the left of Nora, and Leo at the end of their group. Leo had insisted on sitting at the end so he be would first in line to slow and stop anyone who came at them from the center of the stage.

Once they were settled, Glenn could do nothing but work not to fidget as preparations continued. As more people arrived and took the stage, Glenn was relieved to see the colosseum crowd filling out as well. People had simply left to grab a bite or relieve themselves, and now the crowd was swelling more closely to its original size.

Finally, Mayor Whitley stepped forward and stopped before a simple wooden lectern. A tall Town Guard took up position to either side of Whitley, and not just as an honor guard. Glenn had learned almost too late that the officiants of the **<Sandsea Cup>** weren't fools.

They wouldn't allow even those who won contests to shout anything they liked to thousands of spectators, which is why the Town Guards were here. Each Adventurer who made a speech would make it to the Town Guard, who would repeat their words while using **[-Public Address-]**. This had the dual benefit of ensuring the Town Guard could censor anything unpleasant while also ensuring that everyone could hear a speech given from a stage all the way in the cheap seats.

[-Public Address-] was, in this case, the final trick that would allow Glenn to reveal the truth. As a former Town Guard, he *knew* **[-Public Address-]**... and he had slotted it at the temporary Shrine of Celes before reporting to the stage. Tonight, *no one* would be able to censor his words.

Mayor Whitley launched into a speech so long-winded and annoying that Mayor Coleman would have appreciated it. The crowd cheered and hollered for some reason. After that, the Gospel of Celes rose and walked to the podium. Glenn was glad she wasn't a conspirator. She had a kind face.

The Head Gospel offered the typical tribulations to the Gods and led the crowd in the arena in prayers. Glenn closed his eyes and joined in with them as genuinely as he had every time he'd prayed in Richard Deepscar's chapel back in Wolfpine. The Gods might test him every day... but he had to believe they had the best interests of everyone at heart. They were, after all, giving him back Zack.

Once the Gospel of Celes finished her speech, she returned to her seat. Whitley again took the stage, spent far too much time reminding everyone present how great the **<Sandsea Cup>** had been so far (and who, like him, was responsible) before finally announcing the moment Glenn had waited for.

"And now, it's time to present the experience scrolls earned by the brave and skilled Adventurers who reminded us all that the 10-15 level range is as filled with talent as the higher level brackets. To start, I'd like to call Kaden Tallhorn to the stage! Kaden, get up here!"

Kaden rose and hurried to the podium. Out of curiosity more than anything, Glenn checked Kaden's Status sheet. There it was, as he'd expected it would be.

Level 15: *Win an event in the* **<Sandsea Cup>** *(Anonymous)* *(Complete)*

Given the Quest was anonymous, Glenn knew Mayor Whitley wouldn't be confirming it on this stage. That was the very opposite of anonymous. Still, Kaden was going to get halfway to 17 by consuming a 5,000 experience scroll and completing that expensive Quest.

After shaking his hand, Whitley handed Kaden his experience scroll, and Glenn eyed it curiously. It looked almost like the scroll created by a Scribe to create a Quest, and he suspected it was created by a Scribe... like a Preceptor. He also knew it cost a small fortune.

Kaden took his scroll and then bowed to the crowd. As he slipped the scroll behind his back, Glenn marveled as it burst apart in a shower of tiny white particles and vanished. Kaden was, it appeared, wasting no time in using that scroll, likely out of worry he might be exposed as a cheater.

Glenn supposed he might as well do the same. He checked Kaden's Status Sheet and again confirmed what he'd expected. Kaden was level 16 now and sitting at **129,988/136,000** experience. If not for the mysterious benefactors Brennon had mentioned, that scroll would have been Glenn's. He would have reached level 15 tonight and could have resurrected Zack tomorrow.

He hoped his good friend wouldn't mind waiting just a bit longer.

Kaden stepped up to the podium, then looked to the Town Guard. As he spoke, the Town Guard repeated his words verbatim. Kaden thanked Mayor Whitley, of course, followed by the Ten Gospels and the "fantastic audience" in the stands. The only surprise was when he added one bit.

"And lastly, I'd like to thank Glenn Graybreaker for giving me the fight of my life... twice. I know we hit each other hard out there, but I want Glenn to know I bear him no ill will, and that I'm honored to have faced both him and Rebecka Coldbreaker." Kaden turned to Glenn. "Good duels, both of you."

The crowd roared raucously, but this was the first time in forever Glenn had felt less than eager to return a courtesy from a former opponent. That feeling vanished quickly. Both he and Kaden had bent the rules to get where they were now, and Glenn was just sore he'd finally lost a duel.

Glenn stood, thumped his hand to his chest, and nodded to Kaden. Becka waved. The crowd roared even louder at that, and Kaden smiled and looked to a Lifecaster, who then led him off the stage. Kaden had another scroll coming—he and Cullen both had a 1,500 experience scroll reward waiting for taking second in the doubles bracket—but those scrolls would be given to them in private.

To keep the speeches during the awards ceremony to a minimum, only those who won first place got to speak. As Glenn sat, Becka leaned close and patted his knee before she mouthed *"Well done."* It took Glenn a moment to decide why she had said that.

If he had been an ass to Kaden after Kaden had made such a gracious gesture, the crowd would have grown to dislike Glenn before he could even speak. He hadn't returned Kaden's politeness for that reason... but now he was very glad he had done so. He needed people to believe him.

Mayor Whitley returned to the stage. "And now, folks, we'll move onto our second awards presentation of the night. Let's hear a warm round of applause for Glenn Graybreaker and Nora Rapidbloom, the winners of the doubles dueling bracket! Get up here, you two!"

Glenn rose and looked to Nora, who hopped up with a brilliant smile. She looked fully recovered from the arrow she'd taken through her head, though she had said that most of her memories of their duels today were scrambled. At least she hadn't suffered any worse effects from her death.

Carefully, subtly, Glenn removed his enchanted **[Blazer Pin]**. If he showed his Status Sheet to anyone now, they would see his *real* Status Sheet. He would no longer hide that from anyone.

Glenn walked to the podium with Nora at his side, and when they arrived, he motioned for Nora to precede him. She grinned and thumped his arm, then walked forward. Mayor Whitley handed Nora her experience scroll, and she bowed deeply as she tucked it into her **[Unfilled Bag]**.

So she wasn't going to use the scroll immediately? Glenn hoped she wasn't squirreling it away to give to Terry or Carmello or, worse, some impoverished low-level Adventurer who desperately needed a boost. Nora was far too kind and generous, and for once, she needed to do something for herself.

He could talk to her about that later, though. Nora stepped up to the podium, looked to the Town Guard, and spoke as the Town Guard, after a short delay, repeated her words using **[-Public Address-]** for the crowd. Even so, Glenn listened to her words instead of his.

"I never thought I'd be up on this stage, let alone claiming the title of winner in the doubles bracket. But before I say anything else, I have to congratulate a person who's not up here right now, but who will be very soon." Nora looked over her shoulder. "Becka, you're amazing, and I'm honored to have gotten to know you over these past few days." She smiled. "And you and Glenn are *adorable*."

As the Town Guard repeated Nora's words, the crowd once again grew to such a deafening volume the Town Guard (and Nora) had to pause and wait for them to die down. Once they did so, Nora continued her speech. "That's really all I wanted to say. Mom, Dad, I love you! I was honored to fight here, and this was the greatest experience of my life! Thank you, Sun's Cross!"

The crowd roared and cheered as Nora took a quick bow, smiled at Glenn, and then headed off the stage following an attentive Lifecaster. Glenn was next up to the podium. As he stared out over the crowd, he, for a moment, saw Wolfpine and everyone he loved. Everyone he'd left behind.

If he survived this, if Glenn revealed everything, he would finally be able to visit. He could return home and have a drink with Karl Coldbreaker, and play a game of Strat-Go with Erika Willowbraid, and kick back and enjoy mugs with the Wolfpine Town Guards. He could eat supper with his parents.

His time away from home had been a whirlwind of adventures and excitement and terror, and Glenn, despite all he'd seen and suffered, wouldn't take back any of it. He had the life he'd always wanted and the woman he was now certain he'd marry. All that was missing was home.

Wolfpine was home. His family was home. The people who lived there were home. And if he did what he set out to do today, all the Deathcasters forced into service to the church or languishing in secret prisons would also be allowed to go home. To see their families. To sleep in their own beds.

As he thought of Russell Stillwound, in particular, he hoped Russell would find his way home.

Mayor Whitley said something Glenn didn't really hear, then handed Glenn his experience scroll as the second winner of the doubles bracket of the **<Sandsea Cup>**. As Glenn touched it, he sensed that all he would need to acquire its experience was accept.

He accepted. A heady rush of pleasure flooded his body, and then he was 3,000 experience closer to level 15. He imagined Zack pumping his fist from the beyond.

Whitley stepped back. "Now, my boy, simply step up to the podium and speak in a normal tone. Town Guard Mallow will relay your words to the crowd, but keep it short and sweet. Also, keep in mind you can't say anything derogatory about the cup, about me, or about the church." The Mayor chuckled amiably at his own (in his mind) joke. "Not that you'd do anything like that!"

As Whitley winked and stepped back, Glenn decided he definitely didn't hate this man. He wasn't a Mayor Coleman, but he also wasn't a Mayor Earthwhite. He was... annoying. He was perfectly happy to annoy Whitley and move on with his life.

Glenn stepped to the stage and checked the Status Sheet of the Town Guard to his right. His name was Christopher Mallow. Time to make the most important speech of his life.

Glenn looked to Christopher, then spoke in a normal tone. He would start by using Mallow to carry his words and take over with his own once the man balked. It would be useful to see how far Mallow would go before his duty to Mayor Whitley or to Kya, Goddess of Duty, stretched.

"First, I want to personally thank every Adventurer I faced in the singles or doubles brackets of the cup. I feel like I learned something from dueling each and every one of you, and also, I want you to know that I'm sorry I had to rob you of victory in order to win a dueling bracket. I hope, once I'm done up here, you'll understand why I had to win at least one bracket and speak to you tonight."

As he spoke, Glenn kept his eyes on Town Guard Mallow. The man continued bellowing his words, verbatim into the crowd using [-Public Address-]. If Christopher Mallow thought Glenn's speech was odd, he didn't say.

"I also want to thank Mayor Whitley for hosting this cup and everyone who made it run as smoothly as it did. This experience has been amazing, and I wouldn't trade it for anything. How about a round of applause for everyone who works behind the scenes?"

The crowd cheered wildly, and Glenn them. He needed to ease everyone into a false sense of security so they would be slow to react to what he said next. So they wouldn't immediately stop him.

"Finally, I want to thank each and every member of the Church of Celes for traveling here from wherever they lived, worked, or leveled, to keep all of us safe. No matter what happens next, all of you are heroes. Know that I respect each and every one of you in the church tremendously. I always have."

Glenn meant that. Those involved in the Deathcaster conspiracy were a tiny fraction of a very large group of kind, good, and selfless people. People like Lucy Skygazer, Richard Deepscar, and countless others who selflessly worked to protect Luxtera's people all deserved recognition.

"Unfortunately, as much as I'd like to conclude my speech there, there's something else I need to talk about before I step down. Something I need to get off my chest."

Mayor Whitley hopped to Glenn's side and knifed a motion at Town Guard Mallow. "We're out of time! Close out your speech with a thank you to the crowd, and we'll get some dessert!"

Glenn glanced placidly at Whitley. "I can't finish my speech?"

"It was a perfect speech! Let's go out on top, shall we?"

Glenn turned to face the distant crowd and then, in front of Mayor Whitley, the Ten Gospels, the Town Guards, his friends and allies, and thousands gathered in the colosseum, he activated his Town Guard Skill, [-Public Address-]. He spoke his own booming words to the gathered crowd.

"Six of the Ten Gospels are secretly Deathcasters!"

His words boomed out over the stage, the crowd, and the colosseum even more forcefully than those of Town Guard Mallow. Everyone sitting on every bench of the colosseum in every direction could hear him. They might even be able to hear him outside the colosseum.

"And Deathcaster is not a forbidden Class!" Glenn shouted, as Whitley's jaw dropped and Town Guard Mallow reached for his **[Guardian's Mace]**. "Some of the Gospels and others in the Church of Celes have secretly forced young Adventurers to take the Class of Deathcaster! They force those people to use their Desouled to enforce the church's will by violating the Law of Consent!"

Mayor Whitley recovered from his sputtering fit. "Seize him!"

As both Town Guards clomped over, Glenn looked at Mallow and used **[-Soul Scan-]**. At the same time, he willed his Status Sheet to display. Then, he spoke to Mallow without ending **[-Public Address-]**. He didn't deafen the man, but Mallow hunched down as Glenn's words carried to everyone.

"Christopher Mallow, you currently have ninety-four thousand, six hundred sixty-four experience." Glenn read that off Mallow's Status Sheet, followed by his Strength, Vitality, and Luck, in front of Mallow, Whitley, everyone gathered on stage, and the now silent, breathless crowd.

Mallow clanked to a stop as Glenn pointed at his own Status Sheet. "As you can see here, Chris, I'm a Soulseer. It's a new Class the Gods have personally bestowed upon me. It allows me to use **[-Soul Scan-]** to view your Status Sheet without your consent, which is how I know six of the ten Gospels behind me have dual-classed as Death-casters. Kya can't be happy about that."

Mallow didn't slap the cuffs on Glenn. If Mallow tried, Glenn would dance back and complete the rest of his speech at a run. He couldn't use **[-Public Address-]** if he was wearing **[Lawgiver Cuffs]**.

Glenn pointed at **[+Unyielding+]**. "I'm a Town Guard, just like you. Kya would want you to let me finish my speech. She's the Goddess we both serve, and my duty to Her is why I'm speaking here tonight. I can't let this horrific injustice continue one more day."

"Seize him!" Whitley bellowed again.

The Town Guard behind Mallow clanked to a stop. Glenn was relieved when Mallow incrementally shook his head. He had, thank the Gods, lucked into a curious Town Guard.

Christopher Mallow had a responsibility to follow Mayor Whitley's orders, but not if they went against the higher authority Mallow also served: Kya, Goddess of Duty. She was the ultimate authority over every Town Guard in Luxtera, not the elected mayor of the city in which they served.

"Like you, Chris, I stood a gate at Wolfpine for over two years before the Gods chose me to correct this injustice. Worse yet, the Gospels have hidden a great secret. A Scripture of Ralun exists, and its passions prove the Gospel's words are lies. Deathcasters have never been a forbidden Class."

"Arrest him now! Right now!" Whitley shouted. "What are you fools doing?"

Glenn was unsurprised to see dozens of men and women in white robes, Lifecasters, Spiritualists, and Shamanists clustered around the stage with expressions ranging from awe to shock to fury. Some of their stares were directed at him, but others were directed at the Ten Gospels.

The rank-and-file of the church were starting to believe Glenn.

Not a one of the Gospels spoke. None of them rose from their seats. All of them sat silently, placidly, and watched Glenn reveal their secrets with gazes ranging from kind to murderous.

"Some of you will question my words, but I wouldn't be here if I didn't have proof. So now, in front of everyone assembled, I call upon Preceptor Duncan Steelwright, a former Gospel of Ralun, to approach this podium and read to us from the Scripture of Ralun. Ralun's holy book!"

The Gospel of Idros leapt to his feet, followed by the Gospels of Xiva and Ansin. "Town Guards! Seize this man and anyone who aids him! Every word from his mouth is a foul lie!"

Chaos erupted as the huge crowd of Lifecasters, Spiritualists, and Shamanists down below rushed the stage and encountered a wall of Town Guards who were, in absence of order, defaulting to the orders given by Mayor Whitley. Under no circumstances were strangers to get on stage. In the chaos, Duncan Steelwright—Teacher—produced a large tome from his [Unfilled Bag].

As Duncan raised it high above his head, the book glowed with ominous purple energy. Glenn's eyes were instinctively drawn to the scripture, and he suspected it was the same with everyone in the colosseum. Even the Gospels. All of them but Ralun rose.

The six Gospels who'd dual-classed as Deathcasters were Idros, Xiva, Ansin, Dina, Levos, and Isdon. The Gospels who hadn't dual-classed were Celes, Ralun, Kya, and Vox. And as the dual-classed Gospels stormed forward to grab Glenn, the Gospels of Celes, Vox, and Kya interposed themselves.

"Stop there!" Even shouting at the top of her lungs, the Gospel of Celes had no way to make herself heard like the Town Guards or Mayor. "Sit down! I would hear more from Duncan Steelwright and Glenn Graybreaker about this lost scripture! Brothers and sisters, I say he must be heard!"

"Silence him!" the Gospel of Isdon bellowed. "He speaks blasphemy! By a vote of six to four, I say the blasphemers must be arrested and silenced!"

As the Gospels began to argue among themselves and the crush of church clergy below grew so numerous that even the Town Guards had trouble holding them back, the Gospel of Ralun stood at last.

As the others faltered in their arguments, the Gospel of Ralun took three steps. She calmly removed her veil. And then, in a booming voice that turned Glenn's blood to ice, *He* spoke.

"Let him speak." The voice of the God of Endings rumbled through the colosseum.

The silence was so immediate and so complete that Glenn was worried he had lost his ability to hear. Then, from the crowd of seats where the guests of the winners had gathered, Ripper howled. Sara's brave Arctic Wolf offered a long, low, mournful howl that made Glenn long for home.

Glenn turned and walked back to the podium, and no one stopped him. He motioned to Duncan to join him, and then, as he looked out over the crowd, he spoke again using **[-Public Address-]**. "We've now revealed the lies. Worse, there is a truth that's been hidden from you." He looked to Duncan.

Duncan walked to the podium, and then, Glenn couldn't fail to notice his whole body go stiff. Duncan no longer stood like a flesh-and-blood man. He swayed like a Desouled puppet. And when he spoke before the arena again, it was not Duncan who spoke. It was Ralun.

"Passion Sixteen, Refusal of the Climb. Heed well these words, disciple of mine, for I am Ralun, the ending of all things.

You are a child of the Gods, caretaker of a shard of Celes' divine spark. Such a gift is not given without responsibility. The levels you gain are a sacred contract between you and Us. To honor Us, to honor those who freely gave you the spark of divinity that created both your life and your will, you must climb the ladder until you reach the peak of strength or fall bravely in your attempt.

Though your climb may be hard and your challenges great, you must never lose faith in your abilities or abandon your climb. To refuse to level and grow stronger is to stray from the path with which We entrust you. You refuse Our call to action at great peril to both your life and soul."

As he finished speaking those words, Duncan sagged, but then he surged back to unnatural life. He flipped through the Scripture of Ralun as if possessed... which Glenn knew, now, he was. Ralun, it seemed, was done wearing a veil and remaining silent as his chosen Class was kept in chains.

"Passion Two, the Charge of Death. Heed well these words, disciple of mine, for I am Ralun, the ending of all things.

All Classes honor the Gods, but my Class is intended to honor death. As Celes guides you in life, I guide you beyond life. Know that death is not the end, but simply a transition. To remind you of this, and to help you on your climb, I offer my most potent gift. I offer Deathcaster, my chosen Class.

If you choose Deathcaster, your responsibility is not simply to level. It is to remind the world every day that death is not the end. Your diverse Skills will not only allow you to protect your allies, but to save their souls. You can even ensure they remain in their bodies long enough to be resurrected."

Ralun was right. Glenn knew for a fact that there was a Death-caster Skill, [-Flesh Anchor-], that could bind a soul to an ensouled corpse for seventy-two hours. That meant that if someone fell in battle, they could wait six times as long for a [-Resurrect-], and anyone who used that Skill on a friend would make it three times as likely a Spiritualist would be able to use [-Resurrect-] and bring them back.

"Should any tell you not to choose Deathcaster, that it is an impure, immoral, or forbidden Class, you are to tell them this. You serve Ralun, the End of all Things, and Ralun, like death, cannot be denied. If you choose to level as my Class, know that no force in all Luxtera can claim you are not in the right."

Glenn swallowed. There it was. Ralun Himself, while possessing the body of Duncan Steelwright and reading His words from His own tome, had called every single member of the Ten Gospels who'd chosen to engage in the Deathcaster conspiracy a liar. No wonder they had suppressed this.

As he looked at the gathered Gospels, all of whom continued staring in shocked silence, Glenn felt his first hint of rage. Without the knowledge that abandoning Luxtera's Climb could leave them wandering in the dark after death, how many had met that fate? Could their souls still be saved?

Duncan wavered. Glenn rushed over and caught him just as he collapsed, but as Duncan stared up at him, wet tears filled the man's eyes. He was crying, but it was happy crying.

Duncan sobbed. "It's been such a hard road, but... they know now. They know. Thank you."

Mayor Whitley had gone so white he looked like he might pass out. As for the Gospels, those who had favored the conspiracy looked ill as well. Meanwhile, the Gospel of Ralun looked pristine, and as for the Gospel of Celes, her bright smile warmed her whole being. Her eyes also glowed.

The Gospel of Celes all but floated across the stage. And then, as Glenn remained as paralyzed as if he'd been struck by [-Guardian's Smash-], she hugged him and spoke in his ear.

Not the Gospel. Not the woman. This otherworldly voice could only be Celes Herself.

"No matter how many times we think we've seen all you mortals have to offer, one of you always surprises us." Celes squeezed him and stepped back. "You'll see him again soon."

The Gospel staggered and almost fell, but Glenn caught her before she could collapse. The glow in her eyes faded, and then, as Glenn steadied her, she inclined her head. The Gospel of Celes, the most influential and powerful church leader in Luxtera, inclined her head to him.

"This is the end, just as Ralun suggested. We'll all leave our posts after this. You, Glenn, have torn out a sickness I couldn't stop. I only hope the church can heal. Thank you. Bless you."

"Redwood." Glenn swallowed. "My real name is Glenn Redwood, son of Tania and Hal Redwood of Wolfpine. I'm a Town Guard."

She smiled. "Until we speak again, Town Guard Redwood."

The Gospel of Celes walked back to her fellow Gospels, some of whom had already collapsed on their seats in shock. Glenn had hoped his speech would have an effect on people, but he hadn't expected to have Ralun Himself offer His contribution. Then again... Glenn had tempted Him.

Behind him, Mayor Whitley found his voice. "I... well, this is certainly unprecedented."

Glenn turned around to find Becka, Leo, Sara, and Ripper all waiting expectantly. Duncan stood at the podium, staring at the sky. And somewhere out in the huge mass of shocked Church of Celes clergy members, he knew Nora Rapidbloom had to be bursting with questions.

Glenn walked to Mayor Whitley. "You can arrest me now."

"I can... what?"

"I think the best way to get me out of here without being mobbed would be to have an escort of Town Guards. My only duty here was to tell everyone the truth, and I've done that now. I leave my fate in the hands of your Town Guards, whatever Gospels are elected to serve the Church of Celes, and, I suppose, the Blazers. But I'm not going alone."

Glenn walked to Becka and reached into his **[Unfilled Bag]**. He pulled out his **[Lawgiver Cuffs]**, raised them so everyone could see them, and snapped one cuff around his own wrist. Immediately, he lost access to every Skill and Blessing he had slotted. He was once more a mortal man.

He then knelt before Becka, whose eyes were widening by the moment, and offered the other cuff. "My love, I've known you for what feels like as long as I've been alive. I know now I can never stop loving you. I need to ask you one last question which I hope won't come as a surprise." He smiled. "Rebecka Coldbreaker, will you marry me?"

As Sara gasped and slapped her hands over her face in delight,

Ripper panted happily. Leo stared in disbelief, then shook his head. "Of all the times. Really?"

Becka, however, had eyes only for him. As her eyes flooded with tears, she reached for the single remaining cuff. She snapped it around her wrist without hesitation.

Then, as they found themselves mortal and bound together, she gripped his hands and said one word. The word.

"Yes."

TWENTY-NINE

A TRIUMPHANT RETURN

Escorted by Brennon Shadesinger, Rebecka Coldbreaker, Leopold Argentshade, Svara Dawnwhisper (now once again living under her real name), Ripper, and, surprisingly enough, Nora Rapidbloom, Glenn Redwood approached the Shrine of Ralun deep in the wilds of Stillwatch.

Thanks to the dry, parched climate and the rarity of rain or vegetation, this shrine was in better shape than the one he'd seen in Grassea. While sand still covered its surface, Glenn had no problem seeing the central stone where he would touch the sun and moon and enter the Plaza of Selection.

The past few days had been chaotic. Brennon Shadesinger's announcement that all betting on the <Sandsea Cup> was frozen until an investigation into cheating was completed had infuriated thousands. All Ten Gospels had simultaneously resigned, demanding an emergency election. The administration of Sun's Cross, the leadership of the Church of Celes, and even the mighty Blazers were busy with countless arguments and meetings trying to decide where to go from here.

Some among the church and Blazers were demanding that all captive Deathcasters immediately be freed, while others were accurately pointing out that many of the Deathcasters imprisoned by the church had committed serious crimes, including murder. In making his speech, Glenn had likely caused more political chaos than any single person in recent memory.

Even though no one yet knew exactly how everything would shake out, several goals were clear. First, the entire leadership of the Church of Celes—all ten Gospels—had resigned in the aftermath of Glenn's speech. Elections would determine who took those positions anew. Even those Gospels who had opposed the Deathcaster conspiracy had silently allowed it, so everyone had to go.

While everyone who ran and was elected as a new Gospel could not be a secret Deathcaster, there was talk of allowing a Deathcaster to openly serve as a Gospel... in particular, as the Gospel of Ralun. There was already a great deal of talk about electing Duncan Steelwright once more to that position, after, of course, he served his prison sentence for abducting other Adventurers.

The Blazers were particularly worried about having Deathcasters among the Gospels, which surprised Glenn. He had thought the church would have more objections, but they genuinely seemed to want to make amends. Putting one of the people they'd oppressed in power could certainly do that.

He had been right about the church, and knowing he'd been right was a balm on his soul. While a few still questioned if this was the right path, church members overwhelmingly supported electing new leadership and freeing all Deathcasters who had committed no serious crime. Even those who had committed crimes to escape or defend themselves would have their cases reviewed.

Every church member Glenn had talked to, or who had talked to him, seemed adamant in their goal of making this right. Even those who'd had no part in the conspiracy seemed to feel guilty, which was just more proof, in his eyes, of the basic goodness of the average citizen of Luxtera. Russell Stillwound and hundreds of others would languish no more.

Glenn had done it. He had, in one week, unraveled a conspiracy that had vexed the Blazers for over decades and would have taken decades more to end... under current policies. If they didn't promote him and Becka to full Blazers after this, he wasn't sure what else they'd have to accomplish.

Yet for today, all of those concerns and the chaos he'd left behind in Sun's Cross seemed distant. He was out here for one goal and one goal only. A reunion with a long dead friend.

As his party came to a stop at the edge of the shrine, he glanced at Nora. "I'm going to try to talk you out of this just one last time. You earned that scroll, and—"

"It's just 1,500 experience, Glenn." Nora chuckled and handed him the scroll. "I know you could earn it on your own, but I really want to see what happens today. Terry and Carmello are utterly done with the desert, so they insist on heading off to Steel Bay after the cup. I could never forgive myself if I lost the chance to witness a man return from the Forever Death."

Glenn ruefully shook his head. "I hope this isn't disappointing."

Nora laughed. "Given Ralun Himself graced your little celebration speech, I doubt it."

Glenn closed his eyes, felt the scroll, and accepted. A rush of pleasure took him as he absorbed yet another 1,500 experience, putting him over the top. A much more turgid rush filled him as he reached level 15 and moved beyond.

He had earned a new Blessing today, but more importantly, he had earned a second life for his best friend. An annoying man, but still a good one. He had made a promise to Zack and kept it.

Glenn opened his eyes and walked out across the shrine. No one followed. He reached the center of the shrine, knelt, carefully brushed away the gathered sand, and placed his hands as he knew he must. One on the sun, one on the moon. And then the world drained away into nothing.

A moment later, Glenn stood in a familiar void. Ahead, the Brazier of Life sat lifeless and silent. Within a Shrine of Ralun, the Brazier of Life was always silent. Wind rustled his spirit hair, and then the Gods spoke... or, in this case, wrote.

-Welcome, Glenn Graybreaker.-

-You have now reached level 15, which leaves you eligible to complete stage 3 of your Epic Quest, "The Soulseer's Path." However, you must speak to Us at the Evolan Trial Shrine to complete this Quest. Until you do, the Calamity of Evolan remains on the horizon.-

Glenn was annoyed but unsurprised. The Gods had made it clear he had to actually find the Shrine of Balance in Evolan and touch the shrine inside it, just as he had in Grassea. Thanks to how fast he'd leveled, he still had plenty of time to do that. So much time.

-The Gods have taken notice of your recent actions and are pleased with your progress toward your goal. As a reward for your faith in the Gods and devotion to Luxtera's Climb, We will now honor our covenant and Quest. We will resurrect one soul that you request. Say the name and they live again.-

Any person? The Gods would let him bring back anyone? This had to be a trick... or a test.

There were so many great minds that had passed into the beyond. Legendary Adventurers who could do great deeds if they returned and got a second chance at life. Glenn even knew of a few, though only because he'd read about them in books. As amused as he was by this offer, he wasn't tempted.

Given the chance, the man he'd come here to save could end up just as famous... or infamous.

"Thank you for granting me this boon." Glenn smiled as he imagined how all the historians of the world might react if they ever learned he had the chance to bring back literally anyone and chose a level 15 Shadower with questionable taste in jokes. "I wish you to resurrect Zack Silverstone."

- Your choice is made. When you leave this shrine, we will grant Zack Silverstone a second life with all of his experience, levels, and Skills intact.-

Glenn waited, and then the void vanished. He once more found himself on the Plaza of Selection, surrounded by braziers on tiers representing his choices for new Blessings. Words appeared.

—You have two Blessings remaining. Should you not choose them now, you must wait 24 hours before you can choose again. Do you wish to move to Skill selection?—

"Yes," Glenn said. He was too excited to think straight, let alone make choices that would carry on for the rest of his life. He needed to see Zack.

The plaza shifted, but no new braziers appeared. He couldn't unlock a new Skill until level 16, and had no Skill selections left. The void returned, and then the words of the Gods appeared once more.

-Your Skills and Blessings are now locked. You may slot again in 24 hours. Go and challenge the best Luxtera has to offer.-

Darkness took him once more, and then, with a gasp, he was once more in Luxtera, on the Shrine of Ralun, in Stillwatch beneath a hot sun. As he rose and looked to his companions, he found all of them staring anxiously in his direction. Everyone was waiting for a grand show.

Nora was practically bouncing up and down with excitement, Becka was watching him with calm, kind eyes, Leo had his arms crossed and looked bored, and Ripper was panting in the sun. Brennon, oddly, showed no expression at all. He had mastered that ability long ago.

Glenn looked up. The sun beamed down. He looked around the shrine, but nothing much was happening. Then, just when he was on the verge of touching the sun and moon again, the air rippled.

Boom after boom shook the shrine, enough that Glenn feared it might collapse into the earth. He barely kept his feet as the earth rumbled with enough force that Glenn suspected they felt it quake all the way back in Stillwatch. All his hair stood on end.

Glenn took several hurried steps back from the central tile of the Shrine of a Ralun, and not a moment too soon. As the moon slipped in front of the sun and day turned to night, a portal of golden energy twice as tall as Glenn manifested in the center of the Shrine of Ralun. It grew larger and brighter, soon forcing Glenn to shield his eyes against the glare.

In that portal, which seemed to stretch on forever to his eyes, a single shadow appeared. That shadow crept forward as if surprised, then rose to his full height, then walked. Then sauntered. As a dark-skinned man in gleaming leather armor stepped from the portal, it vanished behind him.

The moon slipped away from the sun as light returned. The quaking ended. And then, as he looked around at the barren desert in which he'd found himself, the man's eyes alighted on the blonde-haired woman who was sprinting across the shrine toward him. He grinned.

Glenn grinned as well and stepped aside as Anna threw herself at Zack. Zack yelped as he barely caught her, but neither of them fell. Glenn's vision wavered as tears filled his eyes.

Zack laughed merrily. "Calm down, girl, I'm just back from the dead. You couldn't have mis—"

Anna's kiss shut him up, and when he kissed her back, Glenn offered his new fiancé a knowing glance. She grinned wide and hurried over, along with Sara, Nora, and Ripper, but Glenn was surprised when Brennon simply inclined his head and strode away.

Brennon didn't know Zack, and Glenn supposed he'd seen all he needed to see. Seeing a man resurrected by the Gods was another event filled with details and facts Brennon would file away for use in the future. Glenn wondered if Brennon ever forgot even the tiniest detail.

Once Zack finally got done kissing Anna, or at least got some breath back, he eased away and grinned the grin Glenn had missed. "I'm going to be honest, man, I really didn't think you'd pull it off."

Glenn scowled and moved to slug Zack in the arm, but his now *living* friend somehow avoided Glenn's strike with ease while never releasing his grip on Anna. As Zack raised one hand as a peace offering, Glenn relented. Zack stepped away from Anna and opened his arms.

"But I really am grateful. Seriously, Glenn. You told me you'd bring me back, and then you pulled it off. I still can't believe it, but you... all of you..." Zack swallowed as he choked up. "You did it. You all busted your asses to make up for my mistake, and I... I've missed you. Really."

Anna sobbed quietly. "I'm never letting you go anywhere alone again."

"You know, that's fair."

Glenn stepped forward and grinned through his tears. "Good to see you. Really."

Zack eyed him in amusement. "Want a hug, big man?"

"I'll be honest. I could use one."

"Fine. I know you brought me back from the dead, but just the same, I'm not kissing you."

"You don't have to. You just have to agree to stand as my second at my wedding to Becka."

Zack stared. "What, *that's* happening?"

Glenn hugged his best friend tight and pounded him heartily on the back.

THIRTY
AN EPILOGUE
GLENN

THIRTY-EIGHT YEARS LATER

As he sat on his favorite stump within sight of the gates of the small town he'd called home since the day he was born, Preceptor Soulcaller and retired Blazer Captain Glenn Redwood sipped a mug of Lakebrooke Orchard Mead and enjoyed the sunset. After decades of exploring Luxtera, decades in which he'd faced its many dangers and seen its many wonders, he was long past the point where he was eager to tromp off into the wilds and fight.

Wolfpine was home. His and Becka's cozy house was home. And after the rich life they had lived together, he was more than content to relax in Grassea, mentor young Adventurers, and enjoy supper with all the other old people who gathered at The Mead Beast every few days.

In his time on the road Glenn had become a Town Guard, saved Wolfpine from a plague, unraveled a decades-old conspiracy that had paralyzed the Church of Celes, evolved Soulseer to become the first Soulcaller in Luxtera, helped found and defend an outpost in the 32-36 zone of Stormreach, led an expedition to the newly opened zone of Malia, uncovered an ancient temple that suggested there had once been *eleven* Gods, wrestled at least one of Them in the Six Hells, and, in his most impressive feat yet, raised a child alongside the woman he loved.

That last accomplishment was the one he considered his most satisfying success.

Glenn Redwood was now fifty-six years old, old enough to be a grandfather, though, in his and Becka's case, they had settled for becoming parents instead. Given neither of them had been willing to request a child from the Church of Celes until after they retired from Luxtera's Climb at age 41 and 40, respectively, they'd started raising their child later than most.

Even if a couple requested it, it was rare for the Church of Celes to bequeath a child to retired Adventurers. Glenn and Becka weren't most retired Adventurers. He suspected Lucy Skygazer, who had been elected as the Gospel of Celes eight years ago, had a part in approving their request. Even so, the entire church remained immensely grateful to Glenn, in particular.

Better yet, the <**Festival of Isdon**> was just around the corner. In a few days Adventurers would arrive from all over, including many faces he hadn't seen in years: Leopold Argentshade, Svara Dawnwhisper, Ashley Bloodbraid and her merry band of rogues, Terry, Carmello, and Nora, and even, if the rumors were correct, Alan Starshine, his wife Olivia, and their second daughter Victoria, who was just a bit older than his own. Anna had promised they would come.

Glenn was so excited to see all of them it was difficult to sleep.

A ruckus from the Deepscorn Woods drew Glenn's attention away from his lovely thoughts and the lovely sunset. A moment later two bedraggled and bloodied Adventurers burst from the woods huffing and puffing, running for their lives. One carried a limp, unmoving body.

It was Dylan Stoutmore and Diego Stoutmore, who were themselves a rarity in Luxtera. In one in five hundred cases, the church granted a couple in a starter town twins. The two common age men looked identical save for how they kept their hair. Diego, a level 5 Skirmisher, had his head shaved, while Dylan, a level 5 Shadower, had his hair in cornrows like his idol.

It still amused Glenn that young Shadowers across Luxtera now worshipped the legendary Voidstrider Zack Silverstone as a paragon of power and prowess. Still, Glenn had admired Mammoth Cloudcrusher just as much in his youth. Old heroes might pass on and new ones might rise, but the need for legends to inspire young Adventurers never ended.

Dylan was huffing as he carried the body of Janine Moonmont, and Diego was covering his retreat as best he could. All three were freshly minted level 5s, and one of them was dead. They must have stumbled into a group of Monsters they couldn't handle... or been reckless.

Which left him wondering what the *last* member of their party had gotten up to.

Glenn glanced at the two Town Guards standing alertly at the entrance to Wolfpine, then at the pack of Gloamwolves that were chasing down these two Adventurers and their fallen friend. At the pace Dylan and Diego were moving, and with their wounds, they'd never make it within fifty paces of Wolfpine's town gates before the Gloamwolves surrounded them.

It was an all too chilling repeat of a decades old tragedy. A tragedy that had led to Rafe Slatestriker meeting the Forever Death. This time, however, it would play out differently.

Glenn set down his mug, then rose. He broke into an easy jog and then a full-on sprint, as spry at the age of fifty-six as men half his age. He had [+Regrowth+] to thank for that. Despite how tumultuous his life as an Adventurer had been, he owed a lot to the Gods.

But the Gods no longer had any say in who he could save.

A single Gloamwolf outpaced Dylan and Diego and moved around them to cut them off. Glenn raised one hand as he ran and activated one of his advanced Soulcaller Skills, one only usable on a weakened or low level Monster. He had thirty-five levels on this Gloamwolf.

[-Extract Soul-].

The Gloamwolf instantly dropped dead as a mote of bright blue energy zipped from its body. The wolf ashed a moment later as the mote zipped into Glenn's hand. As the other wolves closed on the lagging Adventurer, Glenn raised his other hand and focused on Diego.

[-Regenerate Soul-].

His powerful Soulcaller Skill restored not just Health Points but Blood as well, and it flooded the flagging Skirmisher with energy. [-Regenerate Soul-] would also continue to tick away for the next twenty seconds, restoring Health Points and Blood. Given the Skill was intended to heal Adventurers of level 20 or higher, Diego was now all but invincible.

Glenn cast [-Regenerate Soul-] on Dylan as well. They each cried out in triumph and redoubled their efforts, but as they continued running toward him, Glenn stepped into their path and smiled. "I've got your back, boys. Hammer away!"

Both of them grinned vengefully and turned around. Dylan set down Janine's ensouled body and once again drew his [-Iron Dagger-]s. What was a battle of four Gloamwolves against two Adventurers became a slaughter as Dylan and Diego fearlessly tore the Gloamwolves apart. Even when they both got bit, the wounds healed almost instantly.

Glenn was pleased at how the twins expertly defeated the Gloamwolves. Both were getting better at avoiding hits, though he doubted Janine, their Lifecaster, would get to relax any time soon. Still, none of them could get better at Adventuring if they were all dead.

Diego had just ashed the last Gloamwolf when one more female figure stumbled out of the Deepscorn Woods. She was breathing heavily in her now tattered [Cloth Armor]. Glenn watched his darkhaired, sixteen-year-old daughter proudly as she spun and expertly unleashed [-Transfer Life-] on one of the Gloamwolves chasing her... and herself.

She didn't slow down. Her wounds healed as the last of the Gloamwolf's Health ashed away, and then the wolf burst into purple ash. She continued running as she unleashed the Skill on the second Gloamwolf, never letting the distance close. She was so fleet-footed!

Even as Diego and Dylan belatedly ran to their fourth party member's aid, the second Gloamwolf snarled and, visually, prepared to use [-Pounce-]. As it did so, the young woman snatched a crackling [-Iron Dagger-] from her belt and set her feet.

Her grandmother had enchanted that dagger for her.

The Gloamwolf pounced on the young woman, pinning her but a second before she drove her [-Volt-] enchanted [-Iron Dagger-] into its chest. That stunned the Gloamwolf before it could so much as bite her, and two more stabs ashed the Monster. The young woman stood, brushed off her tattered [Cloth Armor], and turned to see him for the first time.

"Dad!" As she yelled, level 5 Deathcaster Emma Redwood narrowed her eyes at him in obvious annoyance. "I didn't need any help with those two."

Glenn smiled tolerantly. "I didn't give you any."

She glanced at the two piles of ash, then back at him. Then, she frowned. "Oh."

Diego and Dylan finally reached Emma. Each stumbled over the other to assure her they were so grateful she was safe. Emma rolled her eyes and pushed them both away to hurry toward Janine. Glenn stepped aside as the three of them all gathered around their fallen party member.

Diego looked up at Glenn. "Has Richard resurrected anyone today?"

Richard Deepscar was almost ninety years old and still going strong. When he wasn't using [-Resurrect-] on Wolfpine's young and fallen Adventurers, he was out leveling Deathcaster for the good of Luxtera. So much had changed in the last thirty-eight years.

Now that [-Flesh Anchor-], the Deathcaster Skill that allowed an ensouled corpse to remain ensouled for seventy-two hours instead of twelve, was commonly available, every Preceptor Spiritualist in Luxtera had either picked it up or was planning to. Fatalities among Adventurers had fallen by an order of magnitude as a result, which was good, because it felt like every Monster and Demon in Luxtera had gotten more powerful in the last three decades.

Glenn nodded. "Richard used [-Resurrect-] on Debbie Sunless this afternoon. However, I think his queue is clear if you want to bring Janine to the temple to wait."

Dylan stomped one foot. "Devilspit! We never should have gone after the Gloamwolf Den Mother."

Emma scoffed in annoyance. "We'd have made it all the way to the bottom and killed her if you didn't kick over that bone pile." She spun on Diego. "And you! What were you thinking running off to chase a straggler? Your job was to protect Janine!"

The twins protested almost in unison.

"They were practically invisible bones! No one would have seen those bones."

"It was going to call more Gloamwolves! I couldn't let it call more Gloamwolves."

"One." Emma pointed at Diego. "It wasn't, because we'd killed all the Gloamwolves on that level of the cave. I counted. I was also planning to ash it once I finished with the other."

Diego winced. "Oh."

"As for the bones, *Dylan*, everyone knows about that bone pile. Didn't you read the write up of the Gloamwolf Den that I lent you yesterday? They're on the map on the second page!"

Dylan turned beet red. "I... Emma, there was a huge Strat-Go tournament last night!"

Emma sighed in exasperation. "You're both hopeless. I swear! I don't know how Janine and I manage to keep you alive." She dropped to her knees by Janine and raised one hand.

Purple and black energy coursed from her hand and washed over Janine's ensouled body. As Emma rose, she nodded in satisfaction. She had just cast **[-Flesh Anchor-]** on Janine. Janine could now wait seventy-two hours to be **[-Resurrect-]**ed, which was easily within reach.

Emma pointed at Glenn. "Well? Preceptor Redwood is waiting. You two pay up."

Again, the twins winced in unison. "But, Emma..."

Glenn approached and held out his hand. "You know how this works, boys. I had to heal you to keep you in the fight. That means you pay the fine."

Grumbling, both twins dug out all their life crystals and handed them over, along with ten crescents apiece. It was a pittance compared to the fee for a **[-Resurrect-]**, but Glenn knew they barely had more money than this. He also had no plans to spend their money.

Glenn would donate this money to the Church of Celes, where it would go toward a public fund founded by Mayor Moonmont to pay for Adventurers who couldn't afford a **[-Resurrect-]**. It still vexed him to demand payment for saving young Adventurers, but that was the agreement he had come to with the Town Guards after it became clear he'd keep doing this.

After he effectively robbed the Town Guards of their jobs, Captain Joanne Dewcrest had *politely* insisted Glenn charge Adventurers for his services. In her words, if he was going to be constantly saving Adventurers beyond the gates, they needed to pay *some* penalty for almost getting themselves killed. Otherwise, they'd grow "soft and fragile."

Those were Joanne's words, not his. Even so, even at Glenn's age and with all his accomplishments, he hesitated to annoy Captain Joanne Dewcrest. She was even more feared and respected than the retired Logain Cliffbreeze, and that was saying something.

Once Glenn had collected his "fine" for saving the Stoutmore twins' lives, Emma pointed at Janine's motionless and ensouled body. "Dylan? You carry her to the temple and put her in Richard Deepscar's queue. Diego? Go let Mayor Moonmont know that her daughter has been blessed with [-Flesh Anchor-] so she doesn't worry about her meeting the Forever Death."

The twins looked at each other for help, then at the intimidating Emma Redwood.

Emma glowered at them. "Now, please."

Without another word, Dylan huffed as he balanced Janine's ensouled corpse over his shoulder and stumbled off. Diego gave Glenn one last thankful wave before heading off to notify Mayor Moonmont about today's incident. Unlike Mayor Coleman, everyone loved Mayor Moonmont. Glenn and Becka had voted for her in every election since she first ran.

That left Glenn alone with his daughter on the outskirts of Wolfpine. And when the only person he loved as much as Emma emerged from Wolfpine's gates and stood there imperiously, hands on hips, Glenn chuckled.

"Uh oh, kiddo. Looks like Mom wants a word."

Emma brushed back her bangs. "How do you know she doesn't want a word with you? You did spend another day lazing around at the gates."

As Emma stalked off toward the gates, Glenn strolled after her. "I wasn't lazing. I was reflecting and rehearsing. I only have three more days to devise my speech for the <Festival of Isdon>. You know how much I hate giving speeches."

"You were also drinking."

"If a man my age can't enjoy a mug or two as he watches the sunset, why even level?"

Emma sighed. "She's going to be so mad."

Glenn chuckled and rubbed her shoulder. "Look at the bright side, kiddo. You got all the way to the bottom of the Gloamwolf Den and came back alive. Not many can say that."

"Four different Adventuring groups can say that, Dad. I know. I talk to them every night at the tavern." She huffed and shook her head. "We're going to take that bitch down. We have the composition for it, and we have the gear and Skills. I just don't know what I'm going to do with those twins! I swear, if they both weren't so devilishly handsome..."

She gasped, then glanced at him in alarm. "I didn't say that."

Glenn cleared his throat and rubbed the back of his head. "Let's... talk to your mother."

Becka waited at the entry to Wolfpine. Glenn noted in amusement that both Town Guards, each of whom was not much older than him when Kya had first selected him, were standing stiffly at attention. The young guards always stood a watch, but they only stood at attention for three people: Mayor Moonmont, Captain Dewcrest, and Rebecka Redwood.

As they reached her, Becka fixed Glenn with a knowing gaze. As he held it, he felt Emma sigh in relief. She patted his arm and whistled as she strolled into town.

"Good luck, Dad!"

Becka stepped into her way. "Oh no you don't. What happened today?"

Emma sagged in place. "I... we fought some Gloamwolves."

"You led your party into the Gloamwolf Den today?"

Emma sagged and place. "Yes, mother."

"And did those Stoutmore boys give you trouble again?"

Emma perked up. "It's like they don't pay attention to surrounding Monsters at all!"

Becka nodded in understanding and touched Emma's shoulder. "Boys can be like that. I know you like them, honey, but you really could do better. As it happens, I heard from Erika that her youngest is looking for an Adventuring party. He's—"

"Mom!" Emma made a face. "I'm not leveling with Ethan *Caskshaper*."

"Why wouldn't you? He's a Brutalist. You could use a good Brutalist in your party."

Emma flipped Becka's hand off her. "I'm going to get some soup!

We had a long day and I need food. Also, go easy on Dad. He's been trying to memorize his speech all day."

Becka stepped aside and shook her head ruefully as Emma strode off. Then, she turned on Glenn again. As he reached her, Glenn smiled his most innocent smile.

"Darling? Is something the matter?"

Becka rolled her eyes and shook her head. Even at fifty-five, she remained the most beautiful woman Glenn had ever seen, and not just because she'd chosen to level Entertainer as her second Class. Using him as her only source of experience. They still leveled every night.

Becka made him happy and complete. He would utterly adore Rebecka Redwood for as long as he lived. His wife took his hand and drew him after her, away from the Town Guards.

As they walked through a Wolfpine busy with Townsfolk hurrying back inside the walls to get inside them before sunset, Becka spoke. "Did you know Zack was coming?"

Glenn nearly missed a step. "He's here?"

"In disguise. Apparently, he's finally grown tired of being lavished with adoration in every town he passes through, so he wants us to keep his arrival a secret. He also says you said he could stay in our guest room as long as he likes, which I—"

Glenn scowled. "I did *not* say that! I said he could pop in for a drink if he was in Grassea, but I said nothing about him occupying our guest room for an extended period of time."

Becka glanced back at him. "Well, you tell *him* that."

"Oh, I will!" Glenn softened his expression as he followed Becka toward the home they had inherited from Karl Coldbreaker before making it their own. "Though, if he really has nowhere else to stay, we could give him our room and sleep in the attic."

Becka scoffed. "Really, Redwood?"

"I'm just saying! I have so many good memories of that attic."

She giggled and took his hand. "Husband, how are you still this amorous after all these years? I'm not the young filly I used to be."

He pulled her to a stop, pulled her close, and stared at her. "But you're *my* filly."

She scoffed indignantly. "So you're saying I look like an old mare?"

"Becka, that's not remotely what I meant!"

She laughed merrily, shoved him away, and resumed her journey toward their house. "How *is* your speech going, by the way? About the day you singlehandedly ended the Deathcaster Conspiracy? How does Captain Redwood, retired Blazer Truth Seeker, plan to convince today's legions of skeptics that both Ralun and Celes spoke to him on that day?"

Glenn winced as he followed her. "I actually wasn't going to mention that part."

"That is likely wise."

"Still... kind of curious what Zack wants."

"Knowing him? He wants to drag you away on another temple expedition."

Glenn chuckled. "Well, at least we know that's not happening."

"Don't be so certain of that, love."

As they reached the doorway to their home, Glenn frowned at her. "What do you mean? I'm not leaving you again, and I'm certainly not leaving Emma."

"Who says you need to leave us to go on an adventure?" Becka smiled and touched his chin. "I know how much you love it here in Wolfpine, but I've been thinking. Emma's old enough to travel now, and you're strong enough to wrestle a God and win. Why not show our girl the world outside Wolfpine? She's going to explore it without us if we don't."

Glenn stared in surprise. "You really think we should take Emma to another zone?"

"I'm not saying we should. I'm saying we could. We could discuss it. With Emma."

"And Zack?

The door to their home opened, and then a dark-skinned, gray-haired, brightly-smiling man strode out onto their front porch. "Glenn! So good to see you. Still playing Town Guard?"

Glenn scowled at his best friend. "I'll always be a Town Guard."

"Which is why you're *perfect* for the job I have lined up. Now, before you say no—"

Glenn raised one hand. "Not yet. At least let me eat supper first."

"Right, fair. Wouldn't want you hearing about the best opportunity of your life on an empty stomach. Also, I really want to drink some of that Lakebrooke Orchard mead.

Glenn tiredly rubbed his temples and smiled at Becka. "Should I start cooking?"

His wife clutched his arm and smiled up at him. "Emma and I can handle that, love. Why don't you hear what Zack has to say and see if you can get him a room at The Mead Beast?"

Zack frowned. "But I thought I..."

He trailed off as Glenn and Becka stared at him.

"Yes! I've always loved that place. Haven't had chipwrecks in a year, and I really want to see what Randi has done with the menu."

Becka gave Glenn a gentle shove. "Take our visitor to get himself a room. I'll get supper started and enlist Emma when she returns." She leaned up on tiptoes to kiss him again. "And Glenn? Think about what I said, and remember how much *you* wanted to travel at Emma's age."

He nodded as he stared in adoration at the woman he loved. "I will."

Becka slipped inside the house. Their house. As she closed the door and locked them both on the porch, Zack smiled gamely. "Shall we go grab a drink, hero?"

Glenn gestured grandly with one hand. "Why not lead the way, *legendary hero*?"

Zack fumbled in his **[Unfilled Bag]** for a familiar necklace, then slipped it around his neck. In another moment, he looked like another man entirely. That man winked at Glenn.

"Not today," Zack said proudly. "Today, I'm just another anonymous Preceptor."

"Unless I tell them Voidstrider Silverstone is in town."

Zack's eyes widened in alarm. "Glenn, you *can't* tell them. Anna made me promise I was going to stop doing hero tours. Don't make me break my word to my wife!"

"I'll stay quiet for Anna. Not you. But at least tell me you told your mom."

Zack scoffed. "Of course I told my mother."

"Good. Now... drinks. But no expedition talk until after supper, or I'm telling the whole tavern about you. Anna would understand."

Zack slapped him on the back and strolled off. "Right, fair."

As he followed his best friend through Wolfpine like they were both sixteen-years-old again, Glenn couldn't help but smile. He loved Wolfpine, and he loved his life here, but Becka was right. Emma's wanderlust grew every day, and he could relate to that.

Their daughter, unlike him at her age, could travel all of Luxtera without anything to hold her back but the level of the Monsters she faced. With Glenn along, nothing could harm her. So why not travel a little, again, with his lovely wife and increasingly energetic daughter?

It wasn't like they were going to the Six Hells... again. Unless that was what Zack suggested. In which case, Glenn would toss him out a window.

Though he'd be certain to pay Randi for the window.

FROM THE AUTHOR

Thank you for coming on this journey with me! I hope you enjoyed *Divine Progression*. The journey of Glenn Redwood and his friends is now at an end, but I hope to start another journey with you soon. Please follow me on Amazon and let me know what you thought!

If you'd like to get in touch with me, have a comment, or would like to learn more about Luxtera's Classes, lore, and laws, I hope you'll come visit me at https://www.jakebrannigan.com. Thanks for reading this book! Also, please leave a rating or a review on Amazon if you can.

Until next time!

THANK YOU FOR READING CHAMPION

We hope you enjoyed it as much as we enjoyed bringing it to you. We just wanted to take a moment to encourage you to review the book. Follow this link: Champion to be directed to the book's Amazon product page to leave your review.

Every review helps further the author's reach and, ultimately, helps them continue writing fantastic books for us all to enjoy.

———

Also in series:

DIVINE PROGRESSION
TOWN GUARD
SOUL SEER
BLAZER
TRUTH SEEKER
CHAMPION

———

Want to discuss our books with other readers and even the authors? Join our Discord server today and be a part of the Aethon community.

Facebook | Instagram | Twitter | Website

You can also join our non-spam mailing list by visiting www. subscribepage.com/AethonReadersGroup and never miss out on future releases. You'll also receive three full books completely Free as our thanks to you.

———

Looking for more great LitRPG?

Check out our new releases!

Order Now!

(Tap or Scan)

Complete Quests. Earn Renown. Win. Meet Alexander Krup, your average high school graduate turned video game beta tester. Working for a strange company nobody has ever heard of, he earns his pay by the achievement. After a string of bad luck, including his girlfriend dumping him, he wakes up one seemingly average day and is suddenly faced with blue boxes of text that float in the air. While coming to grips with the fact that he might by hallucinating, a representative of his mysterious employer communicates through the menu boxes to offer a fresh life in another world. With nothing left to lose, Alexander takes the offer and is sent hurtling into a fantasy world both like and unlike any game he's played before. Now, he must choose an alignment. Will he seek Renown or Infamy? One way or another, Alex will leave a mark... or will it be a stain? *Don't miss this exciting new LitRPG Adventure from Kos Play, author of the* **System School Series.** *Join Alex as he rises from zero-to-hero in a new world filled with monsters, a detailed system, magic, power progression, and so much more!*

Get Mayhem Now!

Order Now!

(Tap or Scan)

PATRICK LAPLANTE

*he Gods are dead. The Seven Evils reign. Only Hope stands between humanity
and extinction... When Sorin's parent's mysteriously die, he is starved for truth and
thirsty for revenge. He begs the Eighth Evil, Hope, for assistance, and his prayers are
answered... ...Though not in the way he ever expected. He is made a Poison Cultivator,
a rare class who are shunned by high society. Unable to continue his medical practice,
Sorin turns to adventuring to make ends meet. Though he's only able to afford to team
with a ragtag crew of outcasts as companions — An armored polar bear, a stern archer,
a sleep-deprived pyromancer, and a peeping-tom rogue. Oh, and a rebellious rat
familiar who won't stop eating the party's loot when no one is watching. Things are
looking up, until Sorin discovers his ancestor's hidden research notes about forbidden
medical research. What dark deeds was his family up to? Only he can find out... if he
and his party can survive the coming Demon Tide.* **Don't miss this new
Cultivation Progression Fantasy series from Patrick Laplante, bestselling
author of Painting the Mists. Featuring loads of power progression, demon
slaying, dungeons, loot, crafting, and even a rebellious pet rat, it's got
something for everyone!**

Get Pandora Unchained Now!

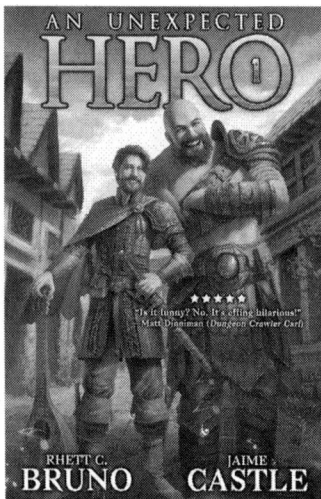

For all our LitRPG books, visit our website.

GET MORE LITRPG

GLOSSARY

Adventurer: A mortal chosen by the Gods to grow stronger by undertaking Luxtera's Climb, where they must fight and defeat successively powerful Monsters, Demons, and Desouled as they strive toward the divine level cap of 40.

Ansin, God of Beasts: One of the four Challenger Gods, also known as the "Savage God." He favors bestial Monsters of all kinds and those who fight only with the strength of their bodies and minds. Patron of Anchorites.

Alchemist (Townsfolk Class): Alchemists craft magical potions which rapidly restore Health Points or Blood, cure Poison, or cleanse ailments inflicted by Monsters, and gain experience from doing so. Their potions may also grant additional benefits like resistance to fire, immunity to poison, or the ability to see in the dark. Finally, Alchemists create offensive potions like **[Slumber Potion]s** and **[Paralyze Potion]s**.

Aquarine: One of the three territories of Luxtera. It is a northern province rich in natural resources that consists of snow-cloaked mountains to the north and a vast interconnected networks of tropic islands to the south. Its capital is Doveport in the zone of Graycoast.

Anchorite (Adventurer Class): A relentless and fearless fighter, the Anchorite specializes in Skills of the unarmed body, including wrestling, grappling, fists, and feet. They can also call upon chakra-based powers to heal and enhance themselves. Their patron is Ansin, God of Beasts.

Auracaster (Adventurer Class): A bastion of support, the Auracaster increases the effectiveness of Skills and weapons wielded by others and themselves with musical prowess. They can also charm enemies or lull them into a slumber. Their patron is Isdon, God of Commerce.

Blacksmith (Townsfolk Class): While anyone can make common weapons and armor, Blacksmiths are the only mortals that can craft weapons and armor of quality uncommon or above, and they gain experience from doing so. Their Skills also make weapons unusually strong and light, which makes them the choice for Adventurers looking for the strongest gear.

Blazers Guild: As the most powerful and respected guild in Luxtera, the Blazers are trusted by the governments of all three provinces to hunt down lawbreakers, settle disputes, and defeat truly terrifying Monsters. As the Blazers recruit both Townsfolk and Adventurers, being chosen by the Blazers Guild is one of the few ways a Townsfolk can venture beyond the walls of their town of birth.

Some Blazers travel the world while others settle in specific zones to act as that zone's final line of defense. Unlike other mortals, Blazers can freely arrest lawbreakers without their consent, though attempting to arrest a lawbreaker allows those lawbreakers to attack the Blazer. Yet given their skill, will, and numbers, few lawbreakers dare to challenge a Blazer in open combat.

. . .

Blessing: A passive magical ability provided to mortals by the Gods. Once slotted, the effects of the Blessing become active upon the mortal and remain active until the Blessing is unslotted. Blessings come in four qualities: uncommon, rare, epic, and legendary, based on how many mortals in Luxtera have acquired that Blessing. Blessings are represented as so: **[+Featherlight+]**.

Once a mortal begins Luxtera's Climb, they may choose one new Blessing every five levels.

Blood: Some Skills, when activated by mortals, consume Blood, which is a magical resource within a mortal's body that restores itself over time. Once a mortal has reduced their Blood pool below a certain number, they can no longer activate Skills that require Blood.

Brutalist (Adventurer Class): A brutal and straightforward fighter, the Brutalist specializes in Skills requiring shields or blunt weapons. They can use Skills to both strengthen their allies and weaken their enemies, and may also force enemies to attack them alone. Their patron is Kya, Goddess of Duty.

Builder (Townsfolk Class): While anyone can build basic structures, Builders can use their Skills to dramatically decrease construction time, quickly excavate foundations, and fortify buildings beyond mortal means, and gain experience from doing so. They are also the only Class who can create Safe Stones, the Kya-blessed stones lining Safe Roads which drive Monsters and Demons away.

Caelfall: One of the three territories of Luxtera, an arid province consisting of sprawling plains, bountiful grasslands, and rain-parched desert. Its capital is Aria in the zone of Fool's March.

. . .

Ceremony of the Path: Once a mortal reaches sixteen years of age, they may undertake the Ceremony of the Path. They must present themselves to a Shrine of Celes within a Chapel of Celes, where the Ten Gods of Luxtera will decide whether they are to become Adventurer or Townsfolk.

The path bestowed by the Gods depends on the needs of the town where the mortal was born and their innate aptitudes. A mortal may not complete the Ceremony of the Path until turning sixteen and must complete it by age seventeen.

If a mortal does not complete the ceremony by age seventeen, the Gods will turn them to salt.

Celes, Goddess of Resurrection: The Mother of All who created Luxtera, the Nurturer and Challenger Gods, and everything that lives and breathes. Patron of life and Lifecasters.

Church of Celes: Primarily composed of Lifecasters and their Evolved Classes, Spiritualists and Shamanists, the church guides all in devotion to the Pantheon. They administer matters of the heart and matters of family, officiating marriages, approving requests for children, and formalizing adoptions. They also maintain the chapels where Adventurers and Townsfolk reslot and resurrect ensouled corpses.

An Adventurer with an official Quest from the Church of Celes can ignore the Pantheon's Law of Consent, provided their target of their Quest is a Deathcaster or another judged by the church to be acting against the Gods. The church has ultimate moral authority in enforcing the laws of Luxtera, so to act against the church is to act against the Gods. Few in Luxtera dare risk that.

Common Age: A mortal of age fourteen or fifteen.

Cooldown: Some Skills, once activated by a mortal, cannot be used again until a set amount of time passes. The time that must pass before the mortal can use the Skill again is its cooldown.

Crescent: A copper coin. The smallest unit of currency in Luxtera.

Culinarian (Townsfolk Class): While anyone can cook food, Culinarians also gain Skills that let them change mundane ingredients into magical ingredients and gain experience from doing so. Their food isn't just mouth-wateringly good. Some dishes can actually speed healing, temporarily increase attributes, or restore Blood.

Cultivator (Townsfolk Class): While anyone can plant crops and run a farm, Cultivators also gain Skills that let them speed the growth of crops and vastly increase their monthly yield from both fields and animals. They gain experience from doing so. They can also grow rare magical ingredients that no other mortal on Luxtera can cultivate.

Deathcaster (Adventurer Class): A disciple of Ralun, the Deathcaster wields power over Desouled and can force the desouled corpses of fallen Monsters to fight as their minions. Their Skills can also drain the life of living beings or sicken them with disease. Their patron is Ralun, God of Endings.

   The Church of Celes currently forbids Adventurers from choosing this Class. Those who defy the church and choose Deathcaster during their Ceremony of the Path are imprisoned for life.

Demons: Created by Xiva, Goddess of the Unseen, Demons challenge the spiritual strength of Adventurers. Demons are intangible beings possessed of animal to human-like intelligence and can gain experience by defeating Adventurers. When defeated they are banished to the Six Hells, though they will eventually respawn at their base level.

Desouled: Twelve hours after a mortal dies in combat, or immediately after a Monster dies in combat, they become a desouled corpse. Their body is now an empty vessel. Deathcasters and some powerful Demons can raise a desouled corpse and force that corpse to do their bidding.

Devilspit: A fairly minor curse common in Luxtera. The saliva of Demons is known to sicken all it touches, hence it is seen as something to be universally loathed and avoided.

Dina, Goddess of the Hunt: One of the four Challenger Gods, also known as the "Predator God." She favors those who hunt and defeat others to grow stronger. Patron of Rangers.

Divine Level Cap: The maximum level a mortal can gain by completing Luxtera's Climb. The Gods encourage all mortals, whether chosen as Adventurer or Townsfolk, to strive to reach the divine level cap. This is 40 for Adventurers and 20 for Townsfolk.

Divinity (Attribute): How close a mortal is to the Gods, increased by fighting with daggers, fighting in light armor or robes, or by casting magical Skills with long cooldowns. It decreases damage inflicted by magical attacks and increases the ability to detect magic, Demons, and spiritual entities. It also increases damage dealt by magic Skills, Health Points cured by restorative Skills, and all damage dealt by magical weapons.

Dual Class: When an Adventurer reaches level 20 in their chosen Class, they may not level it further. Instead, they may choose to select an additional base Class and level that Class instead.

Upon changing their Class, which counts as reslot and can only be done at a Shrine of Celes or Ralun every twenty-four hours, an Adventurer may then level that Class starting at level 1. They retain their current attributes. In addition, they may choose a new Skill upon reaching level 2.

Duel: While the Law of Consent forbids one mortal to harm another without their consent, two mortals who agree to do so may engage in a duel. Once both mortals have given consent, these mortals may attack each other freely. Moreover, no mortals outside the duel may interfere.

A duel ends when one participant yields, is knocked unconscious, or dies.

Duelist (Adventurer Class): A dexterous and skilled fighter, the Duelist specializes in Skills requiring bladed weapons. They can teleport short distances and move blindingly fast when delivering blows. Their patron is Vox, Goddess of Adventurers.

Enchanter (Townsfolk Class): Enchanters use their Skills, along with rare and key materials, to imbue weapons and armor with magical properties that vastly improve the effectiveness of the item, and they gain experience from doing so. They can also craft unique items with magical properties that alter or enhance mortal perceptions.

Ensouled Corpse: When a mortal dies in combat, they become an ensouled corpse, at which point their soul remains bound within their body for twelve hours. If another mortal delivers them to a Chapel of Celes within that twelve hours, a Spiritualist who has gained the Skill **[-Resurrect-]** can restore the mortal to life. Any mortals raised in this way suffer an experience penalty.

In cases where a mortal's body is incinerated, devoured, or otherwise savaged beyond the ability to live upon being resurrected, no resurrection is possible.

Entertainer (Townsfolk Class): Men and women beloved and respected by Townsfolk and Adventurers alike, Entertainers thrill crowds with singing, dancing, and showmanship during the day and offer intimate companionship to those who desire them (and whom they desire) during Luxtera's cold nights. They gain experience by pleasing any who seek their company.

Evolved Class: When an Adventurer reaches level 20 in their chosen Class, they may not level it further. Instead, they must choose one of two Evolved Classes (determined by base Class) that offer increasingly powerful Skills and Blessings. An Evolved Class starts at level 20 and may be leveled to 40.

Experience: When an unclassed, Adventurer, or Townsfolk defeats a Monster, Demon, or Desouled in combat, the Gods award that mortal with 10 experience, given to them alone or split among their party. No experience is given for killing enemies more than three levels below one's own. Mortals also gain experience by completing Quests, crafting items, or using particular Skills that award experience upon use.

All experience is cumulative. Once a mortal gathers a sufficient amount of experience, they will level up. The amount of experience required to level up increases with each level.

Forever Death: After a mortal dies and twelve hours elapse without that mortal being resurrected, their soul departs their body and that body becomes a corpse. When a mortal departs their body, it is known as meeting the forever death.

Guilecaster (Adventurer Class): A wielder of illusion, the Guilecaster confuses and disorients foes with Skills affecting perception. They can also disorient foes and even temporarily trick them into turning upon their former allies. Their patron is Xiva, Goddess of the Unseen.

Half Moon: A silver coin equivalent in value to fifty crescents.

. . .

Harmcaster (Adventurer Class): A wielder of the primal elements, the Harmcaster specializes in offensive and defensive ranged Skills of various elemental types. They can wield all elements equally or specialize in powerful Skills involving only a few. Their patron is Idros, God of Monsters.

Health Points: All entities in Luxtera have a fixed amount of Health Points, which determines how difficult they are to defeat. Successfully striking the entity in combat decreases their Health Points. When the Health Points of any entity reach 0, it dies.

Mortals become ensouled corpses. Monsters turn to ash, Demons are banished back to the Six Hells, and Desouled disintegrate.

Idros, God of Monsters: One of the four Challenger Gods, also known as the "Primal God." He favors tribal Monsters of all kinds and those with strong connections to the raw elemental forces of Luxtera. Patron of Harmcasters.

Isdon, God of Commerce: One of the four Nurturer Gods, also known as "The Townsfolk God." He favors mortals who seek to gain experience and grow wealthy through service to others. A patron of Auracasters, Blacksmiths, Merchants, Tailors, Politicians, Alchemists, Enchanters, Scribes, and Entertainers.

Item: A Townsfolk-crafted object used or worn by Adventurers or Townsfolk, everything from a travel pack to an enchanted breastplate. Items come in five qualities: common, uncommon, rare, epic, and legendary. Items are represented as so: **[Ring-Mail Armor]**.

Any mortal in Luxtera can use and wear common items. Only Adventurers may use or wear items of uncommon or higher quality.

. . .

Kya, Goddess of Duty: One of the four Nurturer Gods, also known as the "Shield Goddess." She favors mortals who devote their lives to growing stronger in the service of protection of others. A patron of Brutalists and Town Guards.

Landers: One of the three provinces of Luxtera, blessed with fertile farmland, bountiful rivers, and mineral-rich mountain ranges. Its capital is Eastwend in the zone of Eastmarch.

Law of Consent: This Divine Law, passively enforced at all times by the power of the Gods, states that no mortal may cause harm to another unless both mortals first consent. As such, while duels between two mortals who feel equally wronged do happen, open war between the three provinces in Luxtera can never occur. Conflict is resolved through diplomacy or spycraft.

The Law of Consent also ensures high level Adventurers cannot lay waste to towns and villages and become despots as they grow in power. It ensures all mortals remain focused on cooperating to fight Monsters, Demons, and Desouled... an undertaking which pleases the Gods.

Laws of Levos: Laws governing what mortals can and cannot do based on their age. The most well-known of these laws are the laws governing when mortals can engage in sexual activities, what activities they can engage in, and who they can engage in those activities with, generally regulated by age.

Level: A number representing a mortal's current progress toward the divine level cap. All mortals begin life at level 1 and remain at that level until they reach fourteen years of age, at which point they may begin Luxtera's Climb.

Once a mortal gains a specified amount of experience, they "level up," increasing their level by 1 and increasing their attributes. They may also gain the chance to select a new divine Skill or Blessing.

. . .

Levos, God of the Hearth: One of the four Nurturer Gods, also known as the "Common Age God"… a name used derisively by those who chafe at the Laws of Levos. He favors mortals who improve themselves by creating resources for their community. A patron of Culinarians and Cultivators.

Lifecaster (Adventurer Class): A disciple of Celes, the Lifecaster specializes in Skills that heal wounds, poisons, and curses. They can also use offensive Skills involving divine magic that are highly effective against Demons and Desouled. Their patron is Celes, Goddess of Resurrection.

Life Crystal: When a Monster, Demon, or Desouled dies, it leaves behind a glowing purple life crystal whose size differs based on the power of the entity that died. Many Townsfolk Classes capable of crafting items have Skills that allow them to use these life crystals to make new items, enchant weapons, or mix potions. Adventurers collect life crystals and sell them to Townsfolk for crescents.

Loophole: Even the Laws of the Pantheon are not without limit, and mortals are endlessly clever at finding ways around the God-imposed limitations on their actions. Such exploits are commonly known as loopholes. Mortals who discover these loopholes guard their secrets jealously.

Luck (Attribute): Whether a mortal is favored by the Gods. Increases the chance that random elements will fall in the mortal's favor. The method to increase this attribute is unknown, but many suspect the Gods grant increases in Luck when they are impressed or amused by a mortal's actions.

    What impresses or amuses the Gods is unknown.

. . .

Luxtera's Climb: The divine commandment of the Gods to gain experience and levels by defeating enemies (if chosen as an Adventurer) or supporting Adventurers (if chosen as Townsfolk). All mortals are charged by the Gods to undertake Luxtera's Climb, though not all mortals complete it. Once a mortal reaches the age of forty, they may choose to leave the ladder and retire.

Merchant (Townsfolk Class): Merchants are the center of all commerce in Luxtera. Only they have the Skills to transmute Monster life crystals into key ingredients necessary for all other crafting Townsfolk Classes. They gain experience from doing so. They typically purchase life crystals from Adventurers for crescents and obtain crescents from other Townsfolk in exchange for those life crystals. They also gain experience from making deals slanted in their favor.

Moon: A golden coin equivalent in value to 100 crescents.

Monster: Created by Idros, God of Monsters, Monsters challenge the physical strength of Adventurers. Monsters are living and physical beings possessed of animal-like intelligence and can gain experience by defeating Adventurers. Once defeated, they will eventually respawn at their base level.

Outpost: A mortal settlement established in zones of level 26 or higher. Unlike towns, outposts lack the divine protection of the Gods as well as a roster of Town Guards. Townsfolk may still settle there, however, no divine power forbids Monsters or Demons from bypassing the walls of an outpost and attacking those within, should they do so unopposed.

The defense of outposts thus falls to high level Adventurers. Evolved Adventurers of level 25 and higher often join an outpost militia in exchange for the bountiful experience gained by defeating the Monsters that attempt to destroy it. Brave or foolhardy Townsfolk also reside in outposts and purchase the rare and valuable crafting materials dropped by high level enemies, which they then sell for a vast profit to Townsfolk in low level zones.

Pantheon, The: Collectively, the ten Gods of Luxtera. While all ten Gods are worshipped by mortals, mortals pay particular tribute to Gods known to favor their Class.

Celes, Goddess of Resurrection, exists at the beginning of all things, while Ralun, God of Endings, exists at the end of time. Together, these two Gods created Luxtera. They gave birth to the Nurturer Gods, who ensure mortals thrive, and the Challenger Gods, who challenge mortals to grow stronger.

Party: A group of Adventurers who make a pact to share experience and life crystals gained by defeating Monsters, Demons, and Desouled. A party may include up to four members. When any member gains experience for any accomplishment, all members split that experience equally, with a small bonus given to those members who contributed most to the victory.

Politician (Townsfolk Class): Politician is simultaneously the most demanding and hardest to level Townsfolk Class, but choosing it offers a benefit all other Townsfolk Classes lack: the ability to hold political office. Politicians must start leveling in starter towns. No Politician can run for an office in a town where they do not meet the minimum level requirement for that town's zone, and can only run for the role of mayor once they reach or exceed the zone's level cap.

Preceptor: An honorific given only to Townsfolk who have reached the divine level cap of 20. These are the only Townsfolk capable of producing the most powerful crafted items created by their Class. Even after they've reached the divine level cap, they continue to craft powerful items for the benefit of all in Luxtera... and an impressive amount of coin.

· · ·

Prowess (Attribute): A mortal's base physical prowess, increasing the ability to pick locks, play instruments, maintain balance, and complete any other difficult tasks requiring flexibility and focus. Increased by accomplishing difficult tasks appropriate to one's Class without the use of a Skill.

Quest: Only Townsfolk can create Quests, a task those they deem eligible must complete. Anyone eligible to take the Quest may do so, and, if they complete it, turn the Quest in by swearing they have completed it to a Politician or the Politician's chosen agent under penalty of divine perjury.

Completing Quests awards experience (an amount designated by the Gods) and coin.

Quarter Moon: A copper coin with a silver border equivalent to twenty-five crescents.

Ranger (Adventurer Class): A deadly ranged combatant, the Ranger specializes in Skills involving the bow and close-range use of daggers. They also have a strong affinity for beast Monsters and can tame a Monster to act as their partner in combat. Their patron is Dina, Goddess of the Hunt.

Ralun, God of Endings: The End of Everything. Ensures Luxtera's population remains in balance and ensures defeated souls pass peacefully to the next realm. Patron of Deathcasters and Shamanists.

Safe Road: Long and winding roads connecting the towns and village of Luxtera. Along these roads stand pillars holding Safe Stones created by Builders and blessed by Kya, Goddess of Duty. These stones are anathema to Monsters, Demons, and Desouled. Travel on a

Safe Road is therefore perfectly safe for even the youngest of Luxtera, so long as the Safe Stones hold.

Scribe (Townsfolk Class): Scribes are the final arbiters of all contracts in Luxtera, both those between mortals and those involving Gods. Only a Scribe can create official documents used by everyone from Politicians to Merchants, including Quests, and gain experience from doing so. Finally, high level Scribes learn the Skill **[-Phantom Pen-]**, which allows them to write messages instantly seen leagues away. This "phantom correspondence" allows instant communication with others in towns zones away.

Shadower (Adventurer Class): A stealthy and dangerous fighter, the Shadower specializes in Skills involving daggers, misdirection, poisons, and stealth. They are especially deadly when launching an initial attack from an unseen position. Their patron is Xiva, Goddess of the Unseen.

Shadowers Guild: The Shadowers Guild operates in all provinces and all zones, though without the official blessing of those zone's rulers. Members in the Shadowers Guild specialize in exploiting loopholes in the supposedly unbreakable laws of the Gods. They complete contracts for coin for those who have decided methods lawful in the eyes of Gods and mortals are insufficient.

By using loopholes only they know to harm those who cannot be harmed and steal that which cannot be stolen, the secretive members of the Shadowers Guild enrich themselves and those who contract their services. Even the province governments contract with the Shadowers Guild from time to time. Sometimes, something needs doing that requires a deft and morally dubious touch.

Skill: An activated magical ability provided to mortals by the Gods, which either consumes Blood upon activation or cannot be used until a cooldown expires. When used, Skills do everything from vastly improving the ability to complete mundane tasks (such as building a particularly strong building foundation) to performing feats entirely impossible for mortals (like summoning fire from the air).

Skills come in four qualities: uncommon, rare, epic, and legendary, based on how many mortals in Luxtera have acquired that Skill. Skills are represented as so: **[-Phantom Slice-]**.

Once a mortal begins Luxtera's Climb, they may choose one new Skill every two levels.

Skirmisher (Adventurer Class): An agile midrange fighter, the Skirmisher specializes in Skills requiring either long-range melee weapons or thrown weapons. They can also wield wind magic to both gain and drop from great heights. Their patron is Vox, Goddess of Adventurers.

Six-Cursed: A strong curse used by mortals wishing to shock others or uttered in the grip of shock or anger. To call something "six-cursed" is to literally suggest it has become associated with the Six Hells. To call a person such is an insult that may instigate a duel.

Six Hells, The: The six vast realms of Demons that exist between Luxtera and the realms of the Gods. Each of the Six Hells is said to be more twisted and horrific than the last. They are the last challenge facing mortals who have reached the divine level cap.

Only the bravest or most foolhardy of Adventurers brave the Six Hells, but the rewards and crafting materials found there are valuable and powerful beyond measure.

Slot: While Adventurers may learn countless Skills and Blessings, they may only "slot" five Skills and three Blessings at any time. To slot Skills and Blessings, a mortal must touch a Shrine of Celes (usually found in a Chapel of Celes) or a Shrine of Ralun (usually found in the wilderness). A mortal can only "reslot" their Skills and Blessings once every 24 hours.

．　．　．

Status Sheet: A divine parchment which a mortal may manifest which records their age, level, attributes, slotted Skills and Blessings, and crafted items. Unless a mortal chooses to allow others to see their Status Sheet, no other mortal may view it. In Luxtera, one's Status Sheet is a private affair, only shared when mandated by the church or willingly shown to dear friends or lovers.

Strength (Attribute): A mortal's base physical strength, increased by pushing oneself to one's physical limits as often as possible. Determines how much a mortal can carry and how rapidly carrying weight affects exhausts their Vitality. It also increases damage dealt with physical weapons.

Tailor (Townsfolk Class): While anyone can make common clothing, Tailors are the only mortals that can craft clothing of quality uncommon or above, and they gain experience from doing so. Uncommon clothing is exceptionally resistant to wear and tear and may even enhance mortal attributes. Some clothing, like Town Guard uniforms, can't be created by any mortal who does not have the proper Tailor Skills.

Tailors also create varieties of cloth armor and robes that remain in high demand among Adventurers who choose caster Classes. Finally, they are the only Townsfolk Class that can create an **[Unfilled Bag]**, the expensive bags that allow Adventurers and others to store multiple heavy items without any worry for space or weight.

Tinker (Townsfolk Class): Tinkers use their Skills, along with rare and key materials, to create marvelous contraptions that are both magic and mundane, and they gain experience from doing so. They can create lamps that burn without oil, magical staffs that store Skill charges, and other wonders. Preceptor Tinkers also create the engines powering the airships that sail the skies above Caelfall.

．　．　．

Town: A mortal settlement, surrounded by walls, in which mortals reside. At least fifty mortals must take up full time residence in a town before it can be declared as such, at which point the Gods then forbid all Monsters, Demons, and Desouled from entering its walls. The permanent inhabitants of a town are generally Townsfolk, though Adventurers may also take up residence there as well.

Townsfolk: A mortal chosen by the Gods to grow stronger by undertaking Luxtera's Climb, where they must complete successively difficult tasks involving cultivation, crafting, or public service on the way to the divine level cap of 20. Once chosen as Townsfolk, Townsfolk remain bound inside the walls of their town of birth until they reach the level of a nearby zone. Townsfolk may travel freely during the day but must enter the walls a town before nightfall, or the Gods will turn them to salt.

Certain exceptions to this policy may be gained by accepting Quests to travel between towns or complete certain tasks. This allows Townsfolk to complete journeys between towns that require multiple days of travel. However, the expense involved discourages casual travel between towns.

Trial Age: A mortal of age sixteen or seventeen.

Unclassed: A mortal whom the Gods have not yet chosen as Adventurer or Townsfolk, anyone under the age of fourteen. These mortals may begin earning experience upon turning fourteen, and may use any Skill they acquire while leveling. Once an unclassed reaches the age of sixteen, they may also undertake the Ceremony of the Path, where the Gods will make them Adventurer or Townsfolk.

Unfilled Bag: A crafted travel pack that contains a magical pocket that can hold a huge number of belongings without any increase in weight. Due to the harsh environment inside the bag, it cannot store anything living. However, it can store any number of inanimate objects.

Vitality (Attribute): A mortal's hardiness, increased by being wounded in battle or exhausting oneself with strenuous physical activity, like running. A mortal gains 10 Health Points for each point of Vitality. It also determines how long a mortal can push themselves beyond their natural limits.

Vox, Goddess of Adventurers: One of the four Nurturer Gods, also known as the "Goddess of Battle." She is worshipped by all who level through combat, and favors those with an adventurous spirit and those who yearn to unlock new discoveries. A patron of Duelists, Skirmishers, and Tinkers.

Wisdom (Attribute): A mortal's knowledge of the world and all its aspects. Increased by memorizing new knowledge and casting Skills that require Blood. A mortal gains 10 Blood for each point of Wisdom.

Xiva, Goddess of the Unseen: One of the four Challenger Gods, also known as the "Goddess of Shadows." She favors Demons and those who defeat their enemies using misdirection and deceit, as well as those who subvert magic. Patron of Shadowers and Guilecasters.

Zone: A discrete geographic area within which all Monsters and Demons fall between a specified lower and upper level. While mortals may travel to zones that are higher than their current level, it is difficult or impossible for those mortals to defeat the Monsters and Demons found there without high level help.

Made in the USA
Coppell, TX
25 February 2025